1635
THE EASTERN FRONT

ERIC FLINT

1635: THE EASTERN FRONT

This is a work of fiction. All the characters and events portrayed in this book are fictional, and any resemblance to real people or incidents is purely coincidental.

Copyright © 2010 by Eric Flint

A Baen Books Original

Baen Publishing Enterprises
P.O. Box 1403
Riverdale, NY 10471
www.baen.com

ISBN: 978-1-4516-3764-9

Cover art by Tom Kidd
Maps by Gorg Huff

First Baen paperback printing, December 2011
Second Baen paperback printing, December 2012

Library of Congress Control Number: 2011036885

Distributed by Simon & Schuster
1230 Avenue of the Americas
New York, NY 10020

Pages by Joy Freeman (www.pagesbyjoy.com)
Printed in the United States of America

To Donald and Michael Davis,

and to Kathryn Diamond.

Contents

Maps   ix

1635: The Eastern Front   1

Cast of Characters   499

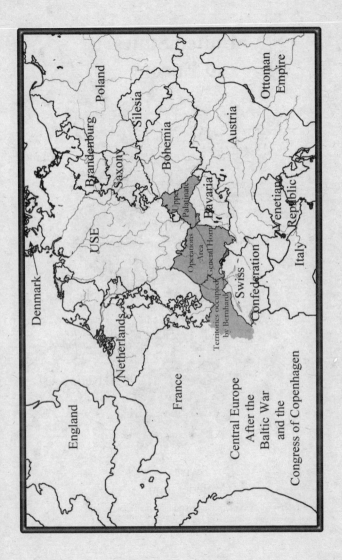

Central Europe After the Baltic War and the Congress of Copenhagen

*Swabia is still under direct imperial administration and not yet a
self-governing province as of March 1635.

Prologue

"They've passed on, Georg," said Wilhelm Kuefer, as soon as he came down the ladder. "I think those soldiers are just deserters, on their way out of Saxony altogether. Probably see no reason to get ground under the Swede's boot."

Georg Kresse nodded. "Probably. If they're some of Holk's men, almost certainly. All those thugs were ever good for was savaging unarmed civilians. The last thing they want is to get caught in a real war."

Neither Kresse nor Kuefer bothered to whisper. This far into the abandoned tin mine that Georg Kresse and his people had taken over as a base of operations, there was no chance that anyone outside the mine could hear him. Kuefer could have shouted and not been noticed by anyone in the open.

That was one of the advantages of using the mine. It offset the many disadvantages, among which darkness and dampness ranked high on Kuefer's list.

Wilhelm had had no trouble seeing Kresse nodding,

1

though. The problem wasn't darkness in itself. They had plenty of lamps, donated to them by their supporters and sympathizers in the Vogtland. The problem was that the oil lamps emitted fumes, which, given the poor air circulation in the mine, added to the problems caused by cooking fires. Whenever they could, Kresse's people did their cooking outside, but that option wasn't always possible.

They did have one "flashlight," as the smokeless American lamp was called, but it was no longer operating. The device required "batteries" to operate, and by the time they made that discovery—by exhausting the energies of said batteries—it was too late to do anything about it. Kresse's agents had made inquiries, to see if the batteries could be replaced. But by now, four years after the Ring of Fire, such batteries had become scarce and extremely expensive. New batteries were being manufactured, they'd learned, using a combination of up-time knowledge and available down-time techniques. They even worked, by all accounts. But they were reportedly much too large and cumbersome to be fit into the slender flashlight.

So, the once-delightful gadget was now useless. It wouldn't even make a very good club. But they kept it anyway, less as a memento than something in the way of a symbol for the future.

That more or less summarized their general attitude toward Americans. For Georg Kresse and his followers in the Vogtland, as for rebels throughout the Germanies—throughout all of Europe, for that matter—the real importance of the up-timers was mostly symbolic rather than practical. Like most such rebel groups, they'd had no significant direct contact with the Americans.

That was hardly surprising. There had only been three and a half thousand Americans to begin with, right after the Ring of Fire had transported their town of Grantville through time back into the seventeenth century. By now, five hundred or so of those had died. Some of the deaths had been casualties of war, and others had resulted from epidemics. For the most part, though, the deaths had been a simple product of human realities. The population of Grantville had been disproportionately elderly, and many of those old people had relied on up-time medicines to stay alive. Most of those medicines had vanished after the Ring of Fire. Now perched in the middle of what the up-timers called the Thirty Years' War, the death rate among those of them who were elderly or sickly had been severe. From the standpoint of the seventeenth century, they'd been living on borrowed time.

The number of Europeans, or even Germans and Bohemians, who had actual relations with the Americans was comparatively minuscule. True, up-time technology was spreading much more widely and rapidly than the up-timers themselves. But, for most people, that technology was still on a level with Kresse's flashlight: one or two minor gadgets. Even an up-time rifle was nothing more than a temporarily handy gadget, in the long run, except insofar as it could be at least partially duplicated.

For all of their partiality toward the up-timers, there were some things about the Americans that irritated Kresse and his people. What they'd heard of them, rather. Except for Anna Piesel, none of them had ever met an American in person, and Anna's contact had been brief and incidental. She'd literally bumped into the man as he came out of a tavern she was entering in Saalfeld. He'd said "Excuse me," in heavily accented Amideutsch, and gone on his way.

The great gift the up-timers had given rebels throughout the Germanies—indeed, throughout Europe—was simply being living proof that rebellion against the established order was not only possible and justified but even, you might say, ordained by history. The biggest irritant was that the Americans seemed to assume, blithely, ignorantly, and arrogantly, that they needed to bring the word of revolution to the benighted and backward Germans. That was a bit absurd as well as aggravating, given that the Germanies had had more in the way of rebellions and revolts over the past two centuries than the Americans had ever experienced. Just to name one example, their leader Georg Kresse was the descendant of one of the leaders of the Peasant War a century ago.

Nor were those two Kresses unusual. Another relative—Hans Kresse, one of Georg's cousins—had been one of the leaders in the town of Mehla when they drove out the soldiers who'd been occupying it.

It was a minor irritant, however—and there was always the possibility that the attitudes of the Americans had become distorted in the process of being passed on. Here in the mountains of the Vogtland, in southwestern Saxony, Kresse and his rebels had been isolated from the developments that had swept over Thuringia and the northerly Germanies after the Ring of Fire. To add to the problems, the enemy against whom they were fighting, the elector of Saxony, John George, had been officially an ally of the Americans and the Swedes. True, the alliance hadn't been a very friendly one, even before John George betrayed Gustav Adolf at the start of the Ostend War. Still, it had apparently been enough for the up-timers to keep a distance from Saxon rebels.

Happily, that situation was now ending. Emperor Gustav Adolf's long-expected invasion of Saxony and Brandenburg was imminent, and that would transform the entire situation. Kresse and his people had hopes that, thereafter, the more admirable qualities of the up-timers would come to the fore.

But that remained to be seen. In the meantime, Georg Kresse had business to attend to. He turned to Kuefer. "Summon the men, Wilhelm."

Kuefer didn't bother to ask why. Given Kresse, the answer was a foregone conclusion. He was a harsh man, when all was said and done. There was no way he would allow a band of deserters from Holk's army to pass through the Upper Vogtland unpunished.

There were certain obligations involved, as well. Heinrich Holk was one of the worst examples of the sort of condottiere who had risen to prominence during the long wars since the Austrian emperor defeated the Bohemian Protestants at the Battle of the White Mountain in November of 1620. He'd been born into a family of Danish Protestants, but had switched his faith and allegiance to the Habsburgs when that suited his advancement as a professional soldier. He'd switched allegiance again and sided with Wallenstein when he seized power in Bohemia.

Not satisfied with a mere triple-cross, Holk then tried to stab Wallenstein in the back by seizing and plundering Prague when Wallenstein led his army out to confront the Austrians at the second battle of the

White Mountain. But he'd been foiled by an alliance of up-timers and the large Jewish community in Prague. Upon hearing that a victorious Wallenstein was on his way back to Prague, Holk had immediately fled north to Saxony, where he'd offered the services of his army to the Saxon elector, John George.

Demonstrating once again his seemingly bottomless stupidity, John George had accepted the offer and placed Holk in charge of "maintaining order" in the Vogtland. Since then, Holk—a man sometimes described as a one-eyed, drunken mass murderer— had turned the unrest in the Vogtland into outright rebellion with his rapacious brutality.

Holk's army was notorious for committing atrocities, and there was no reason to believe that deserters from that army would be any less vicious. A large part of Kresse's success in withstanding the pressure of the Saxon elector's forces was that he had the firm support of the farmers and townsmen in the Upper Vogtland. That support, in turn, was contingent upon Kresse's ability to protect them from the sort of freebooting raids that had become all too common in the course of the long war in the Germanies. Most soldiers were mercenaries and many of those mercenaries were barely more than bandits. Holk's men were a particularly brutal bunch, but they were by no means unique.

Harsh he might be, but Georg Kresse was neither careless nor reckless. He spent three days preparing the attack on the band of deserters. Part of the reason for the delay was because he didn't want anyone associating the attack with the whereabouts of the mine. If need be, Kresse's people could relocate easily enough. They'd done it several times over the past few years. But the abandoned mine was the best of all the bases they'd had, and Kresse didn't want to lose it.

Mostly, though, the delay was simply because Kresse was an experienced commander of irregular forces engaged in the sort of combat that the Americans apparently called "guerrilla warfare." As if a peculiar-sounding Spanish term was needed to depict what was blindingly obvious to any sensible German farmer or townsman! Kresse was always careful to keep his own casualties to a minimum, even when facing a group of undisciplined deserters who didn't number more than perhaps three dozen all told.

One of the methods he used to keep his casualties low was to maneuver his foes in such a way as to take advantage of the local militias. Almost every town and village of any size in the Germanies maintained a militia force. They were often quite effective, within their limits—and the limit was that they generally fought well on the defensive, especially behind fortifications of some sort, but were inept if they were forced to fight in the open field.

Kresse and his men were quite effective in the open field, on the other hand. Kresse used the fortified villages as so many anvils, and used his own troops as a hammer. Against a large force of regular soldiers, such tactics wouldn't succeed. But they worked very nicely against smaller units or simple marauders.

Kresse had the Holk deserters under constant observation throughout those three days. His own scouts provided him with some of that intelligence, but more was provided by the villagers in the area through which the enemy was moving. At least half

a dozen times a day some young lad from one of the
villages would come racing up—"racing," insofar as
the term could be applied to a village plow horse—
to report on the latest movements of the mercenary
band. The youngsters were far more excited than
they were scared. Partly that was because they were
teenagers, but mostly it was because over the past
few years Kresse and his men had demonstrated their
capabilities many times.

Kresse liked to attack at first light. His own people
knew the area quite well—certainly better than their
enemies—and so moving into position under cover of
darkness was not too difficult. Only the most disciplined
military units kept proper vigilance through the night.
Deserters like these would only maintain a small number
of sentries, and those would most likely be careless.

Wilhelm Kuefer's task was harder, in terms of sheer
effort, since Kresse had given him the assignment of
bolstering the militia forces with one of their handful of
cannons. The largest cannon in their possession was a
demi-culverin with a four-inch bore, but the gun taken
by Kuefer on this occasion was a smaller Spanish-built
five-pounder saker. Even the saker weighed almost a
ton, despite having a bore not much more than three
inches. Hauling it through the mountains was no one's
idea of a pleasant outing.

On the other hand, Wilhelm and his squad had
left a day earlier and were taking a more circuitous
route to the selected ambush spot. So, unlike Kresse
and the rest of their forces, they'd been able to move
in daylight. They hadn't had to worry about moving
quietly, either, which was fortunate. The horses didn't

like the saker one little bit, so it required a fair amount of cursing to keep them to the task.

Again, experience counted. Kresse's little army of irregulars had captured quite a few cannons over the years. But they'd learned long since to just destroy—or better yet, sell if they could find a neutral buyer—any guns larger than demi-culverins. Even the smallest full culverin weighed two tons. A cannon that large and heavy was just too difficult to maneuver through the rough terrain of the Upper Vogtland, without having the resources of a large professional army.

When he arrived, Wilhelm was pleased to see that the militiamen had already constructed an abattis to block the road. The militias from three of the local villages would wait in ambush while Kresse and his men drove the Holk deserters toward them. The road had steep slopes on either side here, as it passed through a crest in the mountains. It would be hard to scramble up those slopes while under fire.

The abattis was a sturdy thing. Not up to the standards of a professional army with a corps of engineers, of course, but it was far more than just a haphazard pile of branches and brambles. The war that had raged in central Europe since the Bohemian incident had been going on for seventeen years. Villagers such as these were experienced by now with jury-rigged fieldworks.

This was a well-chosen spot for an ambush in other respects, too. The ambush site was not right on the crest but forty yards below it, just after a bend in the road. Holk's deserters, as they came rushing over the crest, wouldn't spot the abattis until they were within fifteen yards of it. They'd be coming downhill, so the men in front would have a hard time preventing those behind them from piling up.

A pity, of course, that the abatis had to be half-disassembled in order to make room for the cannon. But the militiamen didn't grumble at the added work. As usual, the cannon was proving to be a tremendous morale-booster. Only the militias of the larger towns had such guns. Villages in the mountains rarely even saw the weapons. The fact that Kresse's men possessed several was an important factor in establishing their reputation as a serious military force.

On the positive side, the hand guns owned by the villagers were actually better than those of most soldiers, even regular forces. They were rifles, for the most part, not smoothbore muskets. Far more accurate, especially in the hands of men who'd been hunting all their lives.

Their great limitation on a battlefield was their terribly slow rate of fire compared to smoothbore muskets. That was the reason that professional armies generally used muskets. Wilhelm had heard that the Americans had introduced a method for rapidly rearming front-loading muskets. It involved something called a Minié ball. But he'd never seen one and had no real idea how it was done.

For an ambush like this, however—with Kresse and his men in hot pursuit of the enemy—the villagers didn't really need to worry much about reloading quickly.

Wilhelm Kuefer had participated in many fights under Kresse's command. He knew Georg would launch a savage assault on the deserter camp just as dawn was breaking. Then, as the panicked band of mercenaries tried to escape, he would harry them relentlessly—always keeping them to the road and not letting them veer off into the countryside.

The road would seem like the safest escape route, anyway. So, they'd follow it for two hours after the initial assault—well over six miles of a mountain "road" that was more in the way of a trail for pasturing cows. By the time they arrived at the ambush site where Kuefer and his cannon and militiamen were waiting, they'd be exhausted as well as terrified.

When the first deserters appeared around the bend, the militiamen began shooting them down. But, at Kuefer's prior orders, only a handful of them were firing, their best marksmen, and they were not firing volleys. Their fire was deadly because of its accuracy, but it wouldn't seem to the deserters that they were facing a sizeable opponent. Just some mountaineers trying to defend a local village; at worst, a small number of skirmishers from the same partisan group who'd attacked them.

Either way, especially as they were in a panic over the oncoming and relentless pursuit, Kuefer had figured the deserters would try to rush the barricade and simply drive over the presumed handful of men guarding it.

So it proved. At the last moment, one of the deserters spotted the mouth of cannon barrel hidden behind some branches, and tried to call out a warning.

But by then it was too late. "Fire!" Wilhelm shouted. The saker belched a double load of canister. At that point-blank range—the nearest deserter was less than ten feet away—the canister slaughtered every man in its path. It didn't spread very far, but Kuefer didn't care. The noise and the carnage would be enough to stun the now-completely-disorganized crowd of deserters. And as soon as he shouted the command to fire, all of the militiamen behind the abattis fired a volley. That took down another dozen men. By now, almost half of the band of deserters had been killed or wounded.

Such horrendous casualties would have routed even a disciplined unit of good soldiers. This rabble immediately tried to flee back up the road. Several of them dropped their weapons along the way.

Three of them tried to scramble up the slope to find safety in the forest beyond. But militiamen had been waiting in the woods also, and gunned them down as soon as they reached the crest.

Then, before the last of the Holk deserters had disappeared around the bend, Kuefer could hear more guns firing. Kresse had arrived, obviously.

It was almost comical, in its own way. Now the deserters came racing back. The cannon wasn't reloaded yet, but many of the militiamen had been able to reload their rifles. They started firing again. Not in a volley, but it hardly mattered.

By the time Kresse's men appeared, there weren't more than five deserters left alive and uninjured. You couldn't say "left standing," though, because all five of them were lying on the ground, trying to pretend they were dead.

Wilhelm shook his head. Fat lot of good that would do them.

If it had been left to Kuefer himself, he'd have simply had the men shot right then and there, along with any wounded deserters. But perhaps that was the reason Georg Kresse was in command, rather than him.

Unlike Wilhelm, Georg had taken into account the problem of disposing of the bodies. You simply couldn't leave that many corpses lying around, in an area with as many villages as the Upper Vogtland. Leaving aside the problem of the children—some would be terrified and upset at seeing the bodies; still worse, others would be thrilled and begin mutilating them—there was the ever-present danger of disease.

Digging a grave for that many bodies was a lot of work, though. Hard work. Kresse was a popular commander of irregular soldiers not only because he kept their casualties to a minimum but because he kept their labor to a minimum also.

So, he let the wounded live, and had them dragged off to the side of the road. He provided them with no medical care, though. If they died, they died— and, indeed, several did in the time it took the five survivors to dig a mass grave some thirty yards into the woods. Wilhelm knew that the only reason Georg was keeping the wounded alive at all was to give the toiling grave-diggers the hope that they might be allowed to live.

Digging the grave took almost the whole day. By the time all the bodies were hauled to it and dumped in, it was late afternoon. That work was done by the deserters also, of course. Kresse's men and the militiamen spent a pleasant day lounging in the shade and watching.

By sundown, it was all done, except for shoveling the dirt back over the corpses. Unfortunately, that last bit of work would have to be done by Kresse's people and the militiamen.

At Kresse's command, the five survivors were hauled to the edge of the grave. Two of them began shouting protests, but only one made any attempt to resist. He was immediately clubbed senseless and fell into the grave. The other four were shoved roughly to their knees.

"All right," said Kresse. "Shoot them."

Three of the four bodies fell into the grave on their own. The last one was sent in with a rough boot.

Kresse pointed to the one still-living Holk soldier, the one who'd been beaten unconscious. "Him too."

"Bury him alive!" shouted one of the militiamen. That was old Selig Hirsch, the local tanner. Kuefer didn't blame him. One of his sons had been murdered by soldiers a few years back, along with two of the son's children.

But Kresse shook his head. "We're not savages. Shoot him, I said."

Wilhelm had been expecting that order also, and did the shooting himself. Georg Kresse was as harsh a man as ever lived in these mountains. But only his enemies claimed he was cruel. None of his irregulars would have used that term, not would any of the farmers and townsmen in the Upper Vogtland. He was simply, and fortunately, what the times had produced.

By the time they returned to the mine, Kresse had come to a decision. The first person he spoke to was the woman with whom he shared a small cell in the mine constructed from old timbers. That was Anna Piesel, his betrothed.

"Anna, I want you to go to Magdeburg." He hooked a thumb at Kuefer. "I'll send Wilhelm and some other men as an escort until you're into Thuringia. After that, you should be safe enough. Take Friedrich and Hannelore, also. They could both use some rest in a tavern, and they're old enough to pass as your parents."

He smiled, seeing Piesel's little glare. She was a good woman, but a bit vain about her looks. "I said, 'old enough.' I didn't claim there was any resemblance." Friedrich was downright ugly, and the best you could say for Hannelore's appearance was "dumpy."

"Why do you want me to go to Magdeburg? That'll take weeks, Georg!"

"At least six, I'm figuring. Quite possibly more. But we're not going to be doing much here during that time. It'd be idiotic for us to launch any major attacks, when the Swedes and the USE army are going to be spending those same weeks pounding the Saxon army into a pulp. I figure we may as well just sit and wait. The real struggle will come then, not now. What sort of Saxony will emerge, once the elector's driven out? You know the Swedes, Anna. Gustav Adolf will set up the same sort of military administration he's used in other conquered provinces. That is *not* what we want. We want a republic in Saxony, nothing less."

Kuefer spoke up. "But, Georg...the Americans..."

"What about them? Be realistic, Wilhelm. Even if they're inclined themselves toward a republic, it's not an issue over which they'd risk a rupture with Gustav Adolf." Kresse shook his head. "'Prince of Germany,' the damn fools call Stearns. But I notice that's never stopped him from making compromises with royalty and nobility every time he turns around."

"That's not fair, Georg," Piesel said mildly.

"Maybe not. But I'm still not relying on the good graces of the up-timers. No, we need to get the Committees of Correspondence involved. And that's why I'm sending you to Magdeburg. I want Richter, Anna. Tell her we want her to come to Dresden after the elector's gone."

Anna's eyes got a little wider. "Gretchen Richter *herself*? Do you think she'd really come?"

He shrugged. "I don't know. But if nothing else, we'll test her reputation. We'll see if she's as inclined toward half-measures as the Americans are."

Part One

June 1635

The fever of the world

Chapter 1

Magdeburg, central Germany
Capital of the United States of Europe

After they'd completed the grand tour—Michael's phrase; and a disturbingly appropriate one—of their new home, and had returned to the entrance foyer, Rebecca looked around. Her gaze was simultaneously uncertain, dubious, apprehensive, wary, skittish . . .

She tried to avoid the term "covetous." Not . . . entirely successfully. Compared to the modest working-class house owned by the Stearns family in Grantville, much less the cramped apartments Rebecca and Michael had been occupying since they moved to Magdeburg, this house was both immense and luxurious. In truth, it was more in the way of a mansion than a house, if not a manor as such. The building was immediately adjacent to its neighbors and had almost no yard; what the up-timers called a townhouse. But by the inner city standards of Magdeburg it was as close to a mansion as you could get, short of an outright palace.

The very foyer she was standing in exemplified her mixed feelings. The "foyer" in Mike's house in

Grantville had been a simple entry vestibule, just large enough to provide the house with a heat trap in winter and space to hang some coats. The foyer in *this* house bore a closer resemblance to the hall of an auditorium. You could hold a fairly large party in this space.

Andrew Short came into the foyer from a side door that led to the rooms in the back of the house. "Splendid field of fire," he announced, giving the area a sweeping gaze that had none of Rebecca's doubts and anxieties. He was actually rubbing his hands!

"There's no way in except through that door"—he jabbed a forefinger at the main entrance—"and the service entrance in the rear. And anyone who tries to come through here, we'll slaughter the bastards. Assuming they get in at all."

Rebecca studied the entrance in question. For all its ornate decorations, the "door" looked like it belonged in a castle. It was a double door, huge, made of solid oak further braced with iron, and seemed to have enough in the way of locks and latches to sink a rowboat—not to mention the heavy crossbar resting nearby that could be added in a pinch. The "service entrance" in the back was similar in design and construction, if smaller and completely utilitarian.

There were no other entrances on the ground floor of the mansion. Rebecca had been struck by that: not so much as a single window. Not even a barred one, or an old-style arrow slit. Anyone attempting to assault the house would either have to smash down the heavy doors, blow a hole in the thick stonework of the walls, or scale the second floor using ladders. And those windows *were* barred. True, the bars were tastefully designed. They were also thick and too closely spaced for a human body to pass through.

For all practical purposes, their new home was an urban fortress. That was hardly surprising, since it had been planned and built with that purpose in mind. Michael Stearns had known for more than a year that he'd eventually be leaving Magdeburg for long stretches of time, and he was bound and determined to keep his wife and children as well protected as possible in his absence. By now, more than four years after the Ring of Fire, he had lots of enemies. Many of them were bitter and some of them were prone to violence.

Rebecca had plenty of enemies herself, for that matter. If she wasn't as prominent as her husband in the political affairs of the new United States of Europe, she wasn't that far behind him, either—and had the added distinction of being a Jewess.

Andrew spoke again, now jabbing his finger at the ceiling. "And look there! Murder holes! Ha! They'll be surprised to run into *that*, should the bastards made the attempt."

He didn't specify the names or even the nature of "the bastards." For someone like Andrew Short, it hardly mattered. He and his small clan had transferred their allegiance from the king of England to the person many people called the prince of Germany. Princes had enemies, it was a given; and such enemies were bastards. Also a given.

Rebecca stared up at the ceiling. *Murder holes.* She knew what they were, abstractly, but such devices were something she associated with medieval castles. Here, in a modern town house built as much as possible along up-time lines...

Finally, she spotted them. They were cleverly disguised as further decorations in a heavily decorated ceiling. Wood inlays, to a casual observer. But she had no doubt the wood inlays were slats that could be easily slid aside, exposing any attackers below to fire from above.

She shook her head and looked away. The headshake was simply rueful, not a gesture of denial or criticism. She knew all too well the risks she and her husband—and their children—were taking and had been taking for years. If any reminder were needed, the mayor of Grantville and one of the town's ministers had been assassinated just three months earlier. By fanatic reactionary anti-Semites, it was presumed—exactly the sort of people who hated Rebecca with a passion and had been writing and spreading vicious propaganda about her for at least two years now.

True, the savage response of the Committees of Correspondence to those murders had resulted in the effective destruction of organized anti-Semitism in the Germanies. For a time, at least. But that made it perhaps even more likely that a fanatic or small group of fanatics might seek vengeance by assassinating the most famous Jew in the United States of Europe. Who was now Rebecca herself, without any doubt, much to her surprise.

Her dark thoughts were interrupted by the appearance of her daughter Sepharad, who barreled into the foyer from another of the side doors. "Barreled," at least, insofar as the term could be applied to a toddler still some months shy of her third birthday.

Sepharad also had dark deeds on her mind. "Mommy! Mommy! Barry's messing in the cupboards like he shouldn't!"

Rebecca made a face. Not at the reported crime itself—two-and-a-half-year-old boys were given to rummaging in nooks and crannies; girls too, at that age—but at the name.

Barry. Rebecca detested that nickname and refused to use it herself.

The child's real name was Baruch. Baruch de Spinoza, originally. He'd been orphaned in the siege of Amsterdam and then adopted by Rebecca and Michael.

Yes, *that* Spinoza. *The* Spinoza. Still some years short of his future as a great philosopher, of course. But Rebecca had high hopes. Surely his current investigations were a harbinger of things to come.

Alas, hers was an uphill struggle against doughty antagonists. On this subject, even her husband and daughter were ranked among Rebecca's enemies.

Barry, when it should be Baruch. And Rebecca knew full well that Michael was conspiring with Jeff Higgins to have the innocent boy fitted with a Harley-Davidson jacket and a Cat cap as soon as possible. They'd take him fishing, too, and teach him to ride a motorcycle. They'd already sworn they would.

Before Rebecca could intervene, though, Jenny Hayes appeared in the foyer, holding the selfsame philosopher/young miscreant in her arms. Judging from the smile on the teenager's face, whatever Baruch might have encountered in his adventures had been harmless enough.

"You shouldn't be spreading alarms, Sepharad," Hayes chided the girl. "Baruch couldn't have come to no grief. T'aren't nothing in those cupboards yet anyway, since we've just started unpacking."

Rebecca returned the smile. She considered the

addition of the very large Short-Hayes family to their household a great and unmitigated good.

This, for several reasons. Some of them were obvious. The men were former Yeoman Warders in the Tower of London and would provide the household with the finest security force you could ask for. The women were generally pleasant and invariably hard-working, and would be a great help in managing such a huge establishment. The children were numerous, ranged widely in age, and would make good companions and playmates for her own children.

Best of all, though, was that the family's unquestioned matriarch was Patricia Hayes, and Patricia was of the old school. Whatever the mistress of the house wanted, she got—and Patricia had figured out very quickly that Rebecca's attitude when it came to nicknames was quite unlike her husband's.

And who cared what the husband thought? Michael Stearns was now a general in the army, about to go gallivanting off to some foreign war. The mistress of the house mattered. He didn't.

So, it would be "Baruch," not "Barry." "Sepharad," not the grotesque "Sephie" favored by most up-timers including—

Michael came into the foyer, followed by Anthony Leebrick and Patrick Welch. He looked down at his daughter and smiled.

"And what are you carrying on about, Sephie?"

Her husband.

Later that morning, Michael made his farewells. By then, their younger daughter Kathleen was energetically crawling about the foyer and doing her own investigations. So, she participated in the leave-taking ceremonies along with her mother and siblings. Whether or not the nine-month-old infant understood the nature of the occasion was perhaps doubtful. Although, the way she clutched her father's shoulders when he picked her up for a good-bye kiss would seem to indicate some apprehension on her part at his coming absence.

But maybe she just found the epaulets fascinating. They were the one feature of the uniform of an officer in the USE army that was unabashedly flamboyant. These were not the subdued shoulder straps of the up-time American military, but the sort of golden-tasseled insignia that were used by Napoleonic-era armies. On the otherwise rather subdued field-gray uniform, they quite stood out.

Eventually, Kathleen released her grip and Michael handed her back to her current nursemaid, Mary Hayes. He then gave Rebecca a final kiss—nothing perfunctory, either, she made sure of that—and off he went, with his two new staff officers trailing in his wake.

Some part of Rebecca wondered if she would ever see her husband again, but she squelched that quickly enough.

He's a general, she told herself firmly. Ignoring, just as firmly, her knowledge that in the seventeenth century army generals often led from the front and were quite apt to be killed in battle.

Rebecca spent some time thereafter restlessly moving about the house, doing her own investigations. She spent a fair amount of that time in the several toilets and bathrooms scattered through the huge dwelling, testing their various devices and taking what comfort she could from them.

Which was considerable, actually. Newly designed and built, the house had modern plumbing. Rebecca had grown up with seventeenth-century sanitation facilities, and was certainly capable of managing with such. She'd been doing so again for the past two years, after all. But her stay in Grantville had spoiled her in that regard.

Fortunately, it had done the same thing for every down-timer who passed through the up-time American town. By now, there was a flourishing new industry in central Europe and the Low Countries producing the wherewithal for modern plumbing. The same industries were beginning to appear in France, Italy and Poland, if not yet in Spain and England.

The adoption of those new techniques was especially rapid in the Germanies and Bohemia. That was partly because the industries involved were further developed there. But another important factor was the stance of the Committees of Correspondence, who were more prominent in those areas than they were elsewhere in Europe. The CoCs were firmly convinced—adamant, it would be better to say—that proper sanitation ran a very close second to godliness, and they matched deed to word. The rapidly spreading network of credit unions that was fostered by the CoCs in lower class communities always extended low-interest loans for any sanitation project. And in cities like Magdeburg where they were powerful, the CoCs maintained patrols that were quite prepared to use forceful means to put a stop to unsanitary practices.

There were still towns in the Germanies where people emptied their chamber pots in street gutters as a matter of course. Magdeburg was not one of them. Doing so would certainly result in a public harangue; persisting in the practice would just as certainly lead to a beating.

There were people who denounced the CoCs for that practice, but Rebecca was not one of them. Such people were usually either down-time reactionaries or up-time liberals. The reactionaries were against anything connected to the Ring of Fire. Their objection was not to beatings—they were generally all in favor of *that* practice, applied to lower class folk—but to the cause involved and the persons engaged in it.

As for the up-time liberals, Rebecca understood their qualms. But they'd never lived through a major episode of disease, except the few who'd been in the western Germanies during the ongoing plague epidemic this year or had lived through the diphtheria scare in the Oberpfalz the year before. Any epidemic, even when it was more "benign" than smallpox or typhus, was bad enough. It was quite noticeable that those up-timers who'd survived the experience were not given to wincing at the CoC methods of sanitation enforcement. Better some bruised feelings and even bruised flesh to bodies being carted off by the hundreds, or sometimes thousands.

She then spent some time watching the small horde of children playing with electricity. Within limits, of course. She let them switch the lights on and off in the various rooms, as long as they were reasonably gentle in the process and didn't overdo it. Like most technology patterned on up-time design and theory but constructed using down-time methods and materials, the switches were sturdy things. Still, they could be broken if they were over-stressed, and—again, like almost everything of that nature—they were rather costly. The light bulbs were even more expensive.

She kept them away from the computer. In fact, she kept the door to that room locked. But she allowed them to plug in and operate Michael's battered old up-time toaster in the kitchen. Every child present—there were no fewer than nine participating in the project—got to make and eat his or her own slices of toast.

The toast was on the crumbly side. Down-time bread was much tastier than the up-time varieties which were by now long gone, to no one's regret other than some up-timers themselves. But it didn't slice as cleanly or evenly, probably because it lacked what up-timers called "additives" and down-timers called low-grade poisons.

But the children didn't care. They'd never had toast before, leaving aside some baked flatbreads. They were quite taken by the stuff.

Their interest faded soon enough, though. There were greater thrills in store. It wasn't long before the children were racing down to the basement to start up the mansion's sure and certain center of attraction. For them, anyway.

The toy electric train set. Michael had brought it home just two days ago and finished setting it up last night.

It was one of the very first models produced by the recently launched Fassbinder-Lionel company, from the firm's factory right here in Magdeburg. Completely down-time in construction, albeit obviously based on up-time models. The toy train sets were still fiendishly expensive. As yet, the market was purely a luxury one whose clientele consisted of noblemen and wealthy merchants, manufacturers and bankers.

The only reason Rebecca's husband had been able to afford it was because he'd gotten it for free. The company could just as easily have been named Fassbinder-Stearns, given that Michael was one of the company's two partners, along with Heinrich Fassbinder. He'd insisted on the name Lionel instead of his own, though. For the sake of tradition, he claimed. Rebecca suspected it was more because Michael saw no reason to stir up charges of conflict of interest any more than was necessary.

In truth, there wasn't any in this instance. An army general—even a prime minister, as he'd once been—would have precious little occasion to favor the fortunes of a toy train company. But there were other areas in which Michael's financial dealings were grayer in nature.

This very mansion, for one. They'd only been able to buy the house because of a loan extended to them by some wealthy members of the far-flung Abrabanel family to which Rebecca herself belonged. True, the loan was secured—but the collateral was the royalties that were expected to come in two or three years from the sales of Rebecca's book on current political developments.

Which she hadn't started writing yet. And whose royalties would depend on enforcement of the copyright legislation passed by the USE's parliament so recently the ink was barely dry on the bill sent up to the new prime minister for his signature.

Wilhelm Wettin had signed it readily enough. Whatever other disputes his Crown Loyalists had with Michael and Rebecca's party, they'd agreed that establishing up-time style copyright was a good idea. Still, no one really knew yet how well or easily the new laws could be enforced. There might be wholesale piracy, in which case those royalties would be mostly a chimera.

Not that the Abrabanels who'd extended the loan would care that much. The reason they'd made the loan was political, not economic. Whether or not they ever saw the money paid back, they had a keen interest in seeing to it that the leaders of the July Fourth party stayed alive and well. Their own prosperity, even possibly their very survival, might depend on it.

To be sure, no one thought the new prime minister was himself an anti-Semite, much less a rabid one. Wettin was an eminently civilized man. But it remained to be seen how well he controlled the political forces he'd help to set in motion. The Abrabanels, like many people, thought his control was shaky—and there were people and groups under the umbrella called "the Crown Loyalist Party" who were quite certainly anti-Semites.

Rebecca hadn't hesitated at accepting the loan. She understood the political logic quite well. But she also knew—so did Michael—that there would inevitably be charges of conflict of interest. Especially if it became known that the man who'd arranged the loan was none other than Francisco Nasi, himself a member of the Abrabanel clan and Michael's former head of security and espionage.

Fortunately, Francisco was superbly adept at keeping his doings out of the limelight. And, who was to say? If the copyright laws held up, there might in fact be a large income derived from her book. There would be keen interest in it, certainly. Even if the market was restricted to CoC members and sympathizers, that would be a *lot* of books sold.

Rebecca let the children play with the train set for a full hour. Her magnanimity had a cold purpose to it. The toy train sets, Michael had told her, were much like the train sets his father and grandfather had played with. That was to say, not very concerned with the fussbudget latter-day up-time obsession with child safety.

"There's no way in hell to play with these trains," he'd said, "without getting an electric shock from time to time. No real harm done—and it teaches kids to respect electricity."

So it proved. Only two of the children got shocked, as it turned out—one of them being her own daughter Sepharad, who promptly wailed as loudly as you could ask for. But within an hour, all of the children were being much more careful than they'd been with the toaster or the light switches.

The mission was accomplished. And now she had no further reason to procrastinate. It was time to start writing the book.

Fortunately, she wouldn't have to put up with the troubles and travails of quill pens and ink bottles. Rebecca *loved* her computer.

The title came easily and readily:

An Examination of the Current Political Situation in the Germanies and Europe

She stared at the title. She had no trouble imagining the caustic remarks her husband would have made, had he seen it.

"Why don't you just put a damn footnote in the title while you're at it?" he'd jeer. "Just to make sure and certain everyone understands this is an eye-glazing tract of no conceivable interest to anyone except scholars like you."

After a while, she sighed and suppressed her natural instincts. In this, as in many if not all things, Michael Stearns was correct. So, she deleted the title and, after a few more seconds of consideration, came up with another and more suitable one.

The Road Forward: A Call to Action

Chapter 2

Grantville, State of Thuringia-Franconia

Gretchen Richter's eyes were riveted on the sheet of paper in her hands, her brow creased by a truly magnificent frown. Her husband, Jeff Higgins, was leaning over the back of her chair in order to study the figures himself.

"*How* much?" Gretchen asked again.

Seated across from her in the large couch in the living room of the Dreeson house, David Bartley shrugged his shoulders. "That depends on a lot of variables. But if you sold all your stocks right now—which I don't recommend, since the market's really antsy with another war looming; well, if you had a lot of military industry stocks, I suppose it might be different—they're doing really well, not surprisingly—but you don't, so—"

"David," Gretchen said, half-growling. "Keep it *simple*. If. You. Would. Please."

"But... Look, Gretchen, I'm really not trying to be confusing. It's just that it really *isn't* all that simple. Like, where would you want to sell it? I wouldn't recommend the Grantville or Magdeburg stock exchanges for most of your stocks. They're the ones affected the worst by the war jitters. You'd probably do better in Amsterdam, or in some cases even Venice."

"David!" The "half" left the growl.

Jeff grunted. "Just assume we're morons, David. So, not knowing our asses from our elbows, we go right now to the exchange in downtown Grantville and sell everything—every single stock on this list—for whatever we can get."

Bartley looked at his watch. "You couldn't get there in time today—"

"*David!*" Gretchen's tone left "growl" behind altogether, and began approaching "shriek of fury."

"Calm down, hon," said Jeff soothingly, his big hand caressing her shoulder. "You can't kill him without producing a political crisis. He's way too popular with the CoCs. All over the country, too, not just here."

Gretchen said nothing. She just glared at Bartley.

"Fine," Jeff continued. "So we sell it all tomorrow. How much would we get?"

David's eyes got that slightly-unfocussed look that Jeff had come to be familiar with this afternoon. The one that signified *well-gee-it's-really-complicated-depending-on-this-that-and-the-other.*

"Forget playing with currencies," Jeff added quickly. "Just figure we sell it for USE dollars. Whatever we can get. Soon as the stock exchange opens tomorrow morning."

Bartley looked down at the list of figures in his own hand, which was identical to the one Gretchen and Jeff were looking at. He pursed his lips, an expression that Jeff thought made him look like a young Ichabod Crane. If Bartley had been standing, the likeness would have been even better. David was tall and thin, his gangly frame still not having caught up to his height. He was nineteen years old, and the best-known if not perhaps the richest of the teenage millionaires produced by the Ring of Fire.

"Well... Figure you'd wind up with about two million dollars. Give or take."

Gretchen swallowed. "Two...*million*?"

"About. But like I said, if you waited and sold the stocks on the Amsterdam market—and Venetian market, for that matter—and took your time about it—I think you'd wind up getting closer to two and a half million. But the truth is I don't recommend you sell most of these stocks. It's a good portfolio, Gretchen." His slender shoulders became a bit more square. "We did right by you guys, if I say so myself."

"That seems clear enough," Jeff said dryly. He moved from behind Gretchen's chair and pulled up a chair for himself from a nearby side table. The chair was on the rickety side. Gretchen's grandmother Veronica, Henry Dreeson's widow, used that table for her records and correspondence. She was not a large woman and the chair did fine for her. Under Jeff's weight, it creaked alarmingly. Most of the fat that Higgins had carried as a teenager was gone now. But, if anything, the twenty-three-year-old man who'd replaced that teenager was even bigger—and Jeff had been a big kid to start with.

He ignored the creaks. Whatever else, they could obviously afford to replace the chair now, even if it did collapse under him. And he needed to sit down. He was feeling a bit light-headed.

Two million dollars. Two and a half, if you wait.

The only numbers like that he'd ever dealt with, at least when it came to money, were associated with the role-playing games he and his friends had played in high school. So, trying to get a handle on them and turn the abstract into the concrete, he focused on the chair swaying beneath him.

Go ahead, sucker. Break. See if I care. You're kindling in the fireplace and I go out and buy something sturdier to replace you. Out of pocket change.

That thought steadied him some. He glanced at Gretchen, but saw that his wife was in a rare state of paralysis—an almost unheard of state, in her case. She was normally as uncertain as a calving glacier.

"Whether it's a smart move or not, we will need some cash pretty soon, David. I think you call it liquidity or something like that." Jeff nodded toward his sister-in-law, who was sitting next to David on the couch. The eighteen-year-old girl was studying the figures Bartley held in his hand as intently as a cat watching a mousehole. "Annalise needs to start college in the fall, and that scholarship she got won't be enough to cover the cost."

He lifted his hand and spun the forefinger in a little circle. "Not to mention this gaggle of kids we've got to support. Except for Baldy, anyway. He likes his apprenticeship at KSI, and he's even making enough to support himself."

"That's not a problem. What I recommend is that you sell your shares of Kelly Aviation. They're selling like hotcakes right now on account of the war coming, but I don't personally think that's going to last, so you may as well get out while the getting's good."

Feeling under some sort of vague compulsion to demonstrate his masculine mastery of financial matters in front of the womenfolk, Jeff took off his glasses and started cleaning them with a handkerchief. "You sure? I heard those are pretty good planes they make."

"Technically, yes. Bob Kelly knows his stuff when it comes to designing aircraft. In that respect, he's probably just as good as Hal Smith. The problem's on the other end. He's got the business sense of a jackrabbit and while Kay makes up for it some, she's also, well . . ." He looked uncomfortable. For all his financial acumen, David Bartley wasn't a cutthroat by temperament. He was quite a nice guy, actually, and not given to bad-mouthing others.

"Well," he repeated.

Jeff was less reticent. He'd run into Bob Kelly's wife on several occasions. "Yeah. If pissing people off was an Olympic event, she'd take the gold every time."

David nodded. "I figure you could get three hundred thousand dollars from those stocks. You could set aside twenty-five percent of that as a fund for Annalise, which ought to be plenty even as expensive as Quedlinburg's gotten to be."

Annalise spoke up, her tone a mix of defensiveness and belligerence. "It's the only really good college for women yet. In the USE, anyway. I wouldn't mind going to Prague but Gramma'd pitch a fit."

Jeff put his glasses back on. "That'd leave us with about two hundred and twenty-five thousand. Gretchen wants to move to Magdeburg as soon as possible, now that Ronnie's leaving town, and we'd need to get a house big enough for all the kids. We'd figured on renting, but . . ." He started doing the needed calculations.

Not surprisingly, David did the figuring faster than he did. "You could buy the kind of house you need for . . . I figure about seventy-five thousand dollars. But then you'd own it free and clear and still have a hundred and fifty thousand to live on. Even with all your kids, that's way more than enough."

Gretchen frowned. "Seventy-five thousand? That seems much too high. We're not going to be looking for a home in the rich districts, you know."

"Yeah, sure. You pretty much have to stay in one of the working class areas where the CoCs are strong and can provide you with some protection. You've got a lot of enemies. But for the same reason, you'll need a really solid place. My own advice would be to buy a whole apartment building. Plenty of room for the kids—Ronnie, too, if she wants to move in with you—"

Jeff chuckled. "Not likely. She says she's had enough of babysitting our kids and we can damn well do it on our own from now on. I think she's planning to move in with the Simpsons. She and Mary get along real well, and with the admiral likely to be gone most of the time, Mary'd probably like the company."

Gretchen looked like she was on the verge of choking. "An apartment building? We don't have *that* many kids. Baldy will be staying here and so will Martha, who wants to finish school. That leaves us with only half a dozen who'll be coming to Magdeburg. And I can assure you that I have no intention of becoming a landlady!"

David made a face. Again, the youngster's nature made it hard for him to state the truth bluntly.

Jeff, on the other hand, had no such compunctions left. Being married to Gretchen for four years had pretty well rubbed off whatever delicate sensibilities he'd ever possessed. "Hon, we've got a *lot* of enemies. Well, you do, anyway. Most of them don't have much against me except they've got to get past me to put you in the ground."

Gretchen looked at him, a bit crossly. "So?"

"So figure it out for yourself. If we buy an apartment building—depending on the size, of course, but let's figure twelve units, which is pretty standard in the quarters we'd be looking in—then we can set aside half the space for CoC people."

"What do you mean, 'CoC' people—oh."

He grinned. "Yeah. As in 'CoC people handpicked by Gunther Achterhof.' Good luck, anyone's got it in for you getting through that crowd."

David nodded. "That's what I was figuring."

Gretchen looked back down at the sheet. "I still don't really understand how it happened. And without us even knowing about it!"

Bartley looked a bit defensive. "Hey, we *told* your grandmother what was happening."

Jeff barked a jeering laugh. "Oh, right! And I'm sure you used simple and straightforward language that made lots of sense to Ronnie."

"Well . . ."

Gretchen shook her head. "Explain it to us again. In simple and straightforward language, this time."

"Well . . . Okay. This is simplifying a lot, you understand?"

"I can live with that," said Gretchen. "Whereas you may not, if you do otherwise."

Now, Bartley looked alarmed as well as defensive. "Hey, Gretchen! There's no call for that."

"Relax, David. She's joking." Jeff glanced at his wife. "I . . . think. Do your best."

The young financier cleared his throat. "The gist of it is that, way back when, my grandmother gave you guys some stock in the sewing machine company by way of a belated wedding gift. On account of Jeff's father and my mother were first cousins, which makes me and Jeff second cousins." He rattled off the precise family relationships with the ease of any person raised in a small town. "You remember?"

Jeff and Gretchen nodded simultaneously.

"Well, after that I guess you forgot about it."

"We were . . . ah, busy," said Gretchen.

"Holed up in Amsterdam under Spanish siege, to be precise," added Jeff. "So, yeah. Sewing machine company stocks were not something we thought about much. At all."

"Sure. But as you may have heard, Higgins Sewing Machine Company did really well. And when it went public, you wound up owning five thousand shares— which was two and half percent of the stock."

"The sewing machine company did *that* well?"

David tugged at his ear. "It did really well, yeah. But it wasn't just the sewing machine company. Since you weren't around we talked to Ronnie, and your grandmother told us to handle it however we wanted to." He looked defensive again. "She didn't seem interested when we tried to explain the ins and outs of it."

Jeff wasn't surprised. Depending on who did the explaining—Bartley was actually better at this than most of his partners—Gretchen's grandmother would have probably had as much luck with a short lecture on quantum mechanics. It wasn't that she was dim-witted. She wasn't at all; in fact, in her own way she had a very shrewd grasp of practical finance. But Veronica's idea of practical finance focused on tangibles like property and hard cash. The sort of stock speculations and currency manipulations that David specialized in wouldn't have meant much to her.

David went on. "So Sarah and I diversified your holdings. You've still got the five thousand shares in HSMC, but we invested all the earnings in other stuff. By now, you own sizeable amounts of stock in OPM—"

That was Bartley's own finance company: *Other People's Money.* He was not given to euphemisms, which Jeff found refreshing in a financier.

"—as well as several of the Stone chemical and pharmaceutical companies, Casein Buttons, Kelly Aviation, a little chunk of the Roth jewelry operations, a pretty hefty chunk of the new petroleum operations near Hamburg and an even bigger chunk of the port expansion projects—Hamburg's going to turn into a real boom town—and some railroad stocks. There are some other odds and ends, but that's the heart. Sarah and I didn't want to take too many risks with your money, so we invested most of it in stuff that was safe but reasonably profitable."

It was Jeff's turn to shake his head. "If these are the kinds of returns you get on 'safe' investments, I'd hate to see what you get on something risky that pays off."

Bartley shrugged. "You've got to remember that 'safe' is a relative term. The Ring of Fire triggered off one of the great economic booms in history. At least, that's what Melissa Mailey says. Almost any intelligent investment will pay off well, if you know what you're doing."

Jeff didn't think it was really that straightforward. David Bartley was like most people with a genius streak at something. Doing that something seemed a lot easier to him than it did to most anyone else.

Be that as it may, the end result seemed clear enough. Much to his surprise—and Gretchen's even more so—they'd wound up very well off. So, what had seemed like the sure prospect of several years of hard near-poverty while they finished raising Gretchen's little horde of adopted children had vanished.

He could live with that. Quite easily.

An hour later, when David got up to leave, Jeff escorted him to the front door. "When will we see you again?" he asked.

"I don't know about Gretchen. But you'll be seeing me tomorrow, since your leave's up. We'll be on the same train."

"Huh?"

Bartley got a hurt look on his face. "Didn't you notice that I was wearing my uniform?"

Jeff had noticed, in fact, but hadn't thought much of it. David was a member of the State of Thuringia-Franconia's National Guard. In Jeff's experience—although he'd allow this might just be the sneer of a *real* soldier—weekend warriors wore their uniforms every chance they got. He himself was lounging around in jeans and a sweatshirt. He had no intention of donning his own uniform until he was ready to leave the next morning.

"Yeah. So what?"

"So I'm reporting to the army base in Magdeburg along with you. Mike Stearns asked me to come. He sent me a personal letter, even. Well, I doubt if he actually wrote it. But he signed it, sure enough."

"Leave it to Mike," Jeff said. "He wants you to run his quartermaster operations, doesn't he?"

"Not exactly. He says he wants me as a 'logistics consultant.'"

Jeff grinned. "You may be a financial wizard, but you're a babe in the woods when it comes to the army. Mike's just saying that 'cause he doesn't want to piss off a lot of old-timers. But he'll have you running the show soon enough, in fact if not in name. You watch."

He said it all quite cheerfully. And why not? Logistics was always an officer's biggest headache. But with David Bartley running the supply operations... Jeff figured anybody who could parlay not much of anything into stocks worth over two million dollars could probably also manage to keep food and spare socks and ammunition coming.

Chapter 3

Magdeburg

Caroline Platzer rolled her eyes. "She's still insisting that I have to come with her. I swear, that kid is more stubborn than any mule who ever lived."

Her boss, Maureen Grady, didn't seem noticeably sympathetic. "What do you expect? Not too many mules are in line to inherit a throne—and Kristina's in line to inherit three. Queen of Sweden, empress of the United States of Europe, and—hum. I wonder what the female equivalent would be for high king of the Union of Kalmar? High queen? Sounds silly."

"It's not funny, Maureen! She's been pestering Thorsten too, and now *he's* starting to make noises that I should go."

"Then why don't you? For Pete's sake, Caroline, it's just a trip across the Baltic to Stockholm. Even in this day and age, that's not considered an adventure. At least, not when you've got royal resources to draw on."

Caroline felt stubborn herself. She had an uneasy feeling she probably looked stubborn, too—in that child-mulish sort of way that drove her crazy when Kristina did it to her. "Because."

Now, Maureen rolled her eyes. "Oh, how adult! Caroline, you just don't want to go because you're afraid Thorsten'll get killed when the war starts and you think you ought to be here in case that happens for reasons that defy comprehension, since it's not as if you could do anything about it. Hell, you couldn't even gloom around in widow's weeds since you wouldn't legally be a widow. Unless you marry him just before he ships off, which would be pointless romanticism, seeing as how there isn't any Social Security for spouses in this day and age on account of there's no Social Security for anybody."

Even more astringently, she added, "I suppose you might qualify for a regimental pension, but probably not. Since we administer those funds—that means me, kiddo—and I'm damned if I see why a healthy young woman like you would need to be supported when there are plenty of Deserving Widows around."

Somehow, she verbalized the capital letters. Caroline had never been able to figure out how Maureen managed that.

Still not knowing what to say—beyond another "because," which would just subject her to more ridicule—she satisfied herself with glaring at Maureen. Which brought down more ridicule anyway.

"Oh, stop trying to glare at me. You look like another eight-year-old—except Kristina's one hell of a lot better at it. Which you'd expect, given that she's a genu-ine princess."

There really wasn't much point in trying to out-glare or out-ridicule or out-anything Maureen Grady.

Caroline's boss was a very experienced and successful middle-aged psychiatric social worker, which meant she had the hide of a rhinoceros. It didn't help that she was married to a cop.

"He might get killed!" she half-wailed.

"Yeah, he might," Maureen responded. "He's an officer in command of a flying artillery unit. Maybe in another life Thorsten will choose to do something safer, like being a skydiver or a demolitions expert or a NASCAR driver. But in the here and now—damn fool got himself promoted again, too—he chose to do this instead. My husband chose to be a cop. Did I tell you he turned down an offer to become the manager of the auto parts store he was working in, before he enrolled in the police academy? So there's another damn fool."

Caroline got up and went to the window in Maureen's office. Then, she pushed the curtain aside so she could have the pleasure of gazing out onto Magdeburg from the vantage point of the third floor window.

As visual pleasures went, this was akin to sightseeing Pittsburgh—not the modern and attractive city that Caroline had known in the late twentieth century, but Pittsburgh as it had been a century earlier in its industrial heyday. There were a lot of good things about living in a city which was the center of booming industry as well as the new capital of a new nation. Jobs were plentiful, and they generally paid well. But "looks pretty" was not one of them, and "smells nice" even less so.

Still, staring at Magdeburg's factories was better than dwelling morosely on what might happen to her fiancé, once the war started. Or resumed, depending on how you looked at it. Thorsten's friend Eric Krenz had told her that the historians at the new college he'd been taking classes at were already arguing about it. Should Emperor Gustav Adolf's soon-to-be-launched campaign against Brandenburg and Saxony be considered a new war? And if so, what to call it? The "Eastern War" was advocated by some, but most seem to feel that was excessively expansive. The "East" was a large place, after all, and nobody thought this would be the last war thereabouts.

Still others, Eric said, argued that the looming hostilities should simply be considered another campaign in the Ostend League War—as some called it; other historians preferred "the Baltic War" and there was one fellow who was holding out for "the Richelieu War"—seeing as how the cause of it was the emperor's fury that Brandenburg and Saxony had betrayed him after the League of Ostend launched its attack.

Caroline didn't give a damn what they called it. What difference did it make? No matter what name was given to the upcoming war, Thorsten would be doing the same thing—either leading a charge against well-armed enemies or holding off a charge of theirs. To make things still worse, the "flying" part of "flying artillery" meant Thorsten would be mounted. She couldn't think of anything dumber or more dangerous than perching a man on top of a horse on a battlefield, with about fifty gazillion chunks of metal flying every whichaway.

"So you think I should go," she said.

"Yes. I do. For one thing—if you can tear yourself away from your personal situation for a moment—you'll help keep the trip from becoming a minor disaster.

I'm sure and certain Prince Ulrik will jump for joy. Kristina's a handful at the best of times, and visiting her mother will not be one of them. By all accounts I've heard, the woman's a loon."

Caroline couldn't help but smile. "I don't think 'loon' is one of the approved terms in the *Diagnostic and Statistical Manual of Mental Disorders,* Maureen."

"No, it isn't. Not even in DSM-IV. Who cares? That damn thing was only good for hustling medical insurance companies—and there aren't any of them in the here and now, either. By all accounts, the queen of Sweden is a loon. Or if you prefer, a nut case."

Caroline wasn't inclined to argue the point. She knew that a good part of the reason the young princess was so determined to have Caroline accompany her to Stockholm was because her mother always upset her. That would be even more true this time, Kristina said, because she'd be introducing a future husband in the bargain.

Interestingly, Kristina now seemed more worried that her mother wouldn't approve of Ulrik, rather than being worried about what Ulrik might do. In the short since she'd been introduced to her spouse-to-be, the girl had taken a liking to him. What was perhaps even more important, given the cold realities of royal marriages, was that she was starting to trust Ulrik as well.

That was fine with Caroline. She thought Ulrik was quite trustworthy herself. And that certainly boded well for the future. Unhappy royal marriages usually produced grief that extended far beyond palaces. One of them had even caused the most famous war in history, assuming Homer hadn't made the whole thing up.

"Okay. You said, 'for one thing.' That implies a second reason. What is it?"

Maureen shook her head. "I can't believe how dense you are sometimes. Caroline, we're trying to introduce modern and enlightened attitudes toward mental problems and diseases into a century where they still burn witches. Has it occurred to you that having the future—take your pick, or pick all three—queen of Sweden, empress of the USE and high queen or whatever the hell they call her of the Union of Kalmar being someone friendly to us and to our endeavors might be just a tad helpful?"

"Oh." She thought about that, for a while. "All right," she said eventually. "I'll go."

When he got the news that Caroline Platzer would be accompanying them on their voyage to Stockholm, Ulrik did jump for joy. Not very high, true; and he didn't even think of clicking his heels. But jump he did, grinning from ear to ear.

"Baldur," he announced, "a Herculean task just became a merely difficult one."

The Danish prince's sidekick, technical expert and close friend Baldur Norddahl was less sanguine. "The girl's still who and what she is, and the mother's still no more than half-sane. And that's a long way to go, and the Baltic can be treacherous. And I don't like Stockholm to begin with. Never did."

Ulrik's grin stayed in place. "That's because you were accused of crimes there. Falsely, you say."

"The charges were preposterous in every particular," Baldur said stoutly. "Either I was confused for another—the charitable explanation—or the authorities harbored animosity toward me." He cleared his throat. "For reasons unknown."

"Ha! But have no fear. I will vouch for you myself. Perhaps more to the point, so will the princess. She's taken a liking to you, I think."

Norddahl thought the same himself. He was not sure, though, whether being Kristina's friend or her foe carried more in the way of risk and excitement.

Thorsten Engler reacted to the news very calmly. Equanimity was something the young German ex-farmer did very well. Normally, that was one of her fiancé's traits that Caroline cherished. But less so, of late, once it dawned on her that he probably exhibited that same equanimity in the middle of a battle. She'd be a lot happier if he shared more of his friend Eric's healthy respect for peril. No one would ever accuse Eric Krenz of being a coward, certainly. But the young German ex-gunsmith was the first to say that war was a silly way to settle disputes and that his own happiness and serenity improved in direct measure as he distanced himself from mayhem.

On the other hand, he'd managed somehow to get himself promoted too, so apparently he had some share of damn-fooledness as well. What was it about men, Caroline wondered grumpily, that made them so resistant to common sense? With their skills and personality traits—they were both quite charming men, each in his own way—Thorsten and Eric could easily manage to get themselves transferred to much safer assignments, without leaving themselves open to charges of pusillanimity.

They wouldn't even have to leave the army. Caroline

was no expert on military matters, but even she knew that most soldiers never got very close to combat. Any army had a bigger tail than it did teeth, as they put it. For every damn fool leading a flying artillery charge, there were at least three soldiers way back in the rear hauling up the wherewithal that allowed him to be a damn fool in the first place.

"Better to haul a wagon than be hauled away in a hearse," she muttered.

"What was that, dearest?" asked Thorsten.

Krenz, whose hearing bordered on the supernatural, grinned widely and leaned back in his chair at the table in Caroline's kitchen. "She fears your imminent demise, on account of your recklessness at the front. Always waving a saber where I—an intelligent man— wield a shovel. That's why she's sniffling, too."

"I'm sniffling because I'm cutting onions," Caroline said. Wondering if it were true.

Thorsten and Eric left the next morning. General Torstensson had summoned all officers to their posts. The emperor was arriving with his Swedish forces and the USE army was mobilizing to join him. The war against Brandenburg and Saxony was imminent, and everyone expected the Austrians and the Poles to come to their aid. That would turn what might otherwise be labeled a mere suppression of rebellion into an all-out war.

To Thorsten's surprise, Princess Kristina came to see him off too. He knew she was fond of him—the "Count of Narnia" title bestowed upon him after the battle of Ahrensbök had been at her insistence—but he hadn't thought she'd go to the trouble. One doesn't expect headstrong eight-year-old princesses to think of such things.

"Caroline must have put her up to it," Krenz said, as they rode off. "It never ceases to amaze me, the way that woman dotes on you."

Engler smiled. "When are you going to get your own woman, Eric, so you can stop fussing at me about mine?"

Chapter 4

Near Poznan, Poland

As he watched the archer bringing his horse around again for another run at the target, Lukasz Opalinski leaned toward the man standing next to him. "So, tell me, Jozef. Is Grantville as exotic as its reputation?"

Jozef Wojtowicz didn't answer immediately. He was preoccupied with watching the mounted archer.

"I think he's still the best horseman I've ever seen," he said quietly.

"He's probably the best in Poland, anyway," said Opalinski. "For sure and certain, he's the best archer." The words were spoken in a tone that had more of derision in it than admiration—albeit friendly derision. Then, in the sure tones of man who was still no older than twenty-two, "The archery's a complete waste of time and effort. The horsemanship . . . Well, not so much. But this is still—"

He waved at the man on horseback, now racing past the target and drawing the bow. With his size and splendid costume, he was a magnificent figure.

"Completely ridiculous. We are not Mongols, after

all, nor will we be fighting such. Even the Tatars are outgrowing this foolishness."

The arrow pierced the target, almost right in the center.

Wojtowicz didn't argue the point. But it was still a mesmerizing sight to watch.

"Grantville," nudged his companion.

Josef shook his head. "It's complicated, Lukasz. In some ways, it's incredibly exotic. Yes, they can talk with each at long distance—miles, many miles—using little machines. Yes, they can make moving pictures on glass. Yes, they have flying machines. I watched them many times. Yes, yes, yes—just about every such tale you've heard is either true or is simply an exaggeration of something that is true."

The mounted archer came back around again, still at a full gallop. Jozef, who was an accomplished horseman himself, knew how much skill was required simply to manage that much. The rider's hands, of course, were completely preoccupied with the bow. Add onto that the skill of the archery—again, the arrow hit the target's center—and add onto *that* the preposterous pull of the bow being used. Jozef had no idea what it was, precisely, but he was quite sure that he'd have to struggle to draw the bow even standing flat-footed. And while Jozef was not an especially large man, or a tall man, he was quite strong.

He'd broken off his account, watching. Opalinski nudged him again. "Grantville, Grantville. Let's keep our mind on the future, Jozef, not"—he waved again at the mounted archer, with a dismissive gesture—"this flamboyantly absurd display of prehistoric martial skills."

Jozef smiled. "In other respects, no. Leaving aside

the machines and marvelous mechanism, Grantville seems much like any other town. People going about their business, that's all."

He was fudging here, but he didn't see any alternative. Not, at least, any alternative suitable for a conversation held under these circumstances. The months that Jozef had spent in Grantville had also made clear to him the more subtle—but in some way, even more exotic—differences in social custom that lay beneath the surface of the fantastic machines. He'd also come to understand that those subtleties in social custom were inextricably tied to the mechanical skills that were so much more outwardly evident.

It was not complicated, really, if a man was willing to look at things with clear eyes. If you wanted your serfs to build and operate complex equipment for you, in order to enhance your wealth and power, then . . .

Sooner or later, you'd have to be willing to end their serfdom. The American technology presumed a level of intellect and education even in their so-called "unskilled" laborers that no Polish or Lithuanian or Ruthenian serf could possibly match. And simply instructing them wouldn't work. In the nature of things, education can only be narrowed so far or it becomes useless. And given the necessary breadth, how could a sane man expect an educated serf to keep from being discontented—and, now, far better equipped to struggle against the source of his discontent?

Nor was it simply a matter of education, as such. Another thing had also become clear to Jozef in the time he'd spent in Grantville—and perhaps clearer still, during the months that followed when he'd resided in Magdeburg. The sort of broad-ranging skills that were necessary in a population to create and sustain the technical marvels which the Americans took for granted also presupposed mobility of labor. There was no way around it. Not, certainly, in the long run. The needed skills for that sort of technologically advanced society were simply too complex, too interconnected—most of all, too unpredictable. The demand could only be met by a productive population which was free to move about at will, to learn whatever skills and apply themselves to whatever labor they chose. You could no more regulate it than you could regulate the ocean.

Put it all together, and the conclusion was obvious. Jozef had come to it long before he left Magdeburg. If the Commonwealth of Poland and Lithuania was to have any chance at all of surviving the historical doom so clear and explicit even in Grantville's sketchy historical records of the future of eastern Europe—the Commonwealth had been the one and only major European power which had simply vanished by the end of the eighteenth century—then serfdom had to be destroyed. And Jozef could see only two options. Either the Poles and Lithuanians destroyed serfdom themselves, or someone else would destroy it for them. And, in that second event, might very well destroy the Commonwealth in the process.

But how to explain that, even to the young man standing next to him—much less the mounted archer putting on this impressive display?

The archer was Stanislaw Koniecpolski, who was not only the grand hetman of the Commonwealth but also one of its greatest magnates. The Koniecpolski family was one of the mighty families of the realm, not to mention one of its richest. They owned vast estates in Poland and the Ruthenian lands. The hetman himself owned sixteen districts and had a yearly retinue somewhere in excess of half a million zlotys. He'd even founded a complete new town—Brody, which had manufactories as well as serving as a commercial center. Jozef had heard it said that more than one hundred thousand people lived on Stanislaw Koniecpolski's estates, most of them Ruthenians. And most of them serfs, of course.

He was immensely powerful, too, not just wealthy. King Wladyslaw allowed Koniecpolski what amounted to the powers of a viceroy in the southwestern area of the Commonwealth. Some foreigners even referred to the hetman as the "vice-king of the Ukraine," although no such title actually existed in Polish law. But the king trusted him—and for good reason. So, the hetman negotiated directly with the Ottoman Empire, and the Tatars, and even signed treaties in his own name. He also had perhaps the most extensive spy network in the Commonwealth, which penetrated Muscovy as well as the Ottoman and Tatar realms.

And now, penetrated the United States of Europe as well. Insofar, at least, as his young nephew Jozef had been able to create a spy network in that newest realm of the continent over the past year and a half.

It was a rather extensive network, actually, given the short time available—and, in Jozef's opinion, quite a good one. It turned out that he had a genuine gift for such work.

The young man standing next to Jozef, Lukasz Opalinski, came from the same class of the high nobility. And if the Opalinski family was not as wealthy as the Koniecpolskis and many of the other great magnates, they made up for it by their vigorous involvement in the Commonwealth's political affairs.

They were not stupid men, either of them. Not in the least. Just men so ingrained with generations of unthinking attitudes that Jozef knew how hard it would be for them to even see the problem, much less the solution. He suspected the only reason he'd been able to shed his own szlachta blinders was because he wasn't exactly szlachta to begin with.

"You're smiling, Jozef," said Opalinski. "I don't think I care for that smile."

Jozef chuckled. "I was contemplating the advantages of bastardy."

"What's to contemplate? You get all the advantages of good blood with the added benefit of an excuse whenever you cross someone."

Jozef shook his head. "It seems like an elaborate way to go about the business. Samuel Laszcz manages to cross almost everyone without the benefit of bastardy. Granted, it helps that he has the hetman's favor and protection."

A scowl came to Opalinski. "Laszcz! That shithead." He used the German term, not the Polish equivalent. Like Jozef himself, Lukasz was fluent in several languages. He was particularly fond of German profanity.

So was Wojtowicz, for that matter—although, in recent months, he'd also grown very fond of American vulgarity.

"Finally! He's finished," said Opalinski.

And, indeed, the mounted archer had sheathed his bow and was trotting toward them.

When he drew close, he smiled down at the two young men. "I see from his scowl that Lukasz had not budged from his certainty that I am indulging myself. And what's your opinion, Nephew?"

Jozef squinted up at his uncle. And, as he'd known it would, felt his resolve to break with the man if he couldn't bring him to understand the truth crumbling away. Stanislaw Koniecpolski had that effect on people close to him. Say what you would about the narrow views and limitations of the grand hetman of the Commonwealth, Jozef didn't know a single person who wouldn't agree that he was a fair-minded and honorable man.

The simple fact that he referred openly to Jozef himself as his nephew was but one of many illustrations of Koniecpolski's character. Jozef was a bastard, born of a dalliance by Stanislaw Koniecpolski's younger brother Przedbor. After Przedbor died at the siege of Smolensk during the Dymitriad wars with Muscovy, the hetman had taken in the boy and his mother and raised him in his own household at the great family estate in Koniecpol.

"I wouldn't presume to judge, Uncle."

Koniecpolski laughed. "Always the diplomat! Well, Nephew, I will explain to you the truth, in the hopes that you might see it where stubborn young Opalinski here sees only a pointless melancholy for things past."

He stumbled over the word "melancholy" a bit. The hetman suffered from a speech impediment, and had since he was a boy. He usually avoided long words, in fact, since he tended to stutter on them. That habit of speaking in plain and simple words led some people to assume Koniecpolski was dull-witted, an assumption which was very far from the truth.

Using his bare hands, the hetman mimicked an

archer drawing his bow. He twisted sideways in the saddle as he did so, as if aiming at a target off to his left. "Notice, youngster, how the innate demands of using a bow properly while in a saddle almost force the archer to fire to his side, or even"—here he twisted still further in the saddle, imitating a man aiming behind him—"to his rear. In the nature of the thing, it is very difficult to fire a bow straight ahead while sitting in a saddle—and impossible to do it well, even for an excellent archer."

Jozef nodded. "Yes, I can see that."

The hetman beamed. "Well, then! You understand now—should, at least—what somehow still remains a puzzle to young Lukasz. The reason to practice mounted archery is to ingrain intelligent tactics in a soldier. The pike, the musket, the sword—pfah!" His pronounced mustachios wiggled with the sneer. "These teach a man to be stupid. Straight ahead, straight ahead, straight ahead."

Opalinski sniffed. "That may well be. But that will still be the way the Swede comes at us—and not even you think he can be defeated with bows and arrows."

"Well, of course not. But I also know that I have no chance of defeating the Swede—not so mighty as he has become—if I simply try to match him head to head, like two bulls in a field." Koniecpolski gazed down at the young nobleman, very serenely. "This is why I am the grand hetman of Poland and Lithuania, and you are not."

Opalinski chuckled. "Point taken." He shivered a little, and drew his cloak around him more closely. "And, now, it's cold. Your poor horse looks half-frozen himself. I propose we retire indoors."

In point of fact, the horse—like the hetman—had been exercising far too vigorously to be chilled. And it wasn't that cold, anyway, even this early in the morning. It was summer, after all. Still, the idea of retiring to a comfortable salon and warming one's innards with a stout beverage appealed to Jozef. So, he too drew his cloak around him more tightly, and faked a shiver.

"Weaklings," jeered Koniecpolski. "And at your age! Just another reason to practice mounted archery."

After Koniecpolski left for the stables, Jozef and Lukasz began walking toward the manor, some distance away. Fortunately, they were on one of the Koniecpolski family's smallish estates, this one located near Poznan. Had they been at the great family estate in Koniecpol, their walk would have been much longer. Fortunately, also, it had been a sunny day, so the ground was dry. Had there been a thunderstorm recently, their boots would have been caked with mud by the time they reached their destination.

Still, it was not a short distance, even if the walk was easy. That suited Jozef well enough, though. He needed the time to compose his thoughts.

"So solemn," Opalinski murmured, after a while. "Is it really that bad, Jozef?"

Wojtowicz gave his friend a sideways glance. "Well. Yes, actually. I'm afraid the hetman's not going to like what I have to say. Or you, for that matter."

"Why not?"

"Because I'm going to tell him that it's sheer folly to weigh in on the side of the Saxons and Brandenburgers against the USE. Those are German lands, not

Polish. We should just stay out of the whole business. All that an intervention on our part will accomplish is to give Gustav Adolf an excuse to invade Poland."

"Not that he's ever needed much of one," grunted Lukasz.

"True, true. Still and all, if we stay out—but!" He lifted his hand. "I may as well save it for the hetman. No point giving the same speech twice. It'll probably be wasted on you anyway, dull-witted soldier that you are."

Lukasz called him a very unfavorable term in Lithuanian.

Jozef grinned. "I have the most marvelous American expression."

After he spoke it a few times, Lukasz began practicing the pronunciation. "Modderfooker...mudder—yes, it is nice."

Chapter 5

After Jozef finished presenting his case for staying out of the coming war between the USE and the Saxon-Brandenburgers, Koniecpolski leaned back in his chair. It was a very large and comfortable chair in a very large and comfortable chamber in his manor. Americans would have called it a living room on steroids.

For a few seconds, he stroked his large and prominent nose. Then, as Jozef had expected he would, the hetman sidestepped the issue. "I keep hearing rumors that the Americans are well-disposed toward Poland," he said. "Is that true, Nephew?"

"Well... It's complicated. On the one hand, yes. They tend to have a favorable attitude toward Poles. Quite favorable, actually."

"Why?" asked Lukasz.

"Several reasons. The first and simplest is that the country they came from was a country created by immigrants. Many of those immigrants were Polish."

The hetman grunted, and hefted a wine glass. "So I've heard. But I would assume many of them were Swedes also."

"There were immigrants from Sweden, yes, and other

Scandinavian countries. But most of the Scandinavian immigrants settled elsewhere in America. Places called Minnesota and Wisconsin. There were many more Poles in the area from which Grantville came."

He made a little wagging gesture with his hand. "But that's only one reason, and perhaps not the most important. Some Poles, including noblemen, helped the Americans in their war of independence with England. And, in much more recent times—'recent,' at least, as Americans see it—their principal antagonist was Russia. And since Poland was under Russian control—"

He restrained himself from adding: *because of idiots like those who control the throne and Sejm.*

"—and Poles chafed at the situation, the Americans were favorably disposed toward us."

Koniecpolski finished drinking from his cup. "And on the other hand?" he asked.

Jozef shrugged. "Despite their reputation for fanciful notions—what they themselves call 'romanticism'—the Americans are every bit as inclined toward being practical and hardheaded as anyone else. The fact is, whether they are favorably disposed to us or not, they have formed a close political relationship with the king of Sweden. There are some aspects to that relationship which do not particularly please them, true. Still, by and large, most Americans think their bargain with Gustav Adolf has worked quite well for them. They are not going to jeopardize it because of some favorable sentiments toward us—which, when you come right down to it, are rather vague and nebulous sentiments in the first place."

Koniecpolski nodded again. His eyes never left Jozef's face, though. "And there's something else."

Jozef took a deep breath. "Yes, there is. Whatever favorable sentiments may exist among the Americans toward we Poles as a people, there are no favorable sentiments—not in their leadership, at any rate—toward the Commonwealth as it exists today. I have heard some of their speeches, Uncle, and read a great many more of their writings. That includes, for instance, a speech given by Michael Stearns in which he states that the two great evils which loom before the world today are chattel slavery in the New World and the second serfdom in eastern Europe. Both of which must be destroyed."

"His term?" asked Koniecpolski. "Destroyed?"

"One of his terms. Others were 'eradicated,' 'crushed,' and 'scrubbed from existence.' He is quite serious about it, Uncle. He believes the great evils that afflicted the world he came from were caused, in large part, by the ever-widening divergence between the western and eastern parts of Europe. This, he claims, is what underlay the two great world wars that were fought in the century from which he came, in the course of which tens of millions of people died. And he lays the blame for that divergence upon the fact that, where serfdom vanished in western Europe, it had a resurgence in the eastern lands."

"He's no longer the prime minister of the USE, however," pointed out Lukasz.

"Yes—but that's beside the point. We were talking about the Americans, not the USE. Whether Mike Stearns is the prime minister or not, he still retains the personal allegiance of the big majority of Americans. That even includes Admiral Simpson now, who was once his most prominent opponent among the up-timers." Jozef finished his own glass of wine and set it down on a side table. "Besides, while he is no longer prime minister, he is now one of the three divisional commanders in Torstensson's army. The same army, I remind you, that crushed the French at Ahrensbök. So it's hardly the case that he's vanished from the scene."

The hetman shifted his massive shoulders. The gesture was not quite a shrug. "I may not even disagree with you, Jozef. But it doesn't matter. I am the grand hetman of Poland, not its king. Nor, perhaps more importantly, am I the Sejm. They will make the decision, not me—but I must tell you that King Wladyslaw is strongly inclined to intervene."

Lukasz sniffed. "Of course he is. He's a Vasa himself and thinks he's the rightful king of Sweden, not Gustav Adolf." A bit angrily, he added, "Which is the reason he's constantly embroiling Poland and Lithuania in things we should be staying out of."

Again, Koniecpolski shifted his shoulders. "I may not disagree with you, either, young Opalinski. But—again—I am simply the grand hetman. Whatever decision the Sejm and the king make, I will obey."

Jozef knew there was no point in pursuing the matter. It was odd, in a way. When it came to martial matters, Stanislaw Koniecpolski had a supple and flexible mind. For all the man's personal devotion to ancient methods of warfare—he probably *was* the greatest archer in Poland; certainly the greatest mounted archer—he'd proven quite capable all his life of adapting to new realities. He knew how to use modern infantry, artillery and fortifications; the so-called "Dutch style" of warfare. He had proven to be skilled at combining land and naval operations, too, although he was not a naval commander himself. Yet that same adaptability ended abruptly whenever Koniecpolski confronted a problem of a social or political rather than strictly military nature.

Koniecpolski now looked to Lukasz. "I could very much use some more up-to-date and accurate military information. My iconoclastic young nephew here has proven to be a superb spymaster. Alas, his knowledge of purely military matters is not what it could be. You, on the other hand—as one might expect from an Opalinski—have already made a reputation for yourself as a hussar."

Lukasz made humble noises. Jozef was rather amused. In point of simple fact, despite his youth, Lukasz *was* a noted hussar. A good thing, too. The Opalinski family produced a high number of free-thinkers and heretics. Lukasz's older brother Krzysztof, for instance, was already a notorious radical, who was accused of advocating the overthrow of serfdom and the monarchy—even the nobility to which he himself belonged. The accusation was probably true.

Fortunately, Opalinskis also tended to be skilled at arms. Certainly, Lukasz was.

"How may I be of service?" he asked.

"I do not expect Poland will be fielding any sizeable forces in the opening stages of the coming war, even assuming the Sejm decides to intervene. You know how it is."

Lukasz nodded, wincing a little. Jozef was wincing himself.

You know how it is. In the long and often inglorious annals of the human race, Jozef thought the Polish

Sejm was probably the worst example at any place or any time of all the vices of parliaments and none of their virtues. It was more riddled with factionalism than the ancient Greek city-states—and then added to the mix the absurdity of the individual veto, which even the cantankerous Greeks had had enough sense to eschew. The famous—notorious—Polish Sejm's *liberum veto* required a unanimous decision before anything could be done. The result was that making any decision, even a minor one much less a decision to go to war, invariably required weeks of wrangling. Often enough, months of wrangling.

That situation would only get worse, too, as time went on. The Americans hadn't brought very much in the way of Poland's history with them. Most of what Jozef had been able to discover he'd put together piecemeal, usually from encyclopedia entries. But the *liberum veto* would become so notorious that it had made the passage through the Ring of Fire—more than four centuries after the absurd practice was instituted. In that other universe, by the middle of the next century, it would completely paralyze the Polish state.

The hetman continued. "But I do have the authority, I feel, to send a small unit to fight alongside the Saxons and Brandenburgers. They will be pleased by the gesture, especially with an Opalinski in command." He wagged a large, thick finger. "But don't do anything reckless! From my viewpoint, yours will be simply a scouting mission. I've fought the Swedes before. I've even fought Gustav Adolf himself. But I've never encountered these Americans and their mechanical marvels. I've heard tales of their war machines, but I'd like to get your firsthand impression."

Lukasz nodded. "I understand."

The hetman rose. "And now, I must leave to deal with some other business. Unlike you youngsters, who have the luxury of obsessing over single matters, we men of maturity and substance must deal with many."

Jozef smiled. "Ah, yes. What the Americans call 'multitasking.' But they say only women are really good at it. So perhaps women should be put in charge of the Commonwealth's affairs."

For the first time that day, a trace of alarm came to the hetman's face. "What a dreadful idea!"

Chapter 6

Vienna, Austria

"Yes, I know you're against it," Ferdinand said. The young emperor of Austria settled back in his chair and gave Janos Drugeth a look from under lowered brows that fell short of favorable. Quite a ways short, in fact. "What I wonder is how much of your opposition is based on your attachment to the American woman."

Janos managed not to clench his teeth. For all that he generally approved of Ferdinand III—he even counted himself one of the emperor's few close friends—there were times the man reminded him of his narrow-minded and pigheaded father. Once the emperor made up his mind about something, he could be very hard to dislodge, no matter how foolish the decision might be.

Still, Janos reminded himself, the emperor was only "very hard" to persuade he was wrong. His predecessor, Ferdinand II, had been impossible.

"To begin with," he said mildly, "I am not 'attached' to Noelle Stull. We have exchanged letters, that's all."

"Gifts too."

Drugeth nodded. "Yes, gifts too. But you know perfectly well, Ferdinand, that Americans do not see such exchanges the same way we do. Even between a young man and a young woman."

He was one of the very few people allowed to address the emperor informally, as long as they were speaking in private. Normally, that absence of protocol allowed for considerable ease and warmth in their relationship. On this occasion, Drugeth found himself regretting it. It was easier to oppose such a friend on an important issue when you could call him what he actually was—"Your Majesty," the ruler of the land.

Ferdinand grunted. The noise had a vaguely sour tone. It had more than a vaguely childish tone, as well.

But Drugeth managed not to laugh. On most occasions, he would have been at liberty to disparage his good friend Ferdinand. But with a dispute like this between them, such derision would be unwise. It would certainly be counterproductive. Whatever else they were, Habsburg monarchs were self-assured. They had not become Europe's premier dynasty and held that position for so many centuries because they were given to doubt and uncertainty.

As a rule, that was a good trait. Here, unfortunately, it was not.

Janos was silent for a moment, gauging the emperor's mood. He decided that it would be pointless to continue the line of argument he'd been pursuing so far this morning—to wit, that getting into a war with the USE over the fate of John George and his Brandenburg counterpart George William would be pointless, foolish and shortsighted.

Pointless, because Drugeth had no doubt whatever

that the electors of Saxony and Brandenburg were doomed to defeat. Their armies were not ranked among the best in Europe and would be hopelessly outclassed by Gustav Adolf's forces. The contrast in the quality of military leadership was probably just as severe. The Swedish king was recognized as one of the great captains of the world, and his young lieutenant Torstensson—the same man who had crushed the French at Ahrensbök—ranked not much below him. In contrast, the Brandenburg commanders were mediocre. The Saxon general von Arnim was competent, but some of the Saxon officers—the brute Holk, for instance—had no business being placed in charge of an army.

Foolish, because Austria couldn't intervene directly, in any event. Bohemia stood in the way, and Bohemia was allied to the USE. So, should Austria leap into the fray on the side of Saxony and Brandenburg, it would have only two options: Send an army against Wallenstein, which would reopen a war that Janos believed—and so did Emperor Ferdinand III himself, in his more honest moments—should be ended. Or, send Austrian forces on a long and roundabout march through Poland. That would require bypassing Silesia, which was now also in Wallenstein's possession. The end result would be to leave Austria largely defenseless should Wallenstein decide to reopen the war himself. Janos advocated peace with Bohemia, not because he trusted Wallenstein but because he didn't. A peace settlement would have the great virtue of directing Wallenstein's ambitions to the east instead of southward.

Such a risky gambit would also leave Austria open to attack from the Turk, which was something Drugeth feared quite a bit more than he feared an attack by

Bohemia. The young sultan of the Ottoman Empire, Murad IV, was every bit as ambitious as Wallenstein but he commanded a far more powerful realm than Bohemia.

Finally, it would be shortsighted. Ferdinand's desire to intervene in the coming war was nothing more intelligent or sublime than the instinctive reaction of a dynast to the imminent destruction of two dynasties by a nation that bordered on an outright republic. What made Ferdinand's reaction particularly shortsighted was the fact that one of those dynasties—the Hohenzollerns of Brandenburg—would become the most bitter enemies of the Habsburgs a century hence. That assumed, of course, that the history of this world followed that of the universe the Americans came from, which was now most unlikely.

Janos had spent hours discussing the history of that other universe with the emperor. Grantville's records concerning the Austrian empire had not been as extensive as their histories of England or even France. Still, the basic outlines were clear enough; certainly the two most salient facts, from the standpoint of a Habsburg:

Fact One. Although Austria would survive, as a small landlocked nation in central Europe, all vestiges of the empire would vanish.

Fact Two. So would the Habsburg dynasty, as a ruling family. That would be true of both branches of the family. Indeed, the Spanish branch would die out at the end of this century.

Again, it was highly unlikely that the course of history in this universe would follow that in the other. It couldn't, in fact, because in this world a third branch of the Habsburg had already come into existence in the Low Countries, something which had never happened in the universe Grantville came from.

Still, the patterns were clear. Unless the rulers of Austria carried through a profound transformation of their realm, they would not survive. And it was *that* task which ought to be at the forefront of Ferdinand's mind, not this atavistic desire to come to the rescue of dynasticism. On some level, Janos was certain that even Ferdinand himself knew as much.

But it was probably too much to expect that a scion of the continent's oldest and most powerful family would not suffer the occasional lapse. The thing to do now was to limit the damage until Ferdinand could come to his senses.

The best way to do that was to use Austria's oldest and most powerful enemy. "Point with alarm," was the American phrase, according to Noelle in one of her letters.

Janos got up from his chair and went over to the side table to refill his glass with wine. When he and Ferdinand met privately in this small salon the emperor used for such purposes, there were no servants present. That was a practice that Ferdinand had instituted at Drugeth's insistence.

"Beyond that, Ferdinand, I am concerned about the Turks." He lifted the bottle, offering to pour for the emperor.

Ferdinand shook his head, and gave him another of those suspicious looks from under lowered brows. "You're just trying to frighten me, damn you. What your leman called 'pointing with alarm' in one of those letters you showed me."

Alas. Janos had forgotten that he'd shown that letter of Noelle's to the emperor. Ferdinand served him as an adviser in his courtship of the American woman.

"Still." He resumed his seat and shook his head, trying to seem as firm and certain as he could. "I *am* worried, Ferdinand. The one thing we know for sure is that the Ottomans have purchased a prodigious number of copies of various texts from Grantville. Among them have been histories as well as technical and scientific manuals."

The emperor made a derisive sound. "Yes, they have. Despite that idiotic proclamation of the Turkish sultan that the Ring of Fire never happened, the Americans are witches, and anyone caught saying otherwise will be strangled."

Drugeth shrugged. "But I suspect the proclamation's purpose is primarily to maintain secrecy. One other thing we know for sure is that the Turks have launched some sort of technical project in a location which we haven't yet determined. The purpose is almost certainly to develop new engines of war, using American methods."

Ferdinand frowned. "Do you think they have American advisers and technicians, as we do?"

Janos shook his head. "Possible, but unlikely."

He decided to leave unspoken his growing fears about the band of Americans whom he had himself suborned and escorted into Austria after they defected. It was true that they were providing Austria with a lot of valuable advice and knowledge. But Drugeth didn't trust them. They had betrayed their own people for no more exalted motives than greed and a desire to escape prosecution for criminal activity. Why would people like that hesitate, if the Ottomans offered them still greater rewards? Which, the sultan of the Turks was certainly in a position to do, should he so choose. No realm in the world was as wealthy as the Ottoman Empire, save possibly the empire of the Mughals or that of the Ming dynasty in China. But according to the up-time texts, the Mings were on the eve of collapse at the hands of Manchu invaders. In that other universe, on the other hand, the Ottomans lasted as long as the Habsburgs themselves—and, in 1683, came very close to seizing Vienna after marching an army of 150,000 men into Austria. Like the Mughals in India, the Turks were at the height of their wealth and power.

But Janos had no proof or even solid evidence that any of the Americans now in Austrian service were planning to defect to the Ottomans. If he raised his concerns now, Ferdinand would just accuse him of being an alarmist. Again.

He kept silent, allowing the emperor to mull on the matter. There was nothing at all wrong with Ferdinand's mind, whenever he could shuffle off unthinking royal notions and attitudes. It was better to allow him to come to his own conclusions and decisions. Trying to chivvy him would be counterproductive.

After a minute or so, Ferdinand mused: "It's too late for the Turk to launch an invasion this year."

Drugeth nodded. Like many Hungarian noblemen he was an experienced soldier. The Ottomans would have to mobilize a huge army to attack Vienna—and get that army and its equally enormous supply train through the Balkans. It was impossible to do so in winter, of course. But it was also essential that such an army not be left stranded in the middle of winter.

There would be no way to keep it supplied with enough food, if it failed to seize Vienna.

The end result of these harsh logistical realities was that any attack launched by the Turks against Austria had to follow a rather fixed and rigid timetable. The invasion couldn't possibly be launched until the fresh spring grass arrived, or there wouldn't be enough grazing for the horses and oxen. There was no possibility of hauling enough fodder. Not with the immense number of livestock involved in such a campaign.

Traditionally, the Turks began their campaigning season at or near the time of the festival in honor of Hizir Hyas, the Moslem saint who protected travelers and other people in peril. That came in early May, by the Christian calendar.

Of course, the Turks wouldn't wait that long before they began moving their troops. They'd march them north to Belgrade in March and April, and launch the attack from there once the weather and grazing conditions permitted. Belgrade was roughly half the distance from Istanbul to Vienna, but the terrain over that final stretch was much more difficult for an army. Much of the terrain south of the Danube consisted of marshes and swamps.

The Turkish army was extremely well organized, true. Being honest, he acknowledged that it was better organized than the Austrian—or, indeed, most Christian armies. But it still couldn't move faster than ten or twelve miles a day. The earliest the Ottomans could reach Vienna would be late June or, more likely, sometime in July.

They couldn't afford to arrive much later than that, because once they did arrive they'd only have a few months to succeed in taking the city. If they hadn't done so by late autumn, they'd have no choice but to retreat back to Belgrade. Trying to keep an army of that size in fieldworks through winter would be almost certain disaster. Disease, exposure and hunger would slaughter far more of the sultan's soldiers than his enemy could. Such a disaster had overtaken the Ottoman army in 1529, when Suleiman the Magnificent delayed for too long before ordering a retreat, in hopes that a final assault would take Vienna.

So, Ferdinand was right. It was already June, and thus too late this year for a Turkish invasion.

"All right," said the emperor, a bit grumpily. "I'll agree to hold off any decision until the winter." He raised a rigid forefinger. "But! The price is that you have to undertake an inspection of the frontier fortifications. To see if the Turks really are planning any mischief for next year."

"Again? I inspected those forts less than—"

"Yes, again!" Ferdinand grimaced. There was some sympathy in the expression—not much—along with surly satisfaction at making Janos pay for impeding the royal will. "You can send your letters to the American woman just as well from horseback as from the comfort of your estates in Hungary."

Estates which, in point of fact, Janos hadn't seen in quite a while. That was because he'd been here in Vienna, serving the emperor in the capacity that the up-timers called "right-hand man."

But there was no point arguing the matter. Truth be told, Drugeth wouldn't mind doing such an inspection tour again. It *was* possible that the Ottomans had decided to attack Austria.

Murad was neither stupid nor weak-minded. He could study the up-time texts as well as anyone. Grantville's records with respect to Turkey were assumed to be even scantier than those relating to Austria. But Janos had his own spies in Grantville and he knew that was only true of the *public* records. There was one large private library in the town which, as it turned out, had a copy of a book by a man named Lord Kinross. *The Ottoman Centuries*, was its title. Janos had a copy of it himself, in his chambers in this very palace.

Assuming that Murad had gotten his hands on a copy also—and it would be foolish to assume otherwise—he was quite capable of drawing some lessons from the history recounted therein. The section dealing with Murad's own reign was quite extensive. If Drugeth were the sultan, there was one simple lesson he'd most likely draw from the Kinross book. In the end, the great Turkish power would be brought down not by Persians, the current enemy of the Ottomans, but by the armies of Christian nations.

So, Janos made no further demurral. He finished his glass of wine, rose, and gave his friend and emperor a little bow. "As you command, Your Majesty."

The ruler of the Austrian empire and head of the elder branch of the great Habsburg dynasty looked up at Drugeth. Once again, from under lowered brows.

"Stop gloating," he said.

Chapter 7

A castle in the countryside, near Dessau

"Please have a seat, Michael." Lennart Torstensson waved at a side table against the far wall. "There is wine, but if you prefer I can have some coffee made for you."

The Swedish general who commanded the army of the USE had a sly smile on his face. Americans had a reputation among down-timers for being teetotalers—a reputation which any number of proper hillbillies had found quite disconcerting when they learned about it.

There was some truth to the reputation, though. The Americans came from a land where clean drinking water was taken for granted. Alcohol was generally considered something a person drank in the evening, not something you consumed the whole day long. But for people in the seventeenth century, as had been true for most of human history, alcoholic beverages were a lot safer than water, unless it had been recently boiled.

So, here it was, still before noon—and Torstensson was having himself a little fun. Poking the stiff and proper up-timer, to see how high he would jump.

Mike returned the smile with a frown, as he studied the bottles on the side table.

"No whiskey?" he asked mournfully.

Torstensson chuckled. "I should know better, by now." He gestured toward the other two men in the room, who were already seated. "You have met Dodo, I believe. The more substantial fellow over there is the duke of Brunswick-Lüneburg—and now also the prince of Calenberg."

The very plump nobleman gave Mike a cheerful smile. "Please! Call me George. Staff meetings are dreary enough without everyone stumbling over titles." He half-rose from his seat and extended his hand, which Mike shook.

The other officer in the room did not follow suit, but Mike knew that wasn't due to rudeness. It was just the nature of the man. Dodo Freiherr zu Innhausen und Knyphausen was a professional soldier from East Frisia and had been one all his life. He'd started his career as a teenager fighting for the Dutch, and risen to the rank of captain by the time he was twenty years old. He'd been fighting for the Swedes since 1630. Mike didn't know him very well, but his best friend Frank Jackson thought highly of him. "He ain't what you'd call the life of the party, but he's solid as a rock," had been his summary judgment.

After Mike took his seat, he looked around. He had to struggle a bit to keep from grinning. Talk about chateau generals! This staff meeting of the commander of the USE army and the major generals in charge of the army's three divisions was being held in an actual castle.

Well . . . what the Germans called a "schloss," at any rate. The word was usually translated in up-time dictionaries as "castle," but they didn't resemble the medieval stone fortresses that Americans thought of when they used that term. Most of them, including this one, had been built during or since the Renaissance and they reminded Mike of pocket palaces more than anything else.

The derisive term "chateau generals" came from World War I, and it really wasn't fair applied to these men. They might be meeting in a castle and enjoying for the moment its little luxuries. The chairs in this particular salon were very nicely upholstered, and the walls seemed to be plastered with portraits. But all of these men would soon enough be on a battlefield and placing themselves in harm's way.

That included Mike, he reminded himself, lest his amusement get out of hand.

The four chairs in the room were not positioned evenly. The chair that Torstensson sat in faced the three chairs of his subordinates, which were arranged in a shallow arc. Torstensson's chair seemed slightly more luxurious, too. A large, low table was positioned in the center. Americans would have called it a coffee table.

After he took his seat, Torstensson was silent for a moment. He was giving Mike a look that he couldn't interpret. Slightly embarrassed, perhaps, although that would be quite out of character for the man.

Brunswick-Lüneburg smiled again, even more cheerfully than before. "Poor Lennart! A rustic Swede, he does not really have the aptitude for Machiavellian maneuvers."

The duke transferred the smile onto Mike. "He wants to use you as bait for a trap. I'd urge you to refuse, except it really is quite a delightful scheme."

Torstensson gave him an exasperated look. "Stop clowning, would you? Michael, if we eliminate the buffoonery, what George says is true enough."

Mike spread his hands a little, inviting the Swedish general to continue. But before he could say anything, Knyphausen spoke up.

"The thing is, General Stearns, you are a neophyte and the Saxon commander von Arnim is certainly feeling desperate by now."

The professional soldier had a lean and very long-nosed face that naturally lent itself to lugubrious expressions. He had such an expression now. "Poor bastard, with John George for an employer."

He seemed genuinely aggrieved at the plight faced by the Saxon general. Mike had to fight down another grin. Professional soldiers in the Thirty Years' War tended to have a thoroughly guildlike mindset, when it came to their attitudes toward other officers. There were some exceptions like Heinrich Holk, who were generally despised. But for the most part generals on opposite sides of the battlefield were more likely to feel a closer kinship to their opponent than either one of them felt for their employers.

Knyphausen leaned back, apparently satisfied that his cryptic references to Mike's inexperience and von Arnim's difficulties had made everything clear.

Mike looked back at Torstensson. "Could you perhaps be a bit more precise?"

Torstensson now tugged at his ear. "Well... The thing is, Michael, I would like you to behave recklessly in the coming battle. Pretend to behave recklessly, rather."

Brunswick-Lüneburg's smile seemed fixed in place.

"What he'd *really* prefer would be for you to act the poltroon at the coming battle. Flee at the first sign of a Saxon attack."

"Much as the Saxons did themselves at Breitenfeld," chimed in Knyphausen.

Torstensson gave them both an exasperated glance. "Actually, no. As a theoretical exercise, that would be indeed ideal. But battlefields don't lend themselves well to abstractions. A rout, once started—whether in fakery or not—is extraordinarily hard to stop. And I don't *actually* want your division to leave the field."

Mike settled back in his seat and once again had to suppress an expression. A sigh, this time, not a grin.

"Let me guess. The reason you want to undertake such a gambit—which is bound to be risky, especially with a divisional commander as inexperienced as I am—is because you figure we'll be outnumbered in the coming battle."

"You *do* have an experienced and capable staff," pointed out George. "Just leave it to them."

That was not quite blithering nonsense, but close. Mike's firsthand knowledge of military affairs was limited to a three-year stint as an enlisted man in the up-time American army twenty years back. He'd also done a lot of reading since he'd realized he was most likely going to end up as a general—what Civil War era Americans would have called a "political general"—after he left office as the USE's prime minister. But he knew enough to know that a good staff could only substitute so far for the character of a unit's commander.

Torstensson knew it himself, of course. A bit hastily, he added, "Mostly, it will just require steady nerves on your part. And the emperor himself told me he thought you had nerves of steel."

That last came with a friendly expression. But Mike wasn't about to let himself get sidetracked by a compliment. It was not really a compliment anyway, since he was pretty sure Gustav Adolf had said that to Lennart in a fit of aggravation due to Mike's admittedly hard-nosed approach to political negotiations.

"The more interesting issue," he mused, "is *why* you expect us to be outnumbered in the coming battle. By all accounts I've heard, John George can't field an army any larger than thirty-five thousand men. That's an official count, mind you. In the real world, you have to allow for desertion and illness. There'll be plenty of men just too drunk, too. I've been told by—your words, gentlemen, I remind you—my experienced and capable staff, that we won't actually face more than about twenty-five thousand men on the field of battle."

Torstensson was looking embarrassed again. Given the nature of the man, that was not something that Mike found at all comforting. The truth was, he *did* have an excellent staff.

"Our own army," Mike continued, "—the USE army proper, I mean—officially numbers twenty-seven thousand men. Three divisions, each with a complement of nine thousand officers and enlisted soldiers. Of course, we suffer from desertion, illness and drunkenness too. But certainly not to the same extent as the Saxons. Many of our soldiers are volunteers enlisted by the CoCs, motivated by ideology rather than money. So I've been told by—your words, gentlemen, not mine—that same experienced and excellent staff, that we'll be able to bring at least twenty thousand men onto that battlefield. Probably more like twenty-two or even twenty-three thousand."

Knyphausen and the duke looked away. Torstensson cleared his throat. Mike pressed on relentlessly.

"Then, of course, we need to add the forces which Gustav Adolf will bring onto the field. Even allowing for the troops he'll leave stationed against Bernhard and the French in the Rhineland provinces and in the Oberpfalz against Bavaria, he should still be able to muster a Swedish army numbering around twenty thousand men. And that doesn't include the sizeable forces that some of the provincial rulers might bring. I was told by my experienced and capable staff—such a charming phrase, too bad I didn't coin it myself—that Wilhelm V of Hesse-Kassel will bring at least seven thousand additional men."

"Closer to eight, actually," said Torstensson. Again, he cleared his throat. "Michael..."

"The way I figure it, we'll have around fifty thousand men facing an army not much more than half that size. And that's not allowing for the difference in command. Myself excluded—and allowing for my experienced and capable staff—the quality of our commanding officers greatly exceeds that of the Saxons."

"Von Arnim's pretty good," said Knyphausen stoutly.

The plump duke sniffed. "He's not the Lion of the North. Nor is he Lennart, for that matter."

Torstensson had been holding his breath for the past few seconds. Now, he let it out in a rush. "Michael, enough! As you have obviously already deduced, the emperor will not be with us on the field. He and Wilhelm are marching instead into Brandenburg. The USE army will face the Saxons alone."

By now, Mike had figured out the truth. But he was tired of people dancing around it—starting with Gustav Adolf himself. He was damn well going to get someone to admit it out loud.

"In short, he proposes to divide his forces in order to fight two enemies simultaneously. A military error so basic and egregious—even a neophyte like me knows that much—that it is inconceivable that a general as demonstrably superb as Gustav Adolf would commit it—"

Brunswick-Lüneburg started to say something but Mike drove over it. "—*unless* he had what a suspicious soul would call 'ulterior motives.'"

This time Torstensson tried to interrupt but Mike drove over him too. "And the only such motive a suspicious soul like me can discern is that Gustav Adolf is bound and determined to defeat Saxony and Brandenburg quickly enough to leave most of the campaigning season available for some other purpose. Such purpose, of course, being an invasion of Poland."

He paused, finally.

After a moment, Torstensson said: "Well. Yes. That is his plan." A bit hastily he added, "We have it on good authority that the Poles will be sending a contingent to join the Saxons. So you might say they will begin the hostilities themselves."

Mike chuckled, quite humorlessly. "Exactly how big a contingent are we talking about, Lennart?"

"Not . . . big."

The duke's chuckle, on the other hand, had some real humor in it. "To be precise, one small unit of hussars. But the commander is an Opalinski."

"In other words, a pretext." Mike gave Torstensson a level gaze. "I don't suppose there's any point in expressing my conviction that launching a major war against Poland is folly."

Torstensson shook his head. "No, Michael, there is not. You've made your opinion on this subject clear enough in the past. On several occasions, to the emperor himself. Very bluntly, too."

The two men stared at each other for a few seconds. Then Torstensson said: "You may resign your commission, of course."

Mike shook his head. "In for a penny, in for a pound. Gustav Adolf is the head of state of the United States of Europe. Yes, he's also the king of Sweden and so on and so forth, but that doesn't matter here. He's the commander in chief, according to the agreement we made. So whatever I think of the wisdom of his decisions, I'm duty bound to obey them."

"That agreement does not oblige you to serve personally, Michael," George pointed out. "I've studied your up-time history, you know. So, yes, your President Truman fired your general McDonald's—no, was it McCarthy?—but no one including him felt that McWhateverhisname was obliged to continue serving in the army."

"Technically speaking, you're right. But there are political issues involved here. Given the history of the USE—which is less than two years old, remember—and my position in that history, it would be risky for me to resign my commission over an issue like this one."

"A battlefield is likely to be far more risky," said Knyphausen, "especially one where you're directed to behave recklessly."

"I wasn't referring to the personal danger to me. I was referring to the danger to the nation."

There was silence, for a moment. Then the Frisian professional soldier nodded his head. "Well spoken, Michael," he said softly.

"Say better, well done," chimed in George. He gave Mike another of those cheerful smiles that seemed to come readily to the man. "Maybe there's something to this 'Prince of Germany' business after all."

Torstensson made a derisive sound. Close to a snort, but not quite. "Don't say that in front of the emperor," he muttered. The Swedish general pointed to one of the several side tables against the walls of the room, this one covered with maps instead of bottles of wine. "If you would, Dodo."

Knyphausen rose and went over, then came back with one of the maps and spread it across the low table in the center. As soon as he'd done so, Torstensson leaned over and pointed to a place on the map. After a few seconds to orient himself, Mike realized that the Swedish general was pointing at Leipzig. Near it, rather.

"In this area, gentlemen," said Torstensson. "I think the battle will happen here. It's good, flat terrain that will favor the Saxon cavalry."

"Favor our APCs too," grunted Knyphausen.

Mike cocked an inquisitive eye at Torstensson. "We're going to use the APCs against the Saxons? For God's sake, why?"

Before Torstensson could answer, Mike waved his hand. "Never mind. Same reason."

Torstensson nodded. Mike leaned back in his chair, and couldn't help issuing a sigh. "Well, I say it's stupid—and I don't care if Gustav Adolf is a certified military genius and I'm just a grunt. It's still stupid.

Saxony is not one of the great military powers of Europe, and those so-called 'APCs' are just armored coal trucks—which we can't replace. Not for years, at any rate. So why use them in *this* war? Not to mention that the things are fuel hogs. USE oil production has recovered from Turenne's raid during the Baltic War, true enough, but it was never very large to begin with. The Wietze oil fields just aren't that big. No European oil fields are very big, leaving aside North Sea fields we haven't got the technology to exploit and the Rumanian fields under Ottoman control. We're already lagging further and further behind civilian demand. Until—if—we can get some oil production from the expeditions to North America, we've got a perennial fuel shortage. So why make it worse using the APCs?"

Torstensson had a pained expression on his face. "Michael . . ."

"Never mind," said Mike, waving his head. "I know it's pointless to pursue the matter. I just want my opinion on the record."

The decision to use the APCs was just another indication of how determined Gustav Adolf was to start a war with the Poles as soon as possible. He was willing to use the APCs now rather than hold them back, even though Poland was a much stronger military power than Saxony—or Saxony and Brandenburg combined, for that matter.

But Mike's objection would just be overruled, and Mike would be stuck in the same bind he was stuck in now. The USE was simply too new and too unstable for him to risk precipitating a political crisis over this issue. Especially since he had mixed feelings on the subject, anyway. On the one hand, he thought the Polish situation did not lend itself well to military solutions. On the other hand...

Who could say for sure? The old saying "you can't export a revolution with bayonets" certainly had some truth. But a lot of it was just wishful thinking, too. Mike had read a great deal of history since the Ring of Fire, and one of the things he couldn't help notice was how often history was shaped by the outcome of wars. Napoleon was often denounced as a tyrant, but the fact remained that many of the revolutionary changes he made were not overturned after his defeat—not even by those he'd defeated and forced to accept those changes.

So... There was no way of knowing the outcome of a war between the USE and Poland. If was possible, in the event of a clearcut USE victory, that serfdom in eastern Europe would be destroyed. Not by Gustav Adolf and his armies, maybe. But one thing you could be sure of was that Gretchen Richter and her Committees of Correspondence would be coming into Poland on the heels of those armies. And they hated serfdom with a passion.

In fact, they were already there. Mike knew from his correspondence with Morris Roth in Prague that Red Sybolt and his radical cohorts were active in Poland. Possibly even in the Ukraine by now.

On balance, he thought a military approach to eradicating serfdom in eastern Europe had far more risks than benefits. Still, it was tempting. Military solutions had the great advantage of being clear and definite.

Appearing to be, at any rate. Often, though, that was just a mirage. Mike's friend Frank Jackson was a Vietnam veteran, and could expound for hours on the stupidity of politicians who thought a map was the territory.

He looked back down at the map in front of him and wondered if he was looking at another such mirage.

"Near Lützen, then," said George. "Hopefully, this time there will be a better outcome."

In the universe Mike had come from, the Swedes had won the battle of Lützen in 1632—but Gustav Adolf had also been killed there. So, a tactical victory had become a strategic defeat.

"I will not be leading a reckless cavalry charge," said Torstensson firmly.

But that didn't really matter, thought Mike. There were a thousand ways that tactical victories could turn into strategic defeats.

Part Two

July 1635

The round ocean and the living air

Chapter 8

Magdeburg

Had Gretchen seen the expression on Rebecca's face a month earlier, when Rebecca first inspected her new home in the capital, she would have recognized it. She was wearing much the same expression, after having completed an inspection of her own new home in the city.

Not quite, though. Gretchen had the same uncertain, dubious, apprehensive, wary, and skittish attitude. But, unlike Rebecca, she was making no attempt to avoid covetousness. The last few weeks of having to take care of a small horde of children again—she'd forgotten what it was like, during her long absence in France and Holland—made the prospect of settling them into a large apartment building very attractive.

In her days as a camp follower in a mercenary army, she wouldn't have thought of such things. Lack of privacy had been the least of her worries. But she was not immune to the common tendency of people to have their expectations and aspirations expand along with their blessings. The more you had, it sometimes seemed, the more you wanted. If you weren't careful, that could lead into a bottomless pit.

"And down you'll plunge," she muttered.

Jeff had lagged behind his wife, more interested than she was in the interior design of the building. He came into the vestibule just in time to hear her last remark.

"What was that, hon?" he asked.

Gretchen shook her head. "I was just contemplating the dangers of excessive greed."

Jeff looked around, smiling nostalgically. The structure had been designed by a down-time architect. Where an up-time apartment building was essentially a collection of individual homes all squished together, this "apartment building" reminded Jeff of a hotel more than anything else. Not a newfangled motel, either, but the sort of oldstyle hotels you often found in the downtown areas of small cities.

He'd had a great-aunt in Winchester who'd owned such a hotel. He'd spent a week there, once, when he was eight years old. His great-aunt's hotel had only a few transient customers. Most of the inhabitants of its many rooms had been elderly residents of the town, usually but not always male. There was a common kitchen, and his great-aunt always provided three meals a day in the hotel's dining room.

That was what this apartment building in Magdeburg reminded him of—except this building even came with a resident cook. Two of them, in fact. A middle-aged man and his wife; both, of course, members of the city's Committee of Correspondence.

"So much for those piker Joneses!" He said that

with a melodramatic sneer, twirling a mustachio in the bargain. The seventeenth century had its drawbacks, but it also had its advantages. One of the greatest of those, in Jeff's opinion, was the ubiquitous facial hair sported by men. Jeff ran toward fat, and had been sensitive about it since childhood. He still was, even though he'd replaced of lot of fat with muscle since the Ring of Fire, and even though Gretchen insisted she didn't care. Nothing, in Jeff's opinion, improved a plump lip and jowls like a beard and mustache.

"Who are the Jones?" asked Gretchen.

"They're the next door neighbors that people are always trying to surpass in wealth and ostentatious displays."

"Ah." She nodded wisely. "Bait, dangled by the devil."

This was one of the seventeenth century's drawbacks, on the other hand—the tendency of its inhabitants to inflate all manner of human frailties. There was no peccadillo that someone wouldn't call a sin; no venal sin that couldn't be made into a mortal one; and no mortal sin where a dozen could be described in detail. Even a person as normally levelheaded as Gretchen was prone to the habit.

"Fortunately, we are not guilty," she continued. "I have decided that Gunther is right. We can use this otherwise-far-too-large building for good purposes. The basement, for instance, is perfect for an armory."

And another drawback. This one, the tendency of down-timers to look at everything bloody-mindedly. As his friend Eddie Cantrell had once put it: "These guys make the Hatfields and McCoys look like Phil Donahue and Oprah."

Of course, given the nature of the seventeenth

century, it was hard to blame them. The Hatfields and McCoys would have been right at home here.

Veronica and Annalise came into the vestibule. "It will suit you, I think," said Gretchen's grandmother.

Jeff figured the "I think" part of the sentence was what the British philosopher Bertrand Russell had called a meaningless noise in a collection of essays he'd read once. Gretchen was devoted to her grandmother. Jeff would allow that the old biddy was tough as nails, and some of the time he even liked her. But he often found her view of the universe annoying. Veronica, so far as Jeff could tell, recognized no distinction between an hypothesis, a theorem, and a fact—not, at least, if she was the one expounding the certainty.

Being fair, Jeff himself thought the house would suit them. There was plenty of room for all the kids, even when you factored into the equation the small army of "security experts" that Gunther was determined to foist upon them.

Gunther Achterhof. A kindred spirit of Gretchen's grandmother, if you set aside politics. Achterhof was as radical as they came and Veronica was about as conservative as you could get and still (grudgingly) support Stearns' regime. So what? They both knew what they knew and if you didn't like it, so much the worse for you.

"Security experts." Yeah, sure. Back up-time, Jeff would have labeled them thugs without even thinking about it.

On the other hand, he reminded himself, he *wasn't* up-time any longer. And as many enemies as Gretchen piled up, it was probably just as well that they'd be sharing the apartment building with guys who'd scare motorcycle gangs if there were any such gangs in the here and now. Which there weren't, of course, unless you wanted to count Denise Beasley and Minnie Hugelmair as a two-girl motorcycle gang.

But that'd be silly; and besides, Denise and Minnie would get along fine with Achterhof's guys. Those two teenagers would scare Jeff himself, if he hadn't married a woman who was probably their role model when it came to unflinching pugnacity in the face of danger.

But all he said was, "Yeah, Ronnie, I think it'll suit us just fine."

Veronica met that statement as she would have met a statement that it was raining in the middle of a thunderstorm. A brief dismissive glance.

"So. Annalise and I will be off then. Mary Simpson is meeting us for the journey to Quedlinburg."

Gretchen frowned. "But school won't be starting for two months."

"Yes. Delightful. Two months of quiet with not a squalling child to be found anywhere. I leave that to the two of you. At long last. Come, Annalise."

And off they went. Gretchen's expression was on the sour side.

It got a lot more sour two hours later, when Jimmy Andersen showed up.

In uniform.

"Hey, man, how come you're still in civvies?" he demanded, squinting at Jeff's decidedly unmilitary clothing.

"Already?" Gretchen said, frowning. The word was half a complaint and half a wail. Some of the wailing component, Jeff knew, was because his wife was unhappy at his looming absence. Most of it, though, was because she now faced the prospect of dealing with the kids on her own.

Jimmy looked dense, but he wasn't. Certainly not with regard to technical issues, and occasionally—much less often—with regards to emotional affairs.

"Jeez, Gretchen, what's the problem? Just appoint some of these goons you've got lounging around as babysitters."

Gretchen bestowed an unfavorable look upon him. "There's more to taking care of children than beating them, you know."

"Well, yeah. But I'm pretty sure those guys can feed themselves. As big as they are. All you got to do is make sure they feed the kids, too." He looked her up and down. "They're scared of you, you know."

Gretchen looked dumbfounded. Jeff managed not to laugh. His wife had an odd streak of modesty in her. Odd, at least, given her reputation in the world at large—which he knew Gretchen didn't fully grasp. Her own self-image was still mostly that of a small-town printer's daughter, not the ogress that noble and even royal families were reputed to use to frighten their children into obedience.

Of course, Gunther Achterhof's handpicked CoC muscle didn't really fear that Gretchen would eat them. Still . . .

Gretchen caught his smile. "And what do you think is so funny?"

Jeff, on the other hand, wasn't afraid of her at all. "You. My leave was brief, special, and only happened because I sweet-talked Frank Jackson and he probably sweet-talked Stearns and you knew perfectly well it'd be over soon."

Jimmy nodded. "Way it is, Gretchen. Frank Jackson sent me over himself. So he wouldn't look bad. Well, look worse. On account of every grunt in the army figures Jeff only got that leave 'cause he's your husband. Good thing they're mostly CoC, or they'd be holding a grudge. Still, all good things have to come to an end."

"Fine for you to say!" snapped Gretchen. "You'll be staying here in Magdeburg on Jackson's staff—what do they call them? rear echelon mother-fuckers?—while Jeff goes to the front."

Jimmy looked wounded. "Hey! S'not true! Not any longer. I requested a transfer to the Third Division. Well, okay, Stearns asked me to 'cause he wants a good radio man, but it's not as if I put up an argument or anything."

"Stop picking on him, hon," Jeff said mildly. "You know perfectly well Jimmy's not an REMF. He was with us all through France and Amsterdam, remember."

"We gotta go *now*, Jeff," said Andersen.

Jeff headed for the stairs that led from the huge vestibule to the upper floors. "I have to change into my uniform first."

"Yeah, sure, but how long can that take?"

"The problem is *finding* the uniforms." He started up the stairs. For all his heft, he moved quickly if not lightly. "We just moved in, remember? I got no idea which trunk they're in."

"You got *trunks*? Jeez, I only got a suitcase, myself."

Gretchen's most unfavorable look was back. "And exactly how many children do you have, Jimmy Andersen?"

"Uh. None."

"So shut up."

"We're gonna catch hell," he predicted gloomily.

In the event, they didn't get into trouble for being tardy, because when they finally arrived at the huge army camp outside of Magdeburg, the divisions had been mobilized and were already starting to march toward the Saxon border. In the confusion that inevitably accompanied the movements of over twenty thousand men and almost that many horses and oxen—not to mention the APCs, which only numbered a handful but threw up a lot of dust—Jeff and Jimmy could easily claim that they had been somewhere else doing some necessary if vaguely defined tasks. They were still close enough to being teenagers that lying to authority figures came easily, smoothly, effortlessly, with nary a seam of untruth to be found poking through the tissue of falsehoods.

Not many seams, anyway. But it didn't matter, because the only person who asked them anything was a cook attached to the 2nd Division who mistook them for quartermasters and demanded to know when the flour would be delivered to the mobile kitchen he was in charge of. Jimmy was a little aggrieved, because the insignia on their uniforms—which included some decorations for fighting off pirates in the English Channel and sinking a whole damn Spanish warship during the siege of Amsterdam, for Pete's sake!—should have made it clear to the dimwit that they were real by-God fighting men.

But Jeff took it in good humor. Unlike Jimmy, who'd spent almost his entire army career as a technical specialist, Jeff had a much wider experience with military matters. Cooks were cooks, it didn't matter whether they were army or civilian. They didn't give a damn about anything except their kitchens. He'd worked as a busboy and dishwasher at a restaurant in Fairmont one summer, and had come away from the experience firmly convinced that all professional cooks were either drunks, lunatics, or disguised aliens. It was best to just ignore their foibles.

In the event, they reached Mike Stearns' headquarters with no hassles, not even from the staff officers. Stearns and his staff were mounted already, with the HQ tent being packed up in wagons.

All Mike himself said was "Hi, boys. Where you been?" before he went back to making sure he had his horse under control.

Which, he did. Jeff thought it was a little unfair, the way people like Stearns seemed to be good at anything they turned their hand to. Jeff himself, despite what was now years of experience, still didn't really get along with horses that well. Even his wife told him he rode a horse like a sack of potatoes.

He was relieved when his brigade commander told him that he was assigning Jeff to an infantry battalion.

The relief lasted about two seconds. That was the approximate lapse of time between the end of the sentence wherein Brigadier Schuster informed Jeff he was now an infantryman and the next sentence:

"I am placing you in command of the 12th Battalion."

"*What?*" Jeff managed not to cast his eyes about wildly. But he was pretty sure they were as big as saucers and had a sort of feverish quality to them. "But—but—"

Schuster nodded solemnly. "Yes, I know you are only a captain and would normally serve on the staff of the battalion commander, or be in command of an infantry company. But Major Kruger was badly injured in a horse fall just two days ago and I simply don't have anyone else to replace him." His heavy face now looked glum instead of simply solemn. "There is always a shortage of experienced and qualified officers for this army. Because of the CoC business, you understand. So you will have to manage."

For a moment, Jeff wondered if there was a trace of malice in the brigadier's tone. He knew that a lot of the professional down-time officers in the USE army resented the pressures that often fell upon them due to the political attitudes of the enlisted men. A lot of the soldiers in the USE army had been recruited by the Committees of Correspondence. By no means all of those recruits were what you could fairly call "CoC men," to be sure. But there was no denying that the radical political views of the CoCs were very influential in the lower ranks of the army. Some of the army's officers had joined because they shared that idealism—a fair number, in fact—but most of the officers had the traditional motives of professional soldiers. Whether or not their own political views were conservative didn't really matter. Those soldiers under CoC influence tended to have attitudes on certain matters of discipline that pretty much drove any regular officer half-nuts.

Not on the battlefield, though. Whatever else aggravated professional officers about the enlisted ranks of the USE army, their willingness and ability to fight was not one of them.

After a moment, Jeff decided that Schuster wasn't being motivated by resentment. He really was just strapped for men.

"Uh... Sir. You know I don't have much actual battlefield experience—infantry battles, I mean, if you want somebody to blow up a warship I'm your man—and none at all commanding more than a squad. I'm not sure..."

"You'll do fine, Captain Higgins. The 12th is a good battalion with good companies. And the commander of your regiment is Colonel Friedrich Eichelberger, who is a superb officer."

"But..."

Schuster shook his head firmly. "The decision is made, Captain. I discussed the matter with General Stearns himself, and he concurred in my decision. I suggest you familiarize yourself with the officers of your battalion immediately. The campaign is already underway. We should reach the Saxon border within four days, possibly even three." He cleared his throat. "Whatever might be their other failings, our soldiers march quite well."

It took Jeff until sundown to find his battalion. Somehow or other, it had managed to get shuffled out of its officially allotted place in the marching order.

At least the battalion was ahead of place, not behind. Apparently they were eager-beavers instead of shirkers. Under most circumstances, Jeff would have thought that a positive trait. Under these... he wasn't sure. Bad enough some idiot brigadier had placed a twenty-three-year-old captain with an oddball military resume in charge of a whole battalion, after consulting with a top commander who apparently had the IQ of a turnip. (At a rough count, he'd silently cursed Mike Stearns at least five hundred times that afternoon.) To add to his misery, it seemed that his new battalion was full of vim and vigor and would have absurdly unrealistic expectations of their new commanding officer.

His fears proved too great and too little.

Too great, in that the 12th Battalion turned out to be a veritable CoC hotbed. Every noncommissioned officer, it seemed, as well as half the grunts, were hardcore activists from Magdeburg.

Given that Jeff was married to the woman who was generally viewed as the quintessence of the CoC spirit, his appointment as the battalion's new commander was very highly regarded by the enlisted men.

And that was the bad news too, of course. "Absurdly unrealistic expectations" was putting it mildly.

Chapter 9

After Jeff left, Gretchen didn't spend more than half an hour moping around and feeling sorry for herself. She'd inherited her grandmother's stoic disposition and hardheaded attitude toward life's travails.

Besides, there were the children to be settled down. There weren't as many as Gretchen had handled when she was a camp follower. Baldy and Martha had stayed behind in Grantville, which left only four of her foster children in addition to her own two sons Willi and Joseph. But all four of them were now entering their teen years and were almost the same age—Karl Blume, the oldest, was fourteen; Christian Georg, the youngest, was twelve. The other two, both born in 1622, were thirteen.

So, they were rambunctious. On the other hand, Gretchen was Gretchen. It didn't take her more than half an hour to set them all about various household chores, obediently if not exactly happily.

The problems would come later, once the little devils figured out that the apartment building was as much in the way of a CoC headquarters—national headquarters, at that, with Gretchen in residence—as it was a private dwelling. They'd handle that knowledge each according to his or her own temperament. Otto and Maria Susanna, charmers both, would sweet-talk the various residents into taking on at least some of their tasks; Karl, the most independent, would be ingenious in evading his responsibilities; the very youngest, Christian Georg, would sulk long and mightily.

Gretchen would have none of it, though, sweet-talk and scheme and sulk though they might. She'd never heard the old saw "idle hands are the devil's workshop." That was an English saying that probably originated with Chaucer. Many Americans knew it, especially the more religious ones. But none of them happened to have used the expression in front of her.

Had she heard it, though, she would have agreed immediately and vigorously.

Which brought her to the next problem at hand. The children now dispatched for the moment, Gretchen turned and gazed upon that problem.

Who, for her part, gazed back at Gretchen from her seat on one of the benches scattered about the side walls of the vestibule. The young woman was modestly dressed—enough, even, to minimize a bosom almost as impressive as Gretchen's own—and had her hands clasped demurely in her lap. She was the very picture of an unassuming person. From the style of shoes she was wearing, a town-dweller rather than someone from rural parts. But clearly a commoner, nonetheless.

The last part was true. The girl, who went by the nickname of Tata, was indeed a town-dweller. Her father owned a tavern in Mainz.

Everything else was illusory. Or would be soon enough. Gretchen would see to it herself, if need be.

But she didn't think she'd need to do anything. Tata's story was already spreading through the ranks of the CoCs, all across the Germanies, even though the critical events involved had happened less than two months earlier.

Such is the power of a splendid legend. The CoCs had found their Esther.

A legend it was, too, if Tata herself was to be believed.

"Eberhard came up with the idea all by himself," she insisted. "Not that I didn't think it was a clever move for something so spur-of-the moment, when he told me. But there wasn't time for a lot of deep discussion. He was going to die. Not in minutes, but certainly within hours."

The "he" in question had been Duke Eberhard, the young ruler of Württemberg, who'd been killed in Schorndorf while driving out the Bavarian mercenaries who'd occupied the city.

That was the bare bones of the tale. It got quite a bit less heroic when you added the meat to the bones. The mercenaries had not been driven out in the course of a valiantly fought siege, but by pure luck. An accident in a cook shop had started a fire during high winds which soon spread the flames through the whole town. The duke had been mortally injured in the course of helping a stubborn pastor trying to save valuables from his burning church.

But none of those pedestrian details mattered, because of what had come next. Duke Eberhard's two brothers had already died in the war, so he'd been the sole heir—and, on his deathbed, he'd bequeathed the duchy to its entire population.

Noblemen had relinquished their titles before, to be

sure. The new prime minister of the USE, Wilhelm Wettin, was one of them. He'd given up his title as one of the dukes of Saxe-Weimar in order to make himself eligible to serve as prime minister. But Eberhard had been the first and so far the only nobleman who'd relinquished his entire realm—and given it to the people who'd previously been his subjects, to boot.

It hadn't taken the story more than two weeks to spread all across the USE. So was born the legend of the Good Duke—or, often, the Three Good Dukes, giving credit to Eberhard's younger brothers who had also died in the struggle. So too was born the legend of the young tavern-keeper's daughter whom the duke had loved, that selfsame love presumably being the motive for his righteous deed.

The fact that the girl's father happened to be the head of the Mainz CoC didn't hurt, of course.

The story was mostly nonsense. So much was obvious to Gretchen just from listening to Tata's version. The relationship the girl had had with the duke had fallen quite a ways short of the legend. There was nothing tawdry about it, if you had reasonable standards concerning such things. It was hardly the first time a charming young nobleman and an attractive town girl had had an affair, after all. Tata had been genuinely fond of Eberhard, and he of her. But most likely they'd have drifted apart, had he lived.

As for the duke's motives, Tata insisted that they had nothing to do with her.

"He was just pissed off, the way the Swedes kept jerking him back and forth. You know how they get with their German subordinates, if they're noblemen. So he got even by dumping a mess in their laps."

A mess it was, too. The prime minister's bureaucrats and emperor's lawyers were already trying to get the duke's will invalidated. The lawyers working for the Fourth of July Party were pushing back just as hard. And no matter which way the legal tussles went, the CoCs in Württemberg were having a field day. For once, *they* could claim to be the party of legitimacy. Their popular support in the southwestern province was growing rapidly.

Here, though, Gretchen thought Tata was actually being too modest. She didn't doubt that the driving force behind Duke Eberhard's decision had been his irritation with the often high-handed methods of Gustav Adolf and his officials. Many German noblemen allied to the Swedish king chafed under his rule.

But, without Tata and the CoC to which she belonged, would his deathbed revenge have taken the form that it did?

Gretchen thought not. For all her hostility toward the aristocracy in general, she thought that the dying Eberhard had been moved, at the end, by a genuinely noble impulse. One that Tata could at least claim to have watered, if not seeded.

If even Gretchen was that well-disposed toward the memory of the young duke, she knew full well how the masses of the Germanies would react. Tata could say whatever she wanted. The CoC legend would roll right over it.

Maybe Esther had acne, too. Who cared?

So. Gretchen had a legend on her hands. The question was, what to do with her?

The answer was obvious. The best way to solve a problem is to apply it to another proiblem.

She waggled her hand in a rising motion. "Come, Tata. I want to introduce you to someone."

Obediently, the girl rose.

Once they left the building, a contingent of CoC activists closed in around them. Others stayed in place, guarding the building.

Looked at from one angle, the level of protection being provided to Gretchen was excessive. Here in the heart of Magdeburg's working class district, no large group of enemies would dare to move in force. Not unless an army had already taken the city, in which case a relative handful of security guards would be a moot point.

But conflict had a psychological as well as a physical component, which Gretchen had come to respect as the struggle continued. Spartacus understood that also, and Gunther Achterhof practically worshipped at the shrine of what he like to call "psyops." He was addicted to such Americanisms.

Partly, Gretchen had come to that understanding on her own. Mostly, though, she'd come to it from years of watching Mike Stearns.

Gretchen had suspicions concerning Stearns. His willingness to compromise with the enemy readily and easily was something that rubbed her the wrong way, and always had. At the same time, as the years had passed since the Ring of Fire and her rise to prominence as a leader of Europe's principal revolutionary organization, she'd become a great deal more sophisticated. The girl whose aspirations toward striking back had once been limited to sliding a knife into the brain of a mercenary thug was now a young woman who'd commanded the defending forces of a major city under siege and had negotiated with two princes—one of them a king now—and an archduchess.

One of the things she'd learned from Stearns was that aggressive negotiating—understanding that "negotiating" was a concept much broader than the formalities involved—could often preclude the need for violence altogether. Or, at the very least, reduce the scope of that violence.

So, when she walked in public, Gretchen's stride was sure and confident. So, too, were the strides of the men guarding her. So, at such times, Gretchen's expression was equally sure and confident. And the expressions of the armed men at her side were downright belligerent.

Who could say? Perhaps when his spies reported, an enemy would be moved to negotiate rather than fight. And perhaps, even if he did choose to fight, he would enter the conflict with his self-confidence already frayed.

What still bothered her about Stearns was that she was not sure when negotiation stopped being a means for the man and became an end in itself. There was an insidious dynamic at work. A ruling class had several ways to maintain its domination. One, of course, was brute force. But another was co-option, absorption, seduction. Offer a rebel—usually a man from the lower classes—a prominent place in society. Offer him status; titles; positions—and, of course, a munificent salary. All the things, in short, which he'd never had and whose absence had been, at least in part, the motive for his rebellion.

How long does such a man remain a revolutionary?

In his core, not simply in the trappings and appurtenances?

To be sure, most of Europe's dynasts and noblemen still shook their fists at Mike Stearns and reviled him publicly and privately. But how much did they really fear him, any longer? How much, in their heart of hearts, did they really worry that a man who'd borne the title of a prime minister, bore now the title of a major general, and could easily obtain a loan to buy a mansion for his family, was still their mortal enemy?

The Swedes did not, obviously. The Swedish king Gustav Adolf's relationship with Stearns might be ambivalent, and the Swedish chancellor Oxenstierna might often be downright prickly. So what? They were still willing to let him wield a great deal of power and influence, and never failed to treat him with respect.

So how long would he last? Gretchen simply didn't know. Neither did Spartacus or Gunther Achterhof or any of the central leaders of the Committees of Correspondence. To the lower classes of the Germanies, including those of them who adhered to the CoCs, Mike Stearns was the "prince of Germany." The leadership of the CoCs did not demur publicly. But, more and more, they were beginning to wonder. Might the day come when they would be calling him "the traitor of Germany?"

Gretchen let none of those inner worries show on her face, though, as she moved through the crowded streets of Magdeburg.

"Stop looking nervous," she said quietly to Tata, walking at her side.

The girl grimaced a little. "I've never seen so many people. And it's so crowded."

Actually, it wasn't very crowded—for her and Gretchen. As packed with people as the streets were, on such a fine midsummer day, they gave way for Gretchen and her entourage. Willingly, too, not because they were worried the guards might get rough. Still, even for a girl from a small city like Mainz, Magdeburg would be startling. No city in the Germanies was growing as rapidly as Magdeburg. Its population was still quite a bit less than Paris or London's, but it was already more than twice that of the next largest German city, Hamburg.

"It doesn't matter what the reason is," said Gretchen. "Never look nervous. Our enemies might be watching."

Spartacus and Achterhof were waiting for her in one of the back rooms of the city's central Freedom Arches. This building had served for almost a year as the more-or-less official headquarters for the Committees of Correspondence—everywhere, not simply in Magdeburg. It would no doubt retain that position, even though Gretchen's new apartment building would sometimes double as an informal headquarters.

The building was located next door to Magdeburg's original Freedom Arches, which was still in operation and which still resembled a tavern. The new Freedom Arches, on the other hand...

The first time Melissa Mailey laid eyes on the thing, she'd rolled her eyes. "Oh, swell. It's a cross between Chateau d'If and the Lubyanka. Who was the architect? Frank Lloyd Rack? Mies van der Thumbscrews?"

When informed that the architect had actually been a city employee and one of the mayor's top assistants, she'd been a little dumbfounded. Why would a proper gentleman like Otto Gericke lend his assistance to such a project?

She'd asked Gericke herself, three days later, at one of the soirees hosted by Mary Simpson.

"You see the CoCs as a force for revolution, Melissa. Which you mostly support, albeit with some reservations. But I am in charge of a city—the largest, fastest growing and most dynamic city in the Germanies. In some respects, in the entire world. And from my standpoint, the Magdeburg Committee of Correspondence is a stabilizing force. I hate to think what the situation with disease and crime would be, were it not for the CoC patrols. Not to mention—I am first and foremost a scientist, don't forget—that they have an almost mystical faith in science and invariably support any initiative the city undertakes for scientific education and progress."

She must have had a surprised look on her face. He'd gotten a wry smile. "Melissa, I am often at political loggerheads with the Committees of Correspondence. By and large, however, I think they are a force for good. And regardless of anything else—whatever may be the delusions of the Crown Loyalist party—they cannot be ignored or shuffled aside. That being so, I think it is entirely in my interest to give them institutional validity. Yes, I know that from a purely architectural standpoint that new headquarters of theirs is a blocky monstrosity. But it helps them feel secure, and I find a secure CoC quite a bit easier to deal with than one which is edgy and apprehensive."

Gericke had shaken his head. "However politically radical you Americans may be in some respects, Melissa, you enjoyed a sheltered life as a people.

There was nothing in your history equivalent to the aftermath of the Peasant War, when the aristocracy butchered a hundred thousand farmers after their rebellion was defeated. That was only a century ago. Many of those people sitting right now in the CoC headquarters on October 7th Avenue are the direct descendants of those slaughtered folk. If you were to inquire among the members of the Ram Rebellion— some of whose representatives you can now also find in that same building—the number would be even higher. It would not take much of a provocation for the CoC in Magdeburg to launch a violent uprising. That uprising would succeed rapidly here in the city, be sure of it. Whether it would spread across the USE or be crushed is harder to gauge because there are so many variables involved. But either way, it would be a bloody business. I'd just as soon avoid it, if we can."

He hadn't sounded very optimistic.

The meeting room was on the second floor, where most of the smaller meeting rooms were located, as well as the offices of the city's CoC. The big assembly hall was on the first floor, along with the offices of various organizations affiliated to the CoC. Those included the city's trade unions as well as the regional and national trade union federations; the sanitation commission; credit unions; life and health insurance cooperatives; the retirement insurance association. The smallest office held the just-launched employment insurance cooperative.

The building's basement, just as was true of the city's official Rathaus, was given over to a huge tavern. And, just as with the one in the basement of the

Rathaus on Hans Richter Strasse—or the now famous Thuringen Gardens in Grantville—that tavern was a social and political center.

German traditions of self-organization were already deeply rooted. The up-time Americans, smugly certain as Americans so often were that their own customs were unique, had been surprised to discover the ubiquitous town and city militias with their accompanying shooting clubs. They'd thought the tradition of armed self-defense—not to mention the National Rifle Association—to be quintessentially American.

The up-timers could claim considerable credit for inspiring some of the rapidly growing voluntary associations, true enough, especially the trade unions and the credit unions. Others seemed to them somewhat outlandish. Americans were certainly familiar with sports clubs, but they were quite unaccustomed to seeing such clubs—as with most of the insurance cooperatives—so closely associated with a political movement. But they would have been perfectly familiar to the German Social Democrats of the nineteenth century who had surrounded their powerful political party with such organizations.

Gretchen herself took the situation for granted, including the informal give-and-take between the CoC headquarters and the Rathaus. At any given time of the day or night, you were just as likely to find a city sanitation official discussing his business with CoC activists in their tavern as you were to find CoC activists in the tavern at the Rathaus wrangling over issues involving the city militias with one of the mayor's deputies.

She'd experienced that sort of informal dual power

before, during the siege of Amsterdam. There, too, the CoC she'd organized had been as much the center of authority as the city's official government. And the reason had been much the same: military weakness on the part of the official authorities combined with very real if often informal military strength on the part of the radical plebeians.

When Gretchen entered the meeting room and saw the uncertain and dubious expression on the face of the woman from the Vogtland, it was obvious to her that the Vogtlander did not know what to make of it all. Gretchen was not surprised. The Vogtland, because of its terrain and being under Saxon control, had been isolated from the political developments which had transformed much of the Germanies since the Ring of Fire. The region had shared in those developments, true. In some ways, in fact, the political struggle was even sharper than most places, especially since the Saxon elector had placed Holk in charge of pacifying the region. But the Vogtlander rebels were programmatically limited—"down with the elector!" pretty much summed it up—and were tactically one-sided.

Gretchen took her seat across the table from the Vogtland woman, whose name was Anna Piesel. She was apparently betrothed to Georg Kresse, the recognized leader of the Vogtland rebellion. Tata sat down beside her.

Gretchen had to be careful here. The Committees of Correspondence were the largest and best-known—certainly the best-financed and organized—of Europe's revolutionary organizations. But they were not the only one. In Franconia, for instance, the dominant organization was the Ram movement.

The CoCs were the only revolutionary organization with a national scope, even an international one. So it was inevitable that they would overshadow the other groups, all of whom were regional in character. In times past, overbearing attitudes by CoC activists ignoring local conditions had produced some bad clashes. Gretchen had had to intervene personally in one such conflict, in Suhl, when the local CoC tried to run roughshod over the gun manufacturers who, whatever their political faults, still commanded the loyalty and confidence of the city's population.

The situation in the Vogtland presented a similar problem. There was no question that Kresse's movement had the support and allegiance of most people in the region who were opposed to the elector's rule. Unfortunately, from what Gretchen and the other national CoC leaders could determine, Kresse had a tendency to see political problems through a military lens. That was perhaps inevitable, given the origins of the movement and the conditions in southwestern Saxony. But while that sort of almost-exclusively military approach might work well enough in the mountains of the Vogtland, it was an insufficient basis for establishing a new political regime in the region as a whole.

Saxony was not the Vogtland. Dresden and Leipzig were major cities, cultural as well as population centers. The university at Leipzig, in fact, was the second-oldest in the Germanies. It had been founded in 1409 and was still very prominent, especially in law.

There was simply no way that a movement based in the Vogtland, and one whose approach was almost entirely military, was going to provide the basis for replacing the rule of the elector with a Saxon republic.

On their own, Kresse and his people didn't even have the military strength to overthrow John George. They certainly didn't have the political experience and acumen to handle the situation that would be produced in Saxony if—as Gretchen and all the CoC leaders assumed was going to happen—Gustav Adolf crushed the Saxon army in the coming war.

What then? The same guerrilla tactics that worked well enough against a general like Holk would not work against the sort of military administration the Swedes would set up in Saxony. Gustav Adolf did not rule like John George—and, perhaps more directly to the point, would not try to suppress the Vogtland using the methods of Heinrich Holk. Dealing with him was like dealing with Fredrik Hendrik, the prince of Orange in the Low Countries—or the new Spanish king, for that matter. Such men were not brutes, and they were willing to make accommodations when necessary. Sometimes they were even allies.

On the other hand...

There would be no way to move forward in Saxony in opposition to Kresse and his people, either. Nor would it be correct to do so. Whatever their flaws and limitations, their unyielding struggle against dynasticism and aristocratic rule deserved respect.

Anna Piesel had been scrutinizing her since Gretchen entered the room. She'd barely glanced at Tata. Now she spoke abruptly.

"So, what's your answer? Will you come to Dresden?"

As they'd prearranged, Spartacus answered that question.

"She can't, Anna. From everything we've been able to determine, Wilhelm Wettin is planning to force a drastic reactionary program onto the USE. When that happens, there'll be an explosion—and it'll be centered here in Magdeburg. There's simply no way we could allow such a central leader as Gretchen to leave the capital right now."

Piesel got a pinched look on her face, her eyes narrow. Now Gretchen spoke, gesturing with her hand toward Tata.

"But here's what we *can* do. We'll send a team of organizers into Dresden with Tata here in charge."

Piesel shifted her narrow gaze to Tata. "And who's she?"

Tata looked uncomfortable. Spartacus's eyes widened and his lips tightened, as if distressed that anyone could be so ignorant but too polite to say so.

Gunther Achterhof just chuckled. "We figure if she can persuade a duke to turn over an entire duchy, she can handle the aftermath of the elector's defeat well enough."

Piesel's eyes got wide also. Obviously, although the name hadn't registered, she'd heard the story.

"Oh," she said, after a couple of seconds. Then she gave Tata a shy smile. "Well. I guess that would be okay."

After Piesel left, Tata turned to Gretchen. "This is crazy. I don't have enough experience. And that story's silly and you know it."

Achterhof waved his hand. "Stop worrying, girl. We really *are* sending a team of good organizers, headed by Joachim Kappel. You'll do fine. Just listen to Joachim."

"Why don't you put him in charge, then?"

"Nobody except us has ever heard of him," said Spartacus. "You're famous."

"It's a silly story," she insisted.

Gunther shrugged. "Most stories are. But people still like to listen to them."

Chapter 10

Northeast of Halle, not far from the Saxon border

The countryside between Magdeburg and Saxony reminded Mike Stearns of the American Midwest, except for the absence of corn and soybeans. The crops being grown were different, but the terrain was much the same—flat, and consisting mostly of open farmland but with quite a few wooded areas scattered about. None of the woods could really be called forests, though.

There was one other big difference from the Midwest, but that was not peculiar to this area. It was a common feature throughout central Europe, and Mike suspected you'd find it in most other places in Europe. Unlike the twentieth-century American farm countryside he'd known, with its many scattered individual farmhouses, central European farmers in the seventeenth century all lived in small towns and villages. The farmland itself was largely barren of inhabitants, except during the day when people were working in the fields. By and large, the collective methods and village traditions of the Middle Ages still applied to farm labor in the German countryside.

To the farmers themselves, at any rate, if not necessarily the aristocracy. Seventeenth-century Germany was no longer in any real sense of the term a feudal society. Labor relations might have resisted change, but the same was not true of property relations. In the year 1635, a landlord was just as likely to be a burgher or a well-off farmer as a nobleman—and still more likely to be an institution of some kind rather than a person: a corporation, a city council, a trust, whatever. Still, farmers lived in villages, not in separated and isolated farmhouses; and still, in many ways, worked the land in common.

His musings were interrupted by one of his staff officers, Colonel Christopher Long, who came riding up bearing some new dispatches.

"Anything important?" he asked.

The young colonel shook his head. "Nothing that can't wait until we make camp this evening."

The English officer was a professional soldier who'd come to Magdeburg to join the USE army—not the Swedish forces directly under Gustav Adolf, as did most mercenaries from the British Isles. The reason, Mike had discovered from a conversation a few days earlier, was that Long had been in Spanish service when the Spaniards invading Thuringia had been defeated by the Americans near Eisenach.

In fact, the Englishman was one of the survivors of the destruction of the Wartburg. His depiction of the nightmare of trying to escape the castle as it was being consumed by napalm bombs was horrific, for all that he recounted the tale in a matter-of-fact manner. He'd come away from the experience convinced that the trade of war was about to undergo a drastic transformation—and thus had placed himself at the service of those who seemed to be the principal agents of that change.

In the world Mike had come from, Long's behavior would have bordered on treason. But nationalism and twentieth-century notions of patriotism were just beginning to emerge from dynasticism, in the seventeenth century. Long's pragmatic attitude was the norm for professional soldiers in this day and age, not the exception. The only thing that made Long unusual was that, unlike most mercenary officers, he was quite willing to accept the rambunctious behavior of the CoC-influenced enlisted soldiers in the USE army, as the price for gaining the experience he wanted.

After handing over the dispatches, Long studied Mike for a moment and then said: "Your horsemanship is very good, General Stearns. I'm surprised. I'd have thought you'd ride like the average American."

Mike smiled. "Badly, you mean."

The tall blond officer shook his head. "That would be unfair. I've found that most Americans—assuming they ride horses at all, that is—are reasonably competent at the business. No worse than most farmers and townsmen. But that's a long way short of the sort of horsemanship you need to be a cavalryman."

Mike's eyes widened with alarm. "*Cavalryman?* I thought I was a general. Sit on a horse—way back, you understand—and give orders."

"Alas, no. Even with the radios we have, I'm afraid command methods haven't changed all that much and probably won't for some time." Long's grin seemed a bit on the evil side. "The casualty rate among officers in this day and age—oh, yes, generals too—is usually no better than it is for infantrymen and artillerymen and considerably worse than it is for cavalrymen."

That was *definitely* an evil smile. "The cavalry can run away, you see. Except the generals, who have to stand their ground and set a good example."

Mike had already discovered that Long's casual joking with his commanding officer was normal in the army. Whether that was due to seventeenth-century custom or the egalitarian influence of the rank and file soldiers, he didn't know. Some of both, he expected.

He wasn't going to inquire, though, because whatever the source the attitude suited him just fine. Mike had every intention of succeeding—excelling, actually—at his new occupation. He'd done well at everything he'd turned his hand to in his life, and saw no reason to do otherwise here. But he was not a cocksure fool, either. There was no way a man in his late thirties with no training as an officer and whose only military experience had been a three-year term as an enlisted man in the peacetime U.S. army—twenty years back, to boot—was going to transform himself overnight into what Mike thought of as "a regular general."

Instead, he'd do it his way, by leaning heavily on those traits he already had which he thought would serve him in good stead as a military commander.

First, he was courageous. That wasn't conceit on his part, it was simply a matter-of-fact assessment. He'd faced enough physical threats in his life to know that his immediate reaction to danger was coolheadedness, not panic. He didn't think he was probably Medal-of-Honor material, but he didn't need that sort of superlative bravery. Just enough to keep calm in the middle of a battlefield and think clearly.

Second, he was a very capable leader—and leadership, he thought, probably translated well into any field of endeavor.

Third, he was an experienced organizer. That was, in fact, the channel through which his leadership abilities normally ran. He know how to command outright, and would do so when needed. But his preference and natural inclination was to assemble a capable team and work with them and through them. He saw no reason to think he couldn't do the same with the staff of an army.

One of the things that would require was a certain relaxation in his dealings with his subordinates. And if that sort of casualness would have appalled most of the officers Mike had known in his stint in the up-time army, so be it. He simply wasn't worried that familiarity would lead to contempt. Why should it? Nobody who'd ever gotten to know Mike Stearns in his first almost four decades of life had been contemptuous of him, not even his enemies. The only reason anyone would start now would be if Mike fumbled his new job.

Which, he had no intention of doing. It would be better to say, didn't even consider.

And that, of course, was Mike's fourth relevant trait. His wife Becky had once said—not entirely admiringly—"Michael, you have the self-confidence of a bull."

Well . . . Yes. He did.

"And yourself, Christopher? I wouldn't have imagined an Englishman would ride all that well, either. Your island being so small and all."

Long chuckled. "We're lazy. Why walk when you can make a dumb beast do most of the work? And then, of course, I was in Spanish service for a time. Your proper hidalgo considers it a point of honor to spend most of his life in a saddle. It's an infectious attitude, I found."

About fifty yards to the rear, and as many to the south—they were following parallel roads—Captain Jeff Higgins and his own staff were observing their commanding general.

Jeff's staff was much smaller, of course. It consisted of his adjutant, Lieutenant Eric Krenz, who like Jeff himself was too young and inexperienced for the job. General Schuster had promised Jeff that he'd have experienced and capable company commanders—and so he did. Every one of the battalion's captains was up-to-snuff. So, naturally, following the surrealistic logic that Jeff had decided was inherent to the military mind, they'd put two neophytes in charge.

At least Krenz had been in a battle before. A real one, too, not the sort of firefights and commando raids that constituted the entirely of Jeff's experience. Eric had been part of the flying artillery unit that broke the French cavalry charge at the great battle of Ahrensbök.

"Why don't you ride a horse as well as Stearns does?" Krenz asked him, a sly smile on his face.

Jeff grunted. "Mike's a fricking athlete. Used to— voluntarily, mind you—slug it out with professional prizefighters. Won every fight, even. Me? I'm a fricking geek. Until the Ring of Fire planted me in this madhouse, my idea of physical exercise was rolling the dice in a Dungeons and Dragons game."

He didn't have to explain the reference. Eric Krenz was a natural-born geek himself, and had quickly acclimatized himself to the quirks of American custom. He and two other officers in the regiment, in fact, were planning to launch their own gaming company as soon as their terms of service expired. They intended to plunder Dungeons and Dragons lock, stock, and barrel. Why not? One of the legal principles that had been established by the parliament of the USE was that no copyrights, patents or trademarks for anything brought through the Ring of Fire were still valid except for ones held at the time by residents of Grantville who'd made the passage.

There were a few of those. Seven people were published authors; nothing fancy, just various articles in magazines or journals. Two people held patents for small inventions, Jere Haygood and Diana O'Connor. None of those did them any good, though. O'Connor's patent was for an esoteric aspect of business software which was irrelevant to anything in the here and now. Haygood's two patents were for minor gadgets that no one would probably have any use for until long after the patents expired. On the other hand, Haygood held several patents for devices he'd invented *since* the Ring of Fire—and the same law had established copyrights and patents for the here and now.

Those might be challenged. Haygood's new patents fell into the legal gray area that would afflict any up-time inventor. On the one hand, he had created the devices himself since the Ring of Fire. Nobody questioned that. On the other hand, since there had been nothing close to a complete record in Grantville of all patents, trademarks and copyrights granted by the United States of America, who could say? Maybe Haygood had just copied something that he remembered.

Jeff was pretty sure that the courts would rule in Jere's favor, though, if anyone did challenge him. German jurisprudence was every bit as inclined as the American to see possession as nine-tenths of the law. Unless someone could prove that Haygood had swiped his inventions from something already in existence up-time, his patents would stand.

Jeff was sure enough of that to have been severely tempted when Eric Krenz and his partners had offered to bring him into the business. But, after thinking it over, he'd declined.

The problem was twofold. The first, and lesser, problem was that there might be a conflict of interest involved if the commanding officer of a battalion went into business with some of his subordinates, even if the business wasn't launched until they'd all left the army.

Jeff wasn't sure of that. What he was sure of, however, was how Gretchen would react. His wife wasn't normally given to stuffiness. But he was pretty sure that the recognized central leader of the Committees of Correspondence would cast a cold eye on her husband hustling fantasy games.

Besides, they didn't need the money any longer.

Speaking of cold eyes being cast . . .

Jeff scrutinized Krenz's none-too-relaxed posture. "And you got a lot of nerve making fun of your battalion's commander's horsemanship, Lieutenant. Your own equestrian skills would fit right into a Three Stooges movie."

"What are the three stooges?"

"Ah! An aspect of American high culture you've missed, I see. Well, let me be the first to enlighten you. The Three Stooges were a legend, up-time. Three renowned sages, philosophers one and all, whose wisdom—"

"You're lying to me again, Captain Higgins, aren't you?"

More than a mile farther back in the march, and on yet a different road, Thorsten Engler turned to the man riding next to him and said: "How do you think Eric is getting along in his new post?"

Jason Linn grinned. He was the mechanical repairman who'd replaced Krenz in the flying artillery unit. "He'd have been all right if he'd stayed a grunt. But he went ahead and accepted the commission they offered him. He's an officer now. Officers ride horses. It's a given."

Linn wasn't all that much of a horseman himself, but the redheaded young Scotsman didn't have Krenz's fear of the beasts. And he didn't need any horsemanship beyond the basic skills. He'd be riding the lead near horse of a battery wagon, just as he was doing at the moment.

Thorsten, on the other hand, was riding a cavalry horse. That was expected of the commander of a volley gun company. Fortunately, he was quite a good horseman.

He'd damn well have to be, riding *this* horse. He'd been given the stallion as a gift just three days before the march began, by Princess Kristina. He didn't want to think how much the animal had cost. He was still getting used to the creature. This steed was about as far removed from the plow horses he'd grown up with as a Spanish fighting bull was from a placid steer.

Jason was a good repairman. He was a blacksmith's son and had gotten some further training in one of Grantville's machine shops after he arrived in the up-time town. He'd been all of twenty years old at the time and eager for adventure.

"Scotland's the most boring country on Earth," he insisted. As vigorously as you could ask for, despite having experienced exactly one and a half countries— Scotland and parts of the Germanies—not counting three days each spent in London and Hamburg.

Still, Thorsten missed Eric Krenz. And he certainly envied his friend's position in the march, way up in front with one of the leading infantry units. Where Engler's flying artillery company was positioned, they were almost choking. An army of twenty-some thousand men, many of them mounted, throws up a lot of dust. As it was, they were lucky they were ahead of the supply train.

"Think it'll rain?" asked Jason, his tone half-hoping and half-dreading.

Thorsten felt pretty much the same way about the prospect. On the one hand, rain would eliminate the dust. On the other hand, everything would become a soggy mess and if the rain went on long enough they'd be marching through mud.

"War sucks," he pronounced, using one of the American expressions beloved by every soldier in the army.

It wasn't until an hour later that it occurred to him that he was denouncing war because of the prospect of moderate discomfort. Not death; not mutilation; not madness brought on by horror. Just the possibility of being wet and muddy. As a farm boy, he'd taken getting wet and muddy as a matter of course—but would have been aghast at the carnage of a battlefield.

Thorsten wondered what had happened to that farm boy. Was he still there, beneath the Count of Narnia riding a warhorse given to him by a future empress and betrothed to a woman from a land of fable?

He hoped so.

Chapter 11

Magdeburg

After he entered the mansion, Ed Piazza took a moment to examine the huge vestibule. Then, he whistled softly.

"Wow. You guys have sure come up in the world."

Rebecca got a long-suffering look on her face. "Just once, I would enjoy hearing someone come up with a different remark, the first time they come here."

Piazza grinned. "You've got to admit, it's impressive. Especially for a simple country boy like me."

Rebecca's look got more long-suffering. "'Simple country boy,'" she mimicked. "I doubt you were ever that, Mr. Piazza, even as a toddler. I am firmly convinced you had mastered Machiavelli's *The Prince* by the age of nine. Judging from the evidence."

"Fourteen, actually—and I wouldn't say I 'mastered' it. The truth is, I found it pretty boring."

"Why did you read it, then?"

"I was on my Italian ethnic identity phase at the time. I worked my way through a bunch of stuff. I started with Dante. I read the whole trilogy, too, not just the

Inferno. Damn near turned me into a lapsed Catholic. Heaven seemed deadly dull. Then I read Boccaccio's *Decameron,* which I enjoyed a lot. Then I read Petrarch, which killed my interest in poetry for almost a decade. Then I plowed into Machiavelli. By then, though, I was pretty much going on stubborn determination and *The Prince* did me in. After that, I pursued the search for my cultural roots through the movies. *El Cid, The Fall of the Roman Empire, Marriage Italian Style, Arabesque, The Countess From Hong Kong,* stuff like that."

Rebecca frowned. "Except for the marriage film—and I suppose the one about the Roman Empire—what is their relevance to Italian heritage?"

Piazza grinned. "Sophia Loren. She's in all of them. I delved into quite a few Gina Lollobrigida classics too, although she was a bit before my time. Then I discovered Claudia Cardinale and Monica Vitti and my devotion to Italian culture became boundless. I even watched *Red Desert* three times, and that's some ethnic solidarity, let me tell you. God, that movie's dull. Except for Monica Vitti, of course."

"I think I will not pursue this matter any further. Lest my image of you as an urbane and genteel man of the world suffers terminal harm." Rebecca gestured toward a far door. "This way, please. The others are already here."

Ed could hear Constantin Ableidinger when he was still twenty feet away from the door—which was closed, and thick. The former schoolteacher who'd been the central leader of the Ram Rebellion and was now Bamberg's representative in the USE House of Commons was one of the loudest men Piazza had ever met. Ableidinger seemed to find it impossible to speak in any tone of voice softer than a fog horn.

"—he mad?" were the first two words Ed understood, followed by: "What would possess him to do such a thing?"

Melissa Mailey's much softer response was muffled until Rebecca began opening the door. Ed caught the rest of it:

"—a shame, it really is. Wilhelm always seemed much shrewder than that."

The discussion broke off as Piazza and Rebecca entered the room. The eight people already present turned to look at them. They were sitting at a meeting table made up of four separate tables arranged in a shallow "U" formation. The open end of the "U" was facing away from the door, allowing the participants to look out of a wall of windows which gave a view of Magdeburg's scenery.

Ed wondered why they'd bothered. There was a lot to be said for the capital city of the United States of Europe. It was certainly dynamic—and not just in terms of the booming industries that produced the smoke and soot that turned the sky gray except after a rainfall. Under Mary Simpson's leadership, Magdeburg was becoming the cultural center of the nation, as well. She and Otto Gericke were also pushing hard to have a major university founded in the city.

Scenic, though, Magdeburg was not. The view through the windows was mostly that of blocks of the functional but dull apartment buildings that housed most of the city's working class; with, in the distance, the ubiquitous smokestacks from Magdeburg's many factories, mills, forges and foundries. It was probably the ugliest urban landscape Piazza had ever seen, except the mills lining the Monongahela southeast of Pittsburgh when he'd been a teenager.

Then again, those same working class districts were what gave the Fourth of July Party a political hammerlock over the city and province of Magdeburg. So there was a certain logic to the seating arrangement.

"Where's Helene?" asked Charlotte Kienitz, one of the leaders of the Fourth of July Party from the province of Mecklenburg. She was referring to Helene Gundelfinger, the vice-president of the State of Thuringia-Franconia.

"She should be here by mid-afternoon. She had to sort something out with the abbess of Quedlinburg." Ed got a wry smile on his face. "Who's here visiting Mary Simpson and Veronica Richter, so Helene has to deal with them too."

Melissa, seated at the far end of the tables, barked a little laugh. "I swear, I've never seen anything that generates more wrangling over details than schools do. That's one thing the two worlds on either side of the Ring of Fire have in common."

There was an empty seat next to the mayor of Luebeck, Dieterich Matthesen. After removing a notepad and placing it on the desk, Ed set his briefcase on the floor, leaning it against one of the table legs. Then he pulled out the chair and sat down.

By the time he did so, Rebecca had resumed her own seat. "To bring Ed up to date on what everyone was discussing when he came in, we have received word from reliable sources that Wilhelm Wettin and his Crown Loyalists plan to impose the most sweeping possible variation of their citizenship program. What is sometimes colloquially referred to as Plan B."

James Nichols, sitting next to Melissa, grunted sourly. "Otherwise known as The Bürgermeister's Wet Dream."

"Or the Hochadel Folly," added Anselm Keller. He was an MP from the Province of the Main, and was sitting next to Albert Bugenhagen, the young newly elected mayor of Hamburg. To their right, on the table that form the left end of the U, sat the two remaining attendees at the meeting: Matthias Strigel, the governor of Magdeburg province, and Werner von Dalberg.

Von Dalberg, like Melissa Mailey and James Nichols and Charlotte Kienitz, held no governmental position. His prominence in the Fourth of July Party stemmed from the fact that he was universally acknowledged as the central figure for the party in the Upper Palatinate. Given that he'd had to maneuver with the provincial administrator, Ernst Wettin, and—much worse—the Swedish general Johan Banér, he'd had to be a skilled politician as well as organizer. The political situation for the Fourth of July Party—every political party in the USE, actually—was always tricky in those areas that were still under direct imperial administration.

As of July 1635, there were eleven established provinces in the United States of Europe. The heads of state of each of those provinces, whether elected or appointed by the emperor or established by traditional custom, sat in the USE's upper house, the House of Lords. ("The Senate," in the stubborn parlance of the CoCs.) As such, all eleven of them added the official rank of senator to whatever other posts and positions and titles they held.

Those eleven provinces were:

Magdeburg, which was the name of the province as

well as the capital city. The province's head of state was an elected governor.

The State of Thuringia-Franconia, whose capital had formerly been Grantville and was now Bamberg. Like Magdeburg, this state elected its own governor, although the title of the post—president—remained that of its predecessor, the New United States.

Those were the only two provinces that had a fully republican structure and elected their own heads of state. Not coincidentally, they were the strongholds of the Fourth of July Party and the Committees of Correspondence.

There were three provinces whose heads of state, while not elected, were established by the provinces themselves. Like Magdeburg and the SoTF, these provinces were entirely self-governing within the over-all federal structure and laws of the USE. They were no longer, or had never been, under direct imperial administration.

They were:

Hesse-Kassel, still governed by its traditional ruler, Landgrave Wilhelm V. The Landgrave, along with his wife Amalie Elizabeth, were prominent leaders of the moderate wing of the Crown Loyalist Party that now controlled the USE Parliament and whose leader, Wilhelm Wettin, was the newly elected prime minister.

Brunswick was also governed by its traditional ruler, Duke George of Brunswick-Lüneburg. However, since the duke was now serving as the commander of the USE army's Second Division and was marching this very moment into Saxony, the province was being managed by one of his subordinates, Loring Schultz.

Most recently, the Tyrol had voluntarily joined

the United States of Europe. The agreement made between the Tyrol's regent Claudia de Medici and the USE's envoy Philipp Sattler was that a regency council would be set up under Dr. Wilhelm Bienner, the chancellor of Tyrol, for Claudia's two minor sons. Under the new constitution of the province, they and their heirs would be "hereditary governors."

Four provinces had heads of state who had been appointed by Emperor Gustav II Adolf. However, they were no longer under direct imperial administration and were at least technically self-governing:

Westphalia, whose administrator was Prince Frederik of Denmark. He'd been appointed in June of 1634 as a result of the Congress of Copenhagen. They were still wrangling over the title. Frederik wanted "Prince of Westphalia" but the emperor was reluctant to agree and preferred "Governor." Gustav Adolf would probably give in eventually, though, since his misgivings were general in nature whereas the Danes—both Frederik and his father Christian IV, the king of Denmark—were quite keen on the matter.

The Province of the Upper Rhine, whose administrator was Wilhelm Ludwig of Nassau-Saarbrücken. He'd also been appointed in June of 1634 during the proceedings at Copenhagen. Wilhelm Ludwig, not of royal birth, had been happy enough to settle for the title of governor. His position as the Upper Rhine's head of state was something of a formality, anyway, since he was spending most of his time assisting his father-in-law in Swabia. The actual management of the province was in the hands of his deputy, Johann Moritz of Nassau-Siegen.

The "self-governing" aspect of the remaining two

provinces in this category was questionable, since their official head of state was the emperor himself. Gustav II Adolf, never loath to use medieval precedents, had cheerfully appointed himself the duke of both Mecklenburg and Pomerania.

The provincial independence of Pomerania was pretty much a myth. For all practical purposes, Pomerania was still being ruled by direct imperial fiat. True, Pomeranians did elect members to Parliament. But all of them were vetted by the Swedish chancellor, Axel Oxenstierna. Insofar as the province had any independent politics at all, it tended to be a bastion of the reactionary wing of the Crown Loyalists.

Mecklenburg was quite different. That province had been transformed in the course of the civil war which had taken place there following the Dreeson Incident. With a handful of exceptions, the nobility had fled the province. The Committees of Correspondence were now as dominant on the ground as they were in Magdeburg and the State of Thuringia-Franconia.

A couple of provinces were "self-governing" in the sense that they could elect representatives to Parliament: the Province of the Main and the Oberpfalz. But their heads of state of state were still appointees of the emperor and answered to him directly. The administrator of the Province of the Main was the Swedish general Nils Abrahamsson Brahe. The administrator of the Oberpfalz was the new prime minister's younger brother, Ernst Wettin.

The provinces were split politically. The Province of the Main was solidly Crown Loyalist whereas the Upper Palatinate leaned toward the Fourth of July Party.

Two more provinces would have fallen into the

category of "heads of state, not elected, but established by the provinces themselves," except that their rulers had betrayed the emperor when the Ostend War broke out. That, at least, was how Gustav Adolf saw the matter. Needless to say, the rulers of Saxony and Brandenburg—the electors John George and George William—had a different view. Within a few weeks, the dispute would be settled on the battlefield—and most people figured Gustav Adolf would emerge triumphant.

What would happen then was a matter of speculation. In social and economic terms, Brandenburg was much like Pomerania: relatively backward, with poor farmland and not much in the way of industry. Berlin's position as Germany's premier city was still a long way in the future—and, in the new universe created by the Ring of Fire, might never happen at all. In the year 1635, the city's population was no greater than twelve thousand people.

Furthermore, the elector of Brandenburg was Gustav Adolf's brother-in-law. The emperor was influenced enough by his wife—more precisely, was reluctant enough to upset her—that while he would certainly depose George William he wouldn't strip his family of its political position. The elector would be forced into what amounted to house arrest, and his fifteen-year-old son Frederick William would become the new elector—or, more likely, the new duke. With the effective collapse of the Holy Roman Empire, the title of "Elector" was now meaningless. Until Frederick William reached his majority, of course, Brandenburg would actually be ruled by a regent appointed by the emperor. That might very well wind up being Sweden's own chancellor, Axel Oxenstierna.

In short, Brandenburg would probably wind up playing the same sort of role in the internal politics of the USE that Pomerania did and Mecklenburg used to play: a stronghold of the most conservative elements in the nation.

Saxony was quite different. Its capital city of Dresden was both older and more populous than Berlin. So was its other major city, Leipzig. Dresden was becoming an industrial center and Leipzig had long been commercially prominent—the Leipzig Trade Fair went back well into the middle ages.

The province was far more advanced culturally than Brandenburg, as well. Two of central Europe's major universities were located there: the University of Wittenberg, which produced the great theologians Martin Luther and Philipp Melanchthon, and the even older University of Leipzig.

Most people who paid attention to political affairs thought the situation in Saxony would become very unsettled once Gustav Adolf conquered the province. No one doubted that he would dispossess John George and his family altogether and replace them with his own imperial administration. Nor did anyone doubt that the Committees of Correspondence would be pushing hard to establish the sort of republican structure for the province that already existed in Magdeburg and the State of Thuringia-Franconia.

That left the so-called "Province of Swabia" that had been provided for less than a year earlier by the Congress of Copenhagen. The province was to be created once the region was "fully pacified," with Margrave Georg Friedrich of Baden-Durlach already named as the administrator. But what would actually happen was anyone's guess. The largest single chunk of the projected Province of Swabia was Württemberg, which young duke Eberhard had willed to its population on his deathbed. Lawyers working for the Fourth of July Party were arguing that Württemberg should become its own republican province. Meanwhile, Bernhard of Saxe-Weimar—or "Bernhard, Grand Duke of the County of Burgundy," as he was now styling himself—still had an army nearby and made no secret of his desire to incorporate as much of Swabia as he could into the new independent realm he was busy creating. And just to throw another monkey wrench into the works, several of the cities and towns in the region were now making noises about "turning Swiss."

So, as of July of 1635, the United States of Europe had eleven provinces, with presumably two more to be added soon—or "returned," if you accepted Gustav Adolf's interpretation of the status of Saxony and Brandenburg—and at least one more to be added whenever the situation in Swabia settled down.

In addition, there were the seven imperial cities: Hamburg, Luebeck, Augsburg, Frankfurt am Main, Strassburg, Ulm—and Magdeburg itself. The city was simultaneously the national capital of the USE, the capital of the province of Magdeburg, and an imperial city in its own right. As such, its mayor was Otto Gericke.

It was all very complicated—and, if this latest news was accurate, was going to get still more complicated. Not to mention unsettled and upheaved.

"Is he out of his mind?" Ed demanded.

Chapter 12

Magdeburg

"Wilhelm, this course of action is very reckless." The Landgrave of Hesse-Kassel set down his glass of wine and leaned forward in his chair. That took a bit of effort, since Wilhelm V was a portly man and the armchair in Wilhelm Wettin's salon was plush and deep. "What could have possessed you to decide this?"

Standing behind her husband, with her hand on his shoulder, Amalie Elizabeth knew the argument was probably futile. Wilhelm had that stubborn, grumpy expression that she'd come to know all too well in the three days since she and her husband had returned to the capital. He seemed to have aged a year for every week in office, too.

She wondered what had happened to the charming, gracious, intelligent man who'd been a close friend and confidant of the ruling family of Hesse-Kassel for decades. Had a troll from legend abducted him and left an impostor in his place? This—this—pigheaded, sullen blockhead whom she could barely recognize.

That was just a fancy, though. She knew the real

explanation was prosaic, and shied away from it simply because she hated to admit that even people as acute and perceptive as Wilhelm Wettin—as herself also, she imagined, in the wrong circumstances—could behave so foolishly.

It was a matter of poise. Wilhelm had been mentally off-balance and staggering for at least a year, ever since he smelled the scent of victory and began making shortsighted bargains and compromises in order to gain the support of everyone he could. Being fair, Amalie Elizabeth and her husband had initially inclined in that direction themselves. But once they recognized the danger involved, they'd tried to restrain Wilhelm.

To no avail, apparently. They were bystanders, to a degree, where he was the man at the very center of the maelstrom. What they'd been able to see—as would Wilhelm himself, had he retained his normally judicious temperament—was that the petty obsessions of the average aristocrat and the most prosperous burghers were driving the Crown Loyalist Party off a cliff. Their insistence on retaining all possible privileges was blinding them to the need to abandon many of them if they were to survive at all.

And blinding Wilhelm too—or, at least, putting so much pressure on him that he refused to look.

"If you have to throw these dogs a bone," her husband continued, "then make it the established church. But whatever you do, stay away from trying to impose a uniform solution upon the citizenship problem."

Wettin was sunk far back into his own chair, his hands gripping the armrests tightly. "I've already told you, I can't. Our coalition—which is what it is, never think otherwise—has too many factions which are adamant on both issues. And if they were willing to compromise, it'd be over the established church. They won't budge on citizenship."

It was all Amalie Elizabeth could do not to grind her teeth.

There were two central issues roiling the United States of Europe. It was their differences on these two points that had so sharply distinguished Wilhelm and his opponent Mike Stearns in the recent election.

The first was the matter of an established church. Basically, there were four possible positions:

The position of Stearns and his Fourth of July Party was simple: complete separation of church and state. They wanted no established church of any kind.

On the far opposite side of the political spectrum, some figures in the Crown Loyalist Party—a relatively small minority, thankfully—wanted a single established church for the entire nation. That would have to be Lutheranism, of course. One could hardly do otherwise, given that the emperor was a Lutheran.

Most members of the Crown Loyalist Party, however, took a more moderate stance. They agreed that an established church was a necessary basis for any stable polity, but they felt it would be impossible to impose a single church on the entire country. The USE simply had too many denominations, even leaving aside the issue of the Jews. Those moderate Crown Loyalists had no desire to repeat the century of instability caused by excluding the Calvinists from the Peace of Augsburg in 1555.

Instead, they favored separate established churches in each province. With some exceptions—the only really important one being the State of Thuringia-Franconia,

and *those* people could be counted on to be obstrep-
erous no matter what—the provinces were relatively
uniform, in religious terms. Where an established
church for the entire USE would be an endless source
of conflict, established churches for each separate
province should be stable enough.

Within that broad agreement, however, another division existed: One camp, led by Hesse-Kassel, argued
that the issue of an established church should be settled
entirely on a provincial level. That would allow some
of the more free-thinking provinces, like the SoTF and
Magdeburg, to opt for separation of church and state.

But most of the Crown Loyalists, pigheaded as usual,
would not accept that compromise. They wanted an
established church to be mandatory for every province,
whether that province wanted one or not. In effect,
they insisted on picking a fight with the Committees
of Correspondence in their own strongholds, which
the ruling couple of Hesse-Kassel thought was about
as smart as picking a fight with a bear in its own den.

Still, despite the heat that had been generated over
the question of an established church during the campaign, almost nobody thought it was really a critical
matter. The reason was simple. With the exception of
a very small number of reactionary diehards, who were
considered blockheads even by most Crown Loyalists,
every prominent figure in the political life of the
USE agreed that religious persecution was dead and
buried. No one would be *required* to join the established church, nor would any member of any other
denomination be penalized for not belonging—except,
of course, that some of the taxes they paid would be
used to support a church they didn't belong to.

In private discussions, Mike Stearns had told Amalie Elizabeth and her husband that he would be willing to accept an established church as a compromise solution, if need be. He'd even accept a nation-wide established Lutheran church, provided it was set up the way established churches had been set up in some of the nations from the universe he'd come from, like England and Denmark.

The real heat—the real fury, calling things by their right name—was centered on the other major issue before the nation.

Who was to be considered a citizen of the USE in the first place?

Again, there were basically four positions:

The citizenship program of Mike Stearns and his Fourth of July Party was simple. They lifted it word-for-word, in fact, from the constitution of the United States in the universe they'd left behind, as modified by what the up-timers called the Fourteenth Amendment:

All persons born or naturalized in the United States, and subject to the jurisdiction thereof, are citizens of the United States and of the State wherein they reside. No State shall make or enforce any law which shall abridge the privileges or immunities of citizens of the United States; nor shall any State deprive any person of life, liberty, or property, without due process of law; nor deny to any person within its jurisdiction the equal protection of the laws.

Substitute "Province" for "State" and there you had, in two sentences, the position of the Fourth of July Party. Which, needless to say, was vociferously and belligerently supported by the Committees of Correspondence.

The opposing positions fell into three camps.

The far opposite position, as with the matter of an established church, was subscribed to by few people—in this case, intellectuals rather than reactionaries. These were people so addicted to regularity and precision that they insisted that whatever criteria for citizenship were decided upon needed to be applied to all provinces uniformly.

Most members of the Crown Loyalist Party considered that completely impractical. The variations in local and regional custom when it came to citizenship were simply too great. Trying to come up with any standard criteria applied across the board nationally would tie up the parliament for years.

Instead, as with the established church, most Crown Loyalists felt that each province needed to establish its own criteria for citizenship. Some of them even pointed out that that had been the stance originally taken by the United States the up-timers came from.

(To which Mike Stearns responded bluntly and crudely: "Yup, we sure did, which goes to prove Americans can fuck up like the best of 'em. As a result of which, we saddled ourselves with slavery, property qualifications to vote—you name the stupid limitation on citizenship, we did it—and it took Andy Jackson and a civil war to get rid of all that crap.")

Within that broad camp, a division existed. The moderate wing of the Crown Loyalists, with Hesse-Kassel again in the lead, advocated that citizenship criteria should be established by the provincial governments.

That was simple enough, they argued. In private, Stearns had told them that if his back was to the wall, he'd accept that compromise also.

But most of the Crown Loyalists thought that policy would be disastrous, and for two reasons.

First, they pointed out—correctly enough—that Hesse-Kassel's position amounted to locking the barn after the horse got out. There being as yet no established constitution for the USE, the recent election that had produced the existing provincial governments had willy-nilly been held under the terms dictated by the prime minister in power, Mike Stearns. He had simply decreed that all adult permanent residents were citizens and thus could vote.

To be sure, in many of the provinces still dominated by traditional elites there had been plenty of voter intimidation and vote fraud. Still, from the viewpoint of most Crown Loyalists, the result was hopelessly tainted. Allowing the provincial governments elected under Stearns' dictatorial fiat to turn around and decide citizenship was preposterous. As one prominent Crown Loyalist put it, "You might as well allow a band of robbers to vote on whether their loot is legal."

Abstractly, their position held quite a bit of merit. But Wilhelm V and Amalie Elizabeth thought that was pure folly. In the real world, sensible people—for sure, sensible rulers—had to accept that certain realities, no matter how unpleasant, were too well-established to try to overturn.

Unfortunately, their practical and moderate position was not shared by most of their party. The majority of Crown Loyalists insisted that the decision on who was and who wasn't a citizen had to be made in each province by that province's traditional and established authorities, not the newly elected, bastard legislatures.

Looked at from one angle, this stance was more

than a bit absurd. After all, the Crown Loyalists held state power in the USE because they'd won a majority of the seats in the existing parliament, be that parliament ever so distorted and basely-born.

But that was only true nationally. The majority of the Crown Loyalists were adamant that "proper" citizenship criteria had to be established in every province as well. Left to their own devices, Magdeburg province and the State of Thuringia-Franconia would implement the Fourth of July Party's definition of citizenship. That would give those two very prominent provinces—the SoTF was already the USE's most populous province—even more sway in national affairs. That would be inevitable, since the voter rolls of most other provinces would drop drastically after the provincial elites reestablished traditional citizenship criteria.

Without realizing it, the down-time Crown Loyalists were being sucked into the same quicksand that had trapped the slave-owners in the early up-time United States. The free states—or full-citizenship provinces, in the case of the USE—would inevitably wind up with more voters than the slave states. Or, in this case, more voters than those provinces which sharply limited citizenship.

Amalie Elizabeth and her husband were far more familiar with up-time history than most Crown Loyalists. The landgrave had once suggested at a national gathering of Crown Loyalist leaders, quite sarcastically, that perhaps the Crown Loyalists should demand that all non-citizens in limited-citizenship provinces should be considered 3/5 of a person for the purpose of determining the size of the electorate.

The reference had passed right over the heads of most people present, of course. But it didn't matter. The proposal that was actually adopted by that gathering and then accepted by most Crown Loyalists went beyond Hesse-Kassel's satire: They argued that all non-citizens in a limited-citizenship province should be counted as citizens for the purpose of determining the electoral strength of that province.

That position, needless to say, infuriated the CoCs and the members of the Fourth of July Party. As one wag put it, "Why not simplify things and have just one citizen in every province who exercises all of the votes of the rest of the people who live in the province? What a novel idea! Maybe we could call it 'tyranny.'"

But the traditional elites who provided most of the leadership of the Crown Loyalists ignored the criticisms. For them, steeped in paternalistic traditions and customs, the idea seemed perfectly reasonable. *Of course* all people who live in a province should have their existence reflected in the electoral strength of that province. The decisions made by their legislatures would affect them, would they not? But likewise, *of course* most of those people shouldn't actually be allowed to vote. They weren't competent to do so. You might as well give children in a family the same authority as the parents.

Wilhelm V and Amalie Elizabeth were firmly convinced the end result of forcing limited citizenship on every province would be a civil war. They were not at all sure who would wind up winning that war. But even if they'd been confident their side would win, they didn't think the enormous destruction was a price worth paying.

The landgrave of Hesse-Kassel said so again today, to the prime minister who now had the power to make the decision. And the response was the one he and his wife had feared. A man, trapped in quicksand, who insisted that he was just going for a swim.

"In the long run, we don't have any choice," Wettin said. His tone was mulish, his gaze was downcast. He reminded Amalie of a petulant child. "If we let them set the terms of citizenship, we'll wind up with a civil war for sure. The only way to prevent that is to limit their power from the outset."

Amalie Elizabeth could no longer restrain herself. "Wilhelm, that's wrong from more angles than I can count! Just to begin with, it's absurd to think that you can limit the power of the Committees of Correspondence—not to mention someone like Mike Stearns!—by simply fiddling with the voter rolls. It didn't work in the United States that Grantville came from, did it? What makes you think it will work here?"

Her husband nodded. "Like it or not, their power stems from their political influence over the lower classes. Most of those people are not accustomed to voting anyway. Did the peasants who fought the Peasant War have voting privileges? No. But they still rebelled—and the only thing that crushed them was military force, not stringent voting registrars."

That last came with a sneer, to which Wettin responded with a glare. But the landgrave of Hesse-Kassel was now too angry himself to care about diplomacy.

"And have you given any thought to *that* little problem? How many of those squabbling petty noblemen and burghers you're pandering to have volunteered to raise and fund an army? Or are you lunatic enough to believe you can rely on the USE's army? Which is riddled with CoC agitators and organizers."

Amalie Elizabeth was no more inclined to be polite herself any longer, although she refrained from sneering.

"You *did* notice, I hope—you being the prime minister now—the results of the recent fracas between the CoCs and the anti-Semites?"

Her husband's sneer had never wavered. "Oh, yes. Wasn't that splendid? Thousands of reactionaries dead all over the country, the CoCs triumphant everywhere—and you might ask that pack of semi-literate exile noblemen from Mecklenburg why they haven't returned to their homes. Consider that, Wilhelm, before you get too cocksure about triggering a civil war."

But it was no use. The prime minister's expression might as well have been set in stone. The statue of a dwarf king, perhaps, determined to do what he was damn well determined to do, no matter the consequences.

After Rebecca finished speaking, Gretchen nodded. "Thank you for the information. Would you care for some more tea?" With a little smile, she wiggled her fingers at the large tea pot on the kitchen table between them, with its very ample accompanying provisions of sugar and cream. "It turns out I can afford a lot of tea, these days."

Rebecca shook her head and then cocked it sideways a little. "You don't seem upset by the news."

Gretchen shrugged. "I was expecting it. This clash is inevitable, Rebecca. There won't be any way to negotiate with the Crown Loyalists until they fracture and real political parties emerge from the wreckage. That...*thing* they call a party is nothing of the sort. It's an unholy alliance whose sole basis of agreement is seizing and holding power. Wettin is no more in control of it than a wave controls the sea."

Rebecca sighed. "I fear you may well be right."

She rose from her seat. "I must leave." Hearing the sounds of teenagers quarreling in a nearby room, she smiled. "The demands of children. As you well know."

Gretchen accompanied her to the door. Two Yeoman Warders were waiting in the corridor beyond, ready to escort Rebecca home.

"Thank you," she repeated.

Gretchen had been notified by Rebecca ahead of time that she'd be visiting this morning. That meant important political news, of course. Gretchen, in turn, had sent word to all the CoC leaders in the city.

So, within half an hour of Rebecca's departure, most of them had arrived at the apartment building and were gathered in Gretchen's kitchen. It was a very big kitchen, as it needed to be given that it was the kitchen for the entire complex.

"So it's definite then?" asked Spartacus, who was standing near one of the stoves.

"As definite as any information from Rebecca," she replied. "But, certainly on a subject like this one, that's pretty damn definite."

Across the table from her, Gunther Achterhof nodded. "Yes, I think we can assume it's true. As soon as the parliament begins its session, Wettin will introduce bills that will force through the reactionaries' positions on citizenship and the established church. The only question is: what do we intend to do about it?"

Gretchen reached for the tea pot. "Tea, anyone?"

Achterhof grinned. "Better get a bigger one. We're going to be here for hours."

"Days," predicted Spartacus.

Chapter 13

Stockholm

"Just as ugly as I remembered," Baldur Norddahl said to Prince Ulrik, who was standing next to him on the ship coming slowly into Stockholm's harbor. They were looking up at the Swedish royal palace, known as the Tre Kronor—"Three Crowns"—because of the shape of its central spire.

The palace sat on the island of Stadsholmen, which was the center of Stockholm. In this day and age, there wasn't much of the city lying outside of it. That would change in the future, Ulrik knew, when Stockholm would expand across many of the islands of the great archipelago situated off Sweden's eastern coast where Lake Mälaren met the Baltic. But at least for now, Sweden's capital was a relatively small city.

Stockholm was dominated by two buildings, the Tre Kronor and the Church of St. Nicholas, most commonly known as Storkyrkan and sometimes as the Stockholm Cathedral. The church was an imposing brick edifice located close to the palace, with an even more imposing steeple.

"Ugly" wasn't fair. In its own way, Tre Kronor was quite impressive. But it lacked the grace and style of Frederiksborg Palace in Denmark, in Ulrik's opinion. Admittedly, he could be accused of bias.

They were nearing the dock now, and a flurry of shouts was exchanged between some sailors on the ship and half a dozen men standing on the dock. Ulrik understood Swedish quite well, but some of the profanity being used was unclear to him. Of Finnish origin, perhaps. He was tempted to ask Baldur, who was fluent in all the northern languages including Russian. But he decided he would be damaging his dignity. There was nothing more sublime involved in the exchange than men coordinating the work of docking a small ship. And he was on an important diplomatic mission, after all.

Even if the critical person in that mission was still back on the ironclad that had carried them across the Baltic, having an eight-year-old temper tantrum that even Caroline Platzer was having a hard time coping with. Once it had become clear that Kristina's frenzy wasn't going to fade anytime soon, Ulrik had decided it would be best for him and Baldur to proceed onward in one of the lighters that had arrived to offload the passengers. He didn't think his presence was helping Platzer any, given that at least part of the reason Kristina was so agitated was her sure and certain knowledge that her mother would disapprove of her betrothed.

Besides, he wanted to get off the ironclad. The damn thing made him nervous. He thought it was sheer folly to use such a vessel for this purpose.

Folly, for at least three reasons. First, the vessel

had never been designed as a passenger ship and was very poorly suited for the purpose. Even a regular warship would have been better. It certainly wouldn't have smelled as bad.

Second, using the thing was pure royal extravagance, as grandiose as it was expensive. With a father like Christian IV, Prince Ulrik had had more than enough such wasteful exhibitions.

Finally, it wasn't *safe*. The ironclads didn't handle open seas well at all, and even the Baltic classified as a sea. Admiral Simpson himself had cautioned against using the *Union of Kalmar* to transport Princess Kristina and Prince Ulrik to Stockholm.

But Gustav Adolf and Christian IV had both been adamant on the matter. The ironclad had formerly been the *SSIM President*, in the service of the USE Navy. As part of the elaborate process—"delicate dance," might be a better way of putting it—of forging the Union of Kalmar, Gustav Adolf had insisted that one of the ironclads be turned over to the new Union. That would make Christian IV at least technically the co-owner of the great warship, and the Danish king loved modern gadgets, especially military gadgets.

Well, it was over—assuming the *Union of Kalmar* didn't sink in the harbor, taking down the royal heiress at the same time. But as much as Kristina sometimes aggravated Ulrik, he certainly didn't wish that on her. For the most part, in fact, he'd grown rather fond of the girl.

True, she'd be something of a terror as a wife. At times, at least. But that didn't bother Ulrik very much. He was phlegmatic enough to handle it. His real fear since boyhood when it came to a political marriage—which was inevitable for a prince in line of succession—was that his wife would be dull and boring.

No fear of that with Kristina.

The ship was now tied up to the dock. A large coterie of Swedish court officials came forward. They were trying to spot Kristina, and as it became clear to them that the princess was not aboard, their expressions grew concerned.

"Princess Kristina was ill-disposed for the moment," Ulrik explained, as he came across the gangway to the dock. Norddahl came behind him, followed by four servants toting their baggage.

Once he set foot on the dock, Ulrik nodded toward the *Union of Kalmar.* The ironclad was quite visible in the harbor. In fact, it had drawn a large crowd of sightseers to the various docks and piers. Except this one, of course, which had been blocked off by a unit of Swedish troops. Probably from the palace guard, Ulrik figured.

"She's still aboard the ironclad," he explained. "I imagine she'll be along fairly soon."

The fellow who seemed to be in charge of the contingent of officials was looking very glum by now.

"Her Majesty will be most upset," he said.

"And hence her daughter's indisposition," replied Ulrik cheerily.

Clearly, from his expression, the court official hadn't understood the quip. Just as well. Ulrik's father had once told him: *As a king, you want brave generals, shrewd advisers and diplomats, but—make sure of this, son!—dull-witted court officials. They're insufferable otherwise.*

Judging from the way the court officials were

milling around, talking to each other in low-pitched but agitated tones, nothing would be happening until Kristina set foot on the dock. Quite obviously, none of these men wanted to return to the palace and face the queen without the princess in tow.

So be it. Ulrik had no problem standing around on the dock for a time. It was a very pleasant day, sunny and with just a mild breeze. After spending two days cramped on an ironclad and with the prospect ahead of spending weeks in what looked like a rather chilly royal palace—it would be crowded, too; palaces with royalty in residence always were—he didn't mind at all the pleasures of the moment.

Baldur felt otherwise. "There's got to be a decent tavern hereabouts," he said. "Even a not-so-decent tavern would suit me fine."

Ulrik smiled. "Suit you better, you mean. Unfortunately, this is not the time for carousal. It would look bad."

"Look bad for you," Baldur retorted. "They already think the worst of me."

Actually, from what Ulrik could determine, none of these officials seemed to have any idea of Baldur Norddahl's identity or of his checkered past in Sweden. Neither had any of the Swedish officials they'd encountered before they sailed—and there'd been a veritable drove of those, during the Congress of Copenhagen.

The explanation, of course, was simple—that selfsame dull-wittedness of officials. It simply wouldn't have occurred to any of them that a Danish prince—any sort of prince, even a Hindoo or Mussulman prince—would associate with ruffians. It helped that Ulrik had seen to it that Baldur's wardrobe was suitable.

The name wouldn't matter here. Ulrik had never asked, but he was quite sure that whatever misdeeds Baldur had committed in times past in Sweden, he'd done it under a different name.

There was no reason to press the matter, however, which they'd be doing if they ventured into a disreputable dockside tavern. If there was any place in Stockholm where they might encounter someone who'd known Baldur, it would be there.

A little motion in the distance caught his eye, and he turned to look. Another lighter was coming away from the *Union of Kalmar*. And it was flying the Swedish royal ensign.

"Too late, anyway," he said to Baldur. "Kristina's coming."

When the princess set foot on the dock, she ignored the gaggle of officials and rushed to Ulrik's side. She clutched his elbow with both hands and looked up at him with an expression that combined anxiety, determination and relief.

"Caroline says you won't get upset no matter what happens. Because that's the way you are, she says. So she says I should take my guidance from you."

Ulrik looked over at the gangway, where Caroline Platzer was now coming across. Their eyes met. He didn't know whether he should glare or look thankful.

Instead, he kept his expression neutral. Realizing, at the same time, that the infernally shrewd Platzer woman would have counted on that.

Ah, well. There were advantages to being a phlegmatic prince. Calming the nerves of a younger and very unphlegmatic princess, for one.

He patted her hands. "Everything will be fine."

A smooth and fluent liar, too. Another virtue for a prince.

Vaxholm Island, in the Stockholm Archipelago

When he entered the tavern and saw the men already sitting at the large table in the center, Charles Mademann's eyes widened.

Mathurin Brillard.

Robert Ouvrard.

Gui Ancelin.

Guillaume Locquifier.

Abraham Levasseur.

André Tourneau.

He hissed in a breath. He'd last seen Levasseur and Tourneau in Scotland, just before he left for Sweden. They'd been there with the leaders of their movement, Michel Ducos and Antoine Delerue. The other four men had all been involved in the affair in Grantville back in March. Ancelin was always ready for anything. Locquifier had an unfortunate tendency to obey orders to an excessive degree of fussiness, but he wouldn't be here at all if Michel Ducos and Antoine Delerue hadn't approved the project. Ouvrard, despite his gloomy outlook, was one of the best men in their organization for planning and carrying out decisive actions. So was Brillard, who was a superb marksman to boot. He'd have been the shooter who killed the town's mayor, Henry Dreeson.

They'd known where to find him because he'd sent the information to Scotland soon after he arrived. He had no idea where Levasseur and Tourneau had found the other four, who'd have been on the run after the Dreeson incident. Probably somewhere in Holland.

However they'd managed it, they could be here in Sweden for only one reason.

"Oh, splendid," he said, smiling widely.

Levasseur returned the smile, and gestured to an empty seat at the table. Brillard, on the other hand, was frowning.

"Is this safe, Charles?" he asked quietly, almost whispering. His eyes went to the door at the rear which led to the tavern-keeper's personal dwellings.

Mademann sat down. "Relax, Mathurin. To begin, the owner is a Dutch Gomarist and thus a sympathizer."

That was . . . some ways short of the truth. Geerd Bleecker was indeed a Counter-Remonstrant, as the followers of the theologian Franciscus Gomarus were often called. A stout enough fellow. But his ardor fell quite a bit short of what Mademann and his fellow Huguenots considered necessary for their cause. Bleecker had no idea what Mademann was really planning to do here in Sweden. He thought the Huguenot was just a wealthy exile seeking to recoup his fortunes. Sweden had many industries that were booming due to the influx of American technical knowledge combined with the large and already existing population in Stockholm of Dutch financiers and merchants.

"Perhaps more to the point," Mademann continued, "Geerd is in somewhat desperate financial straits—or was, until I arrived and provided him with a solid and steady source of income." Mademann waved his hand about, indicating the interior of the tavern. The wooden building was well enough made, but it was showing clear signs of disrepair. Nothing that threatened the integrity of the edifice yet. Just the sort of mostly minor problems that ensued when the owner of a building was short of funds.

Mademann smiled ruefully; not at his own situation but that of the tavern-keeper. "When Geerd first settled here he was convinced that many of the Calvinist merchants operating in Stockholm would be more comfortable with a tavern located on another island in the archipelago. Away from the eyes of the Swedish king's Lutheran pastors."

Tourneau cocked an inquisitive eye. "And . . . ?"

Mademann shook his head. "The thing is, Gustav Adolf keeps his pastors on a tight leash. He wants the Dutch here, so he's not about to tolerate harassment. No open worship is allowed, but he makes no effort to suppress Calvinists so long as they remain discreet. And this tavern is on the island of Vaxholm, which is just that little bit too far from the capital."

Ancelin grunted. "Didn't seem that far, from what I could tell when we came in."

Gui was not the most imaginative of men. He'd been born and raised in a port city, but he'd never worked the sea himself. So, incurious by nature, he understood none of the realities involved.

"It's just a few miles," said Mademann. "But it's one thing to walk a few miles, it's another to row a boat across. Especially in a Swedish winter."

"Ah. Hadn't thought of that."

Mademann shrugged. "The distance was enough of an inconvenience that few Dutch merchants have ever even visited here. What little business Geerd has gotten over the years has been from Finnish fisherman and petty traders. Smugglers, most of them, for whom the distance is convenient."

"We can speak freely, then?" asked Ouvrard.

"Not in front of Bleecker or his wife. They don't..." He wiggled his fingers. "I saw no reason to burden them with unnecessary information."

Ancelin grunted again. "Be tough on them after we're done."

He was a crude man, too. Gui was saying nothing that they didn't already understand, so why make a point of the issue? The fate that was sure to befall the tavern-keeper and his wife was unfortunate, of course. But many misfortunes came in the wake of God's purpose.

So Mademann ignored the remark. "But he usually remains in the back. As long as we're not shouting, we can speak freely."

Levasseur leaned forward, placing his weight on his forearms. "You realize why we're here."

"Of course. I was hoping someone would come, once I learned of the princess' visit. On my own, I haven't even been able to find a way to get to the queen."

"Prince, too," said Brillard. "The queen and the heiress would be enough, but we can catch the Danish boy at the same time. That means Christian IV will be as furious as Gustav Adolf."

That would surely mean the wrath of the USE and the Union of Kalmar would be turned upon Cardinal Richelieu, given the evidence they'd be leaving behind. A new war with France would begin, the cardinal would fall, and the Huguenot cause would have another great chance. All seven of the plotters leaned back in their chairs simultaneously, so great was their mutual satisfaction.

Chapter 14

Magdeburg

Gazing out of his office window overlooking the Elbe, Francisco Nasi had the same thought that most people did when they studied that scenery.

What a blighted mess.

In days past—well, you had to go back at least a year—the Elbe itself had been fairly attractive, even if the factories and mills and foundries that lined it in this area were not. But that was no longer true. The river had become rather badly polluted.

According to up-time values of "polluted," at any rate. For someone reared in the seventeenth century, the river might be dirty and ugly but at least it was no longer dangerous. Magdeburg's extensive water and sewer systems saw to that, along with the ferocious patrols maintained constantly by the city's Committee of Correspondence. Whatever other noxious substances might be in that river, human waste was no longer one of them.

Nobody in their right mind would willingly drink from that river. Even after being filtered in the water treatment plants, the Elbe's waters near Magdeburg still tasted pretty foul. If you did drink from it, though, the worst you'd probably suffer was just a bad taste in your mouth, maybe a touch of nausea. But you wouldn't contract dysentery or typhoid fever—as you very well might if you drank the river waters near many towns and cities in Europe.

For that, if nothing else, Francisco's allegiance to the Americans would have been firm. They had their faults, certainly. For someone of Nasi's sophistication and cosmopolitan inclinations, parochialism was perhaps the worst. But wherever the influence of the up-timers went, children lived. Not all, but many more than would have otherwise.

His allegiance to one up-timer in particular was more than firm. By now, it was as solid as granite. That was his former employer, Michael Stearns, whom he'd served for two years as what amounted to his chief of espionage.

Francisco wondered how Mike was faring now. He'd be on the eve of his first battle. Well, not exactly his first battle, but certainly his first battlefield.

He'd do very well, he thought. It was almost impossible to imagine Mike Stearns not doing very well at anything he tried.

But there was no longer anything Francisco could do for the man. Not directly, at least. So, hearing the knock on the door, he turned away from the window and brought his mind to bear on a current problem.

"Come in, Eddie." He'd been expecting Junker's arrival, but Francisco would have known who his visitor was just by the way he knocked. For whatever quirky reason—the man was given to whimsy—Eddie Junker had adopted the habit several months earlier of rapping on a door according to a little up-time jingle: *Shave-and-a-haircut, two bits.*

It was incredibly annoying. Fortunately for Eddie, his employer had studied Maimonides and come away convinced that the great sage's criticism of anthropomorphism could be applied to dealing with petty irritations as well. True, no rabbi he'd encountered agreed with his interpretation of the *Guide For the Perplexed.* So much the worse for them.

Junker came in, moving more lightly that you'd expect for a man as stocky as he was. His hand closing the door was light, too. Nasi could barely hear the latch click.

Proving once again the value of a correct interpretation of Maimonides. Coupled to the aggravating knock was a generally splendid young man.

"Sit."

While Eddie did so, Francisco turned the map that had been lying on his desk so that it faced Junker. That done, he pointed to the place that filled most of the map. He'd been told by people familiar with the city that it was quite a good representation of Dresden.

"Can you land here, if need be? Or anywhere near the city?"

Eddie glanced at the legend. "Dresden, huh? It's a pretty fair likeness."

Nasi's eyebrows raised. "You've been there, then. I hadn't known that."

"Oh, half a dozen times at least. Twice—no, three times—on business for my father. And we have relatives in the city, so I visited them on several occasions also."

He pursed his lips and frowned, studying the map. "As to whether I could land the plane..."

Nasi waited patiently. There was no point trying to hurry Eddie. For such a young man, he was quite deliberate in the way he approached problems. On the positive side, he didn't make many mistakes, either, and no dumb ones.

Finally, Junker leaned back in the chair. "I just don't know, Don Francisco. I...think I probably could. The terrain's flat. As long as you stay away from the Elbe, and it hasn't rained heavily, the ground should be solid enough. But I really wouldn't want to land on a field that hadn't been prepared. Any sort of sizeable rock—"

Nasi waved his hand. "Yes, of course. We'd have to see to that first."

He sat down in his own chair and studied the map pensively.

After a few seconds, Eddie cleared his throat. "If you don't mind my asking—"

Francisco had found that in his line of work one of the worst mistakes you could make was to fetishize security, especially with your immediate subordinates. Not only did it handicap them in their work, but they also invariably resented it. If they were smart, at least, and Nasi had no use for dimwitted assistants.

There were times, of course, when complete secrecy was imperative. But this was not one of them.

"I've been approached by Gretchen Richter. She wanted to know if I could fly someone into Dresden—and if I would be willing to do so."

"The someone being..."

"Herself, I imagine. I know she's been approached by people from that rebellion in the Vogtland. They wanted her to come to Dresden. She refused, at least for the moment, but will send some CoC representatives."

Eddie pursed his lips again. "How solid is that information?"

"As solid as possible, since I got it from Richter herself."

"Really? I'm a little surprised she was that forthcoming."

"She's shrewd. She figures I'd most likely find out about it anyway, if not all the details. This way she maximizes the chances that I'd agree, since I wouldn't be wondering what her motives were."

Eddie stared out the window for a moment. "So you're thinking that she's laying the basis for a later arrival. In case..."

"In case Dresden explodes. Yes. You'll need to take that into account when you investigate the possibilities of landing a plane in the area. There may be hostilities underway."

"Ah, marvelous. What I always wanted. Landing under fire while on a desperate mission."

Nasi smiled. "If it would make you happier, you could take Denise with you. On the exploratory trip, I mean. Not the possible later desperate mission under fire. I wouldn't care to answer to her mother for that."

Eddie winced. "Me neither."

Denise Beasley's mother was a formidable woman. On the other hand, Christin George did not try to rein in her daughter, either—which, given Denise's nature, would have been well-nigh impossible anyway.

Denise and Eddie were more-or-less betrothed now. Not in a manner that down-time Germans would have recognized as legally binding, true. What Denise herself called "going steady." But, perhaps oddly in such a willful girl, Francisco thought she was quite devoted to Junker.

Eddie was back to staring out the window. "We'd have to be gone for at least a month. I'd need to get a chaperone, for that long a trip. Christin is easygoing, but no mother of a seventeen-year-old girl is *that* easygoing." He mused for a few more seconds. "Denise will insist that Minnie come with us, of course. Which I don't mind, except Christin will never agree that Minnie Hugelmair constitutes what any sane person would call a 'chaperone.'"

Nasi nodded judiciously. "That would indeed be madness."

Silence fell upon the room again. After perhaps a minute, Nasi chuckled. "The solution is obvious, I think."

Eddie winced. "She'll kill me."

"Oh, nonsense. I've always found Noelle Stull to be quite the adventuress."

"For God's sake, don't tell her that. Besides, she's all the way down in Bamberg now. And she'd have to get permission from her office, and as overworked as they are—

Francisco shook his head. "Actually, she's been in Grantville for the past week or so, packing her belongings. That's because she's got a new job and a new employer." He cleared his throat. "Who is me. So I foresee no problems."

Junker stared at him, then whistled softly. "I really never thought she'd accept your offer."

"Prague is closer to Vienna."

Eddie chuckled again. "Given that the fellow of her

interest is a Hungarian officer in the service of the Austrians, and the Austrians are officially at war with the king of Bohemia, I'm not quite sure how relocating to Prague really puts Noelle any closer to Janos Drugeth. And who knows where he is these days, anyway?"

Francisco got a smug look at his face. "As it happens, I do."

Györ, Hungary, near the Ottoman border

Janos Drugeth felt an urge to wrap a cloak around himself, even though the temperature atop the bastion was quite warm. As you'd expect on a sunny day in July. He didn't have a cloak with him anyway.

That was just a reflex, from the considerable time he'd spent in his life in one of these Balkan fortresses. The fortifications were of the so-called *trace italienne* design. Medieval perpendicular stone walls, circular or square in design, had been unable to withstand gunpowder artillery. They'd been replaced by fortresses that were generally star-shaped, with triangular bastions that gave the defenders a good field of fire at any enemy getting close to the wall. Later designs—not applied to this particular fortress—added features like ravelins, hornworks and crownworks.

The walls were quite different, too. They sloped rather than being perpendicular. The construction materials used were earth and brick, whenever possible, rather than stone. In every particular, they were designed to absorb artillery fire rather than shed it. Each cannon ball digging into the walls simply became another piece of the structure.

All well and good. But come winter, these new-style fortresses seemed every bit as frigid as their medieval predecessors.

Below him, the Rába River meandered through the town of Györ. The view was pleasant, as was usually the case in the Balkans. Janos had often wondered what God's purpose might be, to couple such a lovely region with so much in the way of strife and misery. Of course, he imagined a Frenchman or an Englishman or a Spaniard—certainly a German—could have recited at least as long a litany of woes as any inhabitant of the Balkans.

Not long ago, Noelle Stull had sent Janos a book of essays written by a famous American writer of the past. The author called himself Mark Twain. That was apparently not his real name, though, which Janos found a bit odd. To be sure, many Europeans of this age and ages past wrote under pseudonyms. But the up-timers insisted they'd had no inquisition in their nation. Why, then, the need for pseudonyms? But perhaps he was missing something.

Among the essays, most of which had been shockingly irreligious, had been one titled "The Damned Human Race." Try as he might, Drugeth had found it difficult to quarrel with Twain's thesis. He'd seen too much cruelty and brutality in his life, some of which—the brutality if not, he hoped, the cruelty—he'd inflicted himself.

He wondered still why Noelle had sent him the book. She was herself a devout Catholic and could not possibly have agreed with Twain's viewpoint, especially that displayed in his *Letters From the Earth*. Had Twain been alive today, that text alone might have gotten him burned at the stake in some countries and in serious trouble with the authorities in most others.

Well... maybe not. In fact, almost certainly not. The manner in which heresy was handled—even the way it was looked upon—had been undergoing a rapid change in Europe since the Ring of Fire. Today, it would be highly unlikely that any nation, even Spain, would actually execute an American for heresy.

Americans themselves would attribute that reluctance to fear of their military capabilities. Which, to be sure, was real enough. But the source of the unease was deeper, something which few Americans really understood themselves. Most of them considered themselves Christians and many of those considered themselves very devout. But with very few exceptions, not even the most religious up-timers really had the same outlook as most people born and bred in the seventeenth century.

The up-timers were, at bottom, a profoundly secular folk. To them, the Ring of Fire had been some sort of cosmic mystery. The more religious would add that God's hand was clearly at work—but they would say the same about almost anything. If they became ill and recuperated, they saw God's hand at work. If their favored sports team won a game, for that matter, they saw God's hand at work.

But there would be no miracle involved. Just God's mysterious ways.

People in the seventeenth century, on the other hand, believed in miracles. And they believed just as firmly—or had, until the Ring of Fire—that the age of miracles was over, and had been over for sixteen hundred years. Every theologian had told them so—and it didn't matter if they were Catholic or Lutheran or Calvinist. On that subject, there had been no real dispute.

True, there were still miracles of a sort. The Catholic church to which Janos himself belonged required evidence of a miracle before it would canonize someone who had not been a martyr. But the sort of miracles one expected to be associated with such "Venerables," as they were called, were modest in scale compared to the miracles that had happened in ancient days. Typically, it would be found that a person was gravely ill, with a disease for which there was no cure or remedy; prayers were then sent to the Venerable, by the victim or by relatives; the afflicted one was cured, spontaneously and completely; for which doctors had no explanation due to natural causes.

Well and good. Janos did not doubt the reality of such miracles. But they were hardly on the order of the parting of the Red Sea or the destruction of Sodom and Gomorrah. Such things had been absent from the earth for over a millennium and a half.

Until the Ring of Fire.

The issue had agonized theologians for years now. There was simply no getting around it. Thousands upon thousands of people—Janos himself was one of them—had gone to Grantville and seen the miracle with their own eyes.

Nor was it just the appearance of a mysterious town of peculiar folk with near-magical mechanical powers. That might possibly have been explained away. But you couldn't explain away the land itself.

There were great cliffs there, nine hundred feet tall—three times the height of the famed White Cliffs of Dover—and completely unnatural in their design. Absolutely sheer, absolutely flat, and with nothing in the way of a scree slope at their base.

More than four years had passed since the Ring of Fire and those cliffs had begun to wear down. But Janos had spoken to eyewitnesses—and there were many of them; Thuringia was a well-populated area—who swore that on the day it happened, those cliffs had gleamed and shone like mirrors. They were simply stone and earth, like any other cliffs, but on the day of the Ring of Fire they had been cut by a blade sharper than any razor. A blade huge enough to cut a perfect circle six miles in diameter,

A blade that no one in his right mind could believe had been wielded by anyone but the Almighty.

So, no American would be burned at the stake. Not even in Spain. As harsh as they might be, not even the inquisitors of the Spanish crown would be willing to take such a risk. Whatever His purpose might have been, God had brought these people here. Executing them for heresy seemed rather perilous.

Theologians all over Europe—as well as political leaders, of course—were still arguing over the meaning of the Ring of Fire. A few even held to the belief that Satan had caused the Ring of Fire. Not in Rome, though, and certainly not in Spain. The Manichean heresy involved was obvious and both the Holy and the Spanish Inquisition were quite willing to subject such persons to *auto-da-fé*.

Most opponents of the up-timers had settled on some version of Cardinal Richelieu's thesis: that God had certainly created the Ring of Fire, but had done so as a subtle caution to princes and peoples. By

showing them a world of the future which had clearly
not been created by demons, he was warning mankind
of the folly of subverting the natural political order.

Janos' own emperor, Ferdinand III, inclined to that
belief. Janos himself had done so, once. Now...He
was no longer sure.

And that, he thought, was the reason Noelle had
sent him the Twain book. Not because she agreed
with Twain, but as a gentle reminder to Drugeth
that God's ways were subtle and mysterious. So how
likely was it that an inquisitor—much less a political
leader with obvious vested interests and biases—could
determine the truth?

Not very, he'd come to conclude.

His musings were interrupted by the sound of
boots clattering up the stone stairs behind him. From
the pattern of the sound, he knew who was coming.
Ágoston Mészáros, one of the four junior officers who
had accompanied him on this expedition. Mészáros
was the most junior of the group, which meant that
he invariably got the assignment of carrying messages.

Just as well. Ágoston was a stout fellow, but not
someone you wanted to assign tasks which required
much in the way of thinking.

As soon as the young officer came onto the bastion,
he extended a slender dispatch. "Just arrived, sir."

Janos broke the seal. The contents of the dispatch
were brief. He read it through, and then read it
through again.

So. Johann Schmid could not come himself. Janos
was not surprised. Schmid served most of the Catholic
countries as their informal ambassador to the Turks.
He was believed to have the best intelligence network

of any European in the Ottoman Empire. Schmid had been a slave of the Turks for twenty years, eventually serving them in the position of dragoman. He had contacts inside and outside of the Ottoman government, and at multiple levels of Turkish society.

Drugeth had met him twice, and wasn't sorry he wouldn't be meeting him again. Schmid was a thoroughly unpleasant man. Potentially dangerous, too. It was believed that he'd tried to poison the diplomat Bratutti, probably in collusion with the Venetians, for no more sublime reason than professional rivalry.

Instead, according to the dispatch, Janos would be meeting with one of Schmid's agents. The name was not given, of course, any more than Schmid had put his own name on the missive. No one spied on the Turks casually, unless he wanted to find a strangler's cord around his neck.

If Janos was lucky, the agent would be the Ragusan physician, Doctor Grassi. The man had probably as extensive a knowledge of Ottoman affairs as Schmid himself and was far more pleasant to deal with.

Janos read through the dispatch a third time. No names were specified when it came to location, either. But from subtle hints, he was quite sure that Osijek was the place the agent would meet him.

That was within Ottoman territory, but Janos had expected as much. In some ways, he would have preferred to meet in Belgrade. There'd be many more Ottoman soldiers there, but the city was also huge—with one hundred thousand inhabitants, it was the largest city in the Turkish empire except Istanbul itself—and had a polyglot population. Serbs, Turks, Armenians, Greeks, Ragusans from Dubrovnik, traders from everywhere. Drugeth would be able to blend in easily. He could probably even do so as a Hungarian merchant.

Still, Osijek would do well enough. It was much smaller than Belgrade, but it was a trade center in its own right. Six roads led into the town. And it was close enough to Hungary that Hungarians were probably more common there than in Belgrade.

"Should we prepare to leave, sir?" asked Ágoston.

Janos shook his head. "No, you'll all be staying here. I'll be leaving tomorrow morning. I should be back within a week or two."

He'd have to go alone. A party of several Hungarians would stand out in Osijek. Besides, none of his subordinates had much experience as anything other than cavalry officers. He doubted any of them could pass themselves off as humble merchants. Mészáros would be hopeless.

Part Three

August 1635

These steep and lofty cliffs

Chapter 15

The Saxon plain, between Merseburg and Lützen

"Lützen's back there," said Eric Krenz. "We've bypassed it already." He turned in his saddle and pointed to the west, almost behind them.

Jeff turned to look. The road they'd been following from Merseburg had continued southward. The army had now turned east. Most of the units, including Jeff's 12th Infantry Battalion, were now marching through fields. Fortunately, cavalry units had already gone ahead of them and partially cleared the way.

Partially cleared the way. That was a euphemistic way of saying that horsemen had already trampled flat most of the local farmers' crops so it was a bit easier for the infantry. Jeff no longer had any trouble understanding why farmers generally detested soldiers, even their own. If this had still been Thuringian territory, the commanders would have given chits to the local authorities, which they could theoretically redeem to get repaid for at least some of the damages. In the State of Thuringia-Franconia, if not all of the USE's provinces, they probably would have gotten something too.

But they wouldn't here. This was Saxon territory, and Torstensson wasn't making any pretense that he'd repay anyone for damages. Looking on the brighter side, he'd also made clear to his soldiers that he wouldn't tolerate any atrocities either.

So be it. War was what it was. Jeff had gotten pretty inured to such things by now. He figured Sherman probably hadn't repaid any Georgia farmers either, during his march to the sea.

When he turned around to face in the direction they were travelling, he had to squint a little. The sun had risen far enough above the horizon to be uncomfortable to look toward.

Eric had turned back too. "Gustav Adolf died very close to here, you know."

Jeff Higgins sniffed. "Last I heard, Gustav Adolf was alive and well and leading his army toward Berlin."

"In that other world, I meant. Your world."

"Not my world any longer."

Krenz looked at him sidewise for a moment. "Do you miss it?"

"I miss my family, sure. I'm the only one who came through the Ring of Fire, you know. But other than that . . ." He shrugged. "I can't say I regret it. I would never have met Gretchen, for one thing. For another . . ."

He paused to check on his horse. The beast seemed placid enough, but you could never be sure what sort of bizarre notions might cross its little mind. Or was it "his" little mind? Jeff wasn't sure of the protocol when it came to geldings.

Geldings weren't really considered suitable war horses by cavalrymen and other such dashing fellows of the time. A *true* warrior would insist on riding a stallion into battle. But as far as Jeff was concerned, that was just more seventeenth-century silliness. Stallions were temperamental and Jeff figured he'd have better things to worry about on a battlefield than a hyperactive half-ton animal.

Krenz wouldn't make fun of him, of course, since he was riding a gelding himself.

"For another..." Eric prompted him.

"It's a little hard to explain. Even leaving Gretchen aside, I feel...I don't know. More alive, I guess. Like what I do here makes a real difference where in the world I left behind it probably never would have."

Krenz chewed his lower lip for a while, thinking about it. "I suppose I understand. But I have to say the thought of being insignificant but alive and healthy seems quite a bit superior than the state of being oh-so-very-important and oh-so-very-dead. If you ask me, Achilles was an idiot."

Jeff chuckled. "Oh, if that's what's bothering you! No, no, you've got it all backwards. You think the world I came from was *safe*?"

He clucked his tongue. "I guess you never heard of thermo-nuclear weapons. There were tens of thousands of those lovely things floating around. Any one of them could have turned the biggest city in the world—that world, forget this one—into a pile of slag."

Ghastly details followed.

"—also had biological and chemical weapons. Take sarin gas, for instance—"

Eric listened intently.

"—course, there probably wasn't any designed weapon as nasty as the Ebola virus. That came out of Central Africa, but I always figured it'd get loose some day. After that..." He made a face. "It's a viral hemorrhagic fever. That means—"

Graphic and gruesome details followed. Jeff moved on to other ills of the twentieth century.

"—overpopulation. Oh, yeah, I figured someday even Fairmont would have skyscrapers and you'd be lucky to get five hundred square feet to—

"—additives in *everything*. I mean, you had no idea what you were really eating. And it was even worse in the fast food joints where—"

He reserved particular venom for what had been his own *bête noire*, automated phone systems.

"—always changed their menus. Call the next day and the lying bastards would insist the menu had changed again. There were stories of people dying of thirst and ruptured bladders trying to figure how to actually talk to anybody. And the one phrase you *never* heard those fucking computer voices say was 'call volumes are unusually low so we'll connect you to your party immediately.' Oh, hell no. Call volumes were *always* high. It was like grading on a bell curve where everybody flunks."

By the time he was done, Krenz was looking downright chipper.

From atop the closest thing his scouts could find to a hill—it was really just a hillock, a slight rise in the landscape—Hans Georg von Arnim studied the surroundings. And, just as Eric Krenz had done, mused on the fact that in another universe the king of Sweden had died in battle not far from this very place.

Exactly where, no one knew. The up-time accounts

referred to "the battle of Lützen," but provided few
details. The battle hadn't taken place in the town itself
but in some field nearby. There was supposed to have
been a monument erected where Gustav Adolf died,
but of course that did not exist in the world on this
side of the Ring of Fire.

Von Arnim himself had once been in Swedish
service, for several years. That had been two decades
back, not long after Gustav Adolf ascended the throne.
The new Swedish king had been seventeen years old
at the time. He was only nineteen when Arnim came
into his employ.

That had been a long time ago. Two decades. Two
decades during which von Arnim, like most professional soldiers of the time, had served many employers.
Having been born in Brandenburger Land, naturally
enough he'd begun his military career as a soldier for
the duchy of Prussia. That had been before Prussia
was absorbed by Brandenburg. He'd had to leave
hastily due to a duel, which was how he'd wound up
on the Swedish payroll.

From there, he'd fought for the Poles for a time.
In 1624, Wallenstein—then a general for the Holy
Roman Emperor Ferdinand II—had hired him. Just
a few years later, the Austrian emperor sent an army
to support the Polish king Sigismund III against the
Swedes. Arnim had been one of the commanders of
those forces.

So, on June 17, 1629, he'd faced Gustav Adolf at
the battle of Trzciana. His Polish allies had been commanded by Stanislaw Koniecpolski. That had been a
ferocious battle, which ended with a slight advantage
for the Poles and imperials. But the Austrian troops

had mutinied when the Poles failed to pay them, and von Arnim had wound up leaving imperial service in disgust and going to work for the elector of Saxony.

Two years later, in one of the twists that were so common in the Thirty Years' War, von Arnim had wound up fighting alongside Gustav Adolf again, when he met Tilly at the battle of Breitenfeld. That had been a great victory for the Swedish king, but the Saxon troops had been ignominiously routed early in the battle.

However, von Arnim himself had not been blamed for the fiasco. It would have been hard to do so, since the elector John George had been present on that battlefield himself and had been one of the first to flee. So von Arnim had remained in Saxon service.

Today, he was regretting it. For the past four years, the elector of Saxony had generally refused to listen to von Arnim's advice. That was true with matters both large and small.

With regard to the largest, John George had ignored von Arnim's advice when the Ostend War broke out. Von Arnim had been confident that Gustav Adolf would eventually emerge triumphant, and thus it would be folly not to support him as Saxony was required to do by the provisions of the agreement that had set up the Confederated Principalities of Europe.

But the elector had chosen to do otherwise. He'd been resentful for years at Gustav Adolf's preeminence among the Protestant nations and principalities of Europe, and John George was unfortunately prone to being sullen and stubborn. His legal argument was based on a differing interpretation of the relevant provisions of the CPE agreement, but von Arnim was sure that the elector's real motive was profoundly irrational.

He felt he'd been dragooned against his will into the CPE by Gustav Adolf's bullying—which was true enough, of course—and now with the Ostend War he saw a chance to get out and regain his independence.

In purely legal terms, John George's position was probably as valid as Gustav Adolf's. Those provisions were not what anyone would call a model of clarity. But regardless of the letter of the agreement, John George was certainly breaking its spirit—and the king of Sweden was just as certain to become furious over the issue. Politics and the law were related but ultimately quite different realms. If Gustav Adolf did triumph over the Ostenders, as von Arnim thought he would and John George insisted he wouldn't, the repercussions on Saxony would be severe.

So it had proved. Once again, Hans Georg von Arnim would face the forces of Gustav Adolf on a battlefield.

Not Gustav Adolf himself, though. Saxon spies had said the Swedish king was taking his own forces north to do battle with Brandenburg. More importantly, since von Arnim had no great confidence in the elector's espionage apparatus, the Poles said the same. It had become clear to von Arnim that Koniecpolski had a very capable spy network in the USE.

Unfortunately, Koniecpolski would be absent from the coming battle. The Polish Sejm was still squabbling over whether or not to come to the aid of Saxony and Brandenburg. King Władysław IV wanted to do so, but without the Sejm's agreement Koniecpolski would not move. And the king was not foolish enough to think his will could override that of the grand hetman of the Polish-Lithuanian Commonwealth.

So, there was only a token Polish force here. Cold-bloodedly, von Arnim intended to order them into the thick of the battle. They'd probably suffer terrible casualties. If von Arnim managed to fend off the USE army—he had no real hope of defeating them—and could prolong the war, then the blood shed by those young Polish hussars might be enough to tip the scale in the Sejm. Their commander was an Opalinski. If all went well, he might be killed himself.

"You watch," grumbled Lubomir Adamczyk. "That Saxon bastard's going to get us all killed."

Lukasz Opalinski glanced at the young hussar riding next to him. "He's Prussian, actually."

Adamczyk sneered. "What's the difference? They're all Lutherans."

Lukasz thought most Brandenburgers were Calvinists, although he wasn't sure what von Arnim's own beliefs were. But there was no point discussing that with Lubomir. Like most hussars, Adamczyk's range of knowledge and interests was limited. It certainly didn't include delving into the fine distinctions between Protestant sects. Why bother? None of them were Catholic and thus all of them were damned. Question closed.

When it came to military matters, on the other hand, Lubomir was no dimwit. Opalinski thought his assessment of the current situation was quite accurate. Von Arnim *would* try to get them killed. A number of them, anyway.

Allowing for perhaps excessive ruthlessness, though, Lukasz didn't really blame him that much. The Saxon elector had placed his army commander in an exceedingly difficult position. Von Arnim, with no significant advantage in numbers, had to face the same army that had recently crushed the French at Ahrensbök. Even allowing that the reputation of the French army had probably been overblown, no one really doubted that it had still been superior to the Saxon army. It was just a fact that the only significant feat of arms of Saxony's forces in recent times had been their ignominious routing at Breitenfeld, less than four years earlier.

Von Arnim had only two factors in his favor. The first was that one of Torstensson's three top lieutenants was the American Mike Stearns. However capable Stearns might have been as a political leader, he had no significant military experience. Von Arnim would surely concentrate his attack on Stearns' units. If, by doing so, he could at least achieve a stalemate at this coming battle...

...and if the small Polish contingent that had come to join him should happen to suffer sadly severe casualties in the doing...

...especially if one of those casualties was from the very influential Opalinski family...

Well, then. Who could say? Perhaps the notoriously temperamental Polish Sejm might cease its bickering and unite furiously in the cause of avenging their wrongs.

No, Lukasz didn't much blame the Saxon commander. On the other hand, he had no intention of obliging him, either.

He leaned in his saddle toward Adamczyk. "Remember. We're mostly just here to observe."

Lubomir made a face. "On a battlefield, that's a lot easier said than done."

Alas, true.

❖   ❖   ❖

Looking across the field at the Saxon army as it came into position, Thorsten Engler felt nervous. Unusually so, he thought. He couldn't remember feeling this nervous when the battle of Ahrensbök began.

But at Ahrensbök he'd just been a noncommissioned officer in charge of a single volley gun battery. Today, he was a captain in charge of an entire company.

No, it was worse than that. Thanks to the whim of a princess, he was now the imperial count of Narnia. A silly title, but it had apparently been enough to draw the attention of the division commander, General Stearns.

And so, Thorsten Engler had been brought into the subtle plans of Stearns and his own commander, General Torstensson, where most officers had not. And so, he'd learned of the trap they hoped to lay for the Saxon commander, von Arnim.

Traps require bait, of course. And so, Thorsten had discovered his role in the coming battle.

Not as bait, though. Oh, no, it was much worse than that. He was the fellow—a child-princess' fantasy of a fairy-tale count—who had to go charging in and *rescue* the bait after the trap had been sprung and the monster had it in his teeth.

One thing had not changed from Ahrensbök, though. Before they began, battles were magnificent. Things of beauty, you could even say. At no other time and place in the world could you see so many men moving together in such immense formations. And all of it to music, too. (Admittedly, the instrumentation was limited. Bugles, fifes and drums only.) It was as if the battlefield was a gigantic stage and an enormous ballet was about to begin.

Chapter 16

The Saxon plain, near Zwenkau

Mike Stearns was stunned the first time he saw a battlefield. He'd expected to be stunned—horrified, rather—by the carnage of a battle's aftermath. What he hadn't expected was the sheer thrill of the spectacle before the battle had started.

He'd seen more people gathered in one place before, of course. There were somewhere around fifty thousand men assembling on this field not far from the small town of Zwenkau. Any modern baseball stadium in the United States they'd left behind would hold that many, and some of the biggest football stadiums could hold twice as many.

But except for a tiny number of athletes on the field, almost all of those people would be sitting down. Their most strenuous activity would be getting up to go to the bathroom.

Here, every single one of those fifty thousand men was doing something—and doing it in unison, to boot. Marching into position, riding horses, hauling up artillery. Most of them were moving fairly slowly, but individual couriers were racing all over carrying messages from commanders to their subordinates.

There were pennants and banners flying everywhere, and the sound of musical instruments filled the air. Drums and fifes mostly, for the moment. Once the battle started, the brass could come to the fore. Over the din of a battle—so Mike had been told; this would be his first personal experience—about the only instruments that could be heard clearly would be bugles and the like. Torstensson had told him that the Republic of Essen favored bells for the purpose, but Torstensson himself thought they'd be too clumsy.

For the first time, Mike really understood the remark made by Robert E. Lee at the battle of Fredericksburg. *It is well that war is so terrible, otherwise we would grow too fond of it.*

That ancient notion of the glory of war had pretty well vanished by the time Mike Stearns had been born. Seeing this incredible display, he understood why. By the end of the nineteenth century, battles had grown so great that they could no longer be encompassed by the human eye and brain. What remained was simply the brutality. Death in the trenches during the First World War. Skirmishing tactics and maneuvers on a gigantic scale during the Second World War, far too huge for a man to really see what was happening beyond his own small corner of it.

But here in the seventeenth century, a battle still fit in its entirety on a single stage. Mike could see all of it, except for some cavalry units scouting on the margins. Just to complete the picture...

He swiveled in his saddle. The observation balloon

Torstensson had brought with the army was hanging in the sky, a mile or so in the rear. The thing was colorfully painted too.

Why not? In the universe Mike had come from, camouflage was an essential part of war. But in this one, military technology was still too primitive. It was more important for a commanding officer to be able to see his troops than for them to be hidden from the enemy. Yes, all units the size of battalions or larger had radios. But the weapons themselves were just coming into the technical range where fighting would have to start taking place at a considerable distance. For a time yet, battlefields would be dominated by men firing in formation.

As for the balloon, why bother camouflaging it when the only other flying objects in the sky were birds? Anyone could and would spot the thing. You might as well make it bright and vivid to improve the morale of your own soldiers.

There should be at least one airplane in that sky, too, but Mike couldn't see it. Gustav Adolf had taken most of the air force with him into Brandenburg. That was fair enough, since he'd left all of the APCs to the USE army. He'd left one plane behind, though—one of the older Belles—so that Torstensson would have a longer-range reconnaissance than the observation balloon could give him.

The plane must be too far away to be spotted. Torstensson had probably ordered it to stay in the vicinity of Dresden. Mike knew that Gustav Adolf had left orders that he wanted John George captured. A reconnaissance plane could hopefully give early warning if the elector tried to make his escape. Torstensson had two cavalry regiments held in reserve, specifically for the purpose of intercepting the Saxon elector if he tried to escape into Poland. He'd already sent one of them to circle around Dresden.

Mike turned back to examine the field where the battle would be taking place soon. There were no woods in sight, and only a handful of trees. The terrain was very flat except for two rises: one where Torstensson had set up his headquarters; the other, across the field to the east, when von Arnim was presumably stationed. The whole area was farmland.

There wasn't much left of the crops by now, though, except for a space of about half a mile between the two armies. That area hadn't been trampled flat yet. It would be soon enough, Mike figured. Fifty thousand men and half as many horses—not to mention artillery balls—would probably turn that area into a wasteland within minutes.

They were no longer oriented directly west to east, in terms of the directions the armies faced. Since the march started at dawn, as he had done for the past two days, Torstensson had continued to move his troops south as well as east. He'd done so in order to force his opponent to come out of Leipzig and meet him on favorable ground. No doubt von Arnim would have preferred to remain in the city and turn a battle into a siege. But by moving around Leipzig to the south, Torstensson had given him no choice. Dresden was not far to the east and whatever else he did, von Arnim was surely under orders from John George to protect the Saxon capital.

There was another advantage to the maneuver, too, Mike now understood. The USE army's orientation this morning meant that the sun wouldn't be directly in their eyes when the battle started. That was a small thing, almost any other time. But Mike could see where it would matter during a battle. With bullets and cannonballs flying every whichaway, the last thing a man wanted to deal with was having to shade his eyes in order to see anything. Which even officers would have to do at least some of time, despite the broad-brimmed hats they favored.

That was Torstensson's experience showing. Experience which Mike himself lacked.

"There's more to this general business than meets the eye," he murmured.

"What was that, sir?" asked Christopher Long, who was writing next to him.

Mike waved his hand. "Just talking to myself."

Mike had originally intended to use all three of the officers he'd rescued from England to serve as his staff, in addition to Long. But it had become clear to him soon enough that Anthony Leebrick was the only one really suited to the task of being a staff officer. Richard Towson and Patrick Welch were much more comfortable commanding their own units. So Mike had given each of them a battalion. For a staff, in addition to Leebrick and Long, he'd taken on a crusty old German veteran. Ulbrecht Duerr had a generally unpleasant personality and was perhaps more foul-mouthed than any man Mike had ever met. Unusually, for this day and age, he was also given to blasphemy. That perhaps explained why a professional soldier who was well into his fifties and seemed to have been in practically every war fought in Europe for the past four decades was still a colonel.

Mike rather liked the man, though. And he found his advice quite helpful.

Those three were his only immediate staff. He planned to enlarge the staff over time, but wanted to wait until he had a better assessment of the many officers in the Third Division. Most of them were still strangers to him.

One was not, of course. As Mike looked to his right he could see the ranks of the 2nd Brigade moving forward. Somewhere among them—they should be right about in the middle—was the Black Falcon Regiment, and somewhere in that regiment was its 12th Battalion, now commanded by the newly-promoted Captain Jeff Higgins.

Mike was feeling doubly guilty today. First, because he'd thrown Jeff into the deep end of the pool by putting him in charge of a battalion. Technically, Brigadier Schuster had made the decision, but Mike had gone along with it.

Second, because he was planning to use Jeff as part of the bait.

No, trebly guilty. He also hadn't told Jeff what he was going to do. He'd been tempted, but from a security standpoint there was really no justification for telling all the battalion commanders what he'd planned for their divisions. He'd told the brigadiers and the regiment commanders, and that was enough. They'd pass along the information to whichever other officers in their units they thought needed to know. Mike was sure that didn't include mere captains, even if they did command battalions.

Mike had known Jeff since he was a kid. He hadn't known him well, since they weren't related and Mike had been a teenager by the time Jeff was born. Still, Grantville was a small town and few of its residents had really been strangers.

And now, he might be responsible for getting him killed.

"Like I said," he murmured again, "there's more to this general business than meets the eye. And a lot of it sucks."

"What was that, sir?" asked Christopher Long.

Jeff never had time to contemplate the strange beauty of armies maneuvering into battle. He was neither a top-hat general who could lounge around on a saddle and let his flunkies handle everything nor an experienced volley gun battery commander who'd been through a big battle before and could afford to let his mind wander.

No, he was a fledgling battalion commander in charge of four hundred men, most of whom were even younger and greener than he was.

Well. Younger, anyway. Maybe not greener. At least half of them were veterans of Ahrensbök. Jeff didn't know if that made him feel better or worse.

And he was just a pitiful captain, to boot. A battalion was *supposed* to be commanded by a major. A dinky little captain was just supposed to take care of a hundred men in a company.

Jeff could have handled that easily enough, he thought. Well. Handled it, anyway. But he was finding that running a battalion was downright nerve-wracking when the fireworks were probably going to start within an hour.

Fortunately, Eric Krenz turned out to be a very

good adjutant. That was armyspeak for right-hand man. What the Navy called an executive officer, if Jeff had the protocol straight.

Jeff was a little surprised, actually. Krenz made so many wisecracks and disparaging remarks about all matters military that Jeff hadn't expected much from him once the shooting started. He'd figured Eric would hold his own well enough. But he hadn't expected him to be the very helpful and quick-thinking officer he was turning out to be.

Thankfully, the worst was over. Sure, there was still the actual battle to go though. But they were in position now and Jeff thought he had everybody pretty well set.

The bugles started up again. That always startled Jeff for an instant. He still thought there was something a little ridiculous about using Stone Age musical instruments—okay, Bronze Age—to signal soldiers on a battlefield. They *did* have radios, after all. Admittedly, given the rather small scale dimensions of a seventeenth-century battlefield, a commander could probably signal more of his soldiers quickly with a bugle than with radio calls. Still, it was...

The signal itself finally registered on Jeff. *Right oblique, MARCH.*

Jeff's mouth fell open. They were already in position—a damn good position, too, with a little rise ahead of them that could give them a bit of cover once the shooting started—already set up, ready to go, everything set—

And some damn fool of a—

Jeff looked around quickly. He'd been about to blame Eichelberger but all three regiments in the brigade were moving out. What sort of an idiot brigadier—?

Belatedly, it dawned on Jeff that the bugle call had specified a divisional move. He couldn't see the other brigades from his position because there were just too many men and horses and artillery pieces and wagons in the way. But he could look behind him.

Sure enough, the divisional commander was coming himself, trotting forward with his staff officers.

That would be Major General Michael Stearns. The newbie. And, apparently, the glory hound. For sure and certain, the fucking idiot.

"General Stearns, this is unwise," said Colonel Long.

"I concur," said Anthony Leebrick. "There's no need—not this early in a battle—for you to come forward and place yourself in harm's way. Should the situation take a bad turn, of course—"

"Pappenheim behaved this way quite regularly. Probably still does. It's amazing the fucker isn't dead yet." That was Ulbrecht Duerr's contribution.

"Gentlemen, leave it alone," said Mike. "It probably is stupid. I'm not at all sure this whole maneuver isn't stupid. But what I know for sure is that there's no way I'm sending my men out there without going with them. I just can't do it."

Long and Leebrick fell silent. But their tight lips indicated their professional disapproval.

Duerr chuckled, on the other hand. "Pappenheim's soldiers adore the bastard, you know."

Lennart Torstensson watched from a distance as Stearns' Third Division moved obliquely forward. That was the entire right wing of his army, now detaching itself in what would appear to be a clumsy flanking maneuver.

"What is Stearns *doing*?" hissed one of his aides. The colonel pointed. "Look! He's going out himself!"

So he was. Lennart could see Stearns and his little group of staff officers trotting past the battalions as they moved slowly forward. Stearns had taken off his hat and was waving it about. Very cheerfully, it seemed. Lennart was quite sure Stearns was accompanying the hat-waving with equally cheerful remarks. The man might be a novice general, but he was a practiced and superb politician.

Even from the distance Torstensson could hear the Third Division cheering.

This had not been part of the plan. There was no reason for Stearns to do this. As soon as the trap was sprung Torstensson was going to throw everything he had at the enemy. That including the five APCs, although he suspected it would be the volley gun batteries who'd do most of the damage. Since Ahrensbök, Lennart had a lot of confidence in his flying artillery.

All Stearns' division had to do, once the enemy attacked, was simply hunker down and fend off the Saxons until the rest of the army came up and broke them. There was no place in all that and certainly no need for the division's commanding general to be gallivanting about on a horse near the front.

No, *at* the front. Stearns and his officers had now passed the lead battalion and were trotted slightly ahead of them.

"What is he *doing*?" repeated the aide.

But Torstensson knew. His monarch had predicted

this would happen. The essence of it, at least, if not the specific details.

"I know that man," Gustav Adolf had told Lennart, some weeks ago. "He's a lot like me, you know, in some ways."

So it seemed. Lennart took off his hat and gave the general in the distance a little tip of recognition.

Chapter 17

"It might be a ploy, sir," said Colonel Carl Bose.

Hans Georg von Arnim continued to examine the peculiar maneuver being undertaken by the enemy's right wing. He'd lowered the eyeglass, though, after he'd confirmed that the commander was the newly-made general Michael Stearns.

"A trap, you mean?" Von Arnim had spent the past few minutes pondering the same problem. But now, he shook his head.

"I don't believe Torstensson would be so reckless. Stearns is a complete novice. If he loses his head—not even that; simply becomes confused and loses control— this could turn into a complete disaster for them."

He wasn't entirely certain of his conclusion, but . . . what choice did he really have, with the odds so heavily against him?

"Tell von der Pforte to move up his troops. But before all else, we have to get Hofkirchen's cavalry engaged." Von Arnim pointed to a creek in a distance, barely visible because it was so narrow. "If at all possible, we have to keep Stearns' division from anchoring its flank on the Pleisse."

✧   ✧   ✧

"He might decide it's a trap," said Colonel Schönbeck. He was leaning forward in his saddle, intently
studying the center of the Saxon lines where von
Arnim was stationed.

Torstensson, who was almost slouched in his own
saddle, gave his head a little shake. "I'm sure he's
considering the possibility. The key is Stearns. I
wouldn't have tried this maneuver with Brunswick-
Lüneburg or Knyphausen. But I'm betting von Arnim
will decide I wouldn't have chanced it with such a
novice as Stearns."

His aide eyed him sidewise. "It *is* a bit risky,
General."

Torstensson shrugged. Like the headshake, the
gesture was minimal. "Stearns may be new at this,
but his soldiers aren't. Most of the units in the Third
Division were at Ahrensbök. So were the flying artillery
companies I lent to him. As long as Stearns doesn't
panic, they'll be able to fend off the counterattack.
Long enough, anyway, which is all that matters."

Schönbeck was still eyeing him sidewise. Torstensson smiled. "I've seen Stearns in a crisis, Colonel."

"The unrest in Magdeburg after Wismar? But there
was no real fighting there, sir."

Again, the USE commander shook his head. The
gesture, this time, was not minimal at all. "That's not
really what matters. The great danger in a crisis is
not that a commander collapses from fear of being
hurt or killed. Most men are not cowards, certainly
not most soldiers. No, the real danger is that they
simply can't think clearly. Their brain freezes. They
exude uncertainty—and that's what begins to create

panic in their subordinates and soldiers. Relax, Colonel Schönbeck. Stearns won't lose his head."

Losing his head never even occurred to Mike Stearns. Although he had no experience with military battle, he had been a prizefighter for a time when he was a young man. Young and stupid, as he liked to say. He'd been quite good at it, too, especially the mental side of fighting. He'd won all eight of his professional bouts. The reason he'd quit—other than a sudden and unexpected lapse of youthful imbecility—was because he'd come to realize that his reflexes simply weren't good enough. Mike was very strong and had superb reflexes. Even now, despite spending the last several years as a sedentary executive, he was still in far better physical condition than most men half his age. But "very strong" and "superb reflexes" were one thing, measured against normal values. Measured against the values of professional boxers, they were something else entirely.

So, he'd quit. Almost twenty years ago, now. But as he moved toward his first battle, Mike felt the familiar mindset closing back in.

The key thing was not to lose your head. To stay in control of the adrenaline rather than letting the adrenaline control you. Ignore the blows. Accept them as inevitable. Concentrate on the enemy. Above all, *watch*. The natural response of a man in a fight was to flail away. To let the fear and rage fuel his physical abilities, so that he might overpower his foe. In essence, to let the animal try to save the man.

Against a capable opponent, that was a recipe for failure. You had to *watch*. Never lose control. Whatever else, stay calm.

✧   ✧   ✧

The officers and soldiers within eyesight were watching him. Quite closely. They knew just as well as Torstensson and von Armim that their commanding officer was a neophyte general. And they knew just as well what the calamitous results might be.

They were reassured. He might not really know what he was doing, but he seemed confident and relaxed. He had good advisers. All he had to do was listen to them.

"The key thing right now, sir, is to anchor ourselves on that river." Colonel Long pointed ahead of them and to the right.

That was the Pleisse, Mike thought. Like most so-called "rivers" in the area, it was really just a creek—and not a particularly large one at that. By North American standards, all the rivers he'd seen in Europe were on the small side. Even major rivers like the Elbe—the Rhine and Danube too, he'd been told, although he hadn't yet seen them himself—were far smaller than the Mississippi.

But while Mike hadn't been in a battle yet, by now he'd had a fair amount of experience in the seemingly simple task of getting an army to move. He'd also read a copy of von Clausewitz's *On War* that Becky had obtained for him. So he'd already learned just how cruelly accurate the military theorist had been.

War is very simple, but in war the simplest things become very difficult.

Now, looking at the little river that his aide Long was pointing to, Mike could see how important it would be for his division to place its right flank against it.

Even a creek ten feet wide and probably not more than a foot or two deep could serve as a significant protection against a possible flank attack. It didn't look like much—and, indeed, to a man enjoying a hike through the countryside, it wasn't much. He could cross it quite easily. At worst, get his boots wet.

But crossing that same creek during a cavalry charge, with bullets and cannonballs flying, would be something else entirely. Horses were big animals, and like all big animals, the prospect of falling made them very nervous, especially falling on a run. An eight-year-old boy weighing fifty pounds would race across that creek without a second thought, shrieking gleefully the whole while. A warhorse weighing a thousand pounds and carrying an armored man weighing another two hundred pounds might balk. Or, if they did wade across, might trip and fall if the bottom was soft or stony or simply uneven.

A balked or spilled cavalryman is likely to be a dead or maimed cavalryman, and nobody knew that better than cavalrymen themselves. So the mere fact that an opponent had his flank anchored against a creek, be that creek never so modest, would automatically shape the battle. Whether or not that creek could be forced was likely to become a purely theoretical exercise, because no general wanted to take the risk of finding out.

"Makes sense to me, Christopher. See to it, if you would."

That lesson, Mike had not learned from an aristocratic Prussian military theorist at the age of forty. He'd learned it from his hillbilly mother, at the age of four. A none-too-gentle slap accompanied by the words *be polite!*

❖   ❖   ❖

Lieutenant Krenz was looking slightly less unhappy. "Well, at least he knows enough to anchor our flank on the river. Now if we could just get off these damned horses."

Jeff shared Eric's opinion on both issues. Especially getting off the horses. Having to ride one was the biggest disadvantage he'd found so far to being an officer, and he was still pretty disgruntled over the issue. He was supposed to be an *infantry* officer. He'd made quite sure of that after he returned from Amsterdam. *I want an infantry assignment,* he'd specified—and he had been assured he'd receive one.

Technically, they hadn't lied. He had been assigned to the infantry. What Jeff hadn't considered—never even crossed his mind, the notion was so absurd—was that in this day and age it was expected that *all* officers had to be mounted.

Laundry officer? Officer in charge of day care for the camp follower kiddies? Didn't matter. *Up you go, buddy.*

There was no logic to it. None whatsover. He had to stay with his troops, didn't he? For Pete's sake, he was the battalion's commander. *Of course* he had to stay with his troops. They were infantry, no? I-N-F-A-N-T-R-Y. That meant they walked into battle. Not rode. Walked. Except for their officers. They had to ride, whether they wanted to or not.

This was one of the disadvantages of being in the seventeenth century that was a lot harder to shrug off than the quality of the toilet paper or (more often) total absence thereof. And that was nothing to shrug off lightly.

"He must be listening to his staff officers," Krenz went on.

Jeff's horse did one of those incomprehensible little jiggly things that horses so often did. Itchy hoofs? Bad hair day? Gelding equivalent of that time of the month? Who knew? By definition, they were dumb animals. What person in his right mind would plant himself on top of one of these huge beasts and place himself at the mercy of a brain which, relative to body mass, probably wasn't much of a step up from a chipmunk?

Would you ride a chipmunk?

The horse did it again. "I can't wait for the battle to start," Jeff groused.

"Me neither," agreed Krenz fervently. "Finally be able to get off these damn things."

A few seconds went by. They grinned simultaneously.

"You realize how insane that is?" asked Eric.

Jeff nodded. "War is hell."

None of those thoughts went through Thorsten Engler's mind. He'd been a good horseman as a farmer. Now that he'd been in the army for almost a year and half, all of which time he'd spent in the flying artillery, his horsemanship rivaled that of most cavalrymen.

That aside, he shared some of Jeff and Eric's relief at seeing the division angling toward the Pleisse. Obviously, their commander Stearns had either had the good sense to anchor his flank against the only significant natural feature in the area or the good sense to listen to one of his staff officers.

Some of the relief, not all. Unlike Higgins and Krenz, Thorsten and the other flying artillery unit commanders had been made privy to Torstensson's plan. They pretty much had to be, given that they'd play the critical role of fending off or at least blunting the cavalry charge that was sure to be the Saxons' initial response. So Engler knew that, anchored on the Pleisse or not, the enemy cavalry was almost certainly going to contest the field—and once that happened, the fact that some infantry battalion was happily nestled against the river wasn't going to do Thorsten and his men much good at all.

In the month of July in the year 1635, cavalry was still the principal offensive arm in a battle. That would change, and pretty rapidly, as the impact of the new rifled muskets spread—and it would certainly change once the new French breechloaders became common. At that point, cavalry charges in a battle would simply become too dangerous to the cavalrymen. The role of cavalry would shift to what it had been during the American civil war, reconnaisance and raiding enemy supply lines. From then on until the introduction of tanks, it would be the infantry and artillery that would be the offensive arms.

In the world the up-timers had come from, that transition had taken three-quarters of a century. In this one, Thorsten didn't think it would even take a decade. Tanks were coming, and probably soon. Thorsten knew that there were at least four newly-formed companies trying to develop the war machines. That was in the USE alone. He was pretty sure the French and Austrians—certainly the Netherlanders—were already developing their own.

But from what he'd been told by a friend who was knowledgeable about technical matters, there was still the great obstacle of the engines. The hybrid technology produced by the Ring of Fire was, like many hybrids, often a peculiar thing. By now, everyone with any scientific or technical knowledge understood the basic principles of the internal combustion engine. The problem that remained was an engineering one. For a variety of reasons, the broad technical capabilities that a large internal engine industry required didn't exist yet. Not to mention that there was a shortage of petroleum.

So, willy-nilly, people had turned to steam technology. In this universe, the first tanks that lumbered into a battlefield would most likely be driven by steam engines.

Steam technology posed its own challenges, but ones that could be met more easily. And that in turn introduced another wrinkle into technological development, which was that the steam technology being introduced into the seventeenth century in this universe was not the primitive steam technology that had first come into existence in the up-timers' world. These new steam engines, even when they were modeled on nineteenth-century designs, were still based on the technology that had been developed—often by hobbyists, since steam had been relegated to a secondary status—by the end of the twentieth century. Especially since, as chance would have it, several of Grantville's residents had been accomplished and experienced steam enthusiasts.

So who could say? Once *that* steam technology was established as the dominant engine technology, it might retain that status for a long time. There had been a lot of accidental and secondary factors that had produced the dominance of internal combustion engines in that other universe. They might never really come into play in this one.

That sort of uneven and combined development had become quite common. Thorsten's friend had told him that a similar situation existed with computer technology. Many down-timers now understood the basic principles of cybernetics. The friend himself, born in the year 1602, was one of them. But recreating the electronic industry the up-timers had relied on for the purpose was simply impossible in the here and now, and would be for some time to come.

Here, his friend had spent half an hour enlightening Thorsten—and Caroline Platzer, who understood no more than he did—on the subtleties of something called "semiconductors." Apparently, the problem of producing those would be enough in itself to stymie the development of up-time-style cybernetics for a long time to come.

But there was an alternative, one which the up-timers themselves had never developed very far because by the time they began creating computers their electronic capacities had been quite advanced. The alternative was called "fluidics," and was based on using the flow of liquids instead of electrons—typically water, but it could be air, and apparently the ideal fluid would be mercury or something similar.

That technology was well within existing seventeenth-century techniques. Already, in fact, there was a little boom developing in Venetian glass manufacturing to provide some of the components needed for fluidics-based computers.

What Thorsten's friend had found most fascinating was that there was no telling where these developments would lead in the long run. Any industry, once established and widely spread, creates an automatic inertia in favor of continuing it. That same inertia handicaps its potential rivals. In the world the up-timers came from, that dynamic had entrenched internal combustion engines and electronic computers. But in this one, that might not be true. There were advantages to steam and fluidics, after all, that had never really been exploited in the universe across the Ring of Fire—but might be in this one.

Across the field, Thorsten could see Saxon cavalry coming forward. It looked as if Torstensson's ploy was going to work.

It occurred to him that this was not the best time to ruminate on possible alternative technologies. For the here and now, cavalry was still the principal offensive arm in a battle, as the Saxons were about to try to demonstrate again—and it was Thorsten's job to stop them.

"Here we go," said Lukasz Opalinski. He and his Polish hussars had been ordered to join the Saxon cavalry in their charge against the overextended right wing of the enemy's army. That would be the Third Division, commanded by the USE's former prime minister.

"The Saxons claim he doesn't know what he's doing," said Lubomir Adamczyk. He sounded more doubtful than hopeful. "Stearns, I mean."

But there was no time to talk any further. The charge was starting. Slightly more than four thousand Saxon horsemen would be hammering that enemy right wing within not much more than a minute. Along with two hundred Polish hussars.

Lukacz wasn't all that hopeful himself. It might well be true that the enemy general didn't know what to do. But he didn't really need to know. Stearns just needed to listen to his staff officers, because they *would* know.

Apparently, he was doing so. To Opalinski, the speed and precision with which the infantry units of the Third Division were moving to anchor themselves on the Pleisse didn't look like the result of confused and amateur orders. Not in the least.

So be it. What remained was simple. As dangerous as it might be, there was nothing in the world quite as exhilarating—to a Polish hussar, anyway—as a cavalry charge.

They were into a canter now. Next to him, Adamczyk started whooping.

Chapter 18

The single thing that Mike Stearns would always remember most clearly about his first battle was the *noise*, the sheer volume of sound. And the second thing he would always remember clearly was the smell; the way the huge clouds of gunsmoke would roll over everything like an acrid fog.

Not the sights of the battle, so much, although he remembered those too. In fact, his whole memory of the battle was actually pretty good. At no point did he feel that his mind had gotten overwhelmed. That was because he expected the sights he saw. Mike had a good imagination and he'd been able to prepare himself for those shocks. Insofar, at least, as anyone can be prepared for such things in the abstract.

But what he hadn't considered—just hadn't thought about, ahead of time—was the incredible effect that firing tens of thousands of gunpowder weapons within a relatively small space would have on the other human senses. Especially the cannon fire. It didn't help, of course, that everyone was still using black powder.

He soon gained an appreciation of the way that same black powder almost immediately shaped control of the battle; what he thought of as its command structure. Within less than five minutes he was fervently wishing a strong wind would spring up—which was not likely, on such a clear and sunny day. He couldn't *see* anything, most of the time. The huge clouds of gunsmoke impeded vision, except when odd and unpredictable eddies would suddenly—and usually all too briefly—clear them away.

Until that moment, Mike had always assumed that Gustav Adolf's recklessness in charging forward into the fog at the battle of Lützen—that's what had gotten the king of Sweden killed in that other universe, in 1632—was because of the man's personal impetuousness. A childish inability to control his emotions, essentially.

No doubt some of that was involved. But Mike could also now understand how much the driving power of pure frustration must have compelled Gustav Adolf. A commanding general was supposed to be in charge of this mayhem, damnation—and he couldn't *see* anything. On at least four occasions, Mike had to restrain himself from riding into the smoke clouds, just so he could find out what the hell was actually happening. On two of those occasions, he might not have managed if Leebrick, Long and Ulbrecht Duerr hadn't been right there to urge him to stay put. Quite forcefully. Indeed, you might almost say impolitely, and in a manner that bordered on disrespect and insubordination.

Leebrick and Long would apologize after the battle. Duerr, true to his nature, would not. His only comment would be, "It's always nice to see that a new commander isn't a coward, even if he sometimes acts like the fucking village idiot." Thereby clearing away again, if such was needed, any uncertainty as to the man's failure to get promoted.

Thorsten Engler had expected the noise and the smoke, so he simply ignored them. In fact, he barely noticed them at all. He was far too preoccupied with the need to get his flying artillery company up to the front in time to blunt the coming cavalry charge.

They'd done that before at Ahrensbök, very successfully, and most of his men were veterans of that battle. So it all went fairly smoothly, in the way that men experienced with a task and confident they could carry it out manage such things.

They had no trouble seeing, either. Hardly surprising, since they were the ones who produced most of the initial gunsmoke—and were happily racing to the rear by the time the resultant clouds obscured the battlefield. It was up to the infantry then, and those oafs were so naturally dull-witted it hardly mattered if they could see anything or not.

They'd learned one lesson from Ahrensbök, though— the infantry had to move up quickly. At Ahrensbök, the volley gun crews had survived because their fire alone had been enough to stop to French cavalry charge. But you couldn't assume that would always be true, and volley gunners were almost helpless against cavalry that got in among them. All they had were partisans and some muskets. Against experienced cavalrymen armed with sabers and lances and wheel-lock pistols, they'd have no chance at all.

That too went smoothly. Not as smoothly, but

smoothly enough. Most of the infantrymen had been at Ahrensbök also.

The flying artillery companies fired three volleys. They might have managed four, but their commanding officer didn't want to take the risk. Colonel Straley had seen how close a thing it had been at Ahrensbök.

The crews could get off those three volleys in less than a minute, and they had four companies on the field instead of the three they'd had at Ahrensbök. That sent over ten thousand balls into the ranks of the oncoming Saxon cavalry. Those weren't musket balls, either. The volley guns fired canister rounds weighing three ounces, twice the weight of the balls fired by the infantry. Any hit on an enemy cavalryman except a glancing one would usually kill or maim.

The Saxons hadn't started their final charge yet, when the volley guns started firing. You simply couldn't start galloping a horse carrying a heavily armed and armored man until you were close to the enemy. A hundred yards or so. Even then, most heavy cavalry wouldn't move at a full gallop. There was just too much risk of tiring out the horses too soon and having your units fall out of formation.

The one exception were Polish hussars. They would gallop into a battle, although the great wings they sometime wore—as they were today—slowed their horses down. Hussars prided themselves on their horsemanship, and with good reason. The same be-damned-to-the-world szlachta insouciance and arrogance that made Polish political disputes so similar to children fighting in a playground also made them brave to the point of sheer recklessness. Nobody who'd ever faced Polish hussars in a battle forgot the experience.

Thorsten never had, himself, but he knew their reputation. So, far more cold-bloodedly than the farmboy he'd once been had slaughtered pigs, he had his volley gun company concentrate their fire on the Poles rather than the Saxons. The hussars were impossible to miss, even at a distance of several hundred yards. The reason they were called "winged" hussars was their bizarre habit of carrying huge feather-covered wooden wings attached to their saddles into battle. The feathers used were usually eagle feathers, or sometimes ostrich feathers.

Why? No one Thorsten had asked really knew—and those of them who'd met Polish hussars in peacetime said that even the hussars themselves had no clear answer. Some claimed they wore the wings to foil the lassos of Tatars seeking to capture slaves. Others claimed the distinctive sound made by the wings frightened the enemy. Still others claimed the sound deafened their own horses so they wouldn't be frightened by the wooden noise-makers used by Tatars and some Ottoman units.

Thorsten's own tentative opinion was that the reason was entirely psychological. From what he knew of Polish hussars, they were the sort of flamboyant people—up-time terms like "narcissist" and "arrested development" would seem to apply here also—who just couldn't resist making a spectacle of themselves.

"I want those silly feathered bastards dead!" he shrieked, in the high-pitched tone of voice he'd learned to use on a battlefield.

From their shouts of surprise and anger, Lukasz Opalinski knew the Saxon cavalrymen hadn't expected to be fired on by volley guns right at the beginning

speed that often panicked enemy infantry or artillery; and, even if they didn't panic, allowed them no time to fire more than one volley, at most.

Instead, they'd been hit by three powerful volleys. At least forty—no, probably fifty—of his hussars were now out of action, dead or wounded or spilled by falling horses. And they were still so far away and moving so slowly that...

Sure enough. Lukasz could see the volley guns being hitched up while infantry units moved up to cover their retreat. The infantrymen fired a volley as soon as the artillerymen were clear.

That volley was just as brutal as the preceding ones. The musket balls were lighter than those fired by the flying artillery, but they were also more accurate. As Josef had warned him, most of the USE army's infantry units had been armed with rifled muskets. Quite obviously, these were.

Out of the corners of his eyes, Opalinski could see that the Saxon cavalry was peeling away. They were reeling from the carnage.

His own men had been hammered just as badly. At a quick glance, he didn't think he had more than half of his unit still in action.

But that still left him a hundred men, and these were Polish hussars, not be-damned Saxon shirkers— and the enemy was finally within reach. He could see the nearest USE infantry officer not more than thirty yards away. A big fellow who'd made the mistake of leading his men a bit too far in the fore.

Lukasz lowered his lance and set his aim on the bastard.

❖   ❖   ❖

"Well, fuck me," Jeff muttered. He'd been so intent on getting his battalion in position to cover the artillery that he hadn't noticed how far ahead of them he'd gotten. The nearest squad of his infantry was a good ten yards behind.

And, at a rough estimate, the Polish hussar bearing down on him was ten feet tall and riding a horse the size of an elephant—and, to make things perfect, was carrying the same lance that Saint George must have used to kill the dragon. Had to be. How many other lances in the world were fifty feet long and had a razor-sharp blade the size of a sword?

Those no-longer-silly-looking wings were making one hell of a scary sound, too.

"Watch out, Jeff!" yelled Eric Krenz. The lieutenant frantically hollered at the nearest squads, waving his sword at the oncoming hussar. "Shoot that Polish fuck!"

But there was too much noise, too much smoke, too much confusion. The infantrymen and their sergeants had shut out everything else in order to do what they'd been trained to do: level their muskets at the enemy in front of them; fire; reload as fast as possible. They weren't even thinking of aiming at specific targets.

Only one of them heard Eric's shouts. That was a nineteen-year-old corporal in charge of a squad who, being a veteran, gave Krenz no more than a dismissive glance. Stupid officers. Getting in the way, like they usually did in a battle.

Eric gave up the attempt and charged forward himself. He might get there just in time to cut the hussar's leg with his sword. No chance of cutting anything higher up. The hussar was at least twenty feet tall, on top of that horse. Still, even a leg wound might distract him enough to save the captain's life.

Jeff dropped the sword he'd been using to encourage his men. Against a charging hussar's lance, that was about as useful as a butter knife. He clawed at the wheel-lock pistol he kept in a holster, bitterly regretting the fact that he'd run out of ammunition for his automatic pistol.

He managed to get it out and cock it just in time to fire a shot at the hussar. Not in time to save his life, though. The lance blade—it was actually fifteen feet long, amazingly enough—was within five yards and was about to split him open.

Opalinski never even thought of ducking. You simply didn't, in the final moments of a charge. If you were struck by a bullet, so be it. The honor of a hussar was concentrated entirely on killing the enemy.

Hussar or not, honorable or not, none of it mattered if a bullet hit your helmet. Lukasz's head was slapped back. The round glanced off his helmet and didn't even scratch his skin. Still, the impact was enough to daze him for a moment.

The lance swung wide of the target. Jeff ducked the blade—but got bowled off his feet by the horse's shoulder.

Eric Krenz squawked and frantically swung his sword. It hit the lance's blade and deflected it just enough to hit him instead of missing him entirely.

The hussar passed by. He was shouting something. Another volley of gunfire drowned out the sound of everything else. Eric stared at Jeff, who was just starting to roll up onto his knees. Then, stared down at the lance lying on the ground some ten feet away. The blade was covered in blood.

Then, stared at his side. The uniform was soaked with blood and there seemed to be more coming. Nothing seemed to be spurting, though, so maybe he'd gotten lucky and no artery had been cut.

"Lucky," of course, only by certain values of luck. Jeff was getting to his feet now, shaking his head as if he was a little confused. He'd lost his helmet in the fall.

"This really sucks," said Eric. He collapsed to the ground.

By the time Lukasz got his senses back, his horse—being no hussar himself, and thus no damn fool—had turned around and was galloping toward the rear. A full-bore gallop, too. A dumb beast he might be, but he wasn't dumb enough to stay in this area any longer than he had to.

In all likelihood, if Opalinski hadn't had the by-now almost instinctive horsemanship of a hussar, he'd have been spilled on the ground. As it was, he needed to use both hands to stay in the saddle. That was easy enough, though, since he'd lost his lance somewhere along the way.

He couldn't remember exactly what had happened. Had he killed that big infantry officer? Or perhaps the little big-eared one who'd come racing up waving his sword?

He simply couldn't remember. He hoped he'd killed at least one of them. Not because he had any personal animus against either of those officers but simply because it was already obvious that this battle was turning into a disaster and he liked to think he'd accomplished *something* in the process.

He looked around, but he simply couldn't tell how many of his hussars had survived. They were too mingled with the Saxon cavalrymen and all of them were racing off. This was not a retreat, this was a pure and simple rout.

Lukasz felt bitterly shamed. This was the first time in his life either he or any hussars he'd fought alongside had been routed in a battle. The worst of it was that he couldn't understand how it had happened.

Opalinski couldn't understand it because he hadn't seen it. He'd been so preoccupied with his personal duel with the two USE officers that he hadn't noticed the effect of the volleys fired by the infantry. Coming on top of the damage already inflicted by the volley guns, that had been enough to bring the charge to a complete halt.

At which point the APCs had arrived. Five of the monstrous machines, charging in from the side and raking the confused cavalrymen with rifle fire from the gunports along the sides of the vehicles. All the while, making the most hideous piercing shrieks from some sort of horns.

The horses had panicked then, and it had all been over.

✧   ✧   ✧

"That's it," said Torstensson. "Send in Dodo and George's divisions. Nothing fancy. Just straight ahead, firing volleys as they go."

Two of his aides raced off. Colonel Schönbeck and three others remained at his side. After a moment, Schönbeck said: "You were right, General. Stearns did quite well."

Torstensson glanced at the Third Division. They were starting to move forward again. He could see that Stearns—or his staff, more likely—had already organized measures to take care of the wounded.

Stearns *had* done well. To all intents and purposes, in fact, his division had won the battle on its own. Allowing, of course, for the critical assistance of the flying artillery and the APCs. Still, he'd kept his men solid, confident, and fully in the fight from beginning to end—and now had them back in action.

"This could get interesting," he said softly.

"Excuse me, sir?"

"Never mind, Colonel Schönbeck." Torstensson saw no point in explaining to a capable but stolid military aide that he really hoped the new prime minister of the USE wouldn't allow himself to be rushed into doing anything rash. Or things could get . . . interesting.

Besides, there were other matters to attend to. He glanced back to make sure the observation balloon was still in place. As an observation balloon, the device had been only minimally useful in this battle. But as a radio platform, it would now prove most useful indeed.

"Colonel Schönbeck—" Torstensson broke off and turned to a different aide. "Major Ziegler, rather. See to it that our cavalry units get word immediately that the Saxon army has been defeated. John George will try to escape now, and I want him intercepted before he can reach the Polish border."

Ziegler was a young man, attuned to the new technological possibilities. He'd use the radios immediately where Schönbeck would probably waste time sending out couriers first.

"Sound the retreat," von Arnim said grimly. "We'll withdraw into Leipzig."

Colonel Carl Bose looked skeptical. "We may not be able to make it, General. They'll be pushing the pursuit hard, from the looks of things."

Von Arnim shook his head. "No, they won't, once they're sure we're retiring from the field. I am quite certain that Torstensson has orders to take Dresden as fast as possible. He won't waste time with us"—*now that he's beaten us out of his way,* but von Arnim left that unspoken—"when he has a chance to catch the elector."

Von Arnim tightened his lips. His military career might be over, as of today. There was no chance he could move his troops into Poland, which was a pity since he was sure King Wladyslaw would hire him. But Torstensson would immediately pursue if the Saxon army—what was left of it—made any move in that direction. If need be, he'd postpone taking Dresden.

The French wouldn't hire him, not given his reputation as a staunch Lutheran. Richelieu wouldn't care himself, but with the political situation as tense as it was in France he couldn't afford to give Monsieur Gaston any more political ammunition. The Bavarians wouldn't even consider the possibility. Not with Duke Maximilian's Catholic fanaticism at the fever pitch it was today.

That left the Austrians. Which... might actually be possible. Von Arnim felt his spirits lifting a bit. Even under Ferdinand II, the Austrians had been willing to employ Protestant soldiers. Now with his son on the throne—Ferdinand III had a reputation for being far more tolerant—and with the tensions with Bohemia...

A detail intruded.

"Oh, yes." He had promised the man, after all. "Colonel Bose, see to it that a courier gets off to Dresden immediately. Warn the elector that we've lost the battle and Torstensson will be moving on Dresden. And..."

He studied the distant enemy observation balloon. He wasn't sure of this, but...

"Also warn the elector that Torstensson has probably got cavalry units watching the Polish border. I'd advise the elector to seek exile in Bavaria instead."

He went back to contemplating more important things. There did, of course, remain the awkwardness that he'd once resigned from Austrian service in something of a high dudgeon and not so long ago at that. Still...

Chapter 19

Eric Krenz never remembered much of what happened after he collapsed from his wound until he woke up in an army hospital tent. All that remained were inchoate images of being moved on a litter and people staring down at him. The clearest of those images was that of a harried surgeon impatiently saying: "This one'll live if he doesn't bleed out. Put him over there."

He had no idea where "over there" was, but some part of his brain understood that he'd just gotten a reprieve from a death sentence. It was probably that same part of his brain which enabled his eyes to observe a line of wounded men lying in a different part of the surgeon's tent who quite obviously had not met the surgeon's criteria for survival. The only attention being paid to them was by a single orderly, and all he was doing was giving them water. Or, more often, giving them cups of a brownish liquid that Eric couldn't identify but which that more-or-less sentient part of his brain figured was probably laudanum. The mixture of opium and liquor had been around for at least a century. Its only real medical use was to comfort the afflicted and serve as a crude anesthetic during surgery.

But these men, clearly enough, weren't going to be operated on. They were just going to die.

Some time later, Eric was given some of the liquid himself. In his case, as an anesthetic. The surgeon was replacing the jury-rigged bandages the medics had used with stitches.

The process hurt. A lot. As far as Krenz was concerned, if that bad-tasting liquor was laudanum, it had a grossly inflated reputation.

When Eric woke up, he was no longer in the surgeon's tent. He was still in a tent, but this one was larger and much cleaner. More precisely, since the surgeons in the USE army did use sterilization and kept their tents washed with antiseptic, this tent had a lot less blood and gore. The cots in a double line on either side of a central aisle were filled with soldiers who, though most of them were heavily bandaged, seemed in far better condition than the ones Krenz had seen in the surgeon's care.

Apparently, then, he'd survive. Eric was quite cheered by the thought. He enjoyed life.

He didn't even lose much of his cheer when Jeff Higgins came to visit and gave him the bad news.

"It's not a magic wound, buddy. Sorry. You'll be out for a while, but they'll have you back in the ranks sooner'n you probably want."

Eric would have shrugged, but he'd already learned that any movement of his upper body hurt. So he grimaced in such a way as to express the same sentiment.

"Just as well. Don't listen to the silly fools, Captain Higgins. Just about any so-called 'magic wound' is going to be awful. You've almost always got to lose some body part you really don't want to lose. Besides—"

He swelled out his chest and immediately regretted it. "Ow! Besides, the girls like the medals, sure, but they like them a lot better if they're attached to a fellow who looks like a fellow instead of a side of beef in a butcher shop."

A dark thought came to him. He gave Higgins a beady-eyed look. "You did put me in for a medal, didn't you? I will remind you that I *did* save your life. All right, I tried to save your life. Probably didn't have much effect on the outcome, but I think intent should count for something."

Jeff grinned. "As it happens, I didn't put you up for a decoration—because I didn't need to. Colonel Straley himself saw your valiant charge and put in for it. He also told me to tell you that only a cretin thinks you can take down a mounted hussar with a sword while you're on the ground, and what the hell happened to your pistol?"

Krenz looked embarrassed for a moment. "I sold the damn thing. It's too heavy to carry around all the time."

Jeff shook his head. "You're lucky it's only the good who die young, Eric." He looked around the inside of the tent. "It's not as bad as the surgeon's tent—you want to talk about a place that'll give you nightmares!—but it still ain't the Ritz. However, you won't be here long."

Krenz got an apprehensive look on his face. "They're not putting me back in the line, are they? *Already?* I just got here! And I must have lost at least ten gallons of blood."

"Nice trick that'd be. Seeing as how there are only five quarts of blood in a man's body to begin with. Probably only four, in a skinny shrimp like you. Well, no, five. Your ears alone must take a whole quart."

Jeff made a little patting motion. "Calm down. That wound you got looks pretty ghastly but it's actually not that serious. The lance blade sliced open your side as messily as you could ask for but didn't penetrate the peritoneum or the abdominal cavity. Once it heals you'll be as good as new—except you'll have a dandy scar to brag about to your grandchildren some decades down the road and girls in the here and now who have the same size brains."

Krenz looked around the tent. "Then why aren't I staying?"

"We'll be marching into Dresden by the day after tomorrow. Torstensson's already announced that all of our wounded are to be billeted in the city as soon as possible."

Eric's smile was a thing to behold. "I'll be in a tavern soon! Probably one filled with good-natured barmaids. With, as you say, the mental acuity of my far-in-the-future tiny little grandchildren."

Jeff grunted. "More likely, you'll be in a stable. With horses a lot smarter and a whole lot more suspicious."

Dresden

Studying the mob packed into the open area south of Dresden's *Residenzschloss*, the seat of the Saxon electors, Noelle Stull thought John George was smart to have gotten out of the city as quickly as he did.

According to the reports she and Eddie Junker had gotten, the elector had left the night before just about the same time Noelle and her party had arrived in Dresden. He'd left with all of his family members who'd still been in the city. Apparently, that only consisted of his wife, Magdalene Sibylle, and their youngest son, Moritz. All three of the older boys—Johann Georg, August and Christian—had been with von Arnim's army which had been defeated in the recent battle of Zwenkau. No one in Dresden seemed to know whether or not they had survived the debacle.

If they had, Noelle thought they'd be wise to stay out of the city as well. Dresdeners didn't seem to be as furious with the elector as the residents of Saxony's rural districts, from what she could tell. But they were obviously angry enough to form an impromptu lynch mob should the occasion arise.

That left the elector's three surviving daughters: Sophia Eleanora, Maria Elizabeth, and the mother's namesake, the eighteen-year-old Magdalene Sibylle. None of them were anywhere near Saxony, however. The two older girls had married noblemen living in the western parts of the Germanies and now resided there. The youngest had just married the Danish crown prince Christian.

She whistled softly. Eddie cocked an eye at her. "What?"

"I was just thinking what a royal mess of a succession crisis we're likely to have, assuming Gustav Adolf unseats John George entirely."

Eddie frowned. "Why? He'd disqualify all the sons from the succession too."

"Sure. But that still leaves the three daughters—each

and every one of whom, I remind you, is married to a loyal subject of the emperor. Assuming we can refer to Prince Christian as a 'loyal subject,' which may be questionable but simply raises other problems."

Eddie thought about it. "Bigger problems, actually. Gustav Adolf can shrug off Hesse-Darmstadt and Holstein-Gottorp's claims easily enough. But if there's no one else in line to inherit Saxony, you can bet that King Christian of Denmark will insist the children of his daughter-in-law should. And Gustav Adolf can't ignore him so readily."

Denise Beasley piped up. "Piece of cake. Throw out all the royal bums and set up a republic."

From the self-satisfied look on her face, the girl would have popped bubble gum by way of emphasis. Had she possessed any bubble gum.

She didn't, of course. Bubble gum had long since gone the way of Ben & Jerry's ice cream and Bic cigarette lighters. But her friend Minnie Hugelmair made up for it by spitting onto the cobblestones. She did that with a skill and assurance that properly belonged to a wizened old farmer.

"I agree," she said firmly. "Just get rid of the shitheads."

The teenage down-timer had lost an eye two years earlier in a brawl started by religious students. Grantville's then-mayor Henry Dreeson had given her his uncle Jim's glass eye to make up the loss as best as possible. He'd then been murdered himself, just a short time ago. The crime was presumed to have been committed by other religious fanatics.

The long and the short of all that history was that insofar as such a thoroughly non-theoretical person as

Minnie Hugelmair could be said to have an ideology, it was awfully simple and clearcut. Get rid of all kings and nobles. Squash all religious zealots. Support the common folk. Support good music. (The last being the influence of her mentor, the old up-time folk singer Benny Pierce.)

She and Denise Beasley saw eye to eye on just about everything, except when they faced each other from Minnie's bad side. Then they saw eye to glass eye on just about everything.

Noelle was fond of both girls. Which was a good thing, given that she sometimes felt like drowning them.

"It's not that simple," she said, in perhaps the thousandth futile effort to instill an appreciation for nuance in the minds of two teenage girls whose view of the world was about as nuanced as that of wolverines.

Eddie just grinned. As well he might, Noelle thought sourly, given that Denise was his girlfriend and had an approach to romance that also had about as much nuance as a wolverine. On any other member of the weasel family, especially minks.

"You're sure of that?" Tata asked sharply. For a pretty young woman on the short and plump side, she had a surprisingly ferocious manner when she was in the mood. The young farmboy she was interrogating flinched a little, even though he really had nothing to fear.

Anna Piesel assumed that was the result of the other woman's CoC training. In point of fact, it was the product of Tata's upbringing as a tavern-keeper's daughter. She'd been pretty since she was thirteen, short all her life, and had the sort of plumpness that

went with very well-filled bodices. By the time she
was fifteen, she'd learned how to intimidate just about
any male. Certainly young ones.

"Yes, I'm sure," he insisted. He turned and pointed
to the southwest. "We saw him. You can't miss that
great big carriage he fancies."

Tata and Anna turned to follow the finger. Of
course, they couldn't really see anything because of the
crowded houses. But Anna had no difficulty picturing
the landscape beyond Dresden.

"He must be headed for Bavaria," she said.

Tata frowned. "Poland's a lot closer. The terrain's
easier too, I think."

"Yes, it is. A lot easier. To get into Bavaria he's got
to pass through the Vogtland, the Erzgebirge and the
Bohemian Forest." Now Anna frowned. "Stupid to try
to do that in a carriage, though."

"He could always swap the carriage for horses when
need be. But why would he go that way at all? Why not
head for Poland? King Wladyslaw would certainly give
him sanctuary. Duke Maximilian probably would too,
but who knows what that crazy Bavarian might do?"

They both turned to stare at the farm boy. Who,
for his part, looked about as unhappy as a sixteen-
year-old boy possibly could when he was the subject
of close scrutiny by two good-looking young women.

"I don't know," he said, almost whining. "How am
I supposed to know what an elector thinks?"

Tata and Anna now looked at each other. The boy's
point was reasonable enough, after all.

"Maybe something's stopping him," ventured Anna.
"I don't know. Whatever. Maybe they sent out cavalry
patrols."

Tata decided she was probably right. She turned back to the farmboy.

"You're sure that's the way he went?" Seeing the hapless expression on his face, she waved her hand. "Never mind. We'll take your word for it."

She looked around. Spotting the towers of the elector's palace not too far distant, she pointed to them. "Up there."

Anna looked doubtful. "How...?"

Tata started striding in that direction. "There'll be a way," she said, with the self-confidence of a tavern-keeper's daughter assuring a patron that if he didn't concentrate on his drinking instead of her rump he would soon be in an ocean of misery.

So it proved. The guards from the city militia who had appointed themselves to maintain order and prevent looting were no match for Tata's will. She got through them in less than a minute—in fact, she even got three of them to serve her and Anna for guides.

"I need the highest place in the palace." She dug into her pack and brought forth a short wave radio transmitter. "We sent one of these to Georg Kresse a while ago. He should have it by now. But I don't know how good the reception will be in those mountains."

The militiamen were suitably impressed by the up-time device. Without argument, they led the two women to the tallest tower in the *Residenzschloss*.

Tata had to consult her notebook to get the Morse code right. She was too much of a novice to have more than a few letters memorized. But the message wasn't all that long anyway.

ELECTOR COMING. STOP. LEFT DRESDEN

LAST NIGHT. STOP. MUST BE HEADED FOR
BAVARIA. STOP. IN CARRIAGE WHEN HE LEFT.
STOP.

The reception in the Vogtland was quite good, as
it happened. But it still took Wilhelm Kuefer a lot
longer to translate the message than it had taken Tata
to send it. His knowledge of Morse was completely
theoretical, to begin with. And secondly, he didn't
have Tata's general familiarity with up-timers and their
peculiar gadgetry.

But, eventually, he got it translated. No sooner had
he finished than he said: "He'll have to swap out the
carriage for horses. No way he can get to Bavaria
unless he does."

Kresse's smile was as cold as a Vogtland winter.
"We'll spot any party that size as soon as it enters
our territory. After that, it won't matter what trans-
portation he's gotten his hands on. Anything will get
you into hell."

Chapter 20

Osijek, the Balkans

"And you're quite certain?" Janos Drugeth asked.

"Oh, yes," replied Doctor Grassi. "There's simply no way to hide that massive a mobilization. And once something like that gets started, as you know, it's almost impossible to stop it."

Drugeth nodded. There was a dynamic power to these things that made them effectively inevitable once a certain point was passed. Could even Zeus have stopped the fleets of Greece once they'd crossed half the Aegean on their way to Troy? And compared to the Ottoman emperor Murad, Agamemnon had been a paragon of prudence and deliberation.

"How soon, then?"

The Ragusan physician shrugged. "Hard to say. You understand that my information is of necessity somewhat outdated—and mostly gathered from a distance?"

Janos smiled. "I don't expect you to give me up-to-the-minute reports on a Turkish army marching into Mesopotamia, Doctor. Still, your guesses are likely to be reasonably accurate."

Grassi took a moment to look around the tavern. It was quite full, and noisy enough to make it impossible to be overheard unless you shouted. The clientele was as polyglot as any in the Balkans, and the Ottomans made no attempt here to enforce the Muslim laws against alcohol consumption.

"Have you read the Kinross book?" he asked.

"Yes. Three times, in fact."

Grassi took a sip of his coffee. Regardless of the situation here, he saw no reason to relax his customary vigilance. He'd gotten by among the Turks for years now, and had even gotten himself appointed as the household physician to several prominent Turkish families. He enjoyed wine and got an occasional bottle from his patron Schmid. But he was careful to drink it only in private.

"Then you know how it transpired in that other universe."

"Murad launched his campaign in the early summer of the year 1638—a little less than three years from now, if the calendars of the two worlds can be matched against each other. He left from Scutari, on the Anatolian coast of the Bosphorus. Baghdad fell in December, after a siege of forty days."

"Yes. From everything I can determine, Murad seems intent to repeat the victory three years earlier—and even more rapidly."

"Can he do it?"

"Quite possibly, I think. I have not been able yet to get definite information, but I am now inclined to believe that the Turks have either obtained up-time military technology or developed it on their own."

"Such as?"

"Rifled muskets, for one. I'm almost certain about that. In addition . . ." The doctor from Dubrovnik hesitated a moment. "They may have developed their own air force," he said, very quietly.

Drugeth was normally imperturbable. But on hearing that, his eyebrows shot up. "An *air force*? Doctor, I think that is highly unlikely. I have a far amount of experience with these matters myself, and it's not so easy as all that to duplicate the American engines."

Grassi shook his head. "You're thinking of the American airplanes. What the Turks would have developed would be . . . what do they call it? Lighter-than-air, I think."

"Balloons? Those might be possible, but what . . . Ah." Idly, Janos drained his wine glass, staring through the open door of the tavern at the busy street beyond.

"Ah," he repeated. "There is also such a thing as a blimp. Or a dirigible. I'm not quite clear on the difference. Either way, they are essentially elongated balloons that are capable of being steered. Very slow, however."

Grassi shrugged. "Such a machine would not need to be quick—if its target was a city. Baghdad will surely be much slower. And if my admittedly scanty information is correct, these machines can lift quite heavy weights."

"I believe that's true," said Janos. "Bombs, you're thinking?"

"That—and the spiritual factor. The Safavids are inclined to mysticism, you know. I do not believe they have paid much attention to the reports coming out of Europe, or given any credence to the ones they have heard. Even though they're farther away, I think the Mughals are more aware of the impact the Americans have had than the Persians are."

"I don't quite understand your point."

The Ragusan smiled. "That's because you have become more accustomed than you realize to this new world created by the Ring of Fire. I mean no offense, Graf. But try to imagine how you would have reacted five years ago—had you seen mysterious flying machines wreaking havoc in Vienna?"

Janos set down his wine and leaned back in his chair. "Now I see your point. Yes . . . The Persians might well panic."

"They don't even need to panic. Confusion alone will probably be enough to let Murad take Baghdad this year."

There was silence, for a minute or so. Then Janos rose to his feet. "I must be off now, Doctor. My thanks for your assistance."

For all the graciousness of his demeanor, it was all Janos could do not to curse aloud.

The Turks attacking Persia. That meant the Austrian emperor would conclude he had no restrictions on his ability to intervene in the war to the north. Which Janos still thought was foolish, whether or not the Ottomans posed an immediate threat.

Besides, who could say what Murad might do the *next* year—if he was triumphant in this one?

Stockholm

"That was a truly miserable experience," said Baldur Norddahl, once they were far enough away from the queen of Sweden's audience chamber not to be overheard.

Prince Ulrik made a sour little noise. "Exhausting, too."

"At least now we know why the princess is sometimes given to moods."

Ulrik made another sour noise, this one not so little. "'Is sometimes given to moods.' Is that Norwegian berserk-speak for 'is sometimes a miniature harridan and others a very short lunatic'?"

"Your words, not mine," Baldur replied serenely. "And that's a terrible way to refer to your future bride. 'Harridan!' 'Lunatic!'"

They reached one of the great doors that led to Slottsbacken, the street that provided the main entrance to the palace. It was more in the way of a plaza than a street, really. Stockholm's great church sat on its western edge.

As soon as they stepped through into the sunlight, Ulrik squared his shoulders. The gesture was half a shrug, half an expression of relief at getting outside. Under the cheeriest of monarchs, the Swedish royal palace would have been on the somber side. Under the influence of Queen Maria Eleonora, it was downright gloomy.

"Kristina is a very intelligent harridan and lunatic," Ulrik said philosophically. "I could do worse. As long as she takes after her father instead of her mother, the marriage should at least be tolerable."

"I certainly hope she doesn't inherit her mother's taste in entertainment."

Ulrik grimaced. The Swedish queen doted on dwarfs and buffoons. The wretched creatures had half-filled the audience chamber.

"Dear God. Yes, let's hope so."

They headed for one of the other wings of the palace, where Ulrik and his entourage had their quarters.

"Look on the bright side, Prince. For at least six more years—no, probably seven or eight or possibly even nine or ten—you won't have to be sharing a bed with the little lunatic harridan. And by the time you do, she won't be so little. Which means—"

"And to think it was you, Baldur, who showed Danish royalty how to execute a man by crushing him in a diving suit."

Baldur smiled, but did not pursue the train of thought further.

Mademann, Locquifier and Brillard watched the prince and his companion from a distance of slightly more than a hundred yards. They were partially hidden in the shade cast by a nearby elm tree.

"Can you do it?" asked Mademann. "I can probably get you one of the new French rifles. I can certainly get you an SRG."

Brillard made a little dismissive gesture. "At this range, Charles, I could do it with any sort of rifled musket. But I think that would be a mistake."

"Why?" asked Locquifier. He and Mademann shared, a bit awkwardly, the joint leadership of the project.

"Because the problem is not the prince. Nor the princess, for that matter. Ulrik is quite active and so is she, every chance she gets."

"Whenever her half-crazed mother lets her roam loose, you mean."

"Yes. But that happens often enough—and when it does, she invariably seeks out the company of the Dane. Not so?"

His companions both nodded. Brillard went on. "And whenever the two of them are together—"

"Three of them," Mademann interrupted. "That Norwegian never leaves Ulrik's side."

"Two, three, it doesn't matter. The point I was making is that they do not restrict themselves to the interior of palace. To the contrary. They always leave it to go elsewhere. More often than not, to the Storkyrkan."

He nodded toward Stockholm's cathedral. "She probably needs the respite, after being for too long with her mother."

Mademann looked back and forth from the palace to the church. "Here, you're saying? Right here in the open?"

"Why not? All of you except me. You can trap them here, and at close range. Between all of you, it should be easy enough."

He shrugged. "Escape may be difficult. But we always understood that."

"And you'd deal with the queen? Alone?"

"It's the only way it can be done anyway. She almost never leaves the palace, and when she does it's under heavy guard."

"And then she goes to the cathedral also. So why not—?" Locquifier broke off as he came to the answer himself.

"The princess never goes at the same time she does," said Mademann. "She waits until the queen has left and is almost back to the palace. Then..."

He whistled softly. "I see your plan now, Mathurin. You position yourself to strike down the queen just as she's passing through the entrance. It'll have to be a sunny day, though, when she's using an open carriage."

"Has to be a sunny day in any event," said Brillard. "You can't risk misfires in the rain."

Locquifier seemed a bit dubious. "A difficult shot."

"Not so difficult as all that—especially if Charles can get me a Cardinal breechloader. An SRG will be a little more accurate, but it won't give me the chance for a second shot."

Mademann had been stroking his beard thoughtfully. "So your shot would be the signal. As soon as we hear it, the rest of us come out into the street. We should be able to hide well enough in the alleys. If all goes well, we'll catch the Dane and the girl before they've reached the cathedral. Then we make our separate escapes."

He, too, now looked a bit dubious. "Tricky timing, though."

But Locquifier's doubts had vanished. "It's the only way," he said firmly. "The instructions from Michel and Antoine were very precise. We *must* succeed in the full task. This is the only way to do it."

Once Guillaume Locquifier came to the conclusion that a given plan was ordained by Michel Ducos, he would be unyielding in his determination to stick to it. Under other circumstances, Mathurin Brillard had often found that annoying. But under these, he didn't mind at all.

He began giving some thought, for the first time, to methods of escape. It was unlikely he could do so, of course, given the ambitious scope of the project. But perhaps not impossible. Especially since the others would draw most of the attention, as numerous as they were and coming out in the open to fire pistols. He hadn't come up with the plan for that reason, to be sure. Mathurin was cold-blooded, but not *that* cold-blooded. Nonetheless, the plan having been agreed to, there was no reason he shouldn't take advantage of its unfortunate but inevitable results.

Part Four

September 1635

The light of setting suns

Chapter 21

Berlin, Capital of Brandenburg

Mike Stearns had never visited Berlin up-time. But he had a distinct memory of a collection of photographs he'd once seen of the city, especially the Brandenburg Gate and the magnificent tree-lined boulevard Unter den Linden.

Neither was here, now. The Brandenburg Gate didn't exist at all. And where Unter den Linden would be in a future world, in this one there was nothing more than a bridle path that led to the elector's hunting ground in the Tiergarten.

There was really no part of Berlin in the year 1635 to attract sightseers, beyond a couple of churches built during the later middle ages. Those were the Marienkirche near the fortified city gate called the Spandauer Thor, and the Nikolaikirche near the Spree river. The Spree divided the two parts of Berlin, the city proper—what Mike thought was called the Mitte—and its adjoining sister city of Cölln.

Both churches were impressive enough, by the standards of the north German plain. But they didn't really compare with such Gothic masterpieces as Notre Dame or the cathedral at Chartres. Of the two, Mike favored the Marienkirche because of its warm brick construction—which was just as well, since that was where Gustav Adolf had chosen to hold his war council.

Mike found the situation a little amusing, given the religious fervor of the seventeenth century. He'd noticed before that the self-professed profound devotion of people of the time—princes and kings, certainly—never stopped them from trampling their very profane boots over holy ground whenever they found it convenient.

Mike wasn't really complaining, though. The only alternative venue for such a large war council would have been to hold it in the elector's palace. But that had been badly burned by a fire that swept through it the night before Gustav Adolf marched into the city. It would take a month to clear away the damage.

The fire hadn't been caused by the Swedes, though. Apparently it was the product of arson committed by persons unknown, but presumed to be acting on the instructions of the Brandenburg elector himself.

In the end, George William hadn't tried to match Gustav Adolf on the battlefield. He'd stayed in his capital until the last minute, and then left with his entourage and his army to seek refuge in Poland.

Mike had found that out the day before he arrived in Berlin. Immediately, he'd understood the implications. There would now be no possibility whatsoever of persuading Gustav Adolf to refrain from launching a war on Poland. There hadn't been much chance of it anyway, of course. Torstensson had made quite clear to Mike that the emperor was determined to do so, even if he had no better pretext than the presence of a small contingent of Polish hussars fighting with the Saxons at Zwenkau.

Now, Gustav Adolf had the sort of pretext that almost anyone would accept—at least, if they thought the way rulers did in this day and age. Being fair about it, probably any day and age. If Jefferson Davis and Robert E. Lee had somehow managed to take their government and army into Mexico in 1865, wouldn't Lincoln have sent Grant and Sherman in pursuit? And if that meant war with Mexico, so much the worse for Mexico.

When Mike entered the vestibule of the church, he found Gustav Adolf there. Waiting for him in order to have a private conversation, clearly enough. None of the Swedish king's subordinates were standing nearby. He was giving Mike the sort of look an eagle might give a hawk who ventured into its territory.

Mike was a skilled and experienced negotiator and had learned long ago that beating a dead horse accomplished nothing but sullying the reputation of the carcass-whacker. He went up to the king and said: "I still think it's a bad idea, but I won't dispute the point any further. George William pretty much pulled the rug out from under me."

Gustav Adolf frowned. "Pulled the rug—? Ah. I understand."

The frown was replaced by stiff nod. "Thank you, Michael. I would like to be able to concentrate on our military plans at this meeting and not get diverted by quarreling over political issues which are"—he cleared his throat—"no longer matters for debate."

Now, Gustav Adolf smiled. A very friendly smile, too. "Lennart tells me you accounted for yourself extremely well at Zwenkau. My congratulations. I will tell you that I was not surprised, however."

"The soldiers did all the work. Mostly, I just sat on a horse and did what my staff suggested I do. And tried to look suitably generalish."

"Do not make light of it, Michael." The emperor shook his head. "I have some skills at this myself, you know. Being a good general is much harder than it looks."

He took Mike by the arm and gestured toward the door leading into the nave. "But let us look to the future. We will face Koniecpolski now. I've fought him before. He's no commander to take lightly."

Magdeburg

"Good news, finally," said Matthias Strigel, as soon as he entered the room. The governor of Magdeburg province closed the door behind him and came over to the large table in the center. Rebecca, Constantin Ableidinger, Helene Gundelfinger and Werner von Dalberg were already seated there.

Strigel pulled out a chair and sat down. "I have it on good authority that Wilhelm Wettin has decided to postpone introducing the new legislation his allies have been demanding. Specifically, the bills dealing with citizenship and an established church."

Rebecca leaned back, her eyes widening a little. "That *is* good news."

Ableidinger was more skeptical. "What 'good authority'? And postpone for how long?"

"As for the first, as good as such authority gets."

Matthias' expression was on the smug side. "I heard it directly from Amalie Elizabeth von Hanau-Münzenberg."

"The landgravine *herself?*" von Dalberg asked sharply.

"Yes. Herself."

Now, all five people in the room leaned back in their chairs. The landgravine of Hesse-Kassel was, along with her husband Wilhelm V, the recognized national leader of what the people in that room thought of as the moderate wing of the Crown Loyalist Party. Nowadays, in fact, Amalie Elizabeth held that position alone, for all immediate purposes. Wilhelm V had taken the army of Hesse-Kassel to join Gustav Adolf's Swedish forces and would presumably be marching into Poland soon. No doubt he and his wife stayed in touch using the emperor's radio resources, but those resources were still limited enough that the landgravine would be operating on her own for the most part.

That was fine with the leaders of the Fourth of July Party, certainly. No one would be so impolitic as to say so aloud, but it was the private opinion of all the people sitting in that room that Amalie Elizabeth was considerably more astute than her husband.

The ramifications were . . . interesting, to say the least. If Amalie Elizabeth was prepared to go so far as to impart such delicate information to one of the central figures in the opposition . . .

"She's trying to keep the peace," said Rebecca. "She must be quite worried."

Ableidinger snorted. Like every sound issued by the former Franconian teacher, it was loud. "No shit, Sherlock, as you up-timers say."

Rebecca looked serene, as she could do so very well. Helene Gundelfinger issued her own snort, which was a far gentler and more ladylike thing. "There is not a single up-timer in the room, Constantin."

"Well..." Ableidinger might have been slightly—oh, so very slightly—abashed. He waved his hand in a vague sort of gesture. "Well. Rebecca, you know. She always seems..."

"I was born in London, actually, and spent most of my life in Amsterdam. All of that, moreover, in this century. Not—" Her own gesture was equally vague. "That other, much later one."

Then, just as serenely, she added: "However, as you say, no shit. It is obvious that the landgravine thinks it unwise to risk stirring up unrest—"

Ableidinger snorted again. "Say better, riot, rebellion and revolution."

Rebecca ignored him. "—while most of the reliable military forces available in the USE are off fighting the Poles and what is left of Brandenburg. And she must have persuaded Wettin of that, as well."

She cocked her head slightly. "As for the question of 'how long,' I think the answer is the same. Wilhelm will stall his allies until he feels he has a secure military force at his disposal."

Werner von Dalberg grimaced skeptically. "I don't know, Rebecca. Given the realities of the USE's own army, 'secure military force' means Gustav Adolf and his Swedes. And I need hardly remind anyone here that the"—he took a dramatically deep breath—"king of Sweden, emperor of the United States of Europe and high king of the Union of Kalmar does not take orders from Wilhelm Wettin. His chancellor Axel Oxenstierna may be a resolute supporter of aristocratic privileges and power, but Gustav Adolf himself is not."

Helene made a little face. "It would probably be more accurate to say that while Gustav Adolf agrees with Oxenstierna in the abstract, he is far more flexible in the concrete."

Ableidinger looked back and forth between them. "Meaning? Please remember, I'm a simple country boy."

"What it means," Rebecca interjected, "is that the king, emperor, high king etc. etc. is far more interested in maintaining his position as the preeminent monarch in Europe—which he certainly is today, even if the Habsburgs might shriek to hear it—than he is in supporting the petty perquisites of every nobleman and patrician in the Germanies."

"Not so petty as all that," said Ableidinger.

"They're petty from Gustav Adolf's standpoint, Constantin," said Dalberg. "He simply doesn't have Oxenstierna's rigidity on the matter. It's obvious, especially if you watch what he does rather that what he says. Is Gustav Adolf going to risk losing his control over the USE—which is now the heart of his power, don't forget, not Sweden and certainly not Denmark—because a pack of Hochadel and Niederadel and city and town patricians can't bear to lose their right to lord it over their lessers? I don't think so."

For all his frequent claims of being a rural bumpkin, Ableidinger was just as politically astute as anyone else in the room. "What you're suggesting, in short, is that the Crown Loyalists are at an impasse. Tied up in knots, as I believe the up-timers say." He smiled. "None of whom, of course, are in the room to correct my possible misquotation."

"That has always been the logic of the situation," said Rebecca. "But it is nice to see that the landgravine has apparently been able to get the prime minister to finally see it."

"To put it another way," said Strigel, "you think there will be no major changes in the political equation until something gets resolved on the military front."

"Precisely."

Rebecca's normal serenity seemed perhaps a bit frayed at the edges. Her hands were now clasped on the table in front of her.

"I understand that congratulations are in order," said Constantin. "With regard to your husband's exploits at Zwenkau."

"Hardly that." She unclasped her hands long enough to make a little wiggling gesture with the fingers of her right. "Michael tells me he did very little except to avoid doing anything stupid."

Ableidinger studied her, for a moment. He didn't miss the speed at which the hands got reclasped. "Perhaps so. But I suspect being a successful general is not as simple as it seems."

Berlin

"We are agreed, then," Gustav Adolf concluded. Standing at the head of the long row of tables that had been set up for the conference, he nodded to Mike Stearns, who was seated four chairs down on the king's left side. "As soon as we defeat the Poles and Brandenburgers in a major battle, General Stearns will take his division to Bohemia. Wallenstein has been requesting our support for months. He fears the Austrians will soon invade."

Gustav Adolf smiled, a bit crookedly. "Personally, I think his fears are excessive. On the other hand, by stationing the Third Division in Bohemia we will certainly forestall any possibility the Austrians might send troops to aid that bastard Wladyslaw."

The last phrase was spoken with real venom. There was a long-standing grudge between the two branches of the Vasa family. The one that ruled Poland felt—with some justification—that it had been swindled out of its rightful claim to the throne of Sweden. For their part, the Vasas who ruled Sweden resented the accusation with the bitterness felt by all usurpers who have convinced themselves they are the rightful heirs. It was a large part of the reason Mike had found Gustav Adolf so unrelenting on the subject of restarting a war with Poland.

As the Swedish king moved on to recapitulate some of the other major decisions made at the conference, Mike pondered the decision that affected him directly.

He was sure that the decision had been dictated by political considerations more than military ones. The Achilles heel of the new USE regime was the allegiance of the military. A very large portion of the soldiers in the army, possibly even a majority, had been recruited by organizers from the Committees of Correspondence. And while the navy and air force had much less of a CoC influence in the ranks, a disproportionate role was played in their leadership by up-timers. In fact, the commanding officers of both services were Americans.

That meant that if the Wettin regime tried to force through the reactionary program demanded by most of its factions, it ran the risk of provoking an open rebellion which, in turn, might very well trigger off a mutiny in the armed forces. The only reliable military units that would leave Wettin would be the king's own Swedish troops—most of whom were actually mercenaries, and most of those from the Germanies—and the forces fielded by some of the provincial rulers. Hesse-Kassel, for instance, had a rather powerful army.

But Hesse-Kassel was here in Berlin and not in Magdeburg—and so were most of his soldiers. In fact, he was sitting across from Mike at this very table, two seats up. Wilhelm V had left just enough troops at home to provide his wife Amalie Elizabeth with a minimal military force.

From the standpoint of the Crown Loyalists and their Swedish allies centered around Chancellor Axel Oxenstierna, the situation was close to intolerable. But so long as the Swedish king himself refused to support any drastic measures, they did not have many options.

They did have a few, though. Mike couldn't prove it, but he was certain that his future assignment to Bohemia was a bone that Gustav Adolf had thrown Oxenstierna and Wettin. He'd remove one-third of the USE's unreliable army from the equation by sending it off to Prague—or České Budějovice in the south, more likely—and the one-third commanded by the most notorious leader of the opposition, at that.

"—quiet situation in the Oberpfalz, we will transfer Ernst Wettin and Johan Báner to Saxony to take charge of the province until its final disposition can be decided. They are an experienced and proven team."

And there was another politically-motivated decision. It was true, in and of itself, that Ernst Wettin as political administrator and Johan Báner as the commander of the military had done a good job of stabilizing the Oberpfalz and beating back the Bavarians. But while no one would have any objections to the prime minister's younger brother being appointed the political administrator of Saxony, the same was not true of Báner.

Ernst Wettin was a judicious, fair-minded and reasonable man, by all accounts Mike had ever heard including from Ed Piazza. The Swedish general, on the other hand—also by all accounts he'd heard, including from Americans who'd dealt with the man—was a pigheaded, narrow-minded militarist whose openly-stated opinion on how to deal with the CoCs was to execute the lot of them.

Sending *him* to Saxony, given the inevitable turmoil that would soon ensue in the province, was not much different from pouring gasoline on an open flame.

Gustav Adolf was perfectly aware of Báner's characteristics and limitations. Báner was the kind of general whom any sensible ruler placed in positions where his undoubted military skills would be of use but which were not politically sensitive. Again, Mike was sure Gustav Adolf was tossing Wettin and Oxenstierna a bone.

Mostly Oxenstierna, actually. All the Wettin brothers except the renegade Bernhard were pretty close. By now, Mike was sure Ernst had privately made clear to Wilhelm his opinion of Báner. It was no secret that Ernst Wettin and the Swedish general had frequently clashed in the Oberpfalz.

Amberg, capital of the Oberpfalz

Ernst Wettin set down the letter he'd just received from his older brother Wilhelm. It might be more accurate to say it slipped from his loose and nerveless fingers onto the desk.

"Saxony?" he groaned aloud. "Me and Báner—*to Saxony*? Have they gone mad?"

Chapter 22

Chemnitz, in southwestern Saxony

John George's face was almost literally red. The elector of Saxony's eyes were bulging, too. Half in disbelief, half in fury.

"What?"

That was the third time he'd said that since Captain Lovrenc Bravnicar had returned and given his report. The young Slovene officer had been told the Saxon ruler could be difficult, but this was his first personal experience dealing him.

"What?" He shrieked the word this time. All traces of disbelief had vanished. The elector's mood was now one of pure rage.

Bravnicar would have had some sympathy for him, under most circumstances. Treachery was indeed a just cause for anger. But what did John George expect if he employed a mercenary like General Heinrich Holk?

What had happened was now clear. The captain had pieced the story together from many sources. As soon as word reached the Vogtland and the Erzbebirge of the Saxon defeat at Zwenkau, Heinrich Holk had mobilized his army and marched to the northeast. The presumption was that he intended to skirt Bohemia and enter Poland, and then offer his services to King Wladyslaw.

Why should anyone be surprised? As a military leader, Heinrich Holk had only two skills: Recognizing a lost cause immediately, and changing sides faster than a snake could molt its skin.

John George's wife stuck her head out of the carriage. "What is wrong?"

"Holk has betrayed us," her husband snarled.

Clearly, she didn't understand the implications. She just shook her head and said: "I never liked that man anyway. When can we get out of this wretched carriage?"

Their son Moritz stuck his head out alongside hers. "Yes, Papa, please. Horses would be so much better."

John George looked back at Bravnicar. For a fleeting moment, the captain wished he had a talent for treason himself. Without Holk's troops, escorting the elector through the Vogtland was going to be dangerous. All Bravnicar had at his disposal were a little over a hundred Slovene cavalrymen, a handful of Croat scouts, less than a hundred and fifty infantry soldiers—and those mostly dregs taken from other units—and exactly one artillery piece and a crew of gunners to service it. A splendid thing, in its own way. A nicely made Italian heavy culverin, which could fire five-inch balls or twenty pounds of canister.

It also weighed two and half tons and, with the forces at his disposal, was impossible to move through this mountainous terrain.

"Perhaps . . . Sir, I strongly recommend that you

make peace with the king of Sweden. As best you can. If we try to pass through the Vogtland without Holk's troops as an escort..."

It was no use. The elector of Saxony spent the new few minutes berating the Slovene captain for presumption, stupidity, ignorance, insubordination, bumptiousness, insolence, effrontery and, most of all, cowardice. By the time he finished, Captain Bravnicar's face was very pale and the knuckles of the hand gripping his sword were prominent and bone-white.

That was quite foolish behavior on the part of the elector. There were any number of mercenary captains who'd have cut him down on the spot and tried to sell his head to Gustav Adolf. Their troops certainly wouldn't object. Mercenary soldiers were loyal to whoever paid them, and only rarely did their pay come directly from their employer. Usually it was passed through the mercenary commanders, and it was those officers to whom the soldiery gave whatever loyalty they had.

Fortunately for John George, the young captain he'd so thoroughly offended was a scion of one of the many noble families in the Balkans who took personal honor very seriously. Often stupidly, too; but always seriously.

So, he simply gave the elector a stiff little bow and said: "As you wish. I do recommend you follow the advice of your wife and son. From here south, carriages are impossible."

They left Chemnitz two hours later, early in the afternoon. They should be able to reach Zwickau by nightfall, now that they'd shed the carriage. After that, it was only fifty miles or so to Hof. Three or four days travel, given the nature of their party and assuming the weather held.

They'd have to bypass Hof in order to avoid possible USE patrols. And, throughout, they'd just have to hope that Gustav Adolf kept all his airplanes in the north carrying out reconnaissance missions against the Poles and Brandenburgers. But once they got into the Bohemian Forest, they should be able to stay hidden within its dense woods until they reached Bavarian territory.

The real problem, however, was that first fifty mile stretch between Zwickau and Hof. That took them right through the heart of the Upper Vogtland.

The region was controlled by Kresse and his bandits, except when large army patrols passed through the area. At such times, Kresse would withdraw into hiding until the patrol passed.

In all, Captain Bravnicar had about two hundred and fifty men. Kresse wouldn't normally attack a force that large. But these were not normal circumstances. Kresse had excellent intelligence. Everyone knew the Saxons had been defeated by the USE and thanks to his tirade, plenty of people in Zwickau now knew that John George was here. Kresse would have no trouble figuring out that the middling-large combined cavalry and infantry force passing through the Upper Vogtland had John George in its midst.

Would he attack then? Two years ago, probably not. Today, after the depredations committed by Holk's mercenaries in these mountains...

Almost certainly.

Magdeburg

"It's a trick," said Achterhof.

Gretchen Richter rolled her eyes. "A trick, Gunther? By whom? Rebecca?"

"And to what purpose?" added Spartacus.

When his paranoid streak was aroused, Gunther Achterhof was as stubborn as the proverbial mule. "No, of course it's not Rebecca. Just means she's been tricked herself. By who? That snake of a landgravine, that's who."

He swiveled in his seat to face Spartacus, who was perched on a stool in a corner of the large kitchen. "To what purpose? You need to ask? It's obvious. To lull us into carelessness and relaxation by making us think we face no immediate danger."

Everyone in the kitchen stared at Achterhof. Not just Gretchen and Spartacus, but the six other CoC leaders present as well. The expressions of all eight people were identical.

After a few seconds, Eduard Gottschalk leaned back against the far wall and said, "Well, of course. How could we not see their scheme? They will trick us into disbanding our militias, dismantling our spy network, and turning all our energies to organizing public festivals."

"We'll get rid of all the associations, too," added Hubert Amsel, who was seated next to Gretchen at the table. He waved his hand. "Insurance cooperatives, sports leagues, the lot—all of them! Into the trash bin. Who needs them, now that we have swooned at the feet of the Hessian lady?"

Achterhof's jaws tightened. "It's not funny."

The young woman standing next to Gottschalk took a step toward the center of the kitchen. "No, but you are. Gunther, this is carrying caution to the point of madness."

Galiena Kirsch pointed her finger at one of the kitchen windows. It was closed, even in midsummer, at Achterhof's insistence. To eliminate the risk of eavesdroppers, he said, and never mind that there were over a dozen CoC security people guarding the apartment building on every side. As a result, of course, the kitchen was stiflingly hot. It would be years before up-time air conditioning became a feature of seventeenth-century life, outside of perhaps a few palaces—and those, small ones.

"Are you blind?" she demanded. "Or do you think our own intelligence people are tricking us?"

"What are you talking about?"

"You know perfectly well," said Gretchen. "For days, the Crown Loyalist legislators and lobbyists have been leaving the city. They'd only be doing so for one of two reasons. Either Wilhelm Wettin is a mastermind and his political party even more disciplined than we are—"

That was good for a burst of laughter. Even Achterhof joined in.

"—and so they're dispersing to all parts of the nation to carry out their fiendish scheme."

"It's possible," said Achterhof, in a surly tone of voice. Gretchen rolled her eyes again. So did half of the other CoC leaders present.

"Or," she continued, "they're leaving because the pack of squabbling dogs finally got tired of trying to force their nominal leader to do as they wish, especially now that he's made clear he refuses to do anything of a major nature until the war situation is resolved. So, their innate selfishness taking over, they are all returning to their manors and mansions. Which is what Rebecca thinks is happening. And so do I."

She decided to try á less confrontational approach. As aggravating as he could sometimes be, Gunther Achterhof was a critical leader in their movement. If he was convinced of the wisdom of a plan and committed to it, then you could be sure the capital city of the nation would remain solid as a rock. In any crisis, that was worth a very great deal.

"Gunther, please. The only specific issue at stake here is whether or not I should move to Dresden. Eduard and Hubert's stupid joking aside"—here she bestowed a stern look of reproof upon the miscreants—"no one is proposing to relax any of our stances or precautions. So what is the harm?"

She saw a slight change in Achterhof's expression. From long experience dealing with the man, she recognized the signs. Gunther was shifting from Absolute Opposition to Resolute Disagreement.

Another half hour, she estimated.

Vienna

"It's in your own report!" exclaimed the Austrian emperor. Ferdinand jabbed an accusing—approving?—finger at the sheaf of papers in his hand. "You say it yourself. The Turks are invading Persia."

Janos Drugeth tried to keep his jaws from tightening. He could not, however, prevent his lips from doing so.

"No, unfortunately they are *not* attacking Persia. If they were, we could relax in the sure and certain knowledge that the Ottomans and the Safavids would be fighting for another decade, at least. They are simply seeking to retake Baghdad, which is in Mesopotamia. And if the results of this same war in that other universe hold true, they will succeed in doing so—and then make a lasting peace with the Safavids. The point being, that while the Turks pose no threat to us this year, they may very well be a threat in the following one."

Ferdinand waved his hand. "You're just guessing. And in the meantime, the Swedish bastard is marching into Poland. *After* taking Saxony and Brandenburg. It's obvious that once he conquers Poland we'll be the next meal on his plate."

Janos took a deep, slow breath. Calm, calm. Always essential, when you were arguing with an emperor.

"Ferdinand, 'once he conquers Poland' is far easier said than done. And even if he succeeds, why would he come south? He'd have to break his alliance with Wallenstein to get to us. Far more likely he'd go after Muscovy."

"Yes, exactly!" The emperor leaned forward in his chair, which was not quite a throne but very close. "He'll keep the alliance with Wallenstein. They'll *both* attack."

Janos saw his chance. "In that case, Ferdinand, the logical thing to do is send all available forces to guard our border with Bohemia." He squared his shoulders, in the manner of man valiantly taking on a perilous task. "I offer to lead them myself."

Ferdinand stared at him suspiciously. The logic of the argument was impeccable, but...

The emperor was very far from being a dull-wit. He understood perfectly well that another effect of Drugeth's proposal would be to keep Austria from taking any irrevocable steps. Any nation had the right to protect its own borders, after all. Gustav Adolf could hardly use such a mobilization as a pretext for invasion. And it would keep Austria's army close to Prague—and close enough to the frontier with the Turks, should Drugeth's fears prove justified.

"I'll think about it," said Ferdinand, in a surly tone of voice.

Wismar, Germany, on the Baltic coast

The up-time radio operator frowned. "Say what?"

"Grain futures," Jozef Wojtowicz repeated.

The tow-headed young fellow's jaws moved, much like a cow chewing a cud. It was difficult to imagine that his people had once, in another world, put a man upon the moon. This particular American seemed about as bright as a sheepdog.

Eventually, Sergeant Trevor Morton confessed. "I don't exactly know what that is."

With a genial expression on his face, Jozef leaned forward across the table.

"It's not complicated. As you know"—which he certainly didn't—"Poland is the world's greatest exporter of wheat."

That might even be true. Close enough for these purposes.

"The grain is shipped through the Baltic. But the process is slow. Grain is bulky." Best to use short sentences. One syllable words as much as possible. "By the time it reaches the market, prices have often changed. Those who speculate"—no way to avoid that term—"in grain can lose a lot of money."

He paused, enabling the sergeant to absorb this mountain of knowledge.

"Yeah, okay, I get it," said that worthy eventually. His jaws were still moving back and forth. Jozef wondered what he could possibly be chewing? It couldn't be the bizarre material the up-timers called "chewing gum." That had vanished years ago. Jozef had never actually laid eyes on the stuff.

Perhaps Sergeant Morton, having gotten into the habit of chewing gum, had simply continued the process when the gum disappeared. Who could say?

"Well, then," Jozef continued. "Nothing has more effect on the travel time of Polish wheat down the rivers and across the sea than the weather."

That was probably true also, although Jozef was grossly overstating its importance to grain speculators. The real effect of the weather on grain prices was seasonal, not daily or weekly. But that wouldn't do for his purposes here.

"Yeah, okay, I can see that."

Jozef smiled. Mission accomplished?

Alas, no.

"But what's that got to do with me?" asked the American sergeant.

It was all Wojtowicz could do not to throw up his hands. Instead, in as gentle a tone of voice as he could manage, he continued the lesson in remedial bribery.

"The weather in northern Europe generally goes from west to east. As you know. Especially over the open waters of the Baltic. Where you are located, here in Wismar."

The reason the sergeant was located here was because of the USE air force base in Wismar. But the base was no longer used much for active air operations. It had become a sleepy garrison post. Hence the presence of sleep-walking soldiers like Morton. In earlier times, Jozef wouldn't have had to do all this, since the weather forecasts were broadcast openly. Lately, though, once it became clear that Gustav Adolf was going to invade Poland, the USE had decided that a knowledge of the upcoming weather might be a military asset, so they now kept the information as private as such information could be kept—which was not at all, as Jozef was now demonstrating. But then, no knowledgeable man expects a government to be any smarter than a cow.

Jozef had paused for a bit, allowing the man across the tavern table to digest that stew of complex data. Now, finally, the sergeant seemed to have done so.

"Yeah, okay, I get that."

"So. You give me a copy of the weather forecast every evening. We can meet in this tavern or anywhere else you'd prefer."

"Here's fine," said Morton. "I come here every day after work anyway. But what good's the forecast going to do you when you need it in Poland?"

A flicker of intelligence. Amazing. Best to stamp it out quickly, lest it spread.

"I'll have couriers ready, on the fastest horses."

Anyone with a knowledge of geography would have understood immediately that that was absurd. No string of horses could possibly get a weather forecast from

Wismar to Poland before the weather itself arrived and made the whole exercise pointless. What Jozef was actually going to do was transmit the information on his own radio. The messages could be easily coded, since they'd be short. Even if a USE radio man should happen to stumble upon the frequency, they wouldn't know what was being transmitted.

But Jozef was certain that Morton wouldn't realize he was being duped. The man obviously had no idea where Poland was in the first place. Nor the name of its capital, the language its people spoke, or... anything. Jozef had once met a man more ignorant of the world than this sergeant. But he had the excuse of being an illiterate Lapp reindeer herder.

Finally, Morton's brain got around to the core of the matter. "How much you say you'll pay me?"

Poznań, Poland

The grand hetman of the Polish-Lithuanian Commonwealth peered down at the object in the hand of his nephew's agent.

"Amazing," he said. "I thought they needed huge towers to work."

The agent shook his head. "That was a lie that the Americans spread at first. They call it 'disinformation.' It's true that radios work better with big towers, especially transmissions, but they're not necessary." He hefted the receiver. "I can only use this effectively in the morning and evenings. What they call the windows. But I'll be able to get the boss's transmissions."

Stanislaw Koniecpolski nodded, and dismissed the

agent with a motion of his hand. He then turned to face young Opalinski, who was seated in a chair in the small salon. Lukasz still had a haunted look on his face.

"It is no crime to be defeated, young man," the grand hetman said gently. "Especially not when you return with such useful information."

Opalinski made a face. "It may not be so useful as all that."

Koniecpolski shrugged. "Anything will help. Gustav Adolf will bring some fifty thousand men into Poland. I will have perhaps forty thousand with which to oppose him, ten thousand of whom are Brandenburgers." He scowled. "I'm not counting Holk's men, assuming the king ignores my advice and hires the swine. Making things still worse, half of the Swede's infantry will be armed with rifled muskets, where I have but a thousand of the French breechloaders."

Opalinski perked up a bit. "You got them, then?"

The grand hetman nodded. "Yes, and I think I'll have at least two thousand SRGs by the time we confront him. They've made enough of those by now to create a sizeable black market and for once"—the scowl came back—"the Sejm isn't being miserly."

He took a seat near Opalinski. "Finally, Gustav Adolf will have his airplanes and his APCs. The first, from what I can determine from the reports I've gotten, have a somewhat limited capability as weapons. On the other hand, they provide superb reconnaissance."

"In good weather," said Lukasz.

"As you say. In good weather. Much like the APCs, which you describe as being invincible war machines against men—"

Lukasz completed the thought. "But by no means invincible against terrain and weather. I warn you, though, I got that mostly from listening to Lubomir Adamczyk and some of the other hussars who survived the battle." His face tightened. "I did not see very much myself, after..."

"After you led an almost successful charge with only two hundred hussars against the same flying artillery that crushed the French cavalry at Ahrensbök. Stop flagellating yourself, young man. We're Catholics, not heathens." A smile removed the sting from the last words and turned them into a jest.

The grand hetman signaled a servant standing by a far wall. "Some wine," he said, when the man came over.

As the servant went about his task, Koniecpolski turned back to Lukasz. "Regardless of who made the observations, I think they're accurate. The only way I can at least partially nullify the Swede's many advantages is to refuse to meet him on terrain and under weather conditions that favor him. I will have to maneuver as long as necessary"—his expression became bleak—"and allow as much ravaging by the enemy as I must, in order to fight a battle under those conditions which favor me. Or, at least, counter some of the enemy's strengths."

The servant returned, with a bottle and two goblets. After he poured the wine and retreated, Koniecpolski raised his goblet.

"Once again, my precious nephew has done right by us. A toast! Here's to drenching rain and blinding fog and the Swedish bastard's downfall."

Chapter 23

Dresden

Dresden was chaos. The cavalrymen escorting the ambulance wagons to the army hospital were making no more headway than an old woman pushing a cart.

So it seemed to Eric Krenz, anyway. He stuck his head out of the rear flap of the covered wagon and tried to look forward. But that was impossible, between the stupid design of the wagon—what idiot thought it a good idea to turn a nice open wagon into a heat trap?—and the relative immobility produced by his healing wound.

Disgusted, he flopped back onto the bench. "What we need are some Finns." He made chopping motions, as if wielding an ax. "*Hakkaa päälle! Hakkaa päälle!* That'd clear the way for us, see if it wouldn't."

"Shut up." A Pomeranian corporal whose name Eric couldn't remember said that through clenched teeth. "You're giving me a headache."

Judging from his condition, Eric didn't think the fellow would be suffering much longer. But perhaps that was just wishful thinking. The corporal had been groaning and moaning most of the way here, when he wasn't snarling at everyone else if they moaned and groaned.

Well, it should be over soon. A nice army hospital, friendly nurses, what could be better?

He must have said it out loud. The soldier slumped next to him, a young lieutenant whose name Eric had also forgotten, raised his head. "You've been to one?"

"Well. No. Never seen one, in fact. But the stories all agree. Especially about the friendly nurses. What's your name again?"

"Nagel. Friedrich Nagel."

"Eric Krenz. A pleasure." They shook hands.

"It's a pigsty," was Nagel's summary. He nodded toward the one and only nurse visible in the huge . . . whatever the room was. Judging by the sour smell and the dank walls, probably one of the adjoining castle's less frequently used storerooms.

"As for that nurse," the lieutenant continued, "let us pray that she never comes near us. Lest she become friendly."

Eric wasn't entirely sure the nurse was a "she" to begin with. The distance was great enough that it was difficult to tell.

The Pomeranian corporal started moaning and groaning again.

"And to think our lives will end here," mused Nagel. "Such is ignominy."

"Do you think we could get something to eat?"

"Must you dredge up my worst fears?"

They got nothing to eat that night beyond a half-loaf of bread. The same nurse came through two hours later, followed by two orderlies carrying baskets full of bread. At each pair of cots, the nurse would take out a loaf, rip it into halves, and hand them to the wounded soldiers, then, without saying a word, move on.

The orderlies were female. Mediocre versions of the gender, to say the least. But definitely female.

Eric still wasn't sure about the nurse.

An hour later, the same trio passed down the line of cots in the great vaulted room again. This time, the orderlies were carrying buckets of water, from which the nurse would fill what looked like an old soup ladle—best not to think about the precise nature of the soup—and place it to the mouth of each soldier. The one poor fool who tried to hold the ladle bowl in his own hand to keep it from spilling got the ladle snatched away and his ear boxed.

Clearly, this was not a nurse to be trifled with.

For the selfsame reason, Krenz refrained from pointing out to the trio of medical geniuses that it would have made more sense to give them water first, and food later. That being every human body's definite priority.

But he kept his silence, swallowed what he could from the ladle—from the taste, he thought it had probably once been a Mongol ladle, used to serve kumiss or whatever the heathens called that horrid fermented milk they drank—and let the nurse and her companions pass on.

He still hadn't determined her gender. "We need a name for it," he whispered to Nagel.

"Leviathan comes to mind," he whispered back. "Though I'd favor Moloch, myself."

"Moloch it is, then."

✧   ✧   ✧

Things did not improve in the morning. Moloch was absent, thankfully, but the nurse who replaced the creature was little improvement. True, she was female. Unfortunately, of the elderly rather than youthful disposition; and, far worse—Eric had a very good-natured grandmother, after all—she subscribed to that school of thought which held that in old age a woman should cultivate the virtues of haggery and witchery. Had there been milk, she would have turned it sour.

There wasn't, of course. Water and bread, as the night before. The bread was stale. The water had a definite green tinge to it.

"I am becoming disillusioned," Eric announced to Friedrich.

His new friend proved to be an educated man. "I had no illusions to begin with. Having studied the classics, I know the fate of man. The best you can hope for is to fuck your mother, put your eyes out, and die in exile."

Eric thought that was something of an exaggeration. Not much, though, judging from current evidence.

"There's one piece of good news," Nagel added.

"What's that?"

The lieutenant jerked a thumb in the direction of the moaner and groaner's cot. "I think the Pomeranian finally died."

Alas, that too was an illusion. No more than two seconds later, the corporal started moaning and groaning again. Calling out for water and bread, if you could believe it.

Reprieve finally came at noon. There was a commotion at the entrance and a small group of people forced their way into the room. "Forced" was the proper term, too. Moloch and the harridan-nurse were trying to prevent them from entering. Quite forcefully, in fact.

That all ended when a short, stout person in the midst of the newcomers knocked the harridan flat with a mighty blow and even caused Moloch to back up a step or two. Thereafter, the nurse-Leviathan was kept pinned to the wall by two more of the newcomers, armed with spears of some sort.

The one who'd sent the old witch flying marched down the aisle in the center of the room. By the time she was within thirty feet, Eric realized she was a woman. Young, too. And what he had taken from a distance for stoutness was mostly something entirely different and far more admirable.

"She's a vision!" he exclaimed.

Nagel was made of sterner stuff. "She might also be your mother. Take care, Saxon. We live in perilous times."

The vision and her cohorts had come to empty the storeroom of its wounded soldiers and place them in billets, as Torstensson had promised. An hour later, Krenz and Nagel found themselves lodged in a house no more than two blocks from the *Residenzschloss* in the direction of the Elbe. Judging by its appearance, the three-story house had been the home of a prosperous burgher. He and his family had apparently left the city, since they'd taken the time to pack up and carry off everything in the house of any value.

With the exception of the furniture. That must have been too bulky. So, Eric and Friedrich found themselves sharing a very comfortable bed on the second floor. There were even pillows of a sort.

Then, blessing piled upon blessing, one of the men who'd been with the group that took them out of the storeroom came through the rooms passing out food. Not just bread, either—and this bread was fresh. He also had cheeses and sausages. Even some cucumbers.

Best of all, he gave them a bottle of wine.

A fine fellow, no doubt about it. Still, he had his flaws. He was neither female nor a vision.

"Who is she?" Krenz asked.

The question was ignored. "You'll be taken care of by the city's Committee of Correspondence from now on," the man announced.

"Who is she?" Krenz asked again.

But the man had left, taking food and wine to soldiers in other rooms of the house.

"If you're that excited," said Nagel, "I'm going to insist on a new bedmate. I'll accept dying in exile after fucking my mother and poking my eyes out. I will not accept being struck down by the Almighty for buggery."

Eric grinned. "Oh, I don't think He's done that since the olden days. But you can relax. I'll do everything in my power to make sure you die many years from now in exile, blind and condemned to eternal torment for unspeakable sins."

"Thank you."

They fell asleep, then, and slept through the day. It had been a very rough few days, and the bed was truly comfortable.

Another CoC man came through after nightfall,

passing out more wine and food. Eric and Friedrich ate, drank, and immediately fell asleep again.

They probably would have slept all through the night, too. Except there was an imperfection in paradise.

The Pomeranian had been moved to this house as well, it turned out. They could hear him moaning and groaning in an adjacent room.

All night. Every hour of the night. Every minute of the hour.

"How does he not die of exhaustion?" wondered Eric.

"Fate won't allow it," replied Friedrich. "He must not have fucked his mother yet."

Dawn came, finally, and with it the vision returned. Not long after he woke up—amazingly, he'd managed to fall asleep in mid-moan—Eric heard a woman's voice in the main room below. It was that of a young woman, from its tone and timber.

Hope sprang alive in his chest. Could it be?

A few seconds later, he heard the sound of a woman's feet clumping up the stairs. He knew it was a woman from subtleties in the sounds being made.

The clumping noises were on the heavy side, too, for a woman as short as she had to be judging from the pace of the footsteps. Hope flared brighter still. Just the sort of sounds that might be made by a shortish woman who was mistaken for being stout at a distance but whose heft was in fact not evenly spread at all.

Then, she appeared in the doorway. Indeed, it was the vision. In the bright light of the room, with its open windows letting in the sun, Krenz could see much more of her than he'd been able to in the dark cavern in the castle.

She was quite pretty, in a modest sort of way. No
Venus here, just an attractive young farm girl or—Eric
raised his head to study her shoes—no, town girl.
Maybe a butcher's daughter. Fox-colored hair—very
rich, too—dark blue eyes. Perfect in every way.

"I'm Eric Krenz," he announced. "From right here
in Saxony. Not Dresden, though. Leipzig."

She greeted that information much the way a milk-
maid greets the sight of flies in a barn. Takes brief
note of the pests; dismisses them as an unavoidable
but minor nuisance.

Eric recognized the symptoms immediately. Mentally, he struck a line through his original guess that
she was a butcher's daughter.

"Your father owns a tavern, doesn't he?"

For the first time, the girl showed some interest
in him that transcended "recognition of pest." After
a couple of seconds, she said: "How did you know?"

Her voice was marvelous. Just the way Eric remembered it from the castle, except without the angry
shouting overtones that went along with putting a
harridan-nurse flat on her ass.

An honest answer would be unwise. *I know from
the long experience of getting clouted by barmaids
annoyed at my advances.*

But an outright lie would be equally unwise, assuming this infatuation had a future. *I know because my
own father owns a tavern* was the sort of claim that
could easily be shredded by a tavern-keeper's daughter.

So, he opted for mysterious silence.

The girl sniffed. "Got boxed on the ears enough
times, did you?"

She took two steps into the bedroom, and planted

her hands on her hips. Very ample hips, Eric was pleased to note.

"My name is Tata and I'm giving you fair warning. I have a short way with irritating men. Give me any trouble and I'll beat you black and blue."

Eric's hand clutched at his chest. "Oh! I adore domineering women!"

Chapter 24

The Vogtland

In the end, all of Captain Lovrenc Bravnicar's efforts to protect the elector of Saxony proved to be pointless. A massive explosion erupted just as John George and his wife and son passed through a narrow defile in the mountains.

The sound was almost deafening. Bravnicar, riding at the front of the column, twisted around in his saddle. The little gorge was filled with gunsmoke. He could hear the sounds of shrieking men and horses. Several riderless horses were already racing away from the disaster. He could see two bodies—presumably their former riders—lying still on the ground. Another horse was dragging a cavalryman whose boot had gotten stuck in a stirrup. His head smashed against a rock and he lost his helmet. Blood spilled out to cover his face.

Lovrenc thought the man was already unconscious. He hoped so. There was no way he was going to survive, the way his horse was dragging him down the rock-strewn incline.

You couldn't even call this a road. It was simply

a trail created by men and animals passing through the mountains for centuries.

"*Gott mit uns*," he whispered. Slovenia was now a Catholic land, but Bravnicar's family were Protestants who'd been driven out at the turn of the century.

Men were starting to stumble out of the smoky gorge. All of them were cavalrymen. The infantry marching behind must have been spared. One of the cavalrymen seemed to have a broken arm, and another's leg was bloody. A third just seemed dazed.

Bravnicar drew his sword and swept it in a half-circle. "Stand guard! We're under attack!"

Immediately, his Slovene veterans began forming a perimeter, drawing out their wheel-lock pistols. For his part, Lovrenc trotted his horse toward the defile. The smoke was beginning to clear away.

On the wooded slopes above, lying hidden on their stomachs, Georg Kresse and Wilhelm Kuefer studied the scene.

"What do you want to do about the Slovenes?" asked Kuefer softly.

"I don't know yet. It depends on whether the elector survived or not."

"Survived *that?* I don't think so." Wilhelm had overseen the laying of the charges himself. They had many former miners in their ranks, who'd done an excellent job of drilling the holes that held the powder. Once they'd covered everything up, the huge mines had been all but invisible, even though each charge had at least ten pounds of iron scrap lying on top to serve as shrapnel.

Wilhelm Kuefer had never heard the term "Claymore mine." But what he had created in that tight and narrow gorge was a line of them on either side. The shrapnel those blasts sent flying would not cover every square inch of the ground, but they would probably cover every square foot. Wilhelm didn't think a rabbit could have survived, not even an armored one.

"He's probably dead," agreed Georg. "But we need to be sure. If he is..." The leader of the Vogtland rebels made as much of a shrugging motion as a man can manage while lying down. "We've got no personal quarrel with the Slovenes, and I'd just as soon avoid unneeded casualties. If they leave, we'll let them go."

Kuefer grunted softly. That seemed reasonable. That was probably Captain Lovrenc Bravnicar's company down there. Wilhelm thought he'd recognized him. If so, just as Georg had said, they had no great quarrel with him or his. The Slovenes had refrained from committing the sort of atrocities that Holk's men were guilty of.

"What about the infantry?"

Kresse's expression hardened. "That's a different story. Not one of those pigs leaves these mountains alive."

That also seemed reasonable.

Bravnicar found the elector soon enough. Most of him, anyway. It took a while longer to find the missing leg, and he never did find the missing hand. Given the incredible force of the explosion, such a small item might well have been blown out of the gorge altogether.

The elector's wife had been scattered more widely, but Lovrenc didn't try to find all the pieces. There was no doubt about her identity. She'd been the only woman in the group and her face was almost unblemished, allowing for the oddly flat shape. It had been blown completely off her head and was plastered onto the hindquarters of a dead horse.

Oddly enough—explosions could be freakish—their sixteen-year-old son Moritz was almost untouched. Only one projectile seemed to have struck him. Unfortunately, that one had come in through one temple and out the other, passing under the helmet.

He heard a volley of gunfire coming from the northern end of the little gorge, followed by more scattered shots. Then, the blast of a cannon. A five-pound saker loaded with canister, by the sound of it.

Lovrenc had dismounted to examine the bodies. Now, he ran toward the noise in a crouch, leaving his steed behind. The stallion was a well-trained warhorse and wouldn't run off unless he was directly attacked.

As he neared the end of the defile, Lovrenc moved more slowly. After half a minute or so, he was able to peek his head around a boulder and see what was happening.

His infantry force—what was left of it; there were at least twenty bodies scattered not far from the gorge entrance—was in full retreat. Rout, rather. No, even "rout" didn't do justice to it. They were racing off like so many mice, discarding their weapons and even their armor as they ran.

Thereby displaying the intelligence of rodents, as well. Disarmed and scattered, in these mountains, they'd never survive the pursuit that Kresse's men were sure to set underway.

Had already set underway, rather. The sounds of gunfire were continuing. Those were all rifles, too. Hunters' weapons.

There was nothing Bravnicar could do about it. All that was left now was to get his Slovenes out of the disaster, if possible.

He had no great hopes.

As soon as Georg Kresse saw the cavalry officer trotting out of the gorge, he stood up and cupped his hands around his mouth.

"Hey there!" he shouted. First in German, then in Slovene. His knowledge of that language was limited, but Kresse knew some words in several of the Balkan tongues. Then, for good measure, he shouted the words again in Czech. He was almost as fluent in that language as he was in his native German.

The Slovene officer had stopped his horse and was staring up at Georg. He'd drawn a wheel-lock pistol from a saddle holster and had it at the ready, but he wasn't pointing it up the slope. At this range, he didn't have much chance of hitting Kresse anyway and they both knew it.

"Parlay!" shouted Georg, in German and Czech. He didn't know the word in Slovene, so he used the term for talk instead. Probably not in a grammatically correct manner—he could be saying "talking!" or "to talk!" instead of "let's talk!"—but he figured the enemy officer would get the point.

After a moment, the officer nodded. He put the pistol back in its holster and then shouted something to the cavalrymen under his command. They were now positioned some fifty yards down the trail and had dismounted and taken up defensive positions. They'd done that fairly well, for cavalrymen.

Not that it would do them much good if fighting

resumed. Georg had no doubt at all that he'd win any battle here. But these Slovenes were tough enough and good enough that he'd lose at least half a dozen men and have twice as many wounded. Some of those would die later.

He saw no point to it. The Slovene officer's behavior made it obvious that he'd found the elector—his body, rather—and had no further duties here. With John George dead, Kresse wanted to intervene as soon as possible and as effectively as he could in the political situation that would already be unfolding in Dresden. By now, the CoC contingent should have arrived in the city and become active. They'd grow very quickly, too. The Saxon capital already had a large number of people who considered themselves members or sympathizers of the CoCs. They hadn't had much organizational experience, but the newly arrived cadre from Magdeburg would take care of that soon enough.

Kresse considered the CoC people to be allies. But allies did not necessarily see everything the same way. After the years he and his people had spent fighting the elector in the mountains of the Vogtland, Georg was determined to have a say in what came next.

To do that, however, he had to get to Dresden, with as many of his people as possible. It would be foolish to delay or suffer casualties in a fracas with Slovene mercenaries with whom he had no real grievance.

He didn't hold their profession against them. These were hard times for any man. Several of his own relatives—an uncle and three cousins—had gone off to fight in the wars. Only one of them had ever come back, a cousin who was now missing his left arm below the elbow.

Once the Slovene officer was satisfied that his men understood the situation and wouldn't unsettle anything, he dismounted from his horse and took several steps away from it. Then, spread his hands a bit to show that he held no weapons. All he was now carrying was the saber belted to his waist.

"Come with me," Georg said to Wilhelm, as he started down the slope. Kuefer followed, just two steps behind.

Once they were on the trail and close enough to see the officer's features, Kuefer leaned over and murmured: "That's Bravnicar, sure enough."

Kresse had never seen the man before, but he took Wilhelm's word for it. As he came up, he extended his hand and said in Slovene: "You are Captain Lovrenc Bravnicar, I believe."

This had to be Kresse himself. Lovrenc had gotten descriptions of the man from several people who'd known him.

His Slovene was heavily accented and he didn't know the tongue as well as he thought he did. What he'd actually said was: "You have been Captain Lovrenc Bravnicar, I have faith."

Fortunately, Lovrenc was fluent in German as well as Czech. He'd been born and raised in exile, mostly in Bohemia. Being honest, he was more comfortable in either of those tongues than he was in his native one.

"Yes, I am he," he replied in German. "And I am guessing that you are Georg Kresse."

Kresse nodded.

This was off to a good start, Lovrenc thought. Well...a start, anyway. But given that he'd thought he and his men were as good as dead ten minutes earlier, any start was good.

It didn't take them more than five minutes to reach an agreement. The only sticking point—not much of one—had been Bravnicar's vague sense that perhaps he had some sort of lingering responsibility for the infantrymen being hunted down.

But he didn't put up a real fight over the issue. Balkan noble honor or not, Bravnicar had seen enough of war to have a very wide practical streak as well. To begin with, those hadn't actually been "his" men. They'd never been on his company's payroll. Most of them had been employed by Colonel Kazimir Zajic, a Bohemian mercenary whom Lovrenc had never met and who was not even here.

Secondly, he had no use for them anyway. They were wretched soldiers and even more wretched human beings. The sort of men who straggled at the best of times and deserted immediately when times got bad. And, invariably, stole and murdered and raped as naturally as a vulture eats carrion.

To the devil with them. "Agreed," he said, and they shook hands on it.

That still left some practical problems. Food and drink, first and foremost. Most of their supplies had been in the wagons, and the wagons had been with the infantry. By now, Kresse's men would have captured all of them.

Lovrenc would have to beg, as much as he disliked the idea. They simply couldn't start foraging, not in these mountains and with Kresse's men all over. In the real world, the antiseptic term "foraging" meant "stealing from the local farmers and villages." The minute they started, they'd be in a battle—and one they were sure to lose.

His thoughts must have shown on his face. Kresse smiled and said: "I'll let you have enough provender to get out of the Vogtland."

Stiffly, Lovrenc nodded. "Thank you."

Kresse shrugged. "Saves me grief, too." He cocked his head a little, a curious expression coming to his face. "Where will you go now?"

Bravnicar took off his helmet and ran his fingers through his thick hair. Even on a September day that wasn't particularly hot, a man's head started to swelter inside a helmet. There was a little breeze, too, which felt very good.

"I don't know," he said, seeing no purpose to lying. "Even if we'd reached Bavaria, I wasn't planning to stay there. Being a Protestant officer in Duke Maximilian's employ could get risky."

Kresse grunted. "And now they say he's gone mad."

Lovrenc had his doubts about that. From everything he'd heard, Bavaria's ruler had always been a little mad.

"You could always go to Bohemia," Kresse said. "I'm sure Wallenstein will be hiring, as tense as things are with the Austrians."

Lovrenc might have flushed a little. "That would be...ah, problematic. At the beginning of my career, I was with General Piccolomini."

"So?"

"So if Wallenstein has read any of the up-time accounts of his life—which you can be sure and certain he has—he'll know that in the universe the Americans came from Piccolomini was one of the central plotters who had him assassinated."

"Ah." Kresse shook his head. "Still, you were not directly involved. Perhaps Wallenstein is not holding a grudge against you."

"Quite possibly not. But would *you* gamble on it?"

Kresse laughed. "I see your point. Austria, then."

This time, Lovrenc was sure he was flushing. "Well... there might be other difficulties in Vienna. A youthful indiscretion..."

That sounded silly even to him, coming as it did from a cavalry captain who was all of twenty-six years old.

Kresse laughed again. Then, said nothing for a few seconds. He had an odd look on his face.

"How much do you need?" he asked abruptly.

"Excuse me?"

"In the way of pay. For you and your company."

Bravnicar frowned. "It's complicated. Depends on which realm—"

Kresse waved his hand impatiently. "Never mind. We have little in the way of coin anyway. Will you work for room and board? For... let's say three months. No, best make it four. Until the end of the year. By then, I may be able to come up with some money to continue your employment. Hard to say. But at least it'd give you a port in the storm for a few months. And I think I could use a good cavalry unit."

Bravnicar was too dumbfounded to reply. He'd never heard of *rebels*—farmers, at that—trying to hire professional soldiers.

Kresse's companion grinned. "It's just like in the movie."

The last term was incomprehensible. It didn't even sound like a German word.

"Like in the . . . what?"

"Movie. Motion picture. It's a device the Americans have to turn lots and lots of images into the illusion of an ongoing story. One of the CoCers we met in Magdeburg explained it to me. I got curious so Anna and I went to one of the theaters they've set up just to watch the things. Some up-timer and his German partners figured out a way to— Well. Never mind. I don't really understand it myself. Anyway, we watched a movie the up-timers had made. Not the Americans, but the Japanese. They called it *The Seven Samurai*. It was about this peasant village in the Japanese islands who hired mercenaries to protect them from bandits."

Bravnicar was now completely confused. "You've got *Japanese* cavalry too? How did they get here?"

Chapter 25

Vaxholm Island, in the Stockholm Archipelago

Charles Mademann had a disgusted look on his face when he came into the tavern. "Well, that's it," he announced. "The word is that Princess Kristina and Prince Ulrik will be returning to Denmark ten days from now."

Guillaume Locquifier, seated at the head of the large table in the center of the tavern's main room, glanced warningly at the door leading to the kitchens. Geerd Bleecker's voice could be heard talking to his wife, although the words couldn't be made out. The two of them were the only ones living here, except for customers—and the only customers at the moment were the Huguenots sitting at the table.

Mathurin Brillard looked up from the book he was reading, a French translation of Melanchthon's *Augsburg Confession*. Despite the rigor and ferocity of their political views and tactics, the group of Huguenots organized around Antoine Delerue and Michel Ducos were rather relaxed about their religious beliefs. They considered themselves members of the

Reformed tradition but lacked the sectarian fervor of many Calvinist groups. Their principal concern was with the political situation in France, not theological doctrine. If one of their members found it interesting to study the views of Lutherans—Brillard even read Catholic and Jewish thinkers on occasion—no one would say anything, not even Ducos. Not when Mathurin was their foremost marksman and had demonstrated for years his loyalty and reliability in the struggle against Cardinal Richelieu and the oppression of France's Protestants.

"This information is solid?" he asked.

Mademann shrugged. "As solid as any such information can be. There's no doubt that the royal party is *planning* to leave at that time. I was told this by servants, porters and stevedores alike, and they all agreed on the date of departure. But who's to say a princess won't change her mind at the last minute?"

"Not likely," grunted Robert Ouvrard. After the many weeks they'd spent watching Princess Kristina, they knew full well how much the heir to the throne disliked being near her mother. If there was any surprise, it was that she had stayed in Stockholm for this long. That was probably the result of strict orders from her father.

Brillard set down his book. "No, it's not likely. Which means we have not much more than a week to get everything in order and hope we get an opportunity to strike."

Mademann pulled out a chair and sat down at the table next to Guillaume. As he did so, he nodded toward the kitchen.

"It's getting more difficult," he said softly. The full

party of Huguenots had been living at the tavern for almost two months. As the time had passed, the tavern-keeper and his wife had begun to wonder what they were really about. Twice, most of them had had to leave for a week or so on a purported business trip just to allay his suspicions—and on one of those occasions, they'd missed the best chance they'd had to complete their mission.

Brillard glanced at Ancelin. The former tailor gave a little nod.

"When the time comes," said Brillard, "Gui and I will take care of the problem."

Mademann didn't doubt they would. There was very little Gui couldn't do quietly with a blade, especially with Mathurin to help him.

He turned to Locquifier. "The forgeries are ready, yes?"

He got an irritated look in response. "Yes, of course they are. I've had them ready since we got here."

Mademann started to press the matter but desisted. Guillaume would just get belligerent. He'd just have to hope the forgeries were up to date.

The problem with Locquifier was that his adulation of Ducos and Delerue was coupled to a tendency to underestimate their opponents. So, having put together and brought to Sweden the needed forgeries, he would ignore or take too lightly the need to make sure the documents reflected the most recent events. Charles had seen the forgeries. At least one of those documents contained a reference to the state of mobilization of the USE's army—while still in their camp near Magdeburg. Weeks had passed since then, weeks during which that army had defeated the forces of John George and occupied Saxony. Would it be logical to have no references to those events in documents that purported to be regular instructions from one of Cardinal Richelieu's top assistants?

Possibly—if none of the documents contained any such references. Perhaps Etienne Servien was a strict taskmaster who saw no need to provide information to his agents. But in that case, why were so many of those forgeries full to the brim of long-winded analyses of contemporary political events—and not just in France but in much of the rest of Europe?

That would have been Antoine Delerue's doing. The man was a brilliant analyst, no doubt about it. But he had little experience with field work and something of a tendency to show off his talents. Charles was sure he hadn't been able to resist filling the forgeries with his version of what he thought the cardinal's minions would think.

It was very frustrating, sometimes. The up-timers had a motto that Mademann wished his own people would maintain: *Keep it simple, stupid.* Instead, the forgeries were complex and intricate, which was all well and good if their internal logic was maintained. But doing so would require creating new forgeries— here in a backwater tavern on a Swedish island, with few of the resources they'd had in their possession in Edinburgh.

Charles was pretty sure Locquifier had simply never bothered to up-date the forgeries. He probably figured the risk of botching the work was worse than the risk of having their inconsistencies spotted after the fact. And . . . he might well be right. The quality of the local constabulary no doubt left much to be desired,

these days. Gustav Adolf's overweening continental
ambitions had stripped Sweden—not a populous nation
to begin with—of a tremendous number of its more
capable people. In all likelihood, the forgeries would
be examined by men who would understand far too
little of the political and military subtleties involved
to see that the forgeries were inconsistent.

That assumed that they succeeded in their task at
all, of course. After weeks of being stymied, Mademann was no longer confident of that. Eleven days
from now, they might be on their way back to the
continent with the forgeries in their luggage, having
accomplished nothing. All they'd leave behind for the
constabulary to investigate would be a double homicide
with no apparent motive.

Robbery perhaps. Mademann considered that, for a
moment. If they also plundered the tavern, suspicion
might fall on the local fishermen.

But... No. *Keep it simple, stupid.* They themselves
would inevitably be the principal suspects, since they'd
stayed here long enough that many people had seen
them. In the unlikely event their escape vessel was
intercepted, it would be best if there were no evidence on board.

Which, now that he thought about it, meant that
they'd have to jettison all the forgeries too, in a
weighted sack of some kind.

He'd have to see to that himself. If he raised it
with Locquifier, the man would have a fit. *We cannot
fail Michel and Antoine!*

Guillaume could be tiresome.

Stockholm

"I'm exhausted," said Baldur Norddahl, as soon as he sat down at the table. "How soon are we leaving? Ten days? I may not last."

Caroline Platzer spooned some pork dumplings into a bowl and handed it to him.

"Dumplings for breakfast?" he complained. "Again? It's no wonder I'm exhausted."

Caroline thought that was amusing, coming from a man who thought a proper breakfast centered around salted fish. She herself had found it hard to adjust to almost all aspects of Scandinavian cuisine, with the exception of pancakes covered in lingonberries. Those were delicious. The best that could be said of the rest of it was that mashed carrots were innocuous enough and meatballs were sometimes decent—if the spices were kept under control, which Swedes seemed to find it difficult to manage.

It was no wonder they'd gone a-viking back in the Dark Ages. Driven by indigestion, drawn by the promise of good English food.

Thankfully, it was almost over. Just another week and a half, and they'd be rid of the Mad Queen and her court full of dwarves.

Kristina looked up from her own bowl of dumplings. "Stop complaining! You think you're exhausted? You get to hide most of the time. Try being me."

The Swedish princess was in a cheerful mood, as she always was in the morning. Within two weeks of their arrival in Stockholm, they'd begun the practice of sharing breakfast in one of the smaller kitchens in the palace that Ulrik and Baldur had appropriated on the grounds that they needed their own Danish cuisine.

The Swedish officials who oversaw the running of the palace accepted that readily enough, even though so far as Caroline could tell the only difference between Swedish and Danish cooking was that the Danes used more cheese and sausages. Like Swedes, they doted on salted fish.

For breakfast. The Ring of Fire had a lot to answer for.

Perhaps the worst of it was that Caroline had had to learn to cook the damn stuff herself. These informal breakfasts also served them as impromptu gripe sessions, and it really wouldn't do to have servants overhearing the conversation.

Naturally, that meant the woman in the group had to do the cooking. The seventeenth century wasn't the bottomless pit of male chauvinism that Caroline would have supposed it to be, in those hard-to-remember days when she'd lived up-time. Assuming she'd ever thought about the seventeenth century at all, which so far as she could remember she'd had the good sense not to. Still, some attitudes were so ingrained that they just weren't worth fighting over, if the issue wasn't really that important.

So, she cooked and the men ate. She served them the food, too. On the plus side, they didn't think anything amiss when she sat down at the table to join them. Even more on the plus side, her willingness to cook minimized Baldur's periodic *let-the-man-show-you-how-it's-done* seizures. On those nightmarish occasions, Norddhal would show off his Norwegian skills at high cuisine.

That meant fish, of course. Salted fish. Smoked fish. Salted smoked fish. Spicy salted smoked fish.

Caroline's father had done the same thing—with hamburgers and steaks, though, not this godawful stuff—in outdoor summer barbecues. She could remember her mother saying on those occasions, "Men. They're still in the caves, you know."

She'd been wiser than she knew. Caroline felt a pang of loss.

"May I have some more dumplings, please?" asked Kristina.

"Just one." Caroline spooned the dumpling into the princess' outstretched bowl, then spooned two more into a bowl of her own and sat down. "Or you'll get fat."

"Ha!" jeered Kristina. With some reason. The eight-year-old girl seemed to have the metabolism of a furnace.

Leaving the food aside, and the unpleasantness of dealing with Kristina's mother, Caroline thought this trip had had a couple of positive effects on the princess. For one thing, without her usual down-time ladies in waiting to keep disorienting the kid and reinforcing her bad habits, Kristina was starting to develop some social graces.

Courtesy, first and foremost. Neither Caroline nor Ulrik—nor Baldur, certainly—treated the girl like she was the sunrise and the morning dew. Once Kristina had started absorbing the initial lessons, she'd quickly figured out that if she was polite to the servants of the palace they would in turn do favors for her. Like helping her hide from her mother and her mother's many obnoxious toadies.

More important, though, Caroline thought, was that the trip had produced a subtle but profound shift in

Kristina's relationship with Ulrik. She'd grown closer to the Danish prince and had begun to rely upon him.

Trust was not something that came easily or readily to the Swedish princess. That had become apparent to Caroline early on in her relationship with the girl. At the time, she'd ascribed it simply to Kristina's innate character, but the experience of this trip had modified that assessment. Caroline could now easily understand how the girl's upbringing would have shaped her in that direction.

If her father had been around more often, things might have been different. In the presence of Gustav Adolf, Kristina was a much happier and less difficult person than she was at most other times. But the king of Sweden, while he was obviously very fond of his daughter, was a man with many ambitions and preoccupations. He simply hadn't been around that often as she grew up.

Ulrik didn't have as much in the way of sheer raw intelligence as Kristina did. The girl was almost frighteningly precocious. But he was still a very smart man in his own right. What was more important, in Caroline's opinion, was that the Danish prince was also a wise man. Amazingly so, in fact, for someone who was only twenty-four years old. Ulrik had an ability to deliberate that you'd expect in a man twice his age—assuming the man in question was a wise man himself. He was prudent without being unduly cautious; temperate without being indecisive; and his automatic first impulse in the face of any problem or challenge was to reason rather than emote.

Caroline Platzer thought very highly of Ulrik, just as she did of Kristina. And, as she ate her dumplings at the same table with them, never thought twice of her presumption in analyzing and guiding the future rulers of much of Europe.

Why should she? She was a social worker, just doing her job, in a time and place that really needed the job done.

A field outside Dresden

"This will do nicely," announced Eddie Junker. Hands on hips, he surveyed the pasture again. "Very nicely."

Noelle Stull turned to the farmer and handed him a pouch full of coins. "Remember, you have to put up a good fence. There's enough in there to cover the cost."

Eddie nodded. "Very important. Or you might have a dead cow and—worse still—I might have a dead me."

The farmer didn't argue the point, once he finished counting the coins. "Not a problem. Keep my sons busy after they finish man-ma"—he stumbled over the English word a bit—"manicuring the pasture. Or they'll waste too much time in the taverns."

"Remember," Eddie said sternly. "Not one stone left in the field bigger than my thumb."

He held up the thumb in question. Standing next to him, Denise Beasley looked up at it and laughed.

"That thumb! A rhino could stumble over it." She held up her own thumb. "No bigger than this one."

The farmer squinted at the much smaller appendage, then shook his head. "Too much work."

"Leave it be, Denise," said Eddie. "My thumb's not all *that* big and—"

"I'm the expert on your thumb, buddy, not you, on account of—"

"Hey!" squawked Noelle.

Denise gave her a cherubic smile. "On account of I've hitchhiked with him."

"It's true," said Minnie. "Eddie's thumb can stop a truck. Of course, it helps when Denise and I"—here she hoisted her skirt and stuck out a leg—"show off too."

The leg was in stockings, but the stockings were very tight. The farmer looked a lot more intrigued at the sight than a man in his late forties with a still-living wife and three sons ought to look. But Noelle supposed it was hard to blame him. Minnie Hugelmair didn't have her best friend Denise Beasley's almost-outrageously good looks, but she was a still a healthy and shapely young woman. True, she had a glass eye and a little scar there, but people of the seventeenth century were more accustomed to such disfigurements than up-timers were. Smallpox left much worse scars on a face.

"I think we're done here," Noelle said. It was less of a statement than a plea.

Part Five

October 1635

The motion of our human blood

Chapter 26

The south bank of the Odra river, near Zielona Góra

"I don't want a repeat of what happened in Świebodzin, Captain Higgins. If you have to, shoot somebody. If that doesn't work, shoot a lot of somebodies. Shoot as many as it takes until they cease and desist. Is that understood?"

Mike Stearns was still icily furious, as he'd been for the last two days. Jeff had never seen him in such a state of mind.

Świebodzin had been hideous, though, sure enough. Some of the Finnish auxiliary cavalry that Gustav Adolf had attached to the Third Division had run amok once they got into the town and got their hands on some of the local vodka, the stuff they called "bread wine." They started sacking the town, with the atrocities that went with it. To make things worse, a couple of companies from an infantry battalion joined in. By the time Mike was able to put a stop to it, half the town had burned down and at least three dozen Polish civilians had been murdered and that many women

315

had been raped. Nine of the dead were children. So were six of the raped girls, including one who was not more than eight years old.

There'd been about twenty of the rioting soldiers who'd been too stupid or too drunk to hide once order starting getting restored. Mike's way of disciplining those soldiers caught in the act had shocked the entire division. He'd had them tied to a wooden fence in a nearby pasture and executed by volley gun batteries at what amounted to point blank range. There hadn't been a single intact corpse left. They'd just gathered up all the pieces and shoved them into a mass grave.

Some of the Finns started to fight back, but Mike soon put a stop to that also. He had his own cavalry now, and they weren't fond of the Finns to begin with. Eight of the Finns were killed outright, and about forty deserted. Mike didn't bother to chase them. A few dozen light cavalrymen simply couldn't survive for very long in a countryside that was as hostile as western Poland. Sooner or later they'd have no choice but to turn themselves in to one of the army units. Of course, they'd choose one of Gustav Adolf's Swedish regiments rather than returning to the USE Third Division. But Mike would deal with that problem when the time came.

The reason the Third Division now had its own cavalry regiment was because Gustav Adolf had decided to march into Poland in six different columns. Dividing his forces like that was risky, of course, but he hadn't really had much choice given that he was determined to move quickly. Marching fifty thousand men through country that had no travel routes except dirt roads and cow trails made spreading out a necessity. Gustav

Adolf figured he could take the risk because the six columns were close enough to be able to reinforce each other fairly quickly.

The northernmost column was made up of units representing about half of his own Swedish forces, under the command of Heinrich Matthias von Thurn. That column's mission was to invest the town of Gorzów from the north, while Wilhelm V and his Hesse-Kassel army would approach Gorzów along the south bank of the Warta river, one of the tributaries of the Oder. Between them, they should be able to take the town. A large part of the population was Lutheran and Gustav Adolf thought they'd be happy to switch sides.

Gustav Adolf himself led the third column, marching south of Hesse-Kassel. That army consisted of the rest of the Swedish army—and all of the APCs. Gustav Adolf's column was going straight for Poznań, the principal city in western Poland. "Going straight," that is, insofar as the terrain allowed. Like most of Poland, the area was quite flat. But it was also quite wet, with lots of winding streams; and while it didn't have the profusion of lakes characteristic of northeast Poland it still had a fair number.

Thankfully, they were mostly little ones. Still, one of the things Mike's short experience as a general had taught him was the geographic variation on Clausewitz's dictum. Terrain that doesn't look too tough is a lot tougher than it looks when you have to move ten thousand men through it. And keep them in some reasonable semblance of order. And provide them with a secure and hopefully dry place to sleep at night, with proper sanitation. And feed them. And do all that while being prepared at any moment to fight the enemy.

Gustav Adolf had put himself in charge of that middle column because he was sure that Koniecpolski would have to defend Poznań. So he would come straight at him while Torstensson and two of the USE army's three divisions would approach Poznań from the southwest.

That left Mike in charge of the sixth and southernmost column. His job was to take and hold Zielona Góra, thereby providing the Swedish and USE forces with a secure southern anchor. Zielona Góra would also serve later as the base for moving down the Odra to take Wroclaw.

The area they were operating in was a border region that, over the centuries, had been controlled at various times by Poland, Brandenburg and Austria. In the timeline the Americans came from, it might well have been in German hands at this time. Many of these border cities had converted to Lutheranism and gotten out from under Polish Catholic control.

In the here and now, however, Poland had taken advantage of the CPE and later the USE's preoccupation with internal affairs and the war against the League of Ostend to reassert its authority over the area. Brandenburg had tacitly acquiesced, probably because George William had figured he might someday need Polish support. The border between Polish and German lands now ran along the Oder-Neisse line just as it had in Mike's universe after World War II. The Odra was completely within Polish territory and Breslau was back to being Wroclaw.

Gustav Adolf didn't expect Stearns would run into

severe opposition. Koniecpolski had fewer forces than Gustav Adolf did, and he'd be hard-pressed to detach any large force to come to the assistance of Zielona Góra. In essence, the king of Sweden had given Mike the easiest and most straightforward assignment. But in order for him to carry out that assignment, Torstensson had had to give Mike one of his cavalry regiments, so he wouldn't be operating blind. The weather was erratic enough this time of year that the Air Force's ability to fly reconnaissance missions couldn't always be counted on.

"Is that understood, Captain Higgins?" Mike repeated.

Jeff nodded. "Yes, sir. But . . . ah . . ."

Mike waited, with a cocked eyebrow.

Jeff took a deep breath. "Why me, Mike? Ah, sir."

For the first time since Jeff had arrived at the Third Division's field headquarters, Mike's expression lightened a little. Not much, but Jeff was still glad to see it, he surely was. He'd known Mike Stearns most of his life. This was the first time the man had ever scared him. Really scared him. An enraged Mike Stearns bore no resemblance at all to the man Jeff had grown accustomed to.

"Why you? It ought to be obvious, Jeff. You're the one commander I've got who's guaranteed to put the fear of God in every man in this division."

Jeff stared at him. He was trying to make sense of that last sentence and coming up blank.

"Huh?"

"That's 'huh, sir.' For Pete's sake, Jeff, do you think there's one single soldier in this division who doesn't know you're Gretchen Richter's husband?"

"Huh? Uh, sir."

"Talk about the innocence of babes. I can guarantee

you that at one time or another every soldier in this division has wondered what she sees in you and come to the conclusion that you must have one huge pair of brass balls. Given that she makes kings and dukes shit their pants."

Mike shook his head. "So do they really want to run the risk of pissing you off, Captain Higgins? No, Colonel Higgins, rather. Now that I think about it, I'll have to jump you up to lieutenant colonel since I'm going to put a whole regiment under your command."

"*Huh?* Ah... Huh, sir. Mike—General, I just got put in charge of a battalion three months ago, and now you want to hand me a whole *regiment*? But—but—"

He was spluttering a little, he was so agitated. "But, first of all—uh, sir—we don't have the rank of lieutenant colonel in the USE army. And second of all—uh, meaning no disrespect, sir—but which regiment are you planning to give me? I mean, that's really gonna piss off whichever colonel—real colonel—you take it away from." He took another deep breath. "Sir," he added, not knowing what else to say. He didn't *think* Mike would have him put up in front of a volley gun, but...

Mike smiled. There was no humor at all in it, but it beat a scowl hands down. "I'm a major general, Colonel Higgins. That means I can do damn near anything I want. I can sure as hell create the brevet rank of 'lieutenant colonel' for a special purpose. Just to keep all the other colonels happy, you'll stay at a captain's pay grade."

"Thank you, sir. I'd appreciate that. I, ah, don't actually need the money anymore."

Mike's smile widened. There still wasn't any humor in it, though. "As for your other objection, I'm not planning to give you any existing regiment. I'm creating a new one. It'll consist of your Twelfth Battalion, and a battalion taken from the Gray Adder regiment. That'll leave them a rump regiment, and ask me if I care, since they're the shitheads who let two of their companies run wild."

Jeff swallowed. Mike had had the major in command of that battalion executed also, along with the captains in command of the two companies—although he'd done them the courtesy of using a regular firing squad, not the volley guns. Then he'd broken every officer in the battalion to the ranks and replaced them with newly promoted sergeants from other battalions.

As a display of savage discipline, Jeff thought the ghosts of Roman tribunes past were applauding somewhere. The whole division was in something of a state of shock. Until Świebodzin, Stearns had seemed like a very easy-going sort of general.

"Then I'm giving you Captain Engler's flying artillery company instead of a regular artillery unit. For the purpose of your new regiment, he fits the bill perfectly."

Stearns had used Engler's unit to carry out the executions. Between that and the man's well-known composure at Ahrensbök and Zwenkau, everyone in the division would take him dead seriously. Nobody made jokes any longer about "the Count of Narnia."

Well, Eric Krenz probably still did. Jeff wondered how he was doing. And then wondered who he'd put in charge of the 12th now that he was being kicked upstairs. Krenz would have been his natural replacement as battalion commander, but he wasn't available and Jeff had no idea when or if he might be.

"Your new regiment will fight alongside all the others in a battle," Mike continued. "But it has a special function as well whenever I call on it. You're the unit I'll be depending on to keep everyone else in line. Do you understand me, Colonel Higgins? I want no repetition of Świebodzin. *Ever.*"

Jeff looked around. They were holding this private conversation in one of the rooms of the small village tavern Mike had taken for his field headquarters. "Taken" as in "expropriated," although no one had gotten hurt because the people who owned the tavern along with everyone in the village had fled before the division arrived.

You could hardly blame them. The news of Świebodzin had spread widely and rapidly. But the expropriation of the tavern itself illustrated the fundamental problem, which was practical at its very core.

It would be nice if atrocities resulted solely and simply from the wickedness of men. Were that true, they could be suppressed by the simple use of harsh discipline. Unfortunately, the world was more complicated—and if Mike Stearns didn't understand that, Jeff would have to explain it to him.

He hesitated, and took another deep breath.

To hell with it. If he shoots me, he shoots me.

And to hell with military protocol, too.

"Mike, this ain't gonna work. Sure, I can probably put a stop to crazy shit like what happened at Świebodzin. But that's just the tip of the iceberg—and you oughta know it. We have to get supplies. And how are we going to do that? We've already pretty much run out of what we brought with us from Berlin. That means foraging, and foraging means stealing, and the way Koniecpolski's been running us ragged there's no way to round up enough supplies except to send out lots and lots of foraging parties and there's no way in hell you or me or anybody can stay in control of that and before you know it some cavalry unit or some infantry squad is going to kill a farmer who squawks too much when they take one of his pigs and then they're likely to rape his wife or daughter or likely both and kill the rest of the kids while they're at it. And what good is my shiny new regiment gonna be?"

Mike put a hand on Jeff's shoulder. "Relax. I know the realities of this kind of warfare and I'm going to start taking some steps to ameliorate it. I don't expect perfection, Jeff. I know there'll be incidents. And even if I come down on them as I hard as I did after Świebodzin—and you can bet your sweet ass I will—some of those crimes will go unpunished because there's no one left alive to report them except the culprits and they sure as hell won't. But that's still not the same thing as wholesale slaughter. That, we can control—with your new regiment."

Jeff took another deep breath, and slowly blew it out. "Okay, then. We'll need a name."

Somehow or other, the tradition had gotten started in the USE army of using names instead of numbers for the regiments. The names had no official existence, but nobody except idiot accountants used the regiments' numbers anymore.

"Call it the Death Watch," said Mike. "Better yet, call it the Hangman."

Jeff thought about it, for a few seconds. "The guys'll probably like that, actually. Well, the ones *in* the regiment, anyway. Don't know about the others."

"Yeah, I think you're right."

They were silent, for another few seconds. Then Jeff said, "Off the record, Mike, you know how fucked up that is?"

For the first time, a trace of humor crept into Mike's smile. "The Ring of Fire didn't cut us any slack, did it?"

After Mike finished explaining what he wanted, David Bartley frowned. The young financier-turned-army-lieutenant stared at the surface of the table he and Mike were sitting at, in the back room of the tavern that Mike was using for his headquarters. His eyes didn't seem quite in focus.

"Pretty tricky, sir," he said after perhaps a minute. "There's no chance of using TacRail like we did in the Luebeck campaign?"

Mike shook his head. "We're not fighting French and Danes here, Lieutenant Bartley. Leaving aside his own cavalry, Koniecpolski's got several thousand Cossacks under his command. They're probably the best mounted raiders in Eurasia, except for possibly the Tatars. TacRail units would get eaten alive before they'd laid more than a few miles of track, unless we detailed half our battalions to guard them. Which we can't afford to do."

Bartley nodded. "That leaves what you might call creative financing."

"That's what I figured—and it's why I called you in."

The lieutenant looked unhappy. "The regular quartermasters are already kinda mad at me, sir. If I—"

"Don't worry about it. To begin with, I'm pulling you out of the quartermaster corps altogether. You'll be in charge of a new unit which I'm calling the Exchange Corps."

"Exchange? Exchange what, exactly?"

Mike gave David the same humorless grin he'd given Jeff an hour earlier. "That's for you to figure out. Whatever you can come up with that'll enable us to obtain supplies from the locals without completely pissing them off. No way not to piss them off at all, of course. But the Poles have had as much experience with war over the last thirty years as the Germans. They'll take things philosophically enough as long we aren't killing and raping and burning and taking so much that people die over the winter."

Again, Bartley went back to staring at the table top with unfocussed eyes.

"Okay," he said eventually. "I've got some ideas. But I'll need a staff, General. Not too big. Just maybe three or four clerks and, ah, one sort of specialist. His name's Sergeant Beckmann. Well, Corporal Beckmann, now. I got him his stripe back but then he ran afoul of—well, never mind the details—and got busted back to corporal."

"Where is he now? And what sort of specialist is he?"

"He's right here in the Third Division, sir. One of the quartermasters in von Taupadel's brigade. As for his specialty... Well, basically he's a really talented swindler."

Mike laughed. And then realized it was the first time he'd laughed since he saw the carnage in the streets of Świebodzin.

"Okay, you got him—and we'll give the man back his sergeant's stripe. May as well, since I'm promoting you to captain."

David looked very pleased. That was just another of the many peculiar results of the Ring of Fire, Mike thought. Take a rural teenage kid and put him somewhere he can become a millionaire—but he still gets a bigger charge out of getting a promotion to a rank whose monthly salary was about what he earned in three hours of playing the stock market.

The Ring of Fire might not have cut anyone any slack, but here and there it had certainly played favorites.

Chapter 27

Zielona Góra

At least he was off the damn horse. Which was just as well, since another part of the house wall Jeff was crouched behind came down right then, knocked loose by a shot from one of the Poles' culverins. He was barely able to scramble aside and keep from getting half-buried in the rubble. The Polish guns fired balls that weighed at least twenty pounds. They were old-fashioned round shot, not explosive shells, but they could do plenty of damage to anything they hit directly.

Or *anyone* they hit directly. Jeff had seen one of Engler's artillerymen cut right in half. The sight had been as bizarre as it was ghastly. The soldier's body from the waist down had stayed in the saddle, his legs still gripping the horse and his feet still in the stirrups. It had still been there the last Jeff saw the horse, which—the beasts weren't always as dumb as they looked—had turned right around and gone galloping back around a bend in the road.

Meanwhile, spewing blood and intestines, the top half of the soldier had gone pinwheeling into the nearby stream the maps called Złota Łącza, however the hell that was pronounced. The half-corpse was still there, too. The Polish counterattack had been so ferocious that Jeff hadn't yet had the time or the spare men to send out burial parties. If a man was wounded, they'd do their best to rescue him. If he was dead, he'd just have to wait.

Jason Linn came running in a crouch and threw himself down alongside Jeff. The two of them along with three infantrymen were taking shelter behind what was left of the house. During battles, the mechanical repairman who kept the flying artillery's equipment operational served Captain Engler as a gofer. In this case, as a message runner.

The newly formed Hangman Regiment had had six radios in its possession. One of them was not working for reasons yet unclear. Another had been broken when its operator took cover too enthusiastically. A third one had just gone missing. Jeff was pretty sure the operator had sold it on the black market in a drunken stupor. They'd probably never know, however, since the operator in question had gotten himself killed in the first two minutes of the battle.

Of the three remaining radios, only one was still functional. The other two had taken direct hits from musket balls—just the radios; the operators had been completely untouched. Jeff was still outraged at the statistical absurdities involved. Murphy's Law by itself was one thing. Any sane person learned to take it into account by the he or she was fourteen years old. But in time of war, that mythical son-of-a-bitch went on steroids. It was no longer the fairly reasonable and straightforward principle *if it can go wrong, it will go wrong.* Oh, hell, no. Now the clause got added: *it'll go wrong even if it can't, too.*

Jeff had had no choice but to keep the sole remaining radio in reserve, for use whenever he needed to reach divisional headquarters. For the purposes of communicating with his own units, he'd had to fall back on the old-fashioned method. Send somebody and hope they don't get killed and use bugles and hope they could be heard over the unholy racket.

Another little chunk of the wall went flying. That had been caused by a grazing hit. Most of the ball's energy went into turning the rubble that had once been a house thirty yards back into slightly less organized rubble.

The second law of thermodynamics also went into overdrive during wartime, Jeff had learned. Entropy in the fast lane.

"Captain Engler is ready, Colonel!" Even positioned two feet away, Linn had to half-shout. The din wasn't quite as bad as it had been at Zwenkau, for the simple reason that there weren't as many guns involved. But the soldiers manning those various weapons were firing them as enthusiastically as you could ask for, on both sides. And now, here and there, the distinctive claps made by hand grenades were being added to the bedlam.

They'd be hearing more of those, Jeff figured, the farther the regiment pushed into the town.

On the plus side, it wasn't that big a town. On the minus side, every square foot seemed to have a damn Pole in it.

None of them were civilians, either, so far as Jeff could tell. Those had apparently skedaddled before the Third Division got within five miles of the place.

At least Jeff wouldn't have to worry about atrocities committed against innocent bystanders.

Swell. Now he could concentrate on the problem of atrocities committed against him and his. The Poles were no sweethearts, and God help you if you fell into the hands of Cossacks. Whatever romantic notions about them Jeff could vaguely remember having back up-time had vanished the first time he came across the mutilated corpse of one of his soldiers who'd been taken prisoner four days earlier. The Cossacks had obviously spent some time on the project.

About the only virtues possessed by Cossacks other than their strictly martial abilities, so far as Jeff could tell, was the dubious one of being equal opportunity savages. From the evidence he'd seen, they were just as dangerous to Polish civilians as they were to anyone they were fighting.

Jeff had made clear to his men that he wouldn't tolerate atrocities, no matter who they were committed against. But his definition of "atrocity" was reasonably practical. He wasn't going to look into the fact that nobody seemed to be taking Cossack prisoners, as long as there was no evidence they'd been tortured.

Of course, they hadn't taken many prisoners of any kind so far. The only way you'd get a hussar to surrender was if he'd been knocked off his horse, and even then he pretty much had to be knocked senseless. Polish infantrymen weren't as cussed crazy belligerent, but they were still plenty feisty.

Jeff had been surprised by that, more than he'd been surprised by anything else. He'd known the set-up in Poland, in broad outlines. A small class of great landowners—they called them magnates—lording it over a population that was mostly dirt-poor peasants, many of them outright serfs. But what he was now learning was that broad outlines don't really tell you very much about a given people's fighting capabilities.

After all, in broad outline, the antebellum American South had been a land dominated by a small class of great plantation masters who lorded it over the poor whites as well as their black slaves. That hadn't stopped the poor whites—talk about dumb!—from fighting for the slaveowners, had it?

What Jeff was now learning firsthand was just how savagely a class of people will fight to defend whatever small privileges they might have, even if they're purely social privileges, so long as those privileges loom large in their minds. That was especially true if the official *casus belli* was clear and straight-forward. *We've been invaded!*

Southern whites may have been poor, but at least they weren't black. Likewise, most of the szlachta weren't really much if any wealthier than the peasants they lived among. But at least they weren't peasants. They had *status*.

Poland and Lithuania were peculiar in that way, compared to most European countries. Their aristocracy was huge—probably a full ten percent of the population, where England's aristocracy wasn't more than three percent and even the sprawling German one wasn't more than five percent.

Only a few of those szlachta were really what Jeff would consider "large landowners." Those were the magnates, like Koniecpolski himself. Plenty of the szlachta didn't have the proverbial pot to piss in. But that only made them cherish even more their social position. In theory, at least, any member of the szlachta could marry the daughter of the richest magnate in the land and rise to any position in society.

So, the Polish infantry and artillery weren't the half-baked forces Jeff had expected. He'd known the hussars would make ferocious opponents, but he'd figured the rest of the Polish army would be like the Persian foot soldiers who'd faced Alexander the Great and his Macedonian phalanxes. When the crunch came down, they hadn't been worth much.

From what he'd been able to determine so far, however, szlachta made up a big chunk of the infantry and artillery they'd face since they closed in on Zielona Góra and the fighting started in earnest. These were some genuinely tough bastards, much more so than the Saxons had been. The soldiers working for John George—and that was exactly the relationship; a purely commercial one—had been professionals who, once a reasonable fight had been put up, were quite willing to surrender. In fact, any number of them were quite willing to go to work for the same people who'd just defeated them.

This was a whole different kettle of fish, now that they were moving into territory that was clearly and definitively Polish. That wasn't always clear, in border areas. Many of the towns near Brandenburg had been technically Polish in political terms, but the populations were often heavily German and Protestant. That was true of Zielona Góra itself, for that matter. Most of the town's population were Lutherans and they called it by the German name, Grünberg.

But the city's population had fled and the surrounding countryside was Polish, not German. As far as the szlachta were concerned, Gustav Adolf had renewed his longstanding aggression against the Polish lands. And if Poland's aristocracy was notorious for its political fecklessness, nobody in their right mind had ever thought they couldn't fight—assuming they could unite behind a leader.

There were times in Polish history where such a leader had been absent, and the resultant political disunity had left Poland's armies weakened or even largely on the sidelines. But unfortunately for Mrs. Higgins' son Jeffrey, this was not one of them. With his new-found money, Jeff had been able to buy down-time copies of three books on Polish history that had been in Grantville. It turned out—oh, joy—that the Ring of Fire had planted Mrs. Higgins' son Jeffrey right smack in the period of Polish history that had produced some of its most capable military leaders. Grand Hetman Stanislaw Koniecpolski was one of them. He'd been mentioned in all three books.

"Sir?"

Jeff suddenly realized that Linn had now shouted that question three times.

"Tell Engler to wait until I give the signal." That would have to be a bugle signal, now, thanks to Murphy. "Then come in from the north—but whatever he does, don't let himself get trapped in any side streets or alleys."

Because of its specific peculiar purpose, the Hangman Regiment was the only one in the division that didn't have regular artillery attached to it. Jeff was bitterly regretting that absence, now. Volley guns were splendid on an open field, but they weren't much use against the improvised fortifications you ran into in street fighting. Jeff would gladly swap Engler's entire unit right now for just one culverin and half a dozen mortars.

He'd even more gladly swap them for the support of another regiment or three. Where was the rest of the division? Since the fighting started this morning, Jeff hadn't seen any USE units except his own.

Linn nodded and raced off, still in a crouch. He'd have a horse nearby, tethered where it couldn't get hit except by a freak shot. Once he was on the horse, he should be able to reach Engler within fifteen minutes or so. The flying artillery company had been moving around the northern outskirts of Zielona Góra. If Jeff's map was accurate—always a chancy proposition—there should be a fairly wide avenue that led directly into the city's central square. Insofar as there was any city terrain that favored volley guns, that would be it.

Jeff didn't really expect Engler could do much except create a diversion. But he hoped that might be enough to enable him to get his infantry battalions moving again. They'd been completely stalled within ten minutes of the battle's start.

Street fighting sucked.

War sucked.

Murphy really sucked.

Where the hell was Mike Stearns?

Chapter 28

That very moment, Mike Stearns was wondering if Jeff Higgins was still alive. He might very well not be—and if he was dead, Mike would be the one who'd killed him.

He'd deliberately left Jeff's regiment twisting in the wind, and he'd done it for two reasons. The second of those reasons left Mike feeling a little sick to his stomach.

The first reason was straightforward: Higgins and his men had kept the Poles in Zielona Góra preoccupied while Mike moved the rest of the division around the city to the south. Once he launched his attack, he thought he could overwhelm the defenders pretty quickly. He'd be attacking from a direction they wouldn't expect and with overwhelming force.

The maneuver was tough on the Hangman Regiment, of course, but that was just the chances of war.

Hard-boiled, yes. But Mike's other motive had been a lot colder and more ruthless. He was utterly determined that no army under his command would ever again behave the way some of its units had at Świebodzin. That, of course, was the reason he'd formed the Hangman in the first place.

But if Mike was a neophyte at organized warfare, he was no stranger to conflict. He knew perfectly well what would happen if his new regiment simply had a reputation for being hard on soldiers in its own division. They might be feared, but they wouldn't be respected—and fear without respect only took you so far. Over time, they'd be looked on as the boss' toadies. The damage to Mike's reputation would be just as bad as the damage to their own. Nobody respected toadies. Most people didn't think much of a boss who surrounded himself with toadies, either.

The solution had been obvious. At the very first battle, shove the Hangman into the worst of it. If they acquitted themselves well, they'd start developing a very different reputation. People might not like hardasses, but they respected them as long as the hardass led from the front.

And if the inexperienced young colonel whom Mike had known since he was a kid and had forced into command wound up getting killed, so be it.

The Ring of Fire hadn't cut anybody any slack. If it had played favorites with Mike Stearns by skyrocketing him into a position of power and prominence that he almost certainly never would have known in the world he'd left behind, it had done so at a price. The Mike Stearns in that other universe had been a lot nicer man than the one he'd become in this one.

He wasn't sure exactly when the change had started, but Mike knew without a doubt the moment it had crystallized. That had been the day in his office, while he'd still been the USE's prime minister, when his then-spymaster Francisco Nasi had informed him that except for the two of them and the culprits themselves, no one in the world knew that Henry Dreeson had been murdered by French Huguenot fanatics instead of anti-Semites.

That murder had enraged the Committees of Correspondence all over the USE. They'd been primed for a fight, anyway. All Mike had to do was keep his mouth shut and the fury would fall on Germany's anti-Semites. The same sort of people who'd produced a holocaust in another universe, and in this one had been insulting and threatening Mike's own wife for years.

He hadn't agonized over the decision. In fact, he'd made it within two seconds. He'd gone further than keeping his mouth shut, too. At his command, Nasi had turned over to Gretchen Richter and Spartacus and Gunther Achterhof every file he had on the country's anti-Semitic organizations and prominent individuals. There'd been thousands of names in those lists. Not more than half of them had survived what came next.

What bothered Mike wasn't their fates, though. He had no sympathy at all for people like that. As far as he was concerned, they'd gotten what they had coming. Live by the pogrom, die by the pogrom.

No, what bothered him was his own ability to lie so smoothly and cold-bloodedly. Granted, the Mike Stearns he'd left behind hadn't run around compulsively telling everyone about every cherry tree he'd cut down. Still, he'd felt guilty on those occasions he had told a lie—and there hadn't been all that many to begin with.

To this day, he'd never felt the slightest twinge of remorse over his actions after the Dreeson Incident. None.

How many times could a man do something on

the grounds that the end justifies the means before he rubs away his conscience altogether?

Mike didn't know. What he did know was that today he was scraping away some more of it.

Christopher Long came racing up. The English officer was such a superb horseman that he didn't think anything at all about galloping his horse across any terrain as long as it was reasonably flat and dry. Here on the southern edge of Zielona Góra, Long's definition of "reasonably dry" bordered on lunacy as far as Mike was concerned. True, there hadn't been any rain lately so the soil wasn't muddy. But there were little streams and rills all over the place, some of which you couldn't see until the last moment. In fact, Long was about—

The Englishman came to the rill in question and casually leapt his horse over it. Ten seconds later he was drawing his mount alongside Mike's. His face was flushed with excitement, but that had to do with the military situation, not the trivial issue of jumping a horse while going twenty-five or thirty miles per hour.

"The Third Brigade is about to engage the enemy, sir!"

Two things struck Mike immediately.

The first was the invariably antiseptic nature of military terminology, which he had noticed before. "Engage the enemy." That meant that three thousand men under the command of Brigadier Georg Derfflinger were about to start murdering and/or maiming an as-yet-unknown number of Polish soldiers—who, for their part, would do their level best to return the favor. *Do unto others before they do unto you.*

Mike was pretty sure that sort of veiled language had been intrinsic to the military since the foot soldiers of Sargon "engaged" their Sumerian counterparts by running them over with chariots and hacking them to pieces with bronze axes.

The second thing Mike noticed was a lot more modern.

Once again, one of his brigade commanders had forgotten to use his radio. Instead, as commanders on battlefield had done since horses were domesticated, he'd sent a courier. That peculiar forgetfulness seemed to be ingrained in seasoned veterans like Derfflinger, even though the man was only twenty-nine years old.

For that matter, Long had obviously overlooked the radio as well—and he'd just turned twenty-six.

But now was not the time to berate anyone for being technological challenged.

"Where are von Taupadel and Schuster?" They were the commanders, respectively, of the 1st and 2nd Brigades. Along with Derfflinger, they were the Third Division's brigadiers.

Long pointed to the northeast. "Schuster's brigade has closed off the road to Wroclaw. Von Taupadel's continuing to push around the city to the east."

Of the two brigadiers, von Taupadel was the senior. He'd have instructed Schuster to fortify positions cutting the Wroclaw road while he took the more challenging task of continuing the flanking maneuver. That made sense, and it's what Mike would have told him to do had he been there. (Or if von Taupadel had thought to get in touch with him by radio, but never mind.) Schuster's brigade was the weakest in the division because Mike had stripped troops out of

the Black Falcon and Gray Adder regiments to form
Jeff's new Hangman Regiment. Its morale was shaky,
too, because except for the Finnish cavalrymen all
the soldiers who'd been executed for the atrocities at
Świebodzin had come from that brigade.

Mike hadn't punished Schuster or the colonel commanding the Gray Adder regiment. Schuster, because
he'd been elsewhere at the time and couldn't in fair-
ness be held responsible. The colonel, because he was
dead. His killing at the hands of a sniper, in fact, was
one of the things that had triggered off the slaughter.

But while he hadn't penalized Schuster, Mike had
privately made clear to him that if the 2nd Brigade
was guilty of another such incident, the brigadier could
expect to be cashiered on the spot. For a while, at
least, Schuster was bound to be excessively cautious.
So would his soldiers, for that matter. Guarding a road
from behind fixed positions would be a good way to
start rebuilding their confidence.

Mike spent a minute or so considering the situation. Ideally, he'd wait until von Taupadel had moved
his brigade far enough around Zielona Góra to cut
the road to Poznań. But that could take quite a bit
more time. They'd come by a circuitous route, following the Bóbr river and then marching cross-country
in order to approach Zielona Góra directly from the
west. The easier route would have been to follow the
Odra, which would have brought them close to the
city. But, of course, the Poles had planned for that
and built fortifications guarding the river.

The problem that Mike was now presented with was
that the road to Poznań started on the northeast side
of Zielona Góra. The 1st Brigade had to march almost

two-thirds of the way around the city in order to reach it. If Mike waited until they got there, the Hangman Regiment might get destroyed in the meantime.

He decided the chance they might encircle and capture all the Polish forces in Zielona Góra just wasn't worth the possible cost to Higgins and his men. That had always been something of a long shot, anyway.

He turned to Long. "Colonel, we'll send the Third Brigade directly into the city. Let Duerr take the word to Brigadier Derfflinger." Mike pointed to some nearby woods. "He's in there, taking care of urgent business."

Long frowned. "If it's urgent business, he may be occupied for a while yet."

Mike smiled. "He should be finishing up any second now. It's the sort of pressing business that never makes its way into fiction."

After a moment, Long chuckled. "I see. And myself?"

"I want you to get in touch with von Taupadel. I want him to forget about reaching the Poznań road and just go straight at whatever part of the city he'd closest to right now."

Long was back to frowning. "It'll take me some time to reach him, General. By the time I do—"

"Radio," Mike said. "Use. The. Radio."

He turned in his saddle and pointed back to his communications tent, which had been set up twenty yards away. Jimmy Andersen was standing outside the entrance flap, looking lonely and forlorn.

"Sergeant Andersen will operate it. He knows what he's doing. So does Brigadier von Taupadel's radio operator, if he hasn't died of neglect and boredom yet."

Long stared at the tent much the way a man might stare at an ogre's lair.

"The, ah, radio, sir?"

"Use. The. Radio. Now."

Duerr went straight to the radio tent as soon as he got out of the woods. Oddly enough, given his age and acerbic temperament, Duerr was more at ease around electronic technology than most younger officers. Within five minutes, all three brigade commanders had gotten their orders.

A minute later, the artillery barrages began. Ten minutes later, even at a distance of half a mile, Mike could hear the sounds of infantry regiments advancing on the city.

"About fucking time," grumbled Jeff Higgins. He and two of his captains were crouched over a map inside a small bakery. They'd been trying to figure out if there was any route that might extricate them from what had essentially turned into a trap. Unfortunately, the map was in as bad a shape as the regiment was by now. Being fair to the regiment, Jeff was sure that map had been lousy even in its prime.

Within thirty seconds, the noise produced by the artillery barrage made it impossible to talk anyway. Jeff signaled the two captains to return to their units. All they could do now was wait.

After it was all over, Mike's aides estimated that about half of the Polish forces who'd been defending Zielona Góra had made their escape to the northeast. The failure to cut off the Poznań road had allowed for that.

But von Taupadel didn't make more than token

noises of reproach. Except for the Hangman Regiment, the division's casualties had been light. Much lighter, he said, than was usual for an army taking a city as sizeable and as well-defended as this one had been.

"A good day's work, General," was his summary conclusion. "Very good day's work."

"I thought we'd need three days myself," said Derfflinger.

"So did I," chimed in Schuster.

The three brigadiers were giving Mike an odd sort of look. That expression stayed on their faces for the next half hour, too. After they left, he asked his aides if they'd noticed.

Duerr grinned. "They've decided you know what you're doing."

"Not exactly that," said Anthony Leebrick. "Meaning no disrespect, General Stearns, but you're not the subtlest military strategist the world has ever seen and your tactics are not what anyone would call complicated."

Long was grinning also. "You go here and hit them. You go over there and hit them too. Then both of you do it again."

All three officers laughed. Mike couldn't help but join in for a moment. It was true enough, after all.

When the laughter died out, Duerr shook his head. He wasn't smiling anymore.

"None of that really matters, General. Your brigadiers have come to the conclusion that the three of us came to some time ago. You are never indecisive and you are always willing to take the fight to the enemy. In war, that is what's most critical."

Long nodded. "Taking this city so quickly, coming

on top of what you did after Świebodzin. They have confidence in you now, General. They may not agree with your decisions, certainly. Von Taupadel obviously thinks you moved too soon and should have let him take the Poznań road. But those sorts of things do not really matter, so long as they have confidence that their commander will command."

Mike was not a egotist, but he enjoyed compliments as much as any human being does. He wasn't able to savor these, however. Right now, there was only one opinion that really concerned him.

He found Jeff Higgins lying on a cot in one of the back rooms of a somewhat battered but still intact bakery. Jeff didn't seem to be injured, just resting after what had been a nerve-wracking and exhausting day.

When he saw Mike come in, he started to get up, but Mike waved him back down.

"Relax, Jeff. This is an informal personal visit."

Jeff lay back down on the cot, propping his head on folded arms. After a short silence, he frowned and said, "I'm trying to figure something out. Did you set me up?"

The frown was simply an expression of puzzlement, not anger or condemnation.

Mike took off his cap and ran fingers through his hair. "I wouldn't put it that way, exactly. But, yes, I did use you as what amounted to bait in a trap."

Jeff thought about that, for a few seconds, staring up at the ceiling. Then the frown faded and he let out a little sigh.

"About what I figured. Did it work?"

"Sure did. We took the town in one day with light casualties—except for your regiment, that is. I've been told that's pretty unusual by people with a lot more experience at this than I have."

"Rough on the bait, though."

"Yes. It was. And I knew it would be when I sent you in."

Jeff lowered his eyes and looked at him. "You should have told me what you had planned, Mike. That's the only thing that pisses me off. But it really does piss me off. The Mike Stearns I used to know wouldn't have manipulated me like that."

"Fair enough. I won't do it again."

Jeff chuckled, in a dry sort of way. "Yeah, you will—and plenty of times. It's not like I don't understand why you do stuff like that, Mike. Just don't do it to me."

There was silence again, for perhaps a minute. Then Jeff sat up on the cot, swiveling his legs so his feet were on the floor.

"What now, boss?"

Mike shrugged. "Gustav Adolf just told me to take Zielona Góra. I don't think he expected we'd do it this soon. I sent him a radio message earlier but I haven't heard back from him yet."

"Hey, maybe we'll draw garrison duty for the rest of the war."

"I wouldn't count on it."

"You think?"

Chapter 29

Near the Warta river, northwest of Poznań

Wojtowicz's agent came into Stanislaw Koniecpolski's command tent, which had been pitched close to the river. It was more in the way of a pavilion, actually. Like the great magnate that he was, the grand hetman traveled in style even during wartime.

"Another message has arrived from Jozef," the agent announced. "And it's good news this time."

He gave the hand-written message to Koniecpolski.

Big storm coming. May last for days.

"Finally," he said. He turned to his aides, who half-filled the tent. "I want the army moving by dawn tomorrow. There's a Swede who needs killing."

Chapter 30

Vaxholm Island, in the Stockholm Archipelago

"Wonderful," muttered Charles Mademann. He stuck his head out of the tavern doorway and looked up at the early morning sky. It was solid gray everywhere you looked. Very dark gray, too. It was going to start raining soon and from the looks of it, the rain would be heavy and go on for quite a while.

And today was their last chance to carry out their mission. Realistically, at any rate. The princess and her entourage wouldn't leave until tomorrow, but when that happened they'd be under heavy guard and the queen most likely wouldn't make an appearance. She hadn't come out to greet her daughter at the docks when she arrived, so why would she accompany her to the docks on her departure? It was now two and a half months since Kristina had come to Stockholm, and relations between her and her mother had reached a nadir.

So they'd been told, anyway. But the information was almost certainly reliable. The Huguenots had developed good relations with several of the palace's servants, using French *livres* provided by Michel

347

Ducos. He'd embezzled a small fortune from his former French employer, the comte d'Avaux. As a result, for the past two years all of the projects and missions of the group he led with Antoine Delerue had been well funded.

They'd not changed the *livres* into a different currency, of course. For the purposes of their mission, it would be all to the good for the Swedish authorities to discover some of the palace servants had been suborned with French money. That would cast still more suspicion on the target of the whole exercise, Cardinal Richelieu. No one else in the world, after all, had greater access to the coinage of the French crown.

Well, there was no help for it. They'd simply have to take their positions, as they had done so many days before, and hope that perhaps this final day things would work out.

Locquifier came to stand next to him. "We should leave now, I think."

Mademann nodded. There was no reason to stay at the tavern on the island any longer. If nothing happened today, they'd find lodgings for the night in the city. By tomorrow, they'd either be dead or making their escape from Sweden altogether.

He looked over his shoulder. Ancelin and Brillard were sitting at the center table, watching him. They understood the logic of the situation just as well as he did.

He gave them a little nod. Immediately, the two men rose from the table and headed toward the kitchen. The tavern-keeper and his wife would either be there, or—more likely, this time of morning—still asleep in their bed upstairs. Which would be even easier.

"We should plant the forgeries," said Locquifier, stating the obvious as he was prone to do.

"Yes. Let's see to it."

Stockholm

Baldur Norddahl closed the lid of the last trunk. Then, with a little grunt of effort, placed it on top of the stack of trunks piled next to the door that led into the palace suite that he and Prince Ulrik had shared since they arrived.

"That's it," he said. "We're all packed except for the one small valise we'll use tomorrow morning. Hallelujah, and hosanna as well. We're finally almost gone. God willing, we'll never see the witch again."

Referring to the queen of Sweden as a witch was a gross form of disrespect for royalty. The French called it *lèse majesté*, but it was a concept that went all the way back to the Roman emperors. The term itself derived from the Latin *laesa maiestas*.

For more than a millennium and a half, men had lost their heads for committing the offense. But Prince Ulrik couldn't find it in his royal self to take umbrage.

Maria Eleonora *was* a witch, queen of Sweden or not.

In a manner of speaking, at least. Caroline Platzer came into the suite just in time to hear Baldur's quip. She immediately took it upon herself to issue a technical correction.

"Don't be silly. Witches don't exist in the first place. The queen of Sweden probably has what's called borderline personality disorder. BPD, for short."

"Probably?" asked Ulrik.

Platzer shrugged. "I've been trained mostly by Maureen Grady, and Maureen thinks people throw around the diagnosis of BPD way too readily."

"It's the first time I've ever heard the term, actually."

"Well, sure. You're a prince, not a shrink. For you, a borderline personality is either someone you ignore completely or"—here came a gleaming smile—"a prime candidate for the chopping block. They're not a lot of fun to be around, especially if you're family."

Norddahl was always fascinated by up-time concepts, even if he thought many of them were nonsense. "What exactly is it?" he asked. "This borderline personality disorder, I mean."

Caroline grimaced. "Well, that's the problem. It's a pretty vague diagnosis. Maureen doesn't like it much because she thinks it's so sloppy it gets applied too often. But the gist of it is that someone with BPD suffers from instability of moods, unstable personal relationships—chaotic relationships, even—and what we call 'black and white thinking.' The technical term is 'idealization and devaluation.' You're either a good daughter or a bad daughter, there's nothing in between—and your status can flip from one to the other at the drop of a hat."

She gave Ulrik the gleaming smile. "Or a good future son-in-law or a bad one, with nothing in between."

Ulrik snorted. "I've seen that change in mid-sentence."

"That's how it works. People with BPD also tend to have an unstable self-image. In extreme cases, that can even lead to dissociation. That means—"

"She turns into a witch," interjected Baldur. "Just as I said."

Kristina came into the suite just in time to hear the last exchange. She looked quite upset. "Do you think I'll turn into a witch too, when I grow up?"

Caroline put her arm around Kristina's shoulders and gave the girl a little hug. "Of course not. And why are you listening to the diagnosis of a social throwback, anyway? If Baldur Norddahl had ever taken an MMPI or Rorschach test up-time, they'd have put him in a straightjacket right away."

Baldur was intrigued. "What is MMPI and who is Rorschach?"

"MMPI stands for Minnesota Multiphasic Personality Inventory. It was one of the most commonly use personality tests up-time by mental health professionals. The Rorschach test was developed—"

"If I took that MMPI, would I pass it?" asked the princess, still agitated.

"Ah . . . Kristina, it's not the sort of test you pass or fail."

"That's just silly," the girl pronounced, as if she were royalty. Which, of course, she was. She drew herself up like a future empress. Which, of course, she was.

"You must develop a new one of these tests," she commanded. "Where you either pass or fail."

Caroline stared at her.

Ulrik laughed. "You'd have done better to leave it at 'witch,'" he said.

Vaxholm Island, in the Stockholm Archipelago

Rather than hire one of the island's local fishermen to ferry them, as they usually did, Mademann and his associates appropriated Bleecker's boat. It was just big enough to get them all to the capital in one trip.

There was no reason not to take the boat. Geerd Bleecker was no longer in a position to complain. Neither was his shrew of a wife.

Eventually, their bodies would be found, but not soon. Most likely, they'd be uncovered in the course of an investigation launched by the local authorities, rather than because their neighbors spotted anything amiss. The tavern's well-built root cellar would slow the decomposition quite nicely.

Everything was going according to plan—except the weather. The skies had grown darker even as the morning advanced. By mid-day it would probably be raining.

That could be a real problem, if their targets appeared.

The Huguenot zealots had managed over time to acquire a few up-time firearms on the black market. Brillard had used one of them to assassinate Dreeson, but he'd been forced to leave the rifle behind. Of the ones that remained, unfortunately, Ducos had insisted on keeping them in Edinburgh. So all they had in their possession here in Stockholm were down-time guns.

Very good ones, true. Mademann had managed to obtain a Cardinal breech-loading rifle for Mathurin Brillard, their best marksman. He'd gotten percussion cap pistols for himself and Gui Ancelin, which shouldn't be affected too badly by the rain. But they were single-shot weapons and muzzle-loaders. Reloading them would take some time.

The others were all armed with double-barreled flintlock pistols. The weapons were better than wheel-locks, but they were also susceptible to misfiring in wet weather. It was possible to keep a flintlock's firing pan covered from rain, so they should be able to count on firing the two shots already loaded. But if they needed more shots than that, they'd be in a very difficult position. Reloading a flintlock in the rain was impossible unless you could find shelter, and who wanted to be worried about that in the middle of a firefight?

That assumed they'd have any chance at carrying out their mission at all, of course. Or even part of it. By now, the plotters had reconciled themselves to killing any one of the appointed targets if the opportunity arose. Ducos had insisted on all three royals being assassinated but Ducos was in Edinburgh. They'd do what they could.

The boat arrived at one of the docks. Mademann and his companions tied it up. If all went well, some of them would be able to use it to make their escape from Stockholm.

Probably not, though. All of them had understood from the beginning that if their mission succeeded, it would probably be at the cost of their own lives. They'd taken care to leave no evidence that would tie them to Delerue or Ducos, and had planted on their persons some faked evidence that would point to Richelieu. That way, even their corpses could do a service for the cause.

The seven Huguenots moved into the streets of Stockholm. They were headed for Slottsbacken, the very broad avenue that connected the royal palace to the Church of St. Nicholas. If there was any chance to complete the mission, it would be there.

The first drops of rain began to fall.

Stockholm

By early afternoon, the dark skies had produced a downpour. As if the weather outside had magical powers over human personalities, the queen's mood worsened in lock step with the weather.

By mid-afternoon, the rain started to ease off a little, but to make up for it the wind picked up. And, again as if by magic, the queen shifted from being morose to being openly belligerent.

Most of her belligerence was aimed at Ulrik. Maria Eleonora apparently found it useful and necessary to spend her final time with the Danish prince explaining to him in detail.

All of his faults.

All of the reasons he was quite unsuited to be the husband of her only child.

All of the faults of her husband, who had been mad enough to concoct the scheme.

None of it, of course, had any effect on Ulrik. He listened patiently, and outwardly politely, because there was no point in doing anything else. By this time on the morrow, they'd be gone anyway. But he dismissed the criticisms as surely and easily as he would have dismissed reproaches by village idiots, town drunks, and palace courtiers.

Unfortunately, Kristina did not have the Dane's impervious hide. The princess was sensitive to criticism coming from anybody, and she had very few defenses against her mother.

So, by late in the afternoon, Sweden's queen and

princess were shrieking at each other. And it didn't take more than five minutes of that before Kristina raced out of the audience chamber.

That gave Ulrik a reasonable pretext to go after her, and thereby get away from the queen. Which he did immediately, of course, with Baldur right on his heels.

They found Kristina half-running toward the palace's entrance onto Slottsbacken. "I'm going to the church!" she cried.

She often did that when her mother upset her. She found the interior of the old church relaxing. She especially enjoyed looking at the wooden statue of Saint George and the Dragon that was said to have been carved by Bernt Notke. The statue was also supposed to hold relics of several saints, including Saint George himself.

"You'll get soaked out there," Baldur warned.

Kristina didn't slow down at all. "So what? It's better than my mother pissing all over us."

She had a point. Besides, there was an alcove near the entrance where the guards took their lunch. The table in it was big enough to shelter all three of them from the rain, if it was turned upside down. Two guards could carry it easily enough.

Of course, the guards would get wet. But theirs was a dull and tedious existence. A little excitement would do them good.

Inside the audience chamber, the little mob of dwarves and buffoons who attended upon Maria Eleonora were struck dumb.

On every prior occasion—there had been plenty

of them—the queen had reacted to her daughter's angry and abrupt departures by pretending nothing had happened. But this time she was in a fury herself.

The weather, obviously. It had driven her out of her wits.

She rose from the throne and strode toward the door, holding up her skirts. "Guards! To me!" Then, she headed for the main entrance of the palace, trailed by a small military retinue.

She was not trailed by dwarves and buffoons, however. This was a new situation and they did not react well to new situations. When in doubt, it was always best to pretend nothing had happened.

Chapter 31

For a moment, Mademann was paralyzed by the arresting sight of the procession coming out of the palace. Two of the palace guards had an upended table in their hands and were holding it above their heads. They came into Slottsbacken and started moving toward the Church of St. Nicholas.

Then he realized that the Swedish princess and the Danish prince were underneath the table, being sheltered from the rain. Ulrik was in front, with Kristina just behind him. Behind her came the prince's burly Norwegian aide.

Al last! They'd at least be able to take down two of their three targets.

He turned his head and hissed, getting the attention of the five men hiding farther back in the alley. Charles was the lookout at the corner and the only one of them who'd seen the royal party emerge from the palace.

"They're coming," he said. "Kristina and Ulrik, with the Norwegian. Two palace guards also."

In his excitement, he forgot to mention the table.

The five Huguenots moved forward until they were

all gathered near the alley's entrance. Mademann was still the only one who could see the royal party, though. That was as it should be. Even in the pouring rain there was a chance they could be spotted lurking in the alley. One person there might be ignored. Half a dozen would cause alarm.

The soldiers were almost trotting, obviously eager to get out of the rain. The party would come abreast of the alley's entrance within seconds.

Mademann gauged the situation. Tactically, given the downpour, there seemed to be only one sensible strategy. Just rush their targets and shoot them down.

"Get ready," he hissed.

Mathurin Brillard was watching the scene from the other end of Slottsbacken. He was farther away but had a better view because he was looking through a window on the upper floor of a tailor shop. Half an hour earlier, when he'd come into the shop, he'd forced the elderly tailor to close the shop and come with him upstairs. Once in the bedroom above, he'd clubbed him senseless.

Judging from the evidence of the bedroom, there should be a wife somewhere. Wherever she was, though, she wasn't in the shop or in the living quarters above. Perhaps she was running an errand or visiting relatives. It was also possible the tailor was a widower but hadn't been able to bear getting rid of his dead wife's belongings.

Whichever the case, all the woman had to do was stay away for a few more hours and it would all be over, one way or the other.

He saw the party coming out of the palace and

stiffened. That was the princess and the prince. Not his targets, technically, since he was supposed to take care of the queen. But the queen would probably never make an appearance, anyway, so Mathurin raised his rifle. If his comrades' attack on Ulrik and Kristina ran into difficulties, Brillard would come to their aid.

In good weather, he'd have positioned himself farther back in the room in order to avoid being spotted in the window by a passerby. In this downpour, though, he didn't think that was a problem, and the direction of the wind was keeping the rain from coming into the room. He was standing close enough to the window that when he took aim, most of the rifle's barrel would extend outside. It would get wet, but that wasn't a problem with a breech-loading rifle like this one. Mathurin had fired the gun several times on the tavern's island, to get accustomed to the thing. It was very accurate. A truly delightful weapon in every respect except that it was quite heavy. This was a full-sized rifle intended for infantrymen, not the carbine version of the Cardinal. Brillard didn't envy any soldier who had to carry the gun on a long march.

That was not something an assassin had to deal with, thankfully.

Behind him, the tailor let out a soft moan. He was lying on the floor near the bed.

Mathurin must not have hit him as hard as he thought he had. Now that the rifle was loaded, he didn't want to use the gun butt again. So he went over and stamped on the man's head. Once, twice, thrice. That should do it.

Quickly, he returned to the window. The royal party was coming abreast of an alley where Brillard thought

Mademann and the others were probably hiding. The fight should start any moment.

"Now!" shouted Mademann. He rushed out of the alley toward the prince and princess.

A shot rang out almost immediately. Then, another.

The shots had come from behind him. Which idiot—?

To his consternation, Charles saw that at least one of the two shots had struck the soldier holding up the front end of the table. The man was already collapsing. Much worse, so was the table.

And God damn all quick-thinking princes!

Ulrik caught the edge of the table and tipped it so the table would fall on its side and provide them with a barricade.

Tried to, rather. The soldier holding up the rear end was too confused to understand what the prince was trying to do. He was still trying to hold the table up.

Baldur kicked him out from under it. The soldier was flung onto his back, his head hitting the street hard enough to be knocked unconscious. Baldur caught his end of the table. He realized what Ulrik was trying to do and followed suit with his own end. A moment later the table was lying on its side with its heavy top facing their assailants. Ulrik and Baldur crouched down behind it. The princess did so herself, without needing to be told.

What a mess. Still, the situation favored them. Locquifier—another idiot!—fired a shot from his percussion cap pistol at the table top. The wood splintered, but it was thick enough that the bullet didn't penetrate.

That left Locquifier effectively disarmed, of course, because his percussion cap pistol only had one barrel. No way to reload in this downpour.

The first idiot had been Ancelin. At least he'd had the sense to discard his pistol now that he'd fired both barrels. He drew a knife and ran toward the right end of the table.

That was now the only sensible tactic. Get around the ends of the table so they had access to their targets.

Mademann made to follow Ancelin. His foot slipped on one of the wet cobblestones and he fell, dropping his pistol. The weapon skittered off across the cobblestones, coming to rest ten feet away.

"Merde alors!"

By October of the year 1635, the Ring of Fire was four and half years in the past. Over that period of time, even though they numbered in the thousands, up-time firearms had come to be worth a prince's ransom.

Fortunately, Ulrik of Denmark was a prince.

He owned three of the weapons, in fact: a bolt-action Browning .308 rifle, a Smith & Wesson .40 automatic pistol with a ten-round magazine, and a Colt Detective Special .38 caliber snub-nose revolver.

He was carrying the revolver today, as he normally did in everyday matters. The little gun was easy to conceal in regular clothing, which the automatic wasn't. Ulrik had been quite sure the queen would have objected had she realized he was coming into her presence armed. The revolver had a six-round cylinder, but Ulrik only had five of the chambers loaded. He disliked carrying the weapon with a loaded chamber under the hammer, even if the man who'd sold him the gun insisted it was quite safe.

So. Five shots, and he had no way to reload since he wasn't carrying any spare ammunition. He didn't have that much anyway. The ammunition for up-time guns was also very expensive. By now, they were all handmade reloads.

He was pretty sure there were at least six assailants, from what he'd seen before the table came down.

The Americans called it Murphy's Law.

Mademann scrambled after his pistol. On hands and knees because when he'd tried to stand up he'd just slipped again.

Out of the corner of his eye he saw that Ancelin was close to the table. André Tourneau was very close also, at the other end. He had his pistol at the ready.

Suddenly, a figure rose from behind the table. The prince, from the hat, although it was hard to be sure. Hats got rather shapeless in this sort of downpour.

Tourneau immediately fired a shot. He'd rushed it, Charles thought.

So he had. The shot struck the very edge of the table and caromed off somewhere in the distance. The only damage it did was to send a little spray of splinters flying.

One of the splinters struck Ulrik just below the eye. He'd already fired at the gun flash. Now, startled, he pulled the trigger again.

Two shots gone! He had only three bullets left.

✧   ✧   ✧

The prince's first shot struck Tourneau in the arm, just above the wrist. Howling, he jerked around, dropping the gun—and moved right into the path of the second bullet. It was that one, despite being completely unaimed, that killed him instantly. The bullet entered his left temple and destroyed much of his brain before coming to a stop against the occipital bone.

It was already obvious things were going badly. Mathurin took aim at the figure standing up above the table rim. He, also, thought it was probably the prince, although this cursed rain degraded visibility in the most terrible manner. It would not be an easy shot under these conditions, but he thought he could make it. If he missed, he would have time for a second shot.

A sudden noise to the right drew his attention.

The queen was coming out of the palace! Brillard hadn't expected that. She was trailed by half a dozen palace guards.

All of them had now stopped. They were just within the entrance, still out of the rain. The queen was staring at the bizarre tableau in Slottsbacken, her mouth wide open.

The guards wouldn't be much use. They were armed with ceremonial halberds, not firearms. The weapons could still do a lot of damage even if those great blades probably weren't keep very sharp. But it would take them a while to reach the prince and princess.

Mademann would have to manage without his help. Brillard's assigned target was Maria Eleonora.

He brought the rifle around. The queen still hadn't moved. She seemed completely paralyzed with shock.

This was much closer range. Even in the rain, he could hardly miss.

Kristina managed to work the dead guard's sword out of the scabbard. Shakily, she passed it on to Baldur.

"My profound thanks, Your Highness." For once, there was not a trace of mockery in the Norwegian's tone of voice.

One of the assailants came around the table, a knife in his hand. Baldur flung himself straight at him, not even trying to get to his feet. The sword point went into the meat of the attacker's right thigh.

His aim had been off a little. He'd been trying for the femoral artery. Still, the wound was severe enough to stop the assailant. He howled and clutched his leg.

With his free hand, though. He didn't let go of the knife. An experienced brawler, it seemed.

Not that it would do him the least bit of good. Now, Baldur did come to his feet.

It was no contest. Gui Ancelin was indeed considered a formidable man with a blade, in his own circles. But those were the circles of assassins and street fighters. Baldur Norddahl had learned his swordplay as an Algerine corsair and guarding caravans in the Sahara from Tuareg raiders.

Not to mention that Gui had a knife and Baldur had a sword. The knife was razor sharp and the sword blade wasn't, but it hardly mattered since the first thing Baldur did was cut off his right arm just below the elbow. With the Norwegian's strength and experience, the precise condition of the blade didn't matter. Even a relatively dull sword is a sword, not a butter knife.

Ancelin stared down in shock. Not for long. Baldur's next strike severed the right side of his neck down to the spinal column. Blood gushed everywhere and he collapsed to the cobblestones. Slottsbacken was not flat. The rain was coming down so heavily that the blood was carried away almost as fast as it came out.

Brillard fired. The queen was knocked flat on her back. The guards stared down at her, still not moving. Clearly the Swedes were not using elite troops to guard the palace.

They should have spotted the gunsmoke coming from the window where he was positioned. In good weather, even dullards like these couldn't have missed the sound and sight of the shot. But the heavy rain distorted sound and obscured the smoke. He thought he was still undetected.

He began reloading the rifle. There was time for another shot. Perhaps he could still help Charles after all.

Mademann finally had his pistol. He started to get up again—and slipped again.

Down onto one knee, this time, not on his belly. But he'd fallen hard and the knee was badly bruised. If he survived the next few moments, he'd be walking with a limp for a while.

If he was lucky. The knee might also be broken. The pain was intense.

Damn this rain!

Robert Ouvrard fired when was ten feet from the prince. At this range, he could hardly miss.

But he did. Ouvrard was not experienced at this sort of gun fight. He did not understand how often people missed their shots even at what seemed point blank range. They got excited and agitated—as he was—and the surge of adrenaline swept away all fine motor control. Ancient fight-or-flight reflexes took over, designed for crude actions like running or striking with fists, not the comparatively delicate work of aiming a pistol and squeezing a trigger.

Instead, he jerked the trigger wildly—but he would have missed by a foot even if he hadn't. The shot struck the wall of the royal palace, causing no damage at all beyond dimpling a brick.

Ulrik fired back. And also missed, at point blank range.

Both men cursed and both fired again—but Ulrik's shot came just an instant sooner. That was the advantage of the revolver's mechanism over that of the double-barreled flintlock pistol.

His shot struck Ouvrard in the stomach. The Huguenot clutched himself, his pistol swinging wide. The shot he fired by reflex hit the cobblestones and caromed off to strike the wall of the church, where it caromed off again.

With that sort of abdominal wound, Ouvrard was almost sure to die eventually. He was still alive but no longer part of the fight. He was disarmed and already falling to the street.

So, naturally, Ulrik shot him again. A good shot, right in the center mass, certain to cause the man's death even if the first shot didn't.

Also a completely stupid wasted shot, which left the prince with an empty gun.

He was not experienced at this sort of thing either.

But he didn't have time to curse himself. Abraham Levasseur had been just behind Ouvrard and now he fired, also at point blank range.

Two shots in very quick succession. Levasseur was familiar with double-barreled pistols and their somewhat intricate trigger mechanism.

He'd also been in a gun fight before, unlike Ouvrard.

Both of his shots hit the prince. Ulrik slumped to the ground.

Locquifier started to clamber over the upended table, in order to stab the princess huddled behind it. He ignored Baldur altogether. His instruction from Michel had said nothing about irrelevant Norwegian adventurers.

Such is the folly of paying too much instruction to orders.

By now, Kristina had taken one of her jeweled hairpins out of her hair. The thing was only three inches long and not particularly sharp, but it was all she had. As soon as she saw Locquifier coming over the table, with an upraised knife in his hand, she shrieked and lunged upward, jagging at his face.

The hairpin did no damage, because Locquifier flinched away from it. But his attack was delayed for two seconds or so.

That was all the time Baldur needed, now that he'd finished with Ancelin.

Again, the flashing sword sent a hand flying, cut off this time just above the wrist. And again, an instant later, a neck was cut open to the bone. This time, since Baldur hadn't been quite as rushed, the windpipe was severed along with the carotid and jugular.

For all practical purposes, Guillaume Locquifier was dead before his body met the cobblestones.

Mademann shrieked with fury at the sight. He'd never liked Guillaume, but he was still a comrade. In his rage, he fired a shot at the prince's companion who'd killed him.

The shot missed. He fired again—and that put the Norwegian down. At least, Charles thought it had. The man was behind the table again, no longer visible.

Reloading a Cardinal could be done very quickly, but the fight in the street below was moving more quickly still. By the time Mathurin had the rifle reloaded, he had no targets left. Prince Ulrik was down already. Brillard could see his body in the street. And whatever might have happened to the princess, she was hidden somewhere behind that cursed table. It would be foolish to shoot at it blindly.

Besides, he had another target, and the one to which he'd been assigned.

He was almost sure his first shot had killed the queen. But there was no reason not to make sure.

The six guards were no longer standing around her. Three of them had moved into Slottsbacken with their halberds ready, headed toward the table. One of them had vanished altogether. Mathurin assumed he'd gone to get help.

The remaining two were still guarding the queen. Clearly, though, their concept of "guarding" was not that of trained bodyguards. Instead of shielding Maria Eleonora, they were standing at least two feet from her.

Their halberds were posed in most formidably martial

fashion, to be sure. But the bullet Mathurin fired cared not in the least. He'd had time to take careful aim, since the queen was now unmoving, flat on her back in the entrance. The bullet passed between the guards and struck her under the chin. When it exited from the top of her head, brains and blood and bits of bone flew out in a horrid gush.

The guards stared at the sight, their halberds still held at the ready.

The sound of the rifle shot drew Mademann's attention. That was the second shot Brillard had fired. Given the man's marksmanship, that meant the queen was certainly dead.

So was the prince. Of their three targets, only the princess was left.

Charles was tempted. But...

Mathurin would now be making his own escape. Of the others, only Charles himself and Levasseur remained alive. And they'd used all their shots. In this rain, they'd need to find shelter in which to reload, by which time the princess would certainly have fled back into the palace.

They could go after her with their knives, but his knee was uncertain—and the three guards with halberds were fast approaching. Could Levasseur alone kill the princess while fending them off?

No chance. It was time to make their own escape, if possible.

"Abraham!" he shouted. "Help me!"

On his way out of the bedroom, Brillard paused at the door to consider the tailor. He'd intended to let the old man live, assuming he survived the injuries he already had. But now that the mission was over and the possibility of escape was at hand—which Mathurin had never seriously expected—it might not be wise to leave a witness who could identify him.

Mathurin Brillard was not a man to agonize over decisions. He raised the rifle and brought the butt down on the tailor's head. Again, and again, and again. It took only as many seconds as it did blows. Not too long, and there would surely be no witness now.

When Ulrik opened his eyes, he immediately had to close them again because of the rain. It was not quite like being under a waterfall, but close enough.

He could feel a small body clutching him where he lay on the street. A trembling child's body. It was making snuffling noises, too.

Kristina, he thought. She was still alive, then.

He turned his head to get his eyes out of the direct path of the rain and opened the left one, which was now sheltered.

Yes, it was Kristina. The only other things he could see were the upended table and, coming toward him, more halberds than Ulrik had ever seen in one place.

Swedish palace guards were attached to the weapons. Looking very stalwart and none too bright.

He made a mental note to make sure he had guards armed with something more useful, in any palace *he* had any control over. Smarter ones, too.

"What's happening?" he croaked.

Chapter 32

Zielona Góra

The clatter of boots coming into the bakery woke Jeff Higgins. By the time he got himself into a seated position on his cot, the regiment's sergeant major was coming through the door to the back room where he'd made his quarters.

"General Stearns wants all brigade and regiment commanders in the Rathaus, Colonel Higgins."

"When? Now?"

"Immediately, he said."

Jeff started lacing on his boots. He'd fallen asleep still wearing his uniform, so he wouldn't have to take the time to put it on. It had already been wrinkled, so that wasn't an issue. After weeks of campaigning, uniforms in the here and now didn't look much like they did in artists' renditions of battlefield scenes. Jeff figured that had probably been true back up-time as well.

"Any change in the weather?"

Seeing the expression on the sergeant major's face— *and how do I inform a colonel he's a donkey?*—Jeff grinned and shook his head.

371

"Never mind. Stupid question." The sound of rain hammering on the roof was loud and clear, as it had been for more than a day now. Luckily, the damage sustained by the bakery during the battle hadn't compromised the roof, or Jeff would be swimming by now.

They were also lucky that Zielona Góra wasn't located on a river the way most cities and large towns were. The Złota Łącza had started to overflow, but it was a small enough stream that it didn't pose any real problems. Jeff wasn't at all sure that would be true with towns located on the Odra or the Warta.

When he got to the door that led out onto the street, Jeff grabbed a short and wide wooden plank that he'd positioned earlier on a side table. He should have had an oilskin rain cape, since he knew the army had been provided with them. But they were nowhere to be found in the supply wagons. Another thing Jeff had soon learned about big campaigns like this one was that the two most common phrases associated with logistics were "musta got left behind somewhere" and "sorry 'bout that."

There was no chance of finding an umbrella, since they weren't even officially part of the army's supply materials. Umbrellas were in short supply, period, if you didn't have an up-time one—and Jeff, naturally, had left his behind in Magdeburg. They weren't yet in common use in Europe although you could occasionally find ones imported from China. People used cloaks instead.

Jeff had a cloak, in fact. But while cloaks did all right when dealing with a drizzle or a light rain, in heavy rain like this they'd just get soaked completely through. He'd wind up arriving at the Rathaus every bit as wet and ten pounds heavier.

The plank was better. It'd keep off most of the rain.

He hoped. He hadn't actually walked as far as the Rathaus since the storm broke.

He started off running but Jeff gave that up quickly. The city's streets were a sea of mud. He'd be bound to slip and fall, especially because the visibility was pretty lousy. They were at least two hours past sunup, but the overcast was heavy enough to leave everything looking like early evening instead. Not to mention that everything was half-hidden behind sheets of rain. This was one hell of a storm.

He wasn't the last of the regimental commanding officers to arrive. Two other colonels came piling in a minute or so after he did. The three brigadiers seemed to have been in the Rathaus long enough to have started drying off in front of the fire. Jeff figured Mike Stearns had held an initial meeting with them before calling in the next layer of the division's officers. He'd used the city's Rathaus as his headquarters since they'd taken Zielona Góra. The tavern in the basement was well suited for the sort of command meetings he was holding right now.

Mike didn't waste any time. As soon as the last colonel came in, he said, "All hell has broken loose, gentlemen. I received a radio call from General Torstensson a short while ago. The Polish army was able to use the weather to evade Gustav Adolf by moving north without being spotted." He waved his hand at the ceiling. "In this sort of weather, all of the air force's planes are grounded, of course."

He didn't add what he could have, which was that

an overreliance on up-time technology could cause its own problems. Koniecpolski didn't have any airplanes. In good weather, that was a big handicap. In weather like this, though, the advantage shifted to him—because what he did have were a lot of excellent Cossack scouts.

The Swedish army had Finnish equivalents, but there weren't nearly as many of them. And the USE's army was notoriously weak when it came to cavalry. Horsemanship was a skill that was heavily concentrated among noblemen, and there weren't many noblemen who wanted to serve in the regular USE forces.

"Whether by good fortune or good intelligence, Koniecpolski was able to trap Hesse-Kassel and his army against the Warta. Which," Mike continued grimly, "was already overflowing its banks and had them pretty well mired."

He took a deep breath. "They got hammered badly. Torstensson's assessment is that they'll be out of the campaign altogether for at least a week. Torstensson thinks Koniecpolski will now try to come south, maneuvering around Gustav Adolf in order to attack one of the USE divisions. Meanwhile, von Thurn's column—that's about half the Swedish army, don't forget—is on the wrong side of the Warta. There's no way they'll be able to cross the river and come into the fight until the river ebbs and they can get their engineers to build some bridges."

One of the colonels frowned. That was Albert Zingre, a Swiss mercenary who commanded the 1st Brigade's Freiheit Regiment.

"Excuse me, General, but if Koniecpolski has come south, then he's left Gorzów undefended. Why not simply take the city and use its bridges? There are two of them, I believe."

Mike shook his head. "Von Thurn *did* take the city— only to discover that Polish engineers had destroyed the bridges two hours earlier."

The more he heard, the more Jeff was getting worried. What all this added up to was that the Polish grand hetman had launched his campaign as soon as the weather turned sour, which indicated superb planning on his part. Within less than two days, he'd then either destroyed or put out of action two-thirds of Gustav Adolf's own forces. And now, apparently, he was trying to move around what was left of the Swedish army in order to attack the USE Army. He was probably aiming for the most northerly of that army's three columns, Knyphausen's First Division. And if he caught the division before it got reinforced, he'd have a three-to-one or possibly even a four-to-one numerical superiority.

That assumed Koniecpolski had managed to keep his entire army concentrated, but Jeff figured that was a pretty safe bet given the man's track record thus far. What the grand hetman was doing was taking advantage of his enemy's dispersed formations in order to defeat them in detail.

The scheme wouldn't have worked in good weather, of course, since Gustav Adolf would have gotten wind of what Koniecpolski was up to almost at once. He'd had every available plane in the air force keeping up continuous reconnaissance in daylight hours since the campaign began. In retrospect, it was obvious that this was the reason Koniecpolski had been retreating before Gustav Adolf's advancing forces without putting up a major fight. He'd simply left garrisons in the major towns to delay his enemy and buy time in the hope that the weather would change—which, at this time of year, wasn't unlikely at all.

Jesus H. Christ. It was one thing to read about "great captains of war," it was another thing entirely to have to face one of the damn monsters.

All this time, without realizing it consciously, Jeff had been reassured by the fact that he had one of the great captains on *his* side: Gustav Adolf. But even the greatest generals—maybe especially the greatest generals—could get too ambitious.

Remember Napoleon?

Jeff was pretty sure Gustav Adolf had been guilty of that. Instead of mounting a slower and more deliberate campaign, keeping his forces together instead of dividing them into half a dozen separated columns, he'd relied too much on his advantages and had underestimated his opponent.

"That's the situation, gentlemen," Mike said. "Torstensson is with the Second Division and he's bringing it up to reinforce Knyphausen. In the meantime, he's ordered Knyphausen to stand his ground and prepare for a battle. Gustav Adolf, of course, is moving his units south to join Knyphausen also."

Mike glanced at the windows along the upper walls. The tavern was in a half-basement, not a full basement. That normally allowed some light into the place, although with this sort of rain and overcast it was as dark as it would have been in late afternoon.

"In this weather, though, it's hard to know how long it'll take to get those forces together." Mike's jaws tightened for moment. "And there's another problem, which is that we have no good idea where Koniecpolski is right now. Whether by design or chance, he might wind up moving farther south than we expect, in which case he might come at us instead."

"If he does, so much the worse for him." That came from Colonel Leoš Hlavacek, the commander of the Teutoberg Regiment, which was also in the 1st Brigade. "We can hold Zielona Góra against him."

"We can certainly hold it long enough for Torstensson to arrive with the First and Second Divisions," Colonel Jan Svoboda chimed him. Like Hlavacek, he was one of the many Bohemian officers serving in the USE Army. He commanded the Yellow Marten regiment in Derfflinger's 3rd Brigade.

Mike shook his head. "General Torstensson's not worried about holding Zielona Góra. If we lose it, we lose it. He thinks it's more important for us to send as many men as we can to reinforce the 1st and 2nd Division. And that's what he's ordered me to do. So . . ."

Mike looked around the room. "We'll leave Brigadier Schuster and the 2nd Brigade here to hold the city as best they can if Koniecpolski shows up. And we'll also leave all of the regular artillery units. Their guns will be useful on defense, and there's no way we could move them fast enough through the muck out there anyway. Even after the weather clears, the ground will be soggy for days."

"What about the flying artillery?" asked Svoboda. "They'll be handy against hussars."

"We're taking them with us. Their carriages are light enough that I think they'll be able to handle the terrain. It's not as if any of us are going to be marching very fast."

He looked directly at Jeff, now. "I'm also leaving

the Hangman Regiment behind. They suffered the worst casualties when we took this city, and I think they need more time to recuperate. But, Colonel Higgins, please come see me after the meeting is over."

That happened less than a quarter of an hour later. Stearns was driving everyone to move as quickly as possible. He normally ran staff and command meetings in a relaxed manner, but not this one.

When Mike was alone except for Derfflinger, he motioned Jeff to come over.

"You wanted to see me, sir?"

"You know that Colonel Gärtner was badly wounded two days ago," Mike said.

Jeff's stomach felt queasy all of a sudden. "Uh, yes, sir."

"That leaves the Third Brigade's White Horse Regiment without a commanding officer. I can't promote his adjutant because Major Nussbaum was killed right about the same time."

Jeff had always wondered what free fall felt like. Now he knew.

"Uh, yes, sir."

Mike nodded toward the brigadier standing next to him. "Georg thinks you'd do just fine. So I'm putting you in charge of the White Horse."

He got a solemn, reassuring look on his face. "It's just temporary, Jeff. We'll have you back in command of the Hangman as soon as possible."

He made it sound as if being in command of a regiment specifically put together to execute people had been Jeff's lifelong ambition.

But all he said was, "Uh, yes, sir."

Chapter 33

West of Poznań

The Landgrave of Hesse-Kassel died in the middle of the night. Gustav Adolf got word over the radio as soon as it happened.

It came as no surprise. Wilhelm V had suffered terrible wounds in the battle at the Warta, the sort a man almost never survives. Still, the king of Sweden was distressed by the news. Hesse-Kassel was not exactly a friend, but he'd been a staunch supporter for years. He would be missed.

Gustav Adolf didn't spend much time dwelling on the landgrave's death, though. He had much worse problems on his hands, politically as well as on the military front. Hours earlier, the radio had brought news that his wife had been murdered in Stockholm by assailants whose identity was still unknown. The same assailants had also attacked the king's daughter and Prince Ulrik but, thankfully, they had survived. Untouched, in the case of Kristina. Ulrik had been injured, but apparently not too seriously.

Gustav Adolf had not been close to his wife for

many years. In some ways, he'd never really been close. Theirs had been a marriage of political convenience, not of affection. The king of Sweden's romantic attachment since the age of sixteen had been to the noblewoman Ebba Brahe—and still was, although she was now married to Sweden's Lord High Constable, Jacob de la Gardie.

Nonetheless, Maria Eleonora had been his wife, and had borne him a child. Had she died of natural causes, he would have been slightly saddened but no more. Her being killed in such a fashion, however, had left him furious.

He'd already been close to a fury because of the weather. What had seemed a straightforward campaign against a redoubtable but still weaker foe was turning into a nightmare.

Hesse-Kassel was gone now, and his army with him, for all practical purposes. As soon as the landgravine heard the news, she'd undoubtedly recall at least half of her forces to Hesse-Kassel. And the ones she left would be the weakest units, and just enough of them to maintain the pretense that she was not withdrawing Hesse-Kassel's support to the emperor. Unfortunately, the laws of the USE gave the provincial heads a great deal of control over the disposition of provincial troops. Their armies were almost as independent of federal control as the private armies of Polish magnates.

Gustav Adolf had not yet sent her the news of the disaster on the Warta, but he couldn't stall for much longer. There were some disadvantages to radio as well as advantages. In the old days, he could have send a courier with the news and instructed him to have a lamed horse along the way. By the time Amalie Elizabeth found out her husband had been killed and a good portion of her army destroyed, Gustav Adolf would have had the rest of that army back at the front. And he could have kept forestalling the landgravine for weeks, or even months.

He'd come into Poland with fifty thousand men, against what he'd estimated were forty thousand at the disposal of Koniecpolski. He'd lost Hesse-Kassel's eight thousand, and another ten thousand troops under Heinrich Matthias von Thurn were stymied north of the swollen Warta. They'd be out of action for several days; possibly as long as a week, if this wretched weather kept up.

Even if he assumed Koniecpolski had lost as many men in the battle on the Warta as Hesse-Kassel—which he almost certainly hadn't; that had been a very one-sided affair, by all accounts—he'd still have thirty-five thousand troops at his disposal.

There'd have been losses from disease, but those had probably been equally distributed. The same for losses by desertion. Those had probably been unusually low, on both sides. However difficult they might be to handle politically, the soldiers of the USE army tended to have good morale. The same would be true of Polish troops, especially hussars, so long as they had good leadership—and in Koniecpolski they had a commanding general as good as any in the world.

In two days, the tactical situation had turned sour as quickly and as badly as the weather. Gustav Adolf had gone from having a five-to-four numerical superiority to odds that were now no better than even. He'd lost all of his technological advantages except radio. The planes were grounded, the APCs were stuck in the mud miles to the rear.

Finally—this was the factor that really concerned him—his forces had been dispersed when the storm arrived, where Koniecpolski had kept his forces together. Until Gustav Adolf could reunite the four columns still available to fight—his own Swedish forces and the three divisions of the USE army led by Torstensson—he was at a major disadvantage. If Koniecpolski caught any one of those columns on its own, he could crush it.

The king of Sweden was a pious man. He'd even written a number of the hymns sung in Sweden's Lutheran churches. Now, for one of the rare times in his life, he lapsed into blasphemy.

"God damn this rain!"

Hearing that curse, Anders Jönsson got more worried still—and he was already worried. He'd been Gustav Adolf's bodyguard for years and he knew the signs. The one great flaw the king of Sweden possessed as a military commander was his tendency to get headstrong and reckless in the grip of powerful emotions. And right now, the stew of emotions the man was seething in was an unholy combination. The devil himself couldn't have cooked up a more dangerous brew.

Tremendous frustration at the military situation due to the weather.

Anger at himself for having been overconfident and allowing his forces to become divided. Anger at having underestimated an opponent—for which he had no excuse at all. He'd faced Koniecpolski before.

Fury at the murder of his wife. An act which, in the nature of things, was as much a blow struck at the Swedish crown as it was at a woman.

Even greater fury that the same assassins had come very close to murdering his only child.

Anxiety because Kristina *was* an only child, and therefore the sole heir to the throne. That was a risky situation for any dynasty, even if the child in question hadn't been but eight years old. And now, with Maria Eleonora dead, there would be no chance of producing another heir any time soon.

But there was nothing Jönsson could do. Any attempt he made to restrain the king would just make him more furious.

He'd read accounts of the battle of Lützen, in copies of up-time texts that Gustav Adolf had collected. When he read of the king's behavior in that battle in another universe, he'd recognized it instantly. Frustrated by the heavy fog that had covered the battlefield and made it impossible to stay in control of his forces, Gustav Adolf had charged impetuously forward with only a small detachment of guards.

No one knew what happened next, exactly. Battles were chaotic and confusing enough even in good weather conditions. But however it happened, the king had been killed. His soldiers still went on to win that battle, but from that day forward Sweden lost its guiding hand.

It could happen in this universe, too. The details might differ, but the essence would remain the same—a great captain who could not restrain himself enough when his blood ran high.

Magdeburg airfield

"Not a chance, Gretchen," said Eddie Junker. "Flying into that wouldn't be any different from slitting your own throat."

Frowning, Gretchen Richter stared at up the clouds. The rain hadn't let up at all and the sky seemed as dark and foreboding as it had since the storm arrived two days earlier.

Well . . . maybe not quite as much.

"I think it's lightening a bit." She pointed toward the west. "See that patch there?"

Eddie chuckled. "Nice try. But if you think a maybe-just-a-tiny-bit-less horrible set of storm clouds—in exactly the wrong direction, too—is going to get me into that cockpit, you are out of your mind. Insane. Mad. Crazed. If Caroline Platzer were here, no doubt she'd have some elaborate way of saying the same thing."

He leaned still farther back in the rocking chair—which wasn't rocking because Eddie put his feet up on the counter that ran all the way around the top floor of the airfield's control tower. Big glass windows ran all the way around, too, which provided a splendid view of the storm. Which, since Eddie could observe it in dry comfort, was actually rather enjoyable to watch.

"Sit down," he urged Gretchen. "Have some more tea."

But Gretchen was far too frustrated to follow that advice. She was the sort of person who, once she'd made up her mind to do something, wanted to *do* it. Now. Not tomorrow. Not the day after.

Now.

All the more so, since Tata's daily radio reports indicated that Dresden was coming to a boil. With the elector dead and the USE's emperor completely absorbed by his campaign in Poland, there was a power vacuum in Saxony. Then word came that Kresse and his little army of irregulars—the same people who had killed John George—had left the Upper Vogtland and were marching on Dresden. That army wasn't even so little anymore. The militias of many of the villages and towns that Kresse passed through or nearby were joining him.

That news—which Tata and Joachim Kappel had seen got spread widely—had panicked many of Dresden's patricians, prosperous burghers and officials. They'd fled the city, just as the same class of people had fled Amsterdam before the cardinal-infante could begin his siege.

The whole situation sounded much like Amsterdam. There might even be a rough equivalent to Fredrik Hendrik, the prince of Orange with whom Gretchen had been able to negotiate and maintain something of a tacit alliance. Or truce, at least. Gustav Adolf's appointed administrator, Ernst Wettin, had arrived in the city already. Tata's first reports indicated that despite being the prime minister's younger brother, Wettin didn't seem at all inclined toward confrontation.

But that was probably going to be a moot point, soon enough. The Swedish general Báner was also coming to Dresden. More slowly, because he was bringing an army with him.

There'd been a powerful army at Amsterdam, too. But the commander of that army had been Don Fernando, a man with imagination and great ambitions and, somewhere in his core, a very real streak of decency.

None of which was true of Báner, by all accounts Gretchen had heard. He was coarse, pigheaded, narrow-minded, and seemed to have no ambitions beyond being feared by those he wished to fear him.

He was also on record as saying that the most suitable use for a CoC agitator's head was to serve as an adornment for a pike head. And he was bringing a lot of pikes to Saxony.

"I *have* to get to Dresden!" she said. For perhaps the twentieth times in two days. If this kept up, she'd have to use a horse, even if she wasn't much of a horse-woman. Or a boat, maybe, except the Elbe was flooding.

Dresden

Tata and Joachim Kappel had taken over the Residenzschloss a week earlier, once it became clear the CoC was now the most powerful force in the city. Dresden's official militia had shattered into pieces after a big portion of its officers fled the city. Many of the rank-and-file militiamen had joined the CoC outright. Many others had simply retired into their private affairs. Yet another portion of the militia—perhaps a quarter of its original number—had reorganized themselves into something they called the Dresden Defense Corps. They were maintaining a studied neutrality concerning the city's political affairs, insisting that they were simply and solely a body to defend Dresden from any attackers.

Whether the definition of "attackers" included Kresse's forces from the Vogtland, now just two days from the city's walls, remained to be seen. But for the moment, Tata and Joachim were willing to keep the peace with the DDC.

Tata and Joachim had developed a very good working relationship. Kappel was the organizer, the "inside man." Tata had much better skills than he did at dealing with people outside the ranks of the CoC. She had become the public face of their movement in the city, far more widely known than he was.

Partly, of course, that was simply due to their very different appearance. Tata was a pleasant-looking young woman, not threatening in any way. Kappel...

Eric Krenz had put it this way, in front of both of them, "If the forces of reaction ever need a poster boy for the wicked and vicious instigators of bloody-handed riot and revolution, Joachim, you're their man."

The jest had been close enough to the truth to make even Kappel laugh. He was a man in his early forties who was not simply ugly but frighteningly ugly.

Their enemies in Dresden had taken to calling him "the troll."

So did children on the streets.

So did his own CoC cadre, for that matter.

It had been Kappel who first broached the idea of seizing the elector's palace, but it had been Tata who came up with the formal rationale.

She understood, as Kappel often did not, that you had to be careful not to give people the impression that you were simply high-handed. Even when you were being high-handed. In fact, *especially* when you were being high-handed.

So, the official explanation for the seizure of the

palace: They needed its vast expanse, its many rooms and resources, in order to take care of the troops, wounded in brave battle with the enemy.

Say no to *that,* if you dare.

Eric Krenz had been the one who first suggested the idea. Tata had initially dismissed it as just a typical Eric Krenz ploy to improve his creature comforts. Of course he'd want to recuperate from his injuries in a palace bed!

But she'd gotten to know Krenz well enough by then to realize that he had a habit of couching serious ideas and proposals within a frivolous and casual shell. Why he did that was a mystery to her, but she'd come to recognize the pattern.

So, she'd given it a second thought. It hadn't taken her long then to realize what a cunning idea it was.

Two days later, all the recuperating soldiers in the city were moved into the palace. As a mere afterthought, a casual side effect, a stray feather in the wind, the CoC moved in as well. Within a short time, the palace had become their fortress.

Krenz did wind up in a palace bed. But Tata insisted that he had to share it with Lieutenant Nagel.

Who, for his part—he was a very odd young man— kept making peculiar remarks about hidden mothers and sightless men and the iniquity of fate.

Eric had been very disgruntled. Mostly, Tata thought, because having to share a bed with Nagel created obvious difficulties for his campaign to seduce Tata.

Which was part of the reason she'd done it, of course. She hadn't made up her mind yet and didn't like to feel unduly pressured. Krenz could be relentless, in his insouciant sort of way.

❖   ❖   ❖

In a different part of the city, Noelle Stull was also studying the sky, and looking almost as disgruntled as Gretchen.

"This sucks," she pronounced.

"What are you talking about?" countered Denise Beasley. "I think it's way cool. Dresden's where all the excitement is. Or is gonna be, anyway. You watch."

She and Minnie Hugelmair were perched on a divan in the main room of the house, playing cards. Noelle had no idea which particular game they were playing. She'd been only passingly familiar with up-time card games. These down-time games were incomprehensible. The two teenagers were using Italian cards that Eddie had gotten for Denise as a gift. The cards were round, not oblong. And instead of the familiar four suits of spades, hearts, clubs and diamonds, they had five suits: swords, wands, cups, coins and rings.

"How is it 'cool'?" Noelle demanded crossly. "I want to get back home."

"Why? We're moving to Prague soon anyway. And that so-called 'home' you rented in Magdeburg was a tiny little dump."

Minnie nodded, as she laid another card on the cushion between them that they were using as a table. "Yeah. Compared to that place, this is a palace."

It *was* a very nice house, in most respects. The departure of so many of the city's upper crust had left a lot of vacancies—and Noelle was operating with Francisco Nasi's money here in Dresden, not her own. But she'd expected to be here for only a short time, to oversee the preparation of the airfield while Eddie flew back to get Gretchen. She hadn't anticipated getting trapped in the city by a storm.

A very nice house in most respects, yes. But not all—and not the most critical.

"My apartment in Magdeburg may have been tiny—"

"Smelly, too," Denise chipped in.

"Cockroaches everywhere you looked," was Minnie's contribution.

"—but it had *plumbing*."

That shut them up. With few exceptions, even the wealthiest residences in Dresden still had traditional seventeenth-century toilet facilities. The use of such facilities started with the verb "squat" and went downhill from there.

In contrast, buildings in Magdeburg were less than five years old, with very few exceptions. The sack of the city by Tilly's army in 1631 had destroyed almost everything. And since most of the construction that came later had happened after American influence started to spread, and given the CoCs' well-nigh-fanatical observation of sanitary measures, even the most wretched living quarters in Magdeburg had access to running water.

And sewers.

"You think my apartment smelled bad, Minnie? How d'you like the aroma out in the streets here? Should I open the window to remind you?"

"Don't rub it in," said Denise. "Besides, I bet the rain's washed most of it away by now."

"Yeah, I bet it has—right into the river. Where we get our water from. Can we say 'typhus,' girls?"

"She's going to keep rubbing it in, isn't she?" said Minnie.

Denise whooped and swept up the pile of cards on the cushion. Apparently, she'd won something. A hand? A game? A trick? Who knew?

Noelle's grandmother had warned her that cards were an instrument of the devil. Here, she figured, was living proof.

Chapter 34

The Warta river, between Gorzów and Poznań

The reports had been accurate. Hidden within a small grove of trees, Lukasz Opalinski looked onto the Warta. Just as the Cossacks had said, there on the road running by the river was one of the huge American war machines. An "APC," it was called, whatever that meant. Lukasz had forgotten to ask Jozef Wojtowicz what the initials stood for.

The thing was enormous, even bigger than Lukasz remembered from the battle of Zwenkau. It looked every bit as terrifying, too.

Or would have, had there not been one critical difference. At Zwenkau, the APCs had been moving almost as fast as horses. Faster, on good terrain. This APC wasn't moving at all. The rain-soaked road had given way as it passed, and the machine was now stuck.

It must have slid down and sidewise, Lukasz figured. The rear axle and its grotesquely fat wheels—those were called "tires," if he was remembering Jozef's account correctly—were off the road entirely, hanging out over the river.

Hanging *into* the river now, almost. The swollen waters of the Warta were not more than a foot below the tires. What was worse, those same swollen and rushing waters would be undercutting the riverbank. Before too much longer—a day, perhaps; not more than two—the APC would fall completely into the river.

Judging from the expressions on the faces of the machine's crew, who were standing around staring at the APC, they'd come to the same conclusion. They had placed ropes to tether the machine, but eventually those ropes would give way.

Judging from the marks in the mud, they'd tried to use those same ropes to haul the APC to safety.

With no success, obviously. All they had at their disposal were a half dozen horses, from what Lukasz could see. That wasn't nearly enough in the way of draft power to move something as immensely heavy as the war machine. On a dry, flat road, perhaps. But not here, in this pouring rain, on this soil.

No, for this you needed oxen. Lots of oxen.

Happily, since Lukasz had learned from Koniecpolski to trust the reports of Cossack scouts, if not the Cossacks themselves, he had brought oxen with him. He'd expropriated them from a nearby landowner, who'd objected at first but then seen his Polish duty after Opalinski pointed out that with as many Cossacks as he had with him he could easily just rustle the cattle. A process which, sadly—Cossacks being Cossacks—could get out of hand and result in the unfortunate demise of the landowner and his family and retainers after the most hideous travails along with the crops destroyed, the livestock slaughtered, the house burnt to the ground, the flowers in the meadows trampled, the . . .

The oxen weren't with him any longer, of course. They were now at least five or six miles back, and moving slowly as oxen always did. But nobody was going to be moving quickly here, so much was obvious.

This was a backwater in the war, now. The armies had passed on to the south. Gustav Adolf must have left this APC behind, secure in the knowledge that it was too far behind the lines to be at risk. Even if a passing unit of Poles did stumble across it, what could they do besides slaughter the crew and the soldiers he'd left as guards?

There weren't many of those soldiers. Just a platoon, large enough to frighten away bandits.

There was something profoundly satisfying to Lukasz in the thought that Poland was going to capture its first APC with the descendants of draft animals used by the Babylonians.

Southwest of Poznań

He'd miscalculated, Koniecpolski realized. He'd simply underestimated how much the rain-soaked terrain would slow down his own troops. His army had a much larger percentage of cavalry than Gustav Adolf's. A large enough number, in fact, that he'd taken the risk of dividing his own forces in order to maneuver with cavalry and artillery alone—the latter being the Polish equivalent of flying artillery, except they were armed with small sakers instead of volley guns.

He'd left his infantry behind to hold Poznań while he circled around Gustav Adolf's troops in order to attack the northernmost column of Torstensson's USE forces. That was their First Division, under Knyphausen's command. Koniecpolski's Cossacks reported that Knyphausen's column had become dispersed by the difficulties of crossing swollen streams in the area they were passing through. He'd decided that if he moved immediately, taking cavalry and flying artillery alone, he could hammer them badly. By now, with casualties, desertion, illness and the inevitable straggling caused by a march under very difficult conditions, Koniecpolski didn't think Knyphausen had more than seven thousand effective troops. The number was probably closer to six thousand, in fact.

He could bring twelve thousand hussars, giving him an almost two-to-one numerical superiority. He'd decided the risk was worth it. He was more afraid of the USE's army than he was of the Swedes and Hessians. It was a slower-moving army, true, because it was so heavily based in the infantry. But slow as that army might be, it was immensely powerful if any commander ever got the entire army on a single battlefield, as Torstensson had against the French at Ahrensbök. Almost all units of the USE Army had been equipped and trained with rifled muskets by now, for one thing. And those odd-looking volley gun batteries had proved very effective on every battlefield they'd made an appearance.

They'd be the most effective soldiers Gustav Adolf had when it came time for sieges, too. Koniecpolski had always assumed—and still did, despite his recent successes—that any war with the USE would soon enough become a war of sieges and attrition. The Swede had simply become too powerful to hope to defeat him on the open field except under ideal weather conditions such as these.

Koniecpolski hadn't gotten a clear account yet of what had happened at Zielona Góra. His units stationed in the city had had only one radio—not surprisingly, since the Poles had few radios to begin with—and it had somehow been lost or destroyed in the fighting. So the reports he'd gotten had been piecemeal; and, to make it worse, were coming from the sort of men who were the first to flee a battlefield. Koniecpolski had learned long ago to discount much of what such men reported. Invariably, the enemy force had been immense in number, armed with impossibly powerful weapons, which had a rate of fire that would have depleted all of Europe's gunpowder stores within an hour.

Still, although Stearns had managed to take the city with surprising speed, he had to have suffered significant casualties in the doing. Taking cities was a costly business. His division had taken the brunt of the fighting at Zwenkau, as well. By now, the Third Division had to be in fairly bad shape. Not demoralized, probably. They'd won all of their battles, after all. But even soldiers with good morale can only take so much of a beating before exhaustion sets in; an exhaustion that was as much mental as physical.

Let those other bastards do the fighting for a while. Damn shirkers.

That was the attitude that would inevitably spread through the ranks. The one exception would be if their commander was the sort of rare individual who could instill a great sense of pride in them. What his nephew Jozef had told him the up-timers called *esprit de corps,* a French term which the Americans had stolen, as they so often did. When it came to language, they were a tribe of magpies.

In that event, the situation changed. Units which developed a sense of themselves as being special, an elite, the ones who could always be counted on in a crisis—such units would remain dangerous even after suffering heavy casualties.

But was Stearns such a commander? As inexperienced as he was?

Koniecpolski didn't think so. From what he could see—all of it, admittedly, at a distance and filtered through the reports of others—the American general had simply blundered his way to success. A courageous commander, yes; by now that was quite evident. But such a commander would wear out his own men, soon enough.

So. Those were the parameters of the grand hetman's calculations. He'd effectively destroyed the Hessians and he'd stymied the Swedes. One of the USE's three divisions had to be worn out by now. If he could shatter a second division, he'd have created the best possible conditions Poland and Lithuania could have hoped for. The war that followed would be the sort of protracted affair that a people defending their own lands would fight tenaciously, and the invaders would grow weary of soon enough. The great danger had always been that Gustav Adolf could successfully wage a rapid campaign.

He might well have been able to do so, had God not intervened and blessed Poland with such a tremendous storm.

But even this storm would not last for more than another day, possibly two. It was not the Deluge, after all. As slowly as his cavalry was moving, by the time Koniecpolski reached the USE First Division and could grapple with it in battle, it would have regrouped itself. Knyphausen was a competent general.

Koniecpolski had no intention of attacking a USE infantry division with hussars alone, unless it was spread out. Which it would no longer be—and to make things still worse, the weather would probably have cleared by then.

He had only two options left. Retreat back to Poznań—or try to find Gustav Adolf himself. His forces were more than a match for the Swedish units his opponent had at his immediate disposal. If he could fight a battle before the weather cleared . . .

One of his adjutants came into the command tent. "We just got a radio report. Scouts have spotted the Swede. The king himself, that is. He's marching south and his units have gotten spread out a little."

"How far away is he?" the grand hetman asked sharply.

"Ten miles, maybe twelve."

For the first time that day, Koniecpolski smiled. "Mobilize the men. Immediately. We're going to meet the bastard."

After the aide left, Koniecpolski made a mental note to himself. As soon as the war was over, he'd see to it that his nephew was legitimized. No one had done as much to aid the cause of Poland as Jozef Wojtowicz. In addition to his weather reports that had guided the grand hetman's tactics, he'd been the one who obtained the radios for Koniecpolski's army, that had proven so invaluable in the campaign.

Koniecpolski was unusual among hetman for the importance he attached to building an extensive espionage network. An army without such was half-blind, in his opinion. Once again, he'd been proven right.

Wismar, Germany, on the Baltic coast

"All good things come to an end," murmured Jozef Wojtowicz. He turned away from the window and quickly gave the room a final inspection to see if he was leaving anything incriminating behind. It was time to go.

As he'd always done before meeting the American radio operator in the tavern, he'd arrived in the area two hours early and gone to the hotel room he'd rented for the purpose of observing the tavern before he entered. The room was on the third floor and its windows opened onto the same street where the tavern was located, a short distance away.

He had no fear of arousing suspicion. Wismar now had a lot of transient traffic, which had inevitably produced the sort of hotel whose managers asked no questions—didn't even think of the questions, in fact—so long as the room was paid for. Since the Danish fleet had been repelled here two years earlier, Wismar had become a much larger town than it had been before. The air force base was no longer very active, but the navy had built a base of its own here. Wismar's harbor was deep enough to handle fairly large ships. The navy's main base on the Baltic remained at Luebeck, but they found Wismar convenient for many purposes. They'd improved the harbor, too, which had naturally drawn commercial enterprises to the port city as well.

Jozef's German was almost without accent in the most common dialect spoken along the Baltic, but it hardly mattered since the lingua franca in Wismar was the recently arisen Amideutsch. That bastard language, basically German with stripped down English conjugations and a lot of borrowed English terms, was so new that it had no standard pronunciation and probably wouldn't for many years. No one "spoke it like a native," so Jozef didn't stand out at all.

For that matter, even if he'd spoken Polish he probably would have gone unnoticed. Europe in the first half of the seventeenth century was still a place where nationalism was just beginning to develop. War was traditionally viewed as a matter between dynasties, not peoples. Trade went on between countries officially at war with hardly a pause or a stumble. Not more than two blocks from the tavern where Jozef got his weather reports from Sergeant Trevor Morton was a tavern that catered mostly to Polish fishermen. Two blocks from there, toward the west, was another tavern where Polish was also the only language normally spoken. That tavern was what the Americans called "high end," its clientele being mostly Polish grain dealers.

Jozef had never been worried that he'd be spotted as a "hostile alien." Still, he'd learned early on in his career as Koniecpolski's chief espionage agent in the USE that caution was always a virtue for a spy. So, the day after he'd made his arrangement with the American sergeant, he'd rented this room so that he could reconnoiter the tavern before entering it. He rented the room on a monthly basis rather than a weekly or a daily one, but that was so common for this hotel that the managers thought nothing of it— so long as he paid the rent on time. But one of the advantages of being a spy for the grand hetman of

Poland and Lithuania was that Stanislaw Koniecpolski was immensely wealthy and not given to stinginess.

Jozef glanced out the window a last time. Two more uniformed policemen were just entering the tavern. As with the four who'd preceded them a few minutes earlier, these were USE Navy military police, not the city's constabulary. They were probably on loan to the air force, whose base here was too small to maintain its own police force.

Too bad for Morton, of course. But the man was so stupid that the only thing that really surprised Wojto-wicz was that he hadn't been caught sooner. Luckily for Poland, the American sergeant was a sullen sort of man. He had as few friends as he did brains, so he hadn't let anything slip sooner simply because he talked to few people about anything and didn't talk to them for very long.

There was nothing in the room to worry about. There'd never been much anyway, because Jozef never slept here. For that purpose, he had a room in a private boarding house on the outskirts of the city. What little he had in the way of personal possessions was kept there.

He was tempted to retrieve those few belongings but that would be foolish. It was unlikely that any suspicion had been aroused at the boarding house. The owner was an elderly woman so hard of hearing she was almost deaf, and so nearsighted she carried a magnifying glass with her at all times. Whether as a result of those ailments or her innate nature, she was also one of the most incurious people Jozef had ever met. Which made her a perfect landlady for his purposes, of course.

No, Wojtowicz was almost certain that the USE authorities had been alerted by some misstep on the part of Morton, not Jozef himself. And they could torture the sergeant for eternity without learning where Jozef was living, because he'd never told him.

Still, he might be missing something. It was best simply to leave Wismar immediately, abandoning the possessions he had at the boarding room. Nothing there had any sentimental value; it was just practical stuff.

Jozef passed through the door and locked it behind him. He'd leave the key with the concierge on the way out of the hotel, as he always did. Excessive caution led merely to annoyance. Too little caution could lead to far worse places.

Such as the one Sergeant Morton was probably going to inhabit for the rest of his life. Assuming that life didn't end shortly at the end of a hangman's noose or in front of a firing squad.

Jozef's guess, though, was that the USE authorities would be satisfied with a life sentence. They might even be satisfied with the minimum sentence under USE law of twenty years for treason. Anyone who interrogated the sergeant would soon realize the man was every bit as dumb as he seemed. Jozef was quite certain that at no time during his dealings with Morton had it even occurred to the radio operator that the information he was passing on was for any purpose except the one he'd been told—improving the odds for grain speculators.

Sadly for Morton, so far as Jozef knew, the laws of the USE did not allow for a plea of *innocent on account of imbecility*. The laws of Poland certainly didn't, despite the astonishing concentration of imbeciles in its government.

Wojtowicz had never wished any personal ill on the American sergeant, but he'd always thought this day would probably come. So be it. His nation had not invaded the USE, after all. Poland was rather the victim of foreign aggression. If one of the aggressor's minor minions wound up dangling at the end of a rope, the nephew of the grand hetman of Poland and Lithuania would lose no sleep over the matter.

Chapter 35

Southwest of the Wolsztynr

Mike Stearns was irritated but trying not to show it. The last few days had put everyone's nerves on edge. As the crow flies, the distance from Zielona Góra to the town of Wolsztyn was about twenty-five miles. In good weather and with decent roads, an army could march that distance in a day and a half, two days at the outside. But they weren't crows, and the few roads had been in terrible condition. It had taken them three days to get to the town. Mike had pushed the last day's march into the evening, so they'd be able to get a couple of miles north of Wolsztyn. But from here, they still had maybe ten miles to go before they reached Gustav Adolf and his Swedish forces. Mike was going to try to cover that distance by late afternoon, but it was more likely that they wouldn't make it until the following day.

At that, they were doing better than the First or Second Divisions, even though they'd had to come a longer way. Knyphausen and the duke of Brunswick-Lüneburg had discovered—too late to do anything about it—that the area west of the Obra river in their vicinity had been turned into what almost amounted to a swamp. They were lucky if they moved their divisions four miles in a day.

They weren't going to be able to help Gustav Adolf in his coming battle. None of the USE divisions were. The way things looked now, the Third Division would be the first to arrive, but unless Koniecpolski decided not to launch an attack—and Mike could see no reason he would do so—they wouldn't get to Lake Bledno until after the battle was over.

According to the radio reports Mike had gotten, the king of Sweden had taken positions just south of the town of Zbąszyń, on the northeast shore of Lake Bledno. The weather had finally cleared and the planes had been back in the sky for the last two days, so they'd known where Koniecpolski's forces were. They'd arrived in Zbąszyń the night before and would surely be attacking the Swedes right about...

Now, Mike figured.

It was amazing how rapidly the grand hetman had gotten to Zbąszyń. Apparently, Koniecpolski had left his infantry and heavy artillery in Poznań and come south with just his hussars and light artillery. But that still gave him a third again as many men as the king of Sweden had with him. Maybe half again as many. Troop counts made from aircraft were only approximations.

True, all of the Swedish troops were now armed with SRG rifled muskets firing Minié balls. Some of their units, in fact, had copies of the French Cardinal breechloader that USE armories were now making. (It seemed fair enough to swipe the French design, seeing that they'd swiped it from the up-time Sharps rifle.)

The problem was that the officers and noncoms of Gustav Adolf's Swedish army were mostly old school veterans, set in their ways and slow to adjust to the new realities produced by the SRGs. That was quite unlike the situation in the USE Army, which had been created almost from scratch over the past two years. Some of the officers were hidebound, yes; but almost all of the sergeants were young men who'd recently volunteered. They didn't have any bad habits to get rid of.

The fact that Jeff Higgins had taken it upon himself to pester the division's commanding general with a trivial issue he should have taken up with the quartermasters was making Mike even more irritated. Captain David Blodger, the up-time quartermaster who handled technical supplies and material, could have done Jeff a lot more good than Mike.

But since he was still feeling a little guilty over the way he'd handled Jeff at Zielona Góra, Mike did his best not to let his aggravation show. They were taking a brief halt in the march anyway, to let the units in the rear close up the column, so he didn't really have anything pressing at the moment. A "forced march" didn't actually mean soldiers were constantly marching, despite the term itself.

"I don't understand why you brought this problem to me, Colonel Higgins." Mike leaned over in his saddle and looked down at the object in Jeff's hand, a radio transmitter and receiver that had obviously seen better days. At a guess, a horse had stepped on it. "Captain Blodger can get your regiment a replacement radio, I'm sure."

Jeff shook his head. "I guess I didn't make myself clear, sir. This isn't one of the regiment's radios."

Mike was finding it harder and harder not to snarl at Higgins. What was he? A major general doubling as the division's lost and found department?

"Not that I see why you care, but if you're that concerned about it—again, see Blodger. He can find out which regiment lost the damn thing and get—"

"Sir! Excuse me, sir, I'm still not making myself clear. This radio doesn't belong to *anybody* in this division. Anybody in the whole USE Army, in fact."

Mike stared at the radio again. It *looked* like one of the division's radios.

Well...sort of. In a way. The same way any such radio looks about the same as its equivalent to someone who doesn't know much about radios and doesn't really care about the differences anyway so long as the thing works.

In short, someone like Mike Stearns.

"It's not?"

"No, sir. I didn't think I recognized it, but just to be sure I checked with Jimmy Andersen. He says this is a knock-off made in Hamburg of one of the models that the army uses. He says we've never used this brand because the manufacturer had fly-by-night financing and went bankrupt after making not more than a few dozen of them. Jimmy says the whole lot was bought at an auction in Hamburg by somebody in Amsterdam. Well, by an agent for somebody in Amsterdam who was probably serving as an agent for somebody else. You know how it is."

Mike felt his face stiffen. He was probably going pale, too. "Where did you find this?" he asked.

"I just spotted it this morning, by accident, when I was passing by one of the soldiers who had it stuck in his pack. When I asked him, he said he'd found it

in an alley behind one of the houses in Zielona Góra.
He figures a horse stepped on it and broke it. But he
liked it as a war souvenir. It's different."

"Oh, Jesus," Mike whispered. "It's a *Polish* radio.
It's got to be."

Jeff nodded. "That's what I'm thinking. And it's why
I brought it to you. I got to thinking about it and
it occurred to me I've never heard anyone mention
anything about the Poles having radios."

"That's because we didn't know they did—and, like
idiots, blithely assumed they couldn't. Being dumb
Polacks, like they are."

Jeff chuckled. West Virginia had enough people
with Polish ancestry to have a slew of Polack jokes.
Nothing like Chicago or Milwaukee, of course.

"How many Polacks does it take to screw in a light
bulb?" he said.

"It's not funny, Colonel. It really isn't."

Jeff stared at him. Then, his face got stiff too. "Oh,
hell. You mean we really never considered that they
might have radio communication?"

"No, Colonel, we didn't. It goes a long way toward
explaining how and why Koniecpolski's been able to
maneuver his forces so well, doesn't it?"

Mike dismounted. As they always did whenever a
halt was called, Jimmy Andersen and his three assistants had quickly set up a little tent for the radio so
he could get whatever might be the latest reports or
instructions. Mike walked over, opened the flap of the
tent and passed through.

Jeff dismounted and came after him, still carrying
the radio. He didn't really have a good reason to do
so, since the tent was so small there wouldn't be room

for him anyway. He just liked to get off a horse any excuse he got.

A minute later, Mike came out.

As the march was about to resume, Jimmy Andersen came out of the tent and approached the division's commanding general. Behind him, his assistants began taking down the tent and packing away the radio equipment. Colonel Higgins had already left to rejoin his regiment.

Andersen looked up at Mike, back in his saddle. "Bad news, sir. I just got a weather report. It looks like there's another storm coming. It'll probably hit us around noon today."

Mike stared down at him, then stared off to the west. Huge storm clouds covered the sky and were obviously headed their way.

He felt like saying *No shit, Sherlock.* But that would probably be beneath the dignity of a major general and it would certainly hurt Andersen's feelings.

You always had to make allowances for tech people. Their skills were so useful that you just had to accept the fact that if someone like Jimmy Andersen got struck by lightning, the first thing he'd do if he survived was get on the radio to find out if there were thunderstorms in the area. In those halcyon days before the Ring of Fire, of course, he would have gone online to find out.

Schwerin, capital of Mecklenburg Province United States of Europe

Jozef Wojtowicz had set up a safe house for himself in Schwerin before he'd gone to Wismar. He thought he could lie in hiding here until whatever manhunt was launched for him exhausted its energies.

He assumed that the military police who interrogated Morton would deduce soon enough that the agent who'd suborned him was either Polish or working for Poland. Who else would have taken the risk? Any person familiar with the Baltic grain trade would know that the pretext he'd used was preposterous. If there were no USE interrogators with that knowledge in Wismar, all they had to do was walk over to Wieczorek's tavern and ask the Polish grain dealers who habituated the place.

Where would they look for this Polish agent, then?

Magdeburg, of course—but they really wouldn't expect him to hide there. The capital city's CoC was too pervasive, too well organized. A stranger, especially a foreigner, ran a greater risk of being noticed there than anywhere else.

The fact that such a stranger was a foreigner wouldn't be held against him in Magdeburg the way it might in some cities in the USE. Although the CoCs called for the unification of the German people into one nation, their ideology was not particularly nationalistic. There were CoCs in a number of European countries and they all shared the same basic political program. The Italian CoCs also called for national unification.

The problem with hiding in Magdeburg wasn't that people would be hostile, it was simply that he'd be noticed more quickly, and by an organization that was sophisticated and well organized on a city-wide basis.

Hamburg was another obvious possibility, as were Luebeck and Hannover. Big cities where a foreigner could hide easily.

Jozef had considered them, in fact. The problem

was that they were in western provinces and he wanted to be as close to the border as he could manage. If he did have to make a desperate attempt to escape back into Polish territory, he'd find that much easier to do from Mecklenburg than places farther west.

Escaping into Poland from Pomerania would be even easier, of course. But to do that, he'd have to be in Pomerania, which he detested. The only city in the miserable province that would be tolerable would be Stettin, and Stettin was crawling with Swedes. Suspicious Swedes, with a nasty turn of mind when it came to Poles and anything Polish, as you'd expect from a pack of bandits in their ill-gotten lair. (The city's proper name was Szczecin. Always had been, always would be, and damn anyone who said otherwise.)

Ideally, he'd have gone to Grantville. Jozef *loved* Grantville. And with his uncle as his paymaster, he could even afford the outrageous rents.

Alas, it was not to be. He'd spent too much time in Grantville, early in his career as a spy, before he'd learned how to stay invisible. There was too much risk of being spotted.

Where then?

He'd settled on Schwerin because it was the capital of Mecklenburg province. Since the Dreeson Incident just a short time ago, the place had become a hotbed of radicalism, especially its capital. Young firebrands holding forth on every corner.

More importantly for Jozef, such centers of youthful radicalism produced certain cultural developments, almost like a law of nature. For every firebrand spouting ideology on a corner, there would be a poet spouting verses in a tavern.

Jozef wrote poetry, as it happened. Not very good poetry, but that would be all to the good. A mediocre poet would blend in perfectly where a man with literary talent might be noticed.

So it was. His first night in a nearby tavern was uneventful. He made a few acquaintances.

The second night, the same.

The third night, he was urged to recite some of his own poetry. Which he did, to reasonable applause. To fit the crowd's taste, he'd slightly adjusted a poem he'd once written on the subject of sunrise to make it politically appropriate. (Not hard to do. A sun rising, a people rising; the rhymes just had to be tweaked a bit.)

The fourth night, the same, with the added benefit of finding female company. It turned out that for this crowd of people, anything foreign carried a certain romance and panache.

The fifth night, the same again, with the female company more affectionate still.

The sixth day, catastrophe.

"Hey, Mateusz,"—so was he known here; Mateusz Zielinski—"there's somebody you have to meet."

He had no desire to meet anyone, particularly, especially when he was eating a late breakfast. But since the person doing the introduction was the young woman who'd just provided him with another very enjoyable twelve hours, he felt obliged to do as she wished.

The person to whom he was introduced was a young fellow named Karsten Eichel. It took him no more than three minutes to get to the purpose of the introduction.

"You're for the overthrow of serfdom in Poland, I'm sure. I heard your poem about the people rising. Well, I'm in the CoC here and I can introduce you to somebody who knows"—here, a brief intake of breath—"Krzysztof Opalinski. *The* Krzysztof Opalinski, I mean."

Eichel sat there at the table across from Jozef, looking very pleased with himself. Jozef had had a cat once who had almost the same expression on its face when it plopped a freshly caught rodent at Jozef's feet.

The Krzysztof Opalinski. That would be the same Krzysztof Opalinski whom Jozef had known since he was six. His good friend Lukasz Opalinski was Krzysztof's younger brother. Lukasz had set off to become a hussar for Poland's king and Sejm, and with equal vigor and enthusiasm Krzysztof had set off to overthrow that selfsame king and Sejm. Such was the nature of the Opalinski family.

"He's in Poland now, of course, doing his righteous work," continued Eichel. "But my friend can get you across the border so you can rejoin the struggle." He rose and leaned over the table, his voice dropping to a whisper. "I'll bring my friend here tonight."

And off he went.

During his stay in Grantville, Jozef had been introduced to the work of the English playwright Shakespeare—who was almost a contemporary, oddly enough—and become quite taken by it. So the appropriate thought came to him instantly:

Hoist with his own petard.

Indeed. He had to flee Schwerin, at once. To

where? He had no idea, as yet, but surely a destination would come to him.

He rose from the table, gave his companion a most friendly smile—she really had been splendid company if you excluded her final demonic impulse—and said, "I'm afraid I have to leave."

She looked distressed. "Now? But . . . Where are you going?"

He was already walking away. "The seacoast of Bohemia," he said over his shoulder.

Stockholm

Ulrik dumped the documents onto the bed next to him. Had his physical condition allowed, he'd have used a much more dramatic gesture. Hurling them into the fireplace would have been his own preference, albeit counterproductive. Still, even being able to pitch them onto the floor would have been nice.

The problem was that he might want to pick them up later, in order to illustrate a point from some part of the text. He was completely incapable of such a motion and would be for some time to come. Baldur would pick them up for him, if he insisted, but the Norwegian's ensuing sarcasm would be tedious. So would Caroline Platzer, but her ensuing lecture on psychological self-control and the need thereof especially for a prince in line of succession would be even more tedious. Kristina might or might not, depending on her mood of the moment.

It wasn't worth it. Thankfully, his wounds had not impaired his most necessary skills for the task at hand.

The bullet that had broken two of his ribs—thank God for good Danish buff coats, or he'd probably be dead—had also left that whole side of his torso aching and immobile. The bullet that had creased his skull—thank God also for good Norwegian bearskin hats, which had probably kept the bullet from piercing his skull—had stunned him for a moment and left a wound that bled badly, as head wounds always did.

But neither of the injuries had affected his brain. He could safely ignore Caroline's warning that he might have suffered a mild concussion. Americans were notorious for seeing perilous injuries everywhere. Many of them even went so far as to oppose corporal punishment for errant children. Speaking of insane.

Nor, best of all, had the injuries affected his tongue.

"Colonel Forsberg, I repeat: Your theory makes no sense."

The colonel stood by the bed, his head bend slightly downward but his back straight as a ramrod. An instrument which, in Ulrik's considered opinion after dealing with the man, had been inserted into his rectum at the age of two and never been removed since.

Forsberg pointed a finger at the papers. The finger was rigid too. Everything about the colonel was rigid. How did he manage to bathe?

"The evidence is in the documents themselves, Your Highness. It says right there, in black and white, that Richelieu was behind it all."

"I know what the documents *say*, Colonel. But that's not really the issue, is it? The real question is whether we can place any credence in these documents. To put it a different way, why should we assume that documents which were oh-so-conveniently left for us to find by people who planned to murder us—*did* murder Her Majesty—should be taken at face value?"

It was clear from the expression on Forsberg's face that Ulrik was wasting his time.

Again.

But Forsberg didn't really matter, in the end. Kristina had been following Ulrik's logic since the day after the incident, when he'd recovered enough to start thinking. Her brain might be only eight years old, but it was a superior organ—considerably superior—to those taking up space in the skulls of most of Stockholm's officials.

"And why did they leave the documents at all?" she said. "Why not simply destroy them? They came here to kill me and Ulrik and Mama, not to found a library."

That made no dent in Forsberg's certain convictions either, of course.

Ulrik decided to try one last time, before he simply began acting peremptorily. He disliked doing that, since he'd found that imperiousness on the part of a prince invariably produced resentment, and some of those resentments could last for years and create trouble long after their initial cause was half-forgotten.

"And consider this, Colonel Forsberg. This should register because you were there yourself and personally witnessed the deed. What happened when you cornered two of the assassins on Utö island? The one with the limp and his companion?"

That had happened two days after the incident. All reconstructions of the plot, including Ulrik and Baldur's, were agreed that seven assassins had to have been involved. Possibly more, but a minimum of seven.

Four of them had been killed in the course of the attempt itself. Two by Ulrik; two by Baldur.

Two more had fled in a boat but had been eventually tracked to Utö island. Ulrik had recognized one of them after the bodies had been brought back to Stockholm. That had been the man who'd shot him. The other, the one whom the soldiers said had been limping and had a badly bruised knee, he didn't know. But since he'd been caught in the company of the man who shot Ulrik, it was reasonable to conclude that he'd been one of the six men who came directly for him and Kristina in Slottsbacken.

That left whoever had murdered the queen. That had been done with a rifle, not a pistol. Whoever the man was—he might have had an accomplice with him—he remained at large. All they had in the way of evidence was the badly bludgeoned corpse of the old tailor whose shop he'd used as a shooting stand. The tailor's wife had been no help, because she'd been visiting her sister halfway across the city.

Forsberg still hadn't answered Ulrik's question. From the look on his face, he was probably confused by its sheer simplicity.

"What happened, Colonel?" he repeated.

"Well, I don't exactly know what to say, Your Highness. We found them and caught them."

Kristina practically spit. "Didn't! *You* didn't catch them. They were already dead."

The colonel looked offended now. Was there any bottom to this pit?

"That's as may be, Your Highness," Forsberg said stiffly. "But they'd not have killed themselves if we hadn't had them trapped with no way to escape."

Ulrik threw up his hands. "Exactly! That's the whole point, Colonel. Once he saw there was no escape, the man with the limp shot his companion in the back of the head and then turned the pistol on himself. Do you think a professional spy in the employ of the French crown would have done such a thing?"

The colonel's face was blank.

Blank. Blank. Blank.

This was pointless. Ulrik might as well have been arguing with the Black Forest or the Harz Mountains.

"The point, Colonel, is that only a man with powerful ideological convictions would have behaved in such a manner. And the willingness of his companions to join him in such a daring assassination scheme—they had little chance of escaping, and they must have known it—speaks to the same point."

He retrieved some of the documents he'd scattered on the bed sheets, lifted them up, and then dropped them back. The gesture exuded disgust.

"Nothing about the idea that these men were Richelieu's makes any sense. Not their behavior, not the preposterous idea that supposedly professional assassins would scatter about enough documents to bury a moose, and perhaps most of all, the very logic of the documents themselves."

He pointed an accusing finger at one of those documents. Not because it deserved to be singled out for condemnation, but simply because it was the nearest. Ulrik had to economize even his finger-pointing. Any movement of his upper body was likely to trigger off a spasm of pain.

"Colonel, why in the world would Richelieu's *intendant* Etienne Servien have sent these men detailed— even lovingly detailed—analyses of political and military developments in Europe? None of which developments, I will point out, had any relevance to their task at hand

and *all* of which were developments that happened months ago."

He was tired. Very tired. He didn't have much strength.

"Never mind, Colonel. I am superseding your authority in this matter." He cocked an eye at Kristina. "Assuming my betrothed concurs, of course."

Kristina nodded happily. "Sure! But what do you want to do?"

Carefully, Ulrik levered himself a bit more upright. "The wonders of up-time technology. Baldur, go get the palace's radio operator. I'm going to speak directly with the king. If he's not available, then I'll talk to Chancellor Oxenstierna."

Baldur nodded and left. Colonel Forsberg began issuing protests.

"You can go now!" commanded Kristina. And, a protest or two later, so he did.

Baldur returned sooner than Ulrik expected he would. He had a peculiar expression on his face.

"Ah . . . I didn't have to find the radio man, Your Highness." The honorific was unusual, coming from Baldur in private. Norddahl gestured toward the door. "He was on his way here already."

The radio operator came in.

"We're going to talk to Papa!" Kristina's voice was full of cheer.

The radio operator stared at her. His face, Ulrik suddenly realized, was as pale as a sheet. The man looked down at the message in his hand, as if he were helpless; too weak to even lift it.

"Papa!" cried Kristina.

Chapter 36

Lake Bledno, Poland

The Polish sakers should not have been a match for the Swedish artillery. True, they were more powerful than most of the guns Gustav Adolf had on the field today. He had fourteen of the so-called "regimental" guns and only two twelve-pounders. The regimental guns were three-pounder light artillery, made of cast bronze and with short barrels, and using reduced powder charges to keep from overheating. The Polish sakers had longer barrels and fired shot that was about five and a quarter pounds.

Koniecpolski had managed to get a full dozen of the things onto the battlefield, too. Considering the terrain he'd had to bring them through and the speed at which he'd done it, that was in itself a tremendous feat of generalship.

But the difference wasn't the guns, it was the gunners. The Swedish artillery corps was the best in world, bar none. Gustav Adolf had always emphasized artillery—light artillery, in particular—and in young Lennart Torstensson he'd found a superb commanding general and trainer for his artillery.

Torstensson was gone now, having been put in charge of the USE's army. But his training methods and attitudes had become ingrained in Sweden's artillerymen.

So, lighter though the shot of their regimental guns might be, they fired two or three for every one coming across the field from the saker barrels. Even the two Swedish twelve-pounders were almost able to match the Polish rate of fire.

The Swedish fire was more accurate, too. Where the Poles simply fired in the direction of the enemy, the Swedish gunners were skilled enough to fire the sort of grazing shots that caused the most damage on a battlefield. These were not exploding shells that were being fired, but round shot. The only way to use round shot against infantry or cavalry on a open battlefield effectively was to aim for the ground *ahead* of the oncoming foe. The balls would hit the ground and bounce off, sailing into the enemy's ranks at a low trajectory—waist-high was what gunners tried for—and sometimes destroying a dozen men at a time.

All well and good. But on this field today, by the shores of Lake Bledno just south of the Polish town of Zbąszyń, that same Swedish skill was actually working against them. Grazing shots presuppose ground that is reasonably hard. After days of heavy rain, this soil was very far from that. It wasn't what you could call mud, exactly, but it was certainly soggy. A lot of the Swedish artillery rounds simply buried themselves, especially those fired by the big twelve-pounders. The regimental guns could still manage grazing shots perhaps half of the time, but the effectiveness of those shots was drastically reduced. The second bounce would usually end their trajectories; the third invariably would.

The Poles faced the same problem, of course, but the very imprecision of their fire probably worked to their advantage. They weren't trying for grazing shots anyway.

An hour into the battle, Gustav Adolf's artillery commanders realized the problem and adjusted their fire as best they could. But all that meant was that they were now achieving mediocre results instead of poor ones.

For years, Gustav Adolf had been able to rely on his artillery to offset whatever advantages his opponent might have. The greatest victory of his career, at Breitenfeld, had been due to artillery. Today, at Lake Bledno, he was finding that advantage gone.

He almost regretted now his decision the day before not to take Zbąszyń. When he reached the town, he'd discovered that Koniecpolski had managed to get some of his troops into it already. Not very many, true—perhaps two thousand hussars. They had no artillery and hussars were cavalry, not really trained and equipped to defend a town under siege.

On the other hand, they were hussars. That meant that, trained or not, equipped or not, they'd still fight valiantly and ferociously. Gustav Adolf's forces outnumbered them by four-to-one and did have artillery. He didn't doubt that he could take the town within a day; two at the outside.

But Koniecpolski would be here on the morrow. There was no doubt of it. Once again, the USE Air Force was able to give the king of Sweden superb reconnaissance. The last thing Gustav Adolf wanted was for Koniecpolski to catch him in mid-siege. That could be disastrous.

Instead, he'd chosen to move south and take a stand against the lake. He thought he could at the very least fight the Pole to a standstill on open ground. And a standstill was all he needed. Within a day or two, the USE divisions would begin to arrive—Stearns' Third being the first, surprisingly—and the preponderance of forces would shift drastically against Koniecpolski. He'd probably choose to withdraw, in fact, before Stearns even got here. That would mean a siege of Poznań, soon enough, because that was certainly where Koniecpolski would withdraw his forces.

This was not what Gustav Adolf had hoped for, when he began this campaign. The reason he'd driven so hard and taken the risk of separating into six columns was precisely to circumvent the Poles' ability to tie him up in a succession of sieges.

But, war was what it was—above all else, no respecter of persons. There was still enough time before winter came to seize Poznań and possibly Wroclaw. Breslau, rather, as it should be called. The majority of the population in the territory Gustav Adolf had taken so far—in the cities and bigger towns, at any rate—were German Lutherans, not Catholic Poles. If worse came to worst and Gustav Adolf was forced to halt the campaign once winter arrived, at least he would have reclaimed all the territory that his despised cousin Wladyslaw had stolen while Sweden's back was turned.

So. All he had to do today was simply hold the field. And by now, two hours into the battle, Gustav Adolf was confident he could. The artillery barrages that began most battles—this one had been no exception—had been inconclusive. The Poles would now try to break his ranks with cavalry charges. No one did that better than hussars, either. They were without a doubt Europe's premier heavy cavalry, almost a throwback to the knights of the late middle ages.

Still, Gustav Adolf was sure he could withstand them. He'd placed himself against the lake because he'd been confident he could do so. Normally, he wouldn't cut himself off from a route of retreat that way. If the Poles did break his ranks, the result would probably be disastrous. On the other hand, the Poles could no longer use one of the sweeping flank attacks their hussars employed so well, either. They had no choice but to come at him straight on, and he was sure his veteran soldiers could stand against that.

Without talking his eyes off the enemy across the field, Gustav Adolf swiveled his head to speak to Anders Jönsson. The huge Swede and the dozen Scotsmen under his command served Gustav Adolf as his personal bodyguard—on a battlefield, as everywhere else.

"It's going well, I think. Well enough, at least."

He felt a drop of rain strike his hand. Then two, then three. A little patter of raindrops hit his helmet. *"Fuck!"*

Jönsson had been afraid the king hadn't spotted the storm clouds coming. As it always was in a battle, Gustav Adolf's attention had been riveted on the enemy across the field. Some part of his mind had probably noticed that it was getting darker, despite the sun still rising. They hadn't reached noon yet. But that same part of his mind would have discounted the fact. Things often got darker in a battle, from the gunsmoke pouring out everywhere. Especially if there wasn't much in the way of a breeze, which there wasn't today.

Or hadn't been. Anders felt a sudden gust strike his cheek.

This was going to be another bitch of a storm, watch and see.

"Fuck!" repeated the king of Sweden, emperor of the United States of Europe, and high king of the Union of Kalmar.

Once again, war was respecting no person.

"Praise the Lord," murmured Stanislaw Koniecpolski. Technically, that might be blasphemy. But Koniecpolski was a Catholic, not a superstitious Protestant prone to seeing fussy rules and regulations in the way a man put on a button. He was also the grand hetman of Poland and Lithuania and one of its greatest magnates—a class of men who took a very expansive view of their rights and privileges. Much of the reason for Poland's tradition of religious toleration was because no great magnate was about to tolerate anyone—neither king nor pope nor sniveling Jesuit nor even the Sejm itself—telling *him* what he could or could not believe. He might be a Catholic himself, as most of Poland and Lithuania's magnates were, but he damn well had the right to convert to any brand of Protestantism that took his fancy, if he chose to do so.

So, "Praise the Lord," repeated Koniecpolski. Secure in the knowledge that what might be blasphemy for a peasant or a butcher was not for a grand hetman.

The storm clouds were coming fast. The Poles would start charging furiously now, while the soil was still firm enough that their horses could move across it. The condition of the ground was already bad—terribly so for cannon balls—but it wasn't bad enough that Polish warhorses would disobey their masters. A horse could handle such terrain, even if they didn't like it. They wouldn't be galloping, of course. But even a hussar charge at the speed of a canter could hammer down an opponent if they failed to stand their ground.

That was Gustav Adolf's great concern. Modern infantry could withstand cavalry if they were trained and seasoned, which these troops were—*provided* they retained their confidence. And there was nothing that would faster erode a unit's morale than the feeling they were alone, isolated, with their commanders nowhere to be seen.

The feeling, in short, that a heavy rain would bring.

The king of Sweden knew exactly what Koniecpolski would do now. The grand hetman would push his hussars to the utmost in order to take advantage of whatever period existed between the arrival of the rain and the subsequent obscuring of the battlefield and the point at which the rain turned the ground so muddy that cavalry were effectively unusable.

The morale of his troops. That was everything, now. He had to do whatever was necessary to keep them from faltering.

Without even realizing he was doing so, Gustav Adolf eased his sword in and out of its scabbard in order to make sure it would come forth easily if he needed it. Then he did the same with his pistols in their saddle holsters.

Anders Jönsson knew how to read the signs. He swiveled in the saddle and gave his little unit of Scotsmen a fierce and commanding look.

You know what's probably coming. Be ready!

Then he faced forward again. Were it not completely inappropriate in the presence of his monarch, Anders would have shouted his sentiments aloud—and been echoed by a dozen Scot throats.

Fuck!

Chapter 37

The first hussar charge was driven back with a horrible slaughter. This was the first time Stanislaw Koniecpolski had faced the new rifled muskets massed on a battlefield, and he'd underestimated their effectiveness. They could be reloaded as quickly as smoothbore muskets but had two or even three times the effective range. He understood now why the Swedes had such a seemingly-perilous dearth of pikemen. They had only one pike for every two muskets, where the usual ratio was one-to-one or even two-to-one in favor of the long spears.

But those slender ranks of pikemen were enough, given the horrific rate of fire being maintained by the riflemen they were protecting.

Koniecpolski almost lost the battle, right then and there. He surely would have, had he followed his natural urge to hurl more hussars at the enemy. He'd won battles before with that simple tactic, and more than one of them. Hussars were terrifying in a full charge, on their immense horses and with the wings expanding their apparent size and their huge lances. They were like something out of legend. Mounted knights of fable, with the ferocity of ancient warriors.

But not this battle. The Swedes stood their ground and gunned down the Polish cavalry. Shot them and shot and shot them. Not more than twenty or thirty even managed to reach the enemy lines, and they were either killed or driven off by the pikes soon enough.

The grand hetman couldn't afford such casualties. Not even hussars could withstand losses like these, if they kept up.

"Call them back!" he bellowed to his aides. As they raced off to carry out his orders, Koniecpolski turned to the commander of his Cossack units, Severyn Skoropadsky.

"I need you to relieve the pressure, Ataman. Make no frontal attacks, you understand. Just harass them and keep them off balance for..."

He paused to gauge the sky. "Perhaps half an hour. Or a bit longer."

Skoropadsky had a little smile on his face, with perhaps a trace of derision. As if Cossacks were dumb enough to imitate blockhead Polish hussars! Cossacks were raiders of the steppes. Like Tatars and the Mongols before them, their style of warfare was fluid. They mostly used firearms now instead of bows, but their tactics were still basically those of mounted archers.

But if there was any derision in that smile, it was only a trace and more the product of Cossack habit than any disrespect for Koniecpolski himself. The grand hetman of Poland and Lithuania was well-regarded by the Commonwealth's registered Cossacks. Koniecpolski had played a major role in the Polish campaign to crush the Cossack rebellion in 1630 led by Taras Fedorovych. No Cossack doubted that Koniecpolski would have completely crushed the rebels had that been what he saw as his duty. But during the negotiations that finally produced a treaty in August, Koniecpolski had opposed harsh reprisals against the Cossack rebels. He'd thought that the long-standing tensions between Poland-Lithuania and the Cossack hosts would never end until the Commonwealth changed its policies toward the Cossacks.

So, whenever he went on campaign, Koniecpolski had no trouble gaining the adherence of several thousand registered Cossacks—no small accomplishment, given that there were not all that many to begin with. Many of them were no doubt unregistered, of course. In time of war, the atamans would usually look the other way if their ranks were partially filled with Cossacks from the various independent hosts who had no legal standing in the Commonwealth.

So would Stanislaw Koniecpolski. Whatever their faults, Cossacks were fighters.

Whenever a charge was broken as badly as this one had been, there was always the great danger that the retreating cavalrymen would trigger panic in the whole army. The repulse of a charge would then become the rout of an army.

Koniecpolski himself could play the most important part in stifling that danger. He was already riding toward the returning hussars, to steady them with words of assurance and his simple presence. But it would help a great deal if the army could see that the enemy was being engaged by other forces. In truth, the Cossacks couldn't do more than tear at the edges of the Swedish forces. But that would be enough to keep Gustav Adolf from launching any charge of his own. All Koniecpolski needed was enough time for the rain to begin again.

Cavalrymen didn't like to fight in a storm, even less than infantrymen did. The horses were harder to handle, and for good reason. Many of them would inevitably stumble, charging through rain and mud, and a horse fall could kill or cripple a man very easily.

Still, whether they liked it or not, hussars would have the advantage in a heavy rain. Their somewhat archaic style of war would serve them in good stead then.

A musket is hard to reload in a downpour, leaving the soldier with no better weapon than a bayonet—against a sixteen-foot lance that needed no reloading. And when that lance was lost as lances usually were in a battle, the infantryman would then have to face the hussar's saber. A man on foot armed with what amounted to a short clumsy spear, against a man wielding a long saber from atop a horse fourteen to sixteen hands tall.

It would be a bloody, muddy, mess of a battle. But Koniecpolski thought he could win it. No, Koniecpolski was *determined* to win it. This was the third time Gustav Adolf had invaded Poland. Enough was enough.

Given the pace Mike Stearns was demanding, the march had been exhausting already. Then the rain started coming down.

"Well, fuck a duck," said Colonel Jeff Higgins. Wishing, before long, that he was a duck himself.

At the front of the column, Mike and his aides had called another halt. They had no choice, really, since the division was getting spread out too thinly again. There was only one passable road in this area and you could only safely march three men abreast. That meant the Third Division stretched for more than

two miles between its head and its tail. If you didn't
make periodic stops, that stretch got even worse. The
division was like a giant caterpillar moving across the
Polish landscape.

A wet caterpillar—and from the looks of the sky,
it was going to get wetter before the day was over.

"How far, do you think?" he asked his aides.

Duerr shrugged. "In miles? Somewhere between
two and four. Probably around three. In hours? As
long as it may take."

Long made a face. "That's about the truth of it,
sir. In decent weather, even on a road like this, we
could make it in an hour or two hours. Be wiser to
take the two, though."

Leebrick nodded. "There's no point coming to a
battle so quickly that you're in no shape to fight."
He pointed with his thumb to the army stretched
out behind them. You couldn't see the end of it
from here, and probably couldn't have even in good
weather. "You show up at a battle strung out like this,
cavalry will eat you alive. Hussars won't even bother
to salt you first."

Mike listened for the sound of cannon fire. The
battle must have started by now. If they were only
two to four miles away from the battle, you'd expect
to hear the guns.

He couldn't hear anything at all. But with this sort
of heavy rainfall, he had no idea how much the noise
of a battlefield would get suppressed.

Five minutes later, the march resumed.

Anders Jönsson was having no trouble hearing the
guns. But he wasn't paying much attention to them,

because it wasn't cannon fire he was worried about at the moment. He squinted through the rain, shielding his eyes with a hand. The helmet he was wearing was designed to shed bullets and sword blades, not raindrops.

You could barely see the enemy any longer, the downpour was so thick. Surely the Poles wouldn't try—

The huge shape of a winged hussar came into sight, followed by dozens more—hundreds on either side were now visible—no, that must be at least two or three thousand—

Miserable be-damned Poles. Fighting hussars was like fighting armed and armored lunatics.

For a moment, Jönsson felt a fierce yearning for some of his own lunatic ancestors. A field full of berserks charging the other way would be nice, right about now. Swinging great swords, wearing nothing but bearskins, biting their own shields in a fury.

Not much different from hussars, really, except for the wings and not being quite as dumb.

"Again!" Koniecpolski roared. "No mercy on the Swedes!"

Three times he'd sent the hussars against the front ranks of Gustav Adolf's army since the rain began. Three times they'd been driven back. But each time, they returned with renewed fury rather than despair. The hussars were suffering heavy casualties, but they could sense their enemy weakening.

Meanwhile, Koniecpolski kept the Cossacks in the fight. He'd never let them rest once since he first launched them at the enemy's flanks. They couldn't get around those flanks, of course, because the Swedes

were backed up against the lake. But they could keep
Gustav Adolf pinned where he was.

The Swedish king was completely on the defensive
now. He was outnumbered, unable to maneuver, and
had lost all of his advantages. The superb rate of
fire of his artillery had vanished. There was no way
to reload a cannon quickly in a downpour. The same
for reloading a musket. Rifled or smoothbore, it mattered not. The rain equalized everything. The men
handling breechloaders in the Swedish army could
still maintain a fairly decent rate of fire, but there
weren't that many of them. And as for the accuracy
of the rifles, what did it matter if you could hit an
enemy soldier at three hundred yards? You can't shoot
something you can't see. Between the rain and the
gunsmoke, this battlefield was almost as obscured as
it would have been in a fog.

A gust of wind cleared aside the gunsmoke, allowing Gustav Adolf to see most of the field for the first
time in ten minutes.

He felt a little shock of horror. A gap had opened
up between the Västergötlanders and the Green Brigade. It wasn't a huge gap, but hussars wouldn't need
much to start rolling up the lines.

Outnumbered as he was, he hadn't kept much of
a reserve, and he'd already used up what he had.
He'd sent Colonel Hepburn and his men to shore
up his right very early in the battle. What he'd had
left was just the Orange regiment. Ten minutes ago,
he'd sent them to bolster Winkel. They couldn't be
called back in time.

Whatever was to be done, it had to be done now.

The gap had been created by the Green Brigade, which had bunched itself up from the confusion of the battle and the never-to-be-sufficiently cursed rain. Their ranks needed to be spread out again.

He couldn't spot the brigade's commander. He might have been killed already.

The Swedish king spurred his horse and charged forward. In five minutes, he could salvage the situation.

Anders Jönsson did mutter profanities out loud this time as he raced after Gustav Adolf. No reasons not to, now that the king couldn't possibly hear him. Not with the rain and the gunfire and, most of all, the blood rushing through Gustav Adolf's own ears as happened to idiot berserkers.

The Scots came behind him, mouthing their own profanities. Some of which were no doubt Celtic, which was a bit absurd given that the ancestors of those men had once charged into battle stark naked and painted blue.

Chapter 38

The commander of the Green Brigade was dead, as a matter of fact. So was the officer who would have replaced him in command. Both of them had been too far forward when a hussar charge drove over them.

The colonel in command of the Västergötlanders had also been killed. But the two officers who were next in command were not even aware of the fact. They were at the very front, holding the first ranks steady.

So, the young captain whom they'd left behind to keep an eye on things—yes, it was foolish to do so, but men do foolish things in the chaos of a battlefield—was the only officer in the regiment who spotted the gap that had opened between them and the Green Brigade.

He, too, was horrified at the sight. Immediately, he commanded the nearest company to follow as he raced to set things right.

Which they did—thereby opening another gap. The captain hadn't intended to move more than one company. But he hadn't told any other to stay in place, either. Seeing the first company move, the captain in command of its neighbor concluded that he had to move also. As his company moved, yet a third—and then a fourth—was pulled in its train. It wasn't until five of the regiment's eight companies had shifted their positions that the two officers in command realized what was happening.

But by then, it was too late. Gustav Adolf was still closing the first gap when two hundred hussars found the second. They poured through in a flood.

The rain that the Swedish king had cursed was all that saved his army, then. Koniecpolski's view of the battlefield was even more obscured than Gustav Adolf's, because the rain was being driven from the west. So he never spotted the sudden disaster that had fallen upon his enemy. He knew nothing about it, in fact, until he got reports after the battle from the hussars who had survived to tell their happy tale.

Three times the Swedish bastard and his armies had brought murder, destruction and rapine into Poland. There wouldn't be a fourth.

A Scotsman's shout alerted Jönsson. Twisting in his saddle, he saw at least two dozen hussars racing toward him.

No, most of them were racing toward the king. Gustav Adolf wore no distinctive insignia. But he was a big man, and an imperious one on a battlefield. Whether or not the oncoming hussars knew his exact identity, they obviously realized he was some sort of top commander.

As children, Polish hussars-in-the-making heard the same advice children everywhere got from their elders. *To kill a snake, cut off its head.*

A number of them set out to do so.

❖   ❖   ❖

Gustav Adolf heard Anders' cry of warning. When he saw the hussars coming his way, he swung his horse to face them, sword in his hand. He had two wheel-lock pistols in saddle holsters, but he wouldn't have time to use them.

He'd always turned down the many offers of up-time pistols. Despite their obvious advantages, he simply didn't like the things. They didn't *feel* right. Childish, perhaps, but there it was. If the king of Sweden, emperor of the USE, high king of etc., etc., insists he don't need no steenkeeng up-time pistol, how are you going to make him take it?

The first hussar's lance came at him. The king swatted it aside and struck the man down as he passed.

A mighty stroke it was, too. Hussars were heavily armored, but Gustav Adolf had fought them before so he knew what to expect. His blade avoided the heavy cuirass altogether and passed just under the helmet's ear flap, with its characteristic heart emblem decoration. The neck is always a vulnerable part of any armor, especially for a man strong enough to drive a sword through whatever mail protection might be there.

The king of Sweden was a very strong man, and he loved swords and knew how to use them. The hussar's head stayed with the body, but the man was dead before he fell out of the saddle. His neck had been cut halfway through.

A second hussar was there. Frantically, Gustav Adolf swung back his sword.

The lances used by Polish hussars had a distinctive design. They were partially hollow, being made of two pieces of fir glued together. That made them quite light, despite their great length—not more than seven pounds—and easy to handle in battle.

It also made them brittle, of course. Gustav Adolf's sword broke the lance in half.

But Polish hussars expected that their lances would splinter. The weapons had round wooden hand-guards and the Swedish king's stroke had severed the lance just above the heavy ball. The hussar shifted his grip in order to turn the lance-butt into an impromptu mace and slammed the ball into the king's head.

Hard. The Pole was as big as Gustav Adolf and possibly even stronger. The Swede's head reeled back from the blow, his helmet coming loose.

Seeing his chance, the hussar swung the lance butt again. The helmet came off altogether. The hammering stroke came a third time, and this blow caught the side of the king's head unprotected.

Gustav Adolf was still in the saddle—barely—but he was now completely senseless. The Pole finally dropped the lance butt and drew his saber to finish him off.

But Anders Jönsson had arrived by then and he had no reservations at all about up-time pistols. Years ago, the Americans had given him one of the most expensive guns in their possession, an HK .40-caliber USP automatic. The king's bodyguard had never spent a waking moment without it since. He'd even had his armor modified so he could wear his shoulder holster into battle.

The hussar caught sight of the peculiar object in Jönsson's hand and might have been distracted for a split second before he raised his saber to defend himself. If there was a delay in his reaction, though, it didn't matter. He would have been killed anyway.

Jönsson shot him three times, all of the bullets punching into his chest through the cuirass. Two of them penetrated his heart.

Another hussar was there. Gustav Adolf was reeling but was still in the saddle, his legs gripping the horse from long-ingrained reflex. The first hussar to arrive drove his lance at him, ignoring Jönsson. He knew this target was the key one.

Jönsson saved his king again. He shot the hussar twice—center mass, again—and knocked him from the saddle. Had he not done so, the lance would have pierced the king of Sweden in the center of his torso, rupturing his stomach and severing his abdominal aorta. He would have bled out in less than a minute.

As it was, the lance swung aside at the last moment. It passed through the king's body, but well to the side. The peritoneum was pierced, but no major organs were damaged.

Finally, Gustav Adolf began to fall from the saddle. A third hussar tried to lance him as he fell, but his aim was thrown off by the king's now-rapid slump. He drove his lance butt into the Swede's ribs as he passed, but the blow did little damage beyond bruises.

And that was it. Anders shot him out of the saddle, too. Three shots, two in the back of the cuirass and one in the head.

The last shot was an act of pointless anger. Pointless, because the Pole was already mortally wounded. Anger, at the hussar's cowardly strike at a defenseless man.

So Anders Jönsson thought, anyway. And since he was the man with the .40-caliber automatic in his hand, his was the opinion that mattered.

Justified or not, that last shot—the time it took,

more than the round expended—left Jönsson vulnerable. The next hussar lance came at him, not the king, and almost slew him. All that saved his life was his armor; which, not surprisingly for the personal bodyguard of Europe's premier monarch, was the finest armor available.

The lance slid off and Jönsson shot the man dead as he passed. Two shots, both in the neck. The Pole stayed in the saddle, though. Again, the ingrained reflexes of an excellent horseman. He wouldn't come out of that saddle until his mount returned his body to his own lines, and it was removed by human hands. Gently, almost reverently.

The Scots arrived, forming a perimeter. Just in time, because the hussars were still coming. By now, many of them had deduced the king's identity. The ferocity with which Anders had defended Gustav Adolf was enough in itself, even if they didn't recognize his features.

Stanislaw Koniecpolski was not the only Polish soldier who thought the king of Sweden had outlived his welcome. It would have been hard to find one who differed, in fact.

They had their chance to kill him, here and now. They intended to do so.

Anders had used up eight rounds. That left five in this magazine. But he had three more magazines and enough time to swap them out.

He did so—just in time to shoot a Pole who'd gotten by the Scots and was aiming his lance at the king's body. Gustav Adolf was now sprawled on his side in the muddy soil. He was unconscious and bleeding, both from his head and the wound in his side.

Not bleeding profusely enough to pose an immediate danger to his life, though, so Jönsson continued to concentrate on the hussars.

That last Pole had gotten close enough to his target that Anders had used four shots to put him down—and again, with the last shot being fired in anger. He found it infuriating that the hussars were still trying to kill an obviously helpless man.

Had their histories been reversed, he might have had some sympathy for them. Might even have agreed with them, actually. For all Wladislaw IV's posturing and loud claims to being the rightful heir to the Swedish throne, it was not him—nor his father Sigismund III Vasa before him—who had invaded Sweden and laid waste to its lands, after all. The destruction and plunder had gone entirely the other way.

Three times the bastard had invaded and ravaged Poland. There was not going to be a fourth.

The Scots were crumbling. There weren't enough of them to hold off this many hussars.

Jönsson made a quick decision. He'd do better on the ground. He slid off the saddle and took position guarding the fallen king, almost straddling him.

And there he stayed, until a company of Småland cuirassiers arrived and finally drove off the Poles.

He'd emptied two magazines in addition to the eight rounds fired from the first. He'd just loaded the last magazine when a Polish lance finally put him down. Even then, with his blood pouring out of a severed femoral artery, he shot down his killer. He spent the last minute of his life lying across Gustav Adolf's body, shooting any hussar who came into his sight.

He would have died from blood loss, anyway. But a Pole he didn't see rode up and drove his lance all the way through Anders' body. The hussar was actually trying to kill Gustav Adolf, but since most of him was covered by the huge Jönsson, he saw no option but to try to slay the king through the bodyguard.

He succeeded in the second, but not the first. The Pole reversed his grip on the lance and rose up in his stirrups in order to drive the lance straight down with all his might. The lance missed the sternum, passed between two of the ribs, cut open the right ventricle of the heart and almost made it through Jönsson's entire torso. But there was just too much muscle, too much mass. The king beneath was quite untouched.

Chapter 39

The rain was starting to let up. In the distance to the west, Koniecpolski could see patches of clear sky. By evening, the storm would have passed completely. And with it, his great advantage over the Swedes.

The latest hussar charge had been driven back also, although this one had come close to shattering the enemy. If they'd been able to widen that gap just a bit more, a bit faster...

But there was no point dwelling on what might have been. Once again, his men had been repulsed—and they were finally showing the effects. The grand hetman had been in enough battles to know that he'd driven his cavalry almost to the breaking point. They'd done all he asked of them. The time had come to accept that he'd accomplished all he could this day and not drive into ruin. He hadn't destroyed the Swedish army, as he'd hoped to do. But he'd hammered them badly. Added to the destruction of the Hessians, he'd leveled the odds a great deal in Poland's favor. The intelligent thing to do now was return to Poznań. From here on, this was going to be a war of sieges.

Afterward, he would take a small private satisfaction

in the knowledge that he'd already made that decision before developments made it inevitable. No sooner had he turned to give new orders to his adjutants than he saw a Cossack scout racing toward him.

Literally, galloping at full speed—on this treacherous soil. The man was either a superb horseman or utterly reckless.

Or most likely both, being a Cossack.

Koniecpolski waited until the man drew up his horse. Obviously he was bearing important tidings. Not even a Cossack would run his horse like that for any other reasons.

"The enemy is coming, Hetman!" The Cossack turned and rose in his stirrups, pointing a little east of south. "One mile away. No farther. Thousands of men."

Already? He hadn't thought any of the three divisions of the USE army could get here until tomorrow. Even then, not till noon or early afternoon.

Perhaps it was a different enemy force, although Koniecpolski couldn't think of any that would be in this region. Not numberings in the thousands, certainly.

Cossacks could get fairly vague in their numbering. Still, a Cossack scout could tell the difference between hundreds of men and thousands of men at a glance. On horseback, at a full gallop. The scout's estimate wouldn't be off by that much.

Just to make sure, he questioned the scout concerning details of their appearance. It didn't take long at all before he was certain that these approaching forces were part of the USE army. For one thing, Koniecpolski knew of no other large army that inflicted such dull uniforms upon its soldier. Upon its officers, even!

Gray uniforms. Except for the odd stripe here and

there, a bit of flair with the shoulder decorations, they were the sort of vestments that monks would wear.

Dull monks. Boring monks. The sort of monks who took vows of silence and kept them.

Koniecpolski's own full dress uniform was as uniforms should be. He was particularly fond of his leopard skins.

In the distance, he heard a bugle. Marching orders, clearly. Whichever of the three USE divisions this was, it would be here within an hour. After the casualties he'd suffered today, the numerical odds would be even at best. And his men were exhausted. True, the enemy's troops would be tired as well, after the sort of march they'd made. But nothing wears men down like battle. Nothing in the world.

Yes. It was time to go.

The one thing Mike hadn't expected when he finally met up with Gustav Adolf's army was that he would turn out to be the highest ranked officer present.

Highest *conscious* rank, at any rate.

He turned away from the bed where the king of Sweden lay recuperating from his wounds. There was no point in staring at the man any longer. What Gustav Adolf needed was the best doctor who could be found.

That meant James Nichols. But it would probably be at least two days before planes could safely take to the skies again. The sky was clear at the moment—here, not in Magdeburg. It looked as if another storm might be on its way. If that proved true, they wouldn't be able to get Nichols here for a week or more. Assuming they could build a usable airfield, before this mucky soil finally dried out. Mike had his doubts.

"Not a flicker, you're saying?"

The man who served Gustav Adolf's troops as a doctor shook his head. "Nothing. Sometimes his eyes open, but there is nothing behind them."

Weather or not, they *had* to get Gustav Adolf out of here. Leaving aside his terrible head injuries, the lance wound in his side had penetrated the peritoneum. That meant he'd probably come down with peritonitis. If they didn't get him on antibiotics soon—there was a good chance he'd need surgery, too—that would likely kill him even if he recovered from the head trauma.

Mike had been told that the Jupiters, the new commercial aircraft, were equipped with air-cushioned landing gear that could land almost anywhere. If so, and if one of them were available, and if the weather held—that was a lot of ifs—maybe they could airlift the king.

But there was no way to count on that. With the weather as uncertain as it was, even if one of the planes were available they might not be able to use it.

Berlin. It was the only option Mike could see. Gustav Adolf could be taken there on a covered litter carried by a team of horses and guarded by a powerful cavalry force. By the time he got there, Nichols could have gotten to Berlin even if the planes still weren't flying.

Magdeburg would be better, of course. But Magdeburg was just too far away. Berlin wasn't much of a city, but it did have a palace. The elector had even gotten some of the rooms fitted with modern plumbing.

They might be able to get him to Magdeburg anyway, Mike reminded himself. If the weather cleared and one of the ACLG-equipped planes was available—and the boasts about the capabilities of their peculiar landing gear were accurate—then a Jupiter could meet them on the way to Berlin and airlift Gustav Adolf to the capital instead.

Mike glanced around the room he was in now, the main room of what had probably been Zbąszyń's premier tavern. Or possibly its only tavern.

The floor didn't bear thinking about. The sewers of the town . . . didn't exist. There was a well here, but Mike thought he'd have to be really desperate before he drank any of that water without boiling it first.

Berlin. Yes.

Torstensson agreed, when Mike reached him on the radio. So, an hour later, did the chancellor of Sweden, Axel Oxenstierna. He was already in Berlin himself, as it happened, attending to the creation of an interim imperial administration for Brandenburg.

"And you must come to Berlin yourself, General Stearns," said Oxenstierna. "It is imperative that we have a council of our army commanders."

Legally, Oxenstierna was out of bounds. He was Sweden's chancellor, not the USE's, and had no formal authority over Mike. But the proposal—he'd see it as a command, but that was his problem—was sensible enough. Besides, Mike didn't have any doubt that if he got on his high horse about the matter, Oxenstierna would just get hold of Wettin and have the prime minister give him the order instead. Which would be an order he *did* have to obey.

He found Jeff Higgins in the little room in an abandoned house where they'd put the body of Anders Jönsson. Come to pay his last respects, obviously.

Mike wasn't surprised. He'd come for the same reason.

It was a little over three years since the great Croat cavalry raid on Grantville had been driven off. The main target of the raid had been the town's high school.

Jeff had been there, that day. So had Mike's wife Rebecca.

The only reason they were still alive was because of this man here, and the nearby king he'd served who was now very close to death himself. The two of them had led the charge that turned the tide in that battle. With his own sword, Gustav Adolf had struck down the Croat who'd been about to kill Jeff.

"I have to remind myself, sometimes," Mike said softly. "Whenever Gustav Adolf really pisses me off. The world is just sometimes a gray place, and that's all there is to it."

Part Six

November 1635

Green to the very door

Chapter 40

Dresden, capital of Saxony

Eddie crashed the plane.

The soil of the jury-rigged airfield outside of Dresden turned out to be soggier than Noelle or Denise had led him to believe. They'd underestimated the potential problem with landing on such doubtful ground. In Noelle's case, because she was too anxious to get back to Magdeburg; in Denise's, because she was looking forward to seeing Eddie and was by nature given to overconfidence.

Insouciance, too. The girl could have taken the motto of *Mad* magazine's Alfred E. Newman for her own: "What, me worry?"

The front landing gear dug in, the tail came up, the nose buried itself into the ground—so much for the propeller—and slowly, almost gracefully, the plane flipped over onto its back.

When the little crowd on the airfield reached the plane, they found Eddie and Gretchen Richter hanging upside down in the cabin, still held in their seats by their harnesses. Neither was hurt at all. A bit shaken, but otherwise in excellent condition.

Not so the aircraft itself, of course.

Eddie's first words upon emerging were recriminatory in nature. Unusually, for him, he was in a high temper.

"You told me the airfield was in good shape!"

Noelle, with the wisdom of her advanced years of life—she'd just celebrated her twenty-sixth birthday—was profusely apologetic. Denise, sadly, was still in her teenage years and thus ill-equipped for the task. Her own temperament didn't help, either.

So, she started with the sort of mumbled, oatmealish, altogether unsatisfactory sort of phrases like "well" and "hey, look" that wouldn't mollify a saint. Then, under a continued barrage of heated comments from Eddie, retreated into her natural belligerence.

"Hey, buddy, maybe you just fucked up the landing. Ever think of that, huh?"

Peace was not restored for some minutes. Not until Minnie Hugelmair forced Denise to utter the needed words: "Okay, it was my fault. I'm sorry."

Minnie didn't actually believe that herself. She thought the accident probably *had* been Eddie's fault. The soil wasn't *that* muddy. But unlike Denise, she understood that when the male mind was in formal and court-dress High Dudgeon there was nothing for it but that the woman had to take the blame or nobody would get anything to eat that day. Not in peace, anyway.

Gretchen Richter's comments, upon exiting the upended aircraft, were more philosophical in nature.

"That is the first time I have ever flown in an airplane. I believe it will be the last."

Eventually, amity was restored. A workable semblance of it, at least.

Eddie spent some time examining the wreckage, then, ruefully, scratched his head.

"The propeller's scrap. We'll have to get a replacement from Grantville. No way to get one made here that I'd trust flying with."

"What about the plane itself?" Noelle asked.

"The engine seems okay. If we can get the plane into the city, we can probably fix the rest of it. But don't ask me how we're going to manage that."

He, Noelle and everyone else present turned to gaze upon Dresden. The city was well-fortified; surrounded by walls, with a moat in front of those.

Tata, Joachim Kappel and Eric Krenz were present also, having come out to the airfield with Noelle and her party. Tata and Joachim were there because they were the CoC delegation welcoming Gretchen to the city. Krenz was there because Tata was there and she was less and less inclined to order him away. She would always remember Eberhard fondly, but the duke had been dead for half a year now.

"Not a problem," said Tata.

Eddie looked at her. Then, at Kappel and Krenz.

Kappel shrugged. "Can probably be done."

Tata sniffed.

"Not a problem," agreed Krenz. "Tata has a flair for getting her way."

Tata sniffed again.

❖   ❖   ❖

Two days later, it was possible to estimate the expenses involved with reasonable confidence. Tata had indeed gotten her way again. The city had winches and cranes used for construction, did it not? Lots of manpower in the form of soldiers idling about claiming their injuries were much worse than they were, did it not? The plane was designed to be as light as possible, was it not?

So, the plane came over the moat and the walls. Soon enough, it was sitting in a small city square with a shelter already being built around it. By now, the city's artisans had gotten intrigued in the project—assuming that pay would be forthcoming, of course—and the CoC had decided that having an airfield inside the city itself was a matter of civic pride.

Eddie had no idea how they'd manage that, but he had more immediate concerns.

"Don Francisco is going to fire me," he predicted gloomily. "Leaving aside the cost of repairing his aircraft, he has four of his employees doing him no good at all. We're supposed to be in Prague by now."

Denise was more optimistic. "No, he won't. He's a pretty good guy, actually."

Coming from her, that was high praise. But it turned out to be justified. Francisco Nasi's radio message surprised Junker. It surprised Noelle even more.

NOT A PROBLEM. STOP. SPARE NO EXPENSE FIX PLANE. STOP. DRESDEN GOOD PLACE TO BE NOW. STOP. THINGS WILL GET INTEREST-ING. STOP.

"That's a Chinese curse, isn't it?" mused Minnie. "I read it somewhere."

Poznań

"Torture me as much as you want," the American said, his shoulders squared, his expression resolute. "I said it before, I'll say it again. I won't tell you anything."

Lukasz stared at him. Then, turned his head to stare at the two hussars and two Cossacks who were also gathered around the APC outside of Poznań's main gate. The city's walls were packed with people, eager to gaze upon the enormous war machine that Opalinski had captured.

As soon as the grand hetman learned of Lukasz's exploit over the radio, he'd instructed the officers he'd left in charge of the soldiers still in Poznań to do whatever was necessary to bring the APC into the city itself. Or, should that prove impossible, to extend the city's walls to enclose the war machine.

Either project would be massive, especially since the work had to be done before the worst of winter came. They still hadn't decided which one to adopt.

But that wasn't Opalinski's concern. His instructions from the grand hetman had been to concentrate on the technical aspect of the problem. Could the APC be put in Polish service? If so, how soon? If not—better still, in addition—could the APC be used as the model for the construction of Polish war machines?

Hence his interrogation of Mark Johnson Ellis, the only up-timer they'd found among the APC's crew when they captured it. All he'd told them initially was his name, his rank—that was well-nigh incomprehensible; what sort of preposterous rank was a "Speck"?—and what he called his "serial number." That was a string of digits that Lukasz had set aside for later study. Perhaps it was a code of some sort.

Under further questioning by Lukasz as they made their slow oxen-hauled way to the east, the young American had become a bit more expansive, although not on military subjects. He claimed he was not a regular soldier but what he called a "reservist hauled back to duty for another stupid fucking war." He seemed quite aggrieved over the matter, perhaps because he'd recently been married.

He also claimed—this might be subterfuge, of course—that he was what he called a "civil engineer," not a "grease monkey." He said the only reason he'd been assigned as the APC's "mechanic" was because he was the only one in the crew who knew a "crescent wrench" from a "phillips screwdriver."

He seemed aggrieved over that issue also.

Still, despite Ellis' very apparent disgruntlement with the foreign policies of the USE's political leadership— "how many fucking times do we have to refight the Vietnam War in another fucking universe?"—he insisted he was a patriot and would therefore provide Lukasz with no information that might harm his nation.

As he had just done again. Since they'd been speaking in German, the two Cossacks did not understand what the up-timer had said. Had they understood it, they would have burst into riotous laughter.

As it was, the two hussars both grinned.

Lukasz didn't doubt at all that the up-timer would start babbling profusely if he was subjected to torture. But information gotten from tortured men was always questionable. More importantly, Lukasz was almost sure the grand hetman wouldn't want to torture any

Americans for political reasons. Poland had done quite well in the war so far, but any realist knew that in the long run the USE was the stronger party in the conflict. Sooner or later, they'd need to seek a political settlement.

Despite their small numbers, the up-timers were very influential in the USE. From what Jozef had told him earlier, it seemed they were not enthusiastic about the war with Poland, which they saw as the product of Gustav Adolf's dynastic ambitions rather any national interest of the USE itself. Mark Ellis' statements certainly supported that interpretation.

Would it be wise, then, to infuriate the Americans? Which they most likely would be, if they discovered that one of their own had been badly mistreated by his Polish captors.

Finally, it might all be unnecessary anyway.

He turned to the last member of the small party standing by the APC. This was a young Polish nobleman by the name of Walenty Tarnowski. He was in his mid-twenties, about the same age as Mark Ellis, and had been a student at the University of Krakow. He was now teaching at Lubrański Academy right here in Poznań. The reason he was teaching here was because he and a few other young scholars in the Commonwealth were trying to establish a new academic discipline they called "Advanced Mechanics." The University of Krakow was the oldest and most prestigious university in Poland; and, like most such institutions, very set in its ways. It had refused to accept Advanced Mechanics as a suitable subject for scholarly study.

So, being just as stubborn as they were, Tarnowski had come to Poznań. The Lubrański Academy had been founded over a century ago but was still not recognized as a full university. The University of Krakow restricted that status jealously, and refused to allow Lubrański Academy the right to issue degrees. By accepting Tarnowski and allowing him to create a curriculum, the Poznań scholars were thumbing their noses at Krakow.

Opalinski thought the University of Krakow was being very shortsighted. Be that as it may, for his purposes and those of the Poland's grand hetman it didn't matter what they thought. The man and the skills they needed were here in Poznań.

"Can you do it alone?" he asked Tarnowski. Deliberately, he spoke in German, so the up-timer could follow the conversation.

"The question is whether I can do it. Alone or not, doesn't really matter." He gave Ellis a dismissive glance. "He's a civil engineer, not someone knowledgeable in advanced mechanics."

"The difference is . . . ?"

"He designs and build roads. Canals. Dams. Sewers. That sort of thing. Basically, he knows how to assemble dirt and rocks and bricks together in various useful ways."

"Hey!" protested the up-timer.

Tarnowski ignored him. "As to your question itself . . . I believe so, yes. At least, so far as design is concerned. I doubt if we will have the technical skills and mechanical resources to actually make one of the things. We will have to 'gear down,' as the Americans say. Use what we learn to create something much simpler and more crude, but which will serve Poland well enough on the battlefield."

The American was now glaring at Tarnowski.

"Look at it this way," Lukasz said. "Would you rather be tortured?"

A horse-litter along the Elbe river, in Saxony

A covered litter carried by horses was a better form of transport than a carriage, anywhere except on the very best roads. Still, it had gotten pretty miserable once they'd passed out of Magdeburg province and entered Saxony. The former elector's realm had never been part of the CPE or the later USE except as a political technicality. Even that, John George had discarded as soon as he could, to his eventual ruin. The roads here were so bad that the litter lurched and threw Jozef about almost as badly as he would have been in a carriage.

Well, no. That was hyperbole brought on by exasperation. Wojtowicz hadn't gotten a single bruise. In a carriage, he'd probably have broken a bone by now.

Still, despite the discomfort of the moment, Jozef was in excellent spirits. The solution had come to him before he'd even left Schwerin's city limits.

Dresden, of course. What better place for a Polish spy to hide in the USE at the moment? It would the last place they'd ever think to look.

It would be pleasant, too. He'd been to Dresden on three occasions and liked the city.

More than anything, Jozef Wojtowicz dreaded tedium. At least the time he spent in Dresden would be interesting.

Linz, Austria

Janos Drugeth lounged on the river bank, gazing at the Danube. He always found the sight of moving water soothing, for some reason.

He needed soothing, at the moment. He'd decided to take a break from his exhaustive and seemingly endless round of discussions with the officers in command of the Austrian forces stationed in Linz. He'd forgotten how set in their ways garrisons could be. You'd think that sort of rigid and routinized thinking wouldn't infect soldiers who would be the first to feel the blows if Wallenstein invaded. But it did.

It was probably the pastries, Janos thought. They were certainly delicious. An officer who ate such pastries every morning and evening of every day of the year—which most of them did, judging by their waistlines—was probably bound to lapse into a sugary view of the world.

Surely the Bohemians would share that outlook, and not invade. They had excellent pastries in Prague as well.

Janos had brought a tablet and a pen with him. Sitting up straight, he brought them out and began composing a letter to Noelle. He was doing so simply because he felt like it. He wouldn't be able to post the letter for a while since he had no idea where she was at the moment. Possibly Magdeburg, possibly Prague, possibly Grantville.

That she might be in Dresden never crossed his mind at all. Noelle was a sensible woman. Why would she choose to be in a city that was clearly on the edge of chaos and ruin?

Chapter 41

Zielona Góra

"It happened weeks ago!" Thorsten Engler was a very even-tempered man, but he was feeling decidedly peevish at the moment. You could even say, angry.

"Weeks," he repeated.

The radio operator who'd handed him the message was looking simultaneously apprehensive and indignant, the way a man will when he can see he's about to get blamed for something that was no fault of his own.

Jason Linn put a hand on Engler's shoulder. Not to restrain him, simply to remind him that there was an external world that had an objective reality outside of the swirling furies of his mind.

"Captain, there's no sense in yelling at Corporal Schwab. He's just the one the message passed through."

Schwab gave Linn a quick, thankful glance. For his part, Thorsten took a deep breath, held it for a few seconds, and then let it out slowly. He'd first discovered that technique for controlling his temper at the age of six.

"Indeed," he said stiffly. Just as stiffly, he gave the corporal a nod. "Thank you for bringing me this message, Schwab. You may go."

After Schwab left, Thorsten lifted the message sheet above his head, as if to slam it down somewhere. But, again, he took a deep breath, held it for a few seconds, and let it out slowly. Then, quite gently, he set the message down on a table in the officers' mess. The table was one of several that had been brought into the large main room of a house very close to the city's center. It was called the "officers' mess," but it was open to what you might call established sergeants like Jason.

Shaking his head, Thorsten pulled out a chair and sat down.

"I can't believe they didn't tell me right away. That was *weeks* ago."

Jeff Higgins came into the mess. "What was weeks ago?"

"Caroline was *there*—in Stockholm. When the queen was assassinated and Kristina almost was."

Higgins frowned. "I thought you knew that already."

"Of course I knew. But I didn't know what had *happened* to her. She was often at Kristina's side. Was she hurt? *Killed?* There was no news! And with those people in Stockholm, I could hardly assume that no news was good news." The term *those people* could have been milked for venom.

Jeff pursed his lips. "Um . . . Yeah, I see what you mean. They're still pretty traditional up there. That's a polite way of saying 'medieval.' If you're not royalty, nobility or at the very least some sort of official, nobody will think to mention that 'oh, yeah, and Joe the Butcher got killed too.' I take it she *is* okay? Caroline?"

"Yes, she's fine. As it happens—thank God—she wasn't at the site of the crime when it happened. She was still in her room, packing."

Like many down-timers who associated with Americans a lot, Thorsten was more relaxed about blasphemy than most. Eric Krenz had practically turned it into a art form.

"So how'd you finally find out?" asked Jeff.

Engler looked a bit embarrassed. He nodded at Linn, who had taken a seat at an adjoining table. "It was his idea."

Jason grinned. "He was having the radio guys send queries every other day. Waste of time, of course, because he was sending them as 'Thorsten Engler.'" Linn jeered. "Who the hell is that? Sounds like a peasant."

Jeff laughed. "So you finally sent one as the imperial count of Narnia. Don't tell me. I bet you got a response the next day."

Thorsten finally smiled. "The same day, actually. I sent it early this morning."

Higgins took a seat next to Linn and folded his big hands on the table. "I'm lucky that way. The radio operators I deal with are CoC on the other end. You think you got problems, Engler? Where do you think *my* wife is?"

He didn't wait for their guesses. "Dresden. Guess how she got there?"

He didn't wait for their guesses. "Plane crash. Never a dull moment, being married to Gretchen."

Berlin, capital of Brandenburg Province

"So what's the verdict, James?" Mike handed Dr. Nichols a short glass filled halfway with some sort of clear liquid. Liquor, from the smell.

"It's what passes for Korn in Brandenburg," Mike

explained. "The wine's marginally better, but I figured you'd want something stronger."

"You got that right." Nichols drank half of it in one gulp, then made a little face. "The stuff in Thuringia is way better. And it's not very good."

Mike smiled thinly. "Welcome to Brandenburg. And I repeat: what's the verdict?"

"Can I sit down first?"

"Oh, sorry. Sure." Mike waved to one of the chairs in his suite. That was one advantage to being billeted in a palace. There was usually plenty of room.

Nichols sagged into the chair. He looked pretty exhausted. He'd been at the king of Sweden's bedside all day, since early in the morning.

Some of the doctor's weariness, though, was probably still due to the rigors of his journey here. That had ended two days ago, but Nichols was about sixty.

The weather had made any sort of plane travel impossible to Berlin. Impossible, at least, for any aircraft with standard landing gear. There had been some days when the weather would have permitted flying, but there was nowhere to land.

The elector of Brandenburg, George William, had refused to let an airstrip be built anywhere in Brandenburg. He claimed that was to protect his subjects from aircraft falling on top of them, but the real reason was simply that he resented all of the side effects of the Ring of Fire. If he couldn't make the cursed Americans vanish, at least he didn't have to let them foul his sky with their cursed machines.

As bad as the weather had been—and still was, half the time—there'd been no way to construct an airfield in time. And as it turned out, they couldn't use one of the planes with air-cushioned landing gear. There was only one ACLG plane in regular operation yet, because of a shortage of suitable engines, and it was undergoing major maintenance. Even if the airline had raced to put it back together, Mike would have gotten Gustav Adolf to Berlin by then.

There'd also been a hovercraft used to ferry people and supplies on the Saale that might have managed the job, that Mike had forgotten about. But it wasn't available either. A few months ago, a minerals exploration company had chartered it for use somewhere in the far north.

So, a horse-litter it had been, at a forced pace across rough terrain and with new rainstorms coming every second or third day. Mike had been exhausted when they finally reached Berlin. James' trip hadn't been as rough, but it had been rough enough for a man his age.

The doctor stared moodily into his glass. "It's the head trauma that's really got me worried, Mike."

Mike's eyes widened. "That's . . . saying something, given how deadly peritonitis can be."

"Yeah, but I can help that—some, anyway—with surgery. And the antibiotics we've got should help a lot too. Whereas the head trauma . . ."

Nichols shook his head. "Honestly? There's probably nothing at all I can do. Or anybody can do. We'll just have to wait and hope for the best."

"He's not in a coma, though." That was a statement, not a question. Mike had been with the king throughout the journey from Zbąszyń, and there had been times Gustav Adolf had been . . .

Well. Not in a coma. You could hardly say "conscious," though. He'd seemed very delirious.

"No, he's not in a coma. But there are lots of ways the brain can be badly affected that don't manifest themselves in a coma, Mike. He's suffered a serious traumatic brain injury from being clubbed half to death, essentially. The skull wasn't broken, but parts of the brain where he was struck were certainly damaged. Possibly other parts, too."

Nichols set down his glass and held up his hands as if he were cupping something the size of... Well, a skull, actually.

"A live brain has about the same consistency as Jello. It sits inside the skull, which shields it, and it's also sheltered by layers of membranes that are called meninges. It's pretty well protected from most shocks you'd normally encounter day to day. But if your skull gets hammered really hard, then what happens—"

The doctor suddenly jiggled his hands around, very violently. "—your Jello-y brain is essentially being bounced around against your own skull. The worst damage usually happens to the brain tissue nearest the source of the trauma but you can have damage almost anywhere. Call it ricochet damage, if you will."

"All right. Assuming for the moment, though, that the damage is restricted to where he got hit, what's your diagnosis?"

"'Diagnosis' is way too strong a term, Mike. With this sort of brain injury, there's a lot of guessing at first—and would be, even if we were in the intensive care unit of a major up-time hospital. A lot of the diagnosis of brain injuries has to develop over time, since many of the symptoms are behavioral and—"

"*James.* Please. This is not a time for all the complexities and all the details and all the maybes and the we-don't-know-yets and all the caveats or any of that stuff. I need whatever you've got right now, down and dirty. Give me your best guess, if you don't like the word 'diagnosis.' What is wrong with Gustav Adolf's brain?"

Nichols sighed. "I think his right temporal lobe is damaged."

"And that results in...?"

"Assuming Gustav Adolf survives the next few weeks, he might make a complete and quick recovery." He took a deep breath. "What's more likely, though, is that it will take him months to recover, possibly years, and he may never recover completely. Probably won't, in fact, with that bad of an injury."

Mike sagged a little in his chair. "That's...about what I was afraid of. Would one of the symptoms be that he says things that make no sense at all?"

"Gibberish?"

"No, not gibberish. They sound like complete sentences, but it's as if all the words are scrambled. I'll give you an example. At one point when I looked in on him in the litter, he was awake and stared at me as if he had no idea who I was. Then he said—I think I'm remembering this right: 'I ate my tree but the horse will not open the stirrup.'"

James ran fingers through his short, kinky hair. "Yes, that's a symptom of temporal lobe injury. One of the major functions of the temporal lobes is handling speech. What you're describing is a form of aphasia, which can manifest itself in many ways. People suffering from aphasia might be able to speak but not write, or write but not speak. Or they might be able to sing, but can't speak or write. Gustav Adolf's failure to recognize you is because the right temporal lobe is also involved in the visual content processed by the brain. Sound, too. Even if he recovers—this is just one example of what can happen—Gustav Adolf may have so much trouble with tonal recognition that music means nothing to him any longer."

Mike winced. The king of Sweden adored music.

"What else?" he asked.

James spread his hands. "There could be a lot of things, Mike. He might start having seizures."

· "He hasn't had any so far," Mike protested. "I'm sure I'd have noticed or been told by one of his attendants if I wasn't there at the time."

"Doesn't matter. Seizures don't have to develop right away, with something like this. He might start having them a week from now, a month from now, a year from now—or never at all. And if he does start having them, they might last for a short while or the rest of his life. The brain's still a very mysterious organ, Mike."

"What else?"

"He's almost certainly going to have problems with memory retrieval. The problems may be mild, moderate or severe, and it's impossible to know ahead of time how long they might last. His behavior might become childish and/or irritable. He might have sudden unprovoked rages. He might sink into depression. He might find it difficult to concentrate on anything for very long. He might completely lose any sense of humor. His language skills could be chaotic. He might be able to speak but have no understanding of what he is saying. Or he might—for Christ's sake, Mike, how long do you want me to go on? Don't you get the picture yet? I repeat: *the brain is still mostly a mystery*. There's usually not much you can do with an injury like this except take care of the patient's bodily needs and wait and hope for the best. You want to know my diagnosis? Ask me in six months. Better yet, ask me five years from now."

He drained the rest of his liquor and extended the glass to Mike. "Now why don't you do something useful and pour me some more of this godawful stuff? Did I tell you some sainted soul in Bamberg is trying to distill sourmash whiskey? Of all the things I miss about Ye Olde Up-time, Jack Daniels is right at the top of the list."

Chapter 42

Magdeburg, central Germany
Capital of the United States of Europe

When Rebecca finished her analysis, there was silence around the table for a moment. Then, Anselm Keller cleared his throat.

"Are you sure you are not...ah..."

Rebecca smiled. "Overinterpreting my husband's radio messages?"

The member of Parliament from the Province of the Main made a face. "Ah, yes. You did give us the exact working of the messages, after all. Most of it seemed...well..."

"Personal? Innocuous?"

"Well, yes."

Constantin Ableidinger had been slouched in his chair. Now, he sat erect. "Don't be naïve, Anselm. How else should we interpret phrases such as 'Axel seems extraordinarily vigorous despite the king's condition,' and 'I've noticed the prime minister and the chancellor are spending a lot of time together'?"

Matthias Strigel grunted. "Not to mention: 'Lennart

seems to share some of my misgivings, but the council feels we are obliged to respect Gustav Adolf's last wishes. So it's off to Bohemia I go. As soon as possible, the prime minister has instructed me.'"

Melissa Mailey spoke. "You're all missing the key phrase. Even Becky."

Everyone looked at her. "Which is?" asked Rebecca. She was simply curious, not offended.

Melissa looked down at the sheets of paper in her hand and shuffled through them. "It's...this one. On page four." Her voice got that little singsong pitch people often fall into when they quote something. "Wilhelm seems in quite good health. But I can't help notice how much he's starting to look like my uncle Billy Conn as he gets older."

Rebecca nodded. "Yes, I did wonder about that. He's never mentioned this relative to me before. Or any relative with that surname, in fact."

Melissa chuckled. "Mike Stearns doesn't have an uncle by that name. It's an allusion he must have figured would escape any down-timer's notice—even yours—but I guess he figured I'd be able to decipher it. Although why"—she drew herself up a little—"he would imagine for one moment that I would be familiar with the sordid details of the history of such a brutal so-called sport is quite beyond me."

Rebecca smiled. "Perhaps he assumed Ed Piazza would be here. He has quite low tastes, you know." Her smile widened. "But since you apparently *do* know these sordid details—this particular one, at least—why don't you share it with us?"

Melissa looked slightly embarrassed. "Well...It happened back up-time at some point during the 1930s or 1940s, I don't remember the exact date, and, yes, I realize how preposterous it seems to refer 'back' to a year that won't come for another three centuries, but there it is. Anyway, the heavyweight champion boxer at the time was a man by the name of Joe Louis. He was, among other things, a tremendously powerful man who ended most of his fights by knocking out his opponents. Ah, that means punching them so hard that they are knocked down for a while, and sometimes unconscious.'"

She took a breath. "Billy Conn, on the other hand, was a smaller boxer—what they called a 'light heavyweight'—and one whose great skill was boxing itself. He would often win bouts by outscoring his opponents rather than knocking them out."

Ableidinger frowned. "How do you score something like that?"

"Never mind. Just take my word for it. Billy Conn challenged Joe Louis for the heavyweight title. To everyone's surprise, he won the first twelve rounds—there are fifteen rounds to a championship match, by the way—by outmaneuvering Louis, avoiding his powerful punches and scoring many points with his own much lighter punches. Coming into the thirteenth round, he was far ahead on points and on the verge of winning the match."

She took another breath. "But then Billy Conn got overconfident. He decided he could win the match with a knockout—always the more prestigious method. So he started mixing it up with Louis, as the expression goes. Trading punch for punch, blow for blow."

"Ha!" boomed Ableidinger. "And thereby lost the match, because the Louis ogre knocked him out."

Melissa scowled at him. "Joe Louis was *not* an ogre. He was...Well. A very important man in the history of the United States, for reasons I'm not going to get into here. But, yes, that is what happened. Billy Conn didn't even make it to the end of the thirteenth round."

Everyone at the table sat back in their chairs, contemplating this new data.

"Do you *still* think Rebecca is 'overinterpreting' her husband's radio messages, Anselm?" asked Matthias Strigel.

"Uh, no," he replied.

Constantin was examining Rebecca. "Your husband was one of these American pugilists, wasn't he?"

"He was very young then," she replied, a bit defensively. "Foolish. He says it himself."

Ableidinger waved his hand. "Yes, yes. Still, he was a pugilist. So I'm curious. Was he also one of these superb boxers like this Billy Conn?"

Rebecca seemed at a loss for words. Quite unusual that was, for her. Her mouth opened, closed. Opened again. Closed.

"Ah..." she said.

Melissa spoke up. Her voice was firm, her words a bit clipped. "Mike Stearns had eight professional fights. All of them were fought at the Grand Olympic Auditorium in Los Angeles. He won seven of them by knock-out, all within the first four rounds."

She cleared her throat. "So, no. He bears very little resemblance to his not-uncle Billy Conn." She gave Constantin an unfriendly glance. "Some might even call him an ogre."

"Not I," said Ableidinger, smiling like a cherub. "Not I."

"How do you know all this about boxing?" asked Rebecca. "I did not even know those details concerning Michael's career."

"Just picked it up here and there," Melissa said. "By accident."

"Oh, surely not," said Rebecca.

"That's my story and I'm sticking to it."

Stockholm

The first thing Princess Kristina said when she came into Prince Ulrik's salon was: "Uncle Axel says I have to come to Berlin. Right away. To be with Papa."

Ulrik set down the newspaper he was reading on the low table in front of his chair. Americans would have called it a "coffee table," except no American with a net worth less than fifty million dollars would have dared place a coffee cup on it in the first place.

He was glad enough to put down the newspaper. It was a five-day-old copy of the *Leubecker Zeitung*, a journal that was just marginally tolerable. Unfortunately, none of the Hamburg or Magdeburg newspapers arrived in Stockholm regularly.

Still, anything from the continent was better than what passed for news in Swedish journals. The combination of being isolated and victorious—not to mention the chancellor's heavy hand when it came to censorship—made Stockholm quite a provincial place, despite its objective political importance. Ulrik had been in small town taverns in the Germanies where the political analysis was superior to the drivel you heard here, even in the palace.

Especially in the palace, now that he thought about it.

Caroline Platzer had followed the princess into the salon. From the expression on her face, it was obvious she was worried.

As well she might be, thought Ulrik.

"Do you wish to go?" he asked the girl.

Kristina frowned. "Well...yes, I suppose. I'd very much like to see Papa."

Ulrik volunteered the unspoken word at the end of that sentence. "But...?"

Kristina stamped her foot. "I don't like Berlin! I was there once, with Mama, visiting her brother. He was stupid and everybody in the palace was stupid and the whole city was stupid. I've never been so bored in my life."

"That's not a good enough reason not to go, Kristina." He smiled. "Mind you, I don't disagree. I've been to Berlin twice. It's quite boring, yes."

He waited. Ulrik was fairly certain they had come to a critical point. He was also fairly certain that he knew the right course of action. But it was not something that could be done—or should be done—against Kristina's will.

She was pouting a little, staring down at her shoes.

"Is there any other reason not to go, Kristina?"

The princess glanced at Caroline. The American woman made a little gesture with her head, a nod in Ulrik's direction. Combined with the rather stern expression on her face, Ulrik interpreted it to mean: *Tell him. But you have to do it yourself. I can't do it for you.*

Kristina looked back at Ulrik. "I don't know that I should. It doesn't seem right to me."

That was enough, Ulrik thought. To start, at least.

"It's certainly not right from a legal standpoint," he said firmly.

"I don't have to obey Uncle Axel?" There was a little lift in the girl's voice. Hope, you might call it, if you were the sort of person who saw oak trees in acorns.

Which Ulrik did, as it happened. He fancied himself something of a botanist.

"No, of course you don't have to obey him. To begin with, he's not your uncle. Secondly, no one has appointed him regent. He's simply the chancellor of Sweden. Someone whose opinion you should listen to, of course, but he has no authority over you."

Shrewd as always, Baldur played the devil's advocate. "Not yet. But he can summon the council and the riksdag and have himself declared regent."

Ulrik shrugged. "So? The riksdag's authority extends only to the kingdom of Sweden. Not to the United States of Europe, not to the Union of Kalmar. Never forget that Gustav II Adolf wears three crowns, not one."

He nodded at Kristina. "And so will she."

"Ah!" said Baldur, as if he has just been enlightened. "I hadn't thought of that. And the equivalent authority of the riksdag when it comes to the Union of Kalmar is . . . ?"

The Americans had a term for it that Ulrik had learned from Eddie Cochrane. *Throwing soft pitches.* Or was it *softball pitches? Easy pitches?*

Whatever it was called, Baldur did it superbly.

"Well, that's a very interesting question," said Ulrik. "The final structure of the Union of Kalmar hasn't been settled yet. A union council was created, but its authority remains unclear. There's certainly nothing in the laws established thus far to give the council the right to create a regent."

He cleared his throat. "To the contrary. The only hard and fast rule when it comes to determining the source of final authority in the Union—which was enshrined by law, right there at the Congress of Copenhagen—is that until such time as what they chose to call the 'organic royal line' of the Union comes to the throne—"

He pointed a forefinger at Kristina; a thumb at himself. "That's us, and then our children, and so on. But until that time, the Congress clearly stipulated that the king of Sweden was the premier political figure in the Union, followed by—"

He cleared his throat again. "My father, Christian IV, the king of Denmark. So the authority to create a regent for the Union of Kalmar clearly lies with him, given that Gustav II Adolf is incapacitated. Not Axel Oxenstierna, who has no formal standing at all in the government of the Union."

Kristina was looking brighter by the moment. "What about the United States?"

"Aye, that's the question," said Baldur. "Isn't it?"

"Well, yes, I think so."

Kristina was standing very close to him, now. Ulrik reached out and took her little hands in his. "What you are faced with, my betrothed, is something that no child should have to deal with. But it happens. It has happened before, it will happen again. It's called a succession crisis."

Kristina looked up at Caroline. "Have you heard of that?"

At the time of the Ring of Fire, Caroline Platzer had had the same knowledge of history that most Americans had. Not too bad when it came to American history itself, allowing for big gaps of knowledge between the Revolution and the Civil War and the Civil War and the Great Depression. Abysmal when it came to everything else.

The Greeks invented democracy and were the smartest people who ever lived even if they couldn't run anything bigger than a city. The Romans were very powerful and sometimes majestic but they had a lot of nasty personal habits and killed a lot of Christians. The Dark Ages came next and... Moving right along the Middle Ages were in the middle and there were knights and stuff. Then the English were mean to the Puritans which is why most people in England came to America, and the French had a revolution that went sour and somewhere around that time Napoleon was really big and then you got to modern times and there were two big world wars. And then history ended and current affairs started. That was fourth period class, taught by Mrs. Abrams.

But after the Ring of Fire, she'd taken the study of history much more seriously. To paraphrase Dr. Johnson, being plunged into the Thirty Years' War concentrates the mind wonderfully.

So, today, she knew the answer.

"Yes, and Ulrik's right. It seems like half the wars you Europeans fought were because of succession crises. War of the Spanish Succession, War of the Austrian Succession, War of the Polish Succession. You name the war, and if you dig a little you'll find out it usually got triggered off because King Whatsisname keeled over without leaving any heirs or—this is often worse—did leave an heir but the heir was just a kid."

She was almost glaring, now. "You've heard of Alexander the Great?"

Kristina nodded.

"Well, that was probably the great-grand-daddy succession crisis of them all. He died leaving as his only heir a still unborn son. Guess what happened to his empire?"

Kristina was wide-eyed, mute.

"It got carved into pieces by his generals. Guess what happened to his wife and son?"

Still wide-eyed, still mute.

"They got carved up, too."

Kristina turned the wide eyes onto Ulrik. Her hand had never left his grip. "Would Uncle Axel really cut me up?"

Ulrik shook his head. "No. Oxenstierna has been your father's friend and close adviser for many years. He wouldn't harm your father or you, of that I am quite sure." He paused a moment. "Not *himself*. But succession crises have a dynamic of their own. They're like wild horses. Set them loose—which is exactly what I fear Oxenstierna is doing—and you're likely to get trampled."

He gave the girl's hands a reassuring little squeeze. "So, no. I don't think Uncle Axel means you any harm. But he does believe—with great certainty—that he knows what is best for you. And for your incapacitated father. And for Sweden. And for the Germanies." His jaws tightened. "And probably for Denmark, when it comes to it. Which it will."

Kristina made a valiant last stand. She'd been told

many times—including by Ulrik—that she needed to think for herself and especially to consider all sides of a question instead of just jumping onto the conclusion that pleased her the most. Caroline could get downright tedious on the subject.

"But what about Papa? I really would like to be with him. And Uncle Axel says that maybe just by being there I might help Papa get back his wits."

Ulrik's jaws got tighter still. He'd just bent over backward not to blacken Oxenstierna's name. In fact, he had come to a much darker assessment of the man. Oxenstierna might not wish any harm on Gustav Adolf and his only child. But Ulrik was now certain that the man wouldn't let their well-being restrain him, either, if the situation came to what he considered a critical juncture.

"And he may be right, Kristina," he said. "But I would like the answer to a different question. Several questions, actually."

Ulrik nodded toward the table. The *Leubecker Zeitung* was only the latest newspaper and journal and broadsheet stacked on it. The pile was so big it threatened to spill off entirely. If it did, it would cover a good portion of the floor.

"I have been following the news closely, Kristina, as you know. Why did the chancellor of Sweden send away the American Moor Nichols? Everyone knows he's the best doctor in the world. So why is he no longer at your father's bedside in Berlin?"

Kristina looked uncertain. "I . . . I don't know, Ulrik. But maybe Uncle Axel has a reason."

"Oh, yes, I'm sure he does. In fact, I'm sure I know what he would say to me right now if he were in this room and I asked him the question directly. He'd say that he sent Dr. Nichols away because the doctor himself said there was not much more he could do, now that he'd saved the king from the infection in his body. And so—being as he is such an important physician—it would really be best if he returned to Magdeburg, since everyone knows Magdeburg is becoming the great center of medicine in the Germanies. It might even have surpassed Grantville and Jena, by now."

"Well...doesn't that makes sense? It sounds like it does."

"In and of itself, yes. But it simply raises the next question, which is—"

Caroline interrupted. There was real anger in her voice.

"Which is why the hell didn't James Nichols take your father back to Magdeburg with him? So what if there's not much more that can be done for him? 'Not much' isn't the same thing as 'nothing,' and whatever can be done for your daddy can be done a lot better in Magdeburg than it can in Berlin."

So. Platzer had come to the same dark conclusion as Ulrik had. Axel Oxenstierna would not kill his own king. But he was willing to risk letting him die, wasn't he?

Still, Kristina soldiered on. Ulrik was very proud of her.

"But...maybe the travel would be too hard on Papa."

Ulrik shook his head. "I'm sure that's what the chancellor would say. But it's simply not true."

Baldur finally gave up the softball act. "To put it mildly!" he said, in a caustic tone. It sounded so much more like him, too, it really did.

He'd been leaning against a nearby wall. Now, he levered himself away from it with a little heave of his shoulders and took two steps toward Kristina. "They hauled your father in a horse-litter across western Poland and Brandenburg—which is to say, along cow trails—for five and a half days, didn't they? And he survived, didn't he? Don't let anybody ever tell you otherwise, girl. King or not, emperor or not, your Papa is as tough as men come."

Kristina looked pleased, as well she might. Baldur Norddahl passed out praise the way a miser passes out coins to the needy.

The Norwegian shook his head. "It's all crap. You've ridden in a plane."

"Yes, it's wonderful!"

Baldur smiled. "Probably not so wonderful if you're badly injured. Still, if the pilot is being careful, the ride won't be any rougher than a trip in a horse-litter."

He raised a finger. "But with one great difference! It took Stearns almost six days to get your Papa to Berlin. How long would it take to fly him from Berlin to Magdeburg?"

The princess frowned. "Well, I've flown from Luebeck to Magdeburg. And that's even farther, isn't it?"

"A lot farther," Ulrik said. "Berlin is less than a hundred miles from Magdeburg. The truth is, Kristina, there are several ways your father could be brought to Magdeburg, where he'd be able to get the best medical care available in the world. An airplane would be the fastest, but it's not actually the one I'd propose. Speed isn't critical any longer."

"Barge," said Baldur. "The Havel river runs right by Berlin. It's navigable—for a shallow barge, but it doesn't need to have much of a draft for this purpose—and it will take you down to the Elbe. The Havel enters the Elbe near Werben. Then you'd transfer him onto one of the newer and bigger powered barges and bring him up the Elbe to the Magdeburg."

"It's a roundabout route," said Ulrik. "Still, it can't be more than three hundred miles all told. Three hundred miles on river barges which could be prepared beforehand for the trip would take far less time than the trip your father already took to Berlin. And be far more comfortable and easier on him."

"I'd *rather* be on a well-made river barge," added Baldur, "than be stuck in Berlin."

Kristina's jaws got tight. "I'm getting mad now."

"As well you should," Ulrik said.

"So what should we do?" she asked. "We can't stay here. Uncle Axel's word is law here. It really is. I never liked Stockholm anyway. Should we go to Copenhagen?"

Caroline Platzer looked alarmed, until she saw that Ulrik was already shaking his head.

"No. That would be a very bad mistake. I think it's essential that you and I stay together and—"

"Oh, yes!" Kristina exclaimed. "You have to stay with me, Ulrik! You have to!"

Her hands were gripping his as tightly as they could, now. Her eyes were wider than ever, her face as pale as he'd ever seen it.

"You have to!"

He drew her near and gently kissed her forehead. "You are my betrothed, Kristina," he said softly. "And I am not a man who takes my vows lightly. I will not leave you. I swear that on my honor, here before God."

She released his hands and threw her arms around

him, clutching him tightly. "Good. That's very, very, very good. It would be so hard for me, without you."

After perhaps a minute, she relaxed her hug and stepped back a foot or so.

"But why not go to Copenhagen?"

"Because if we both go—and we would have to, since we've agreed to stay together—it would look as if I'd coerced you. And was trying to take advantage of the crisis to advance the interests of Denmark."

"Oh." She thought about that for a moment and then nodded. "That makes sense."

Caroline spoke up. "We probably don't have much time left, do we?"

Ulrik glanced at the pile of newspapers. "Not much, no. Uncle Ax—Oxenstierna is summoning all of them to Berlin. Well, Wettin is, officially. But I'm sure the chancellor is really the driving force now."

Ulrik had met Wilhelm Wettin and spent several hours in his company. He liked the man. But like him or not, the prime minister of the USE had recklessly plunged into the depths. Ulrik did not think those waters would suit him much. But into them he'd gone, nevertheless.

"Summoning all of who?" Caroline asked, frowning.

"Who do you think? Most of the major figures in the Crown Loyalist Party, to start with. But this goes beyond narrow politics. Important disgruntled noblemen, of course. Wealthy and resentful burghers. If a man has influence and wishes profoundly that the Ring of Fire had never happened, he's probably on his way to Berlin by now. He certainly got an invitation."

Caroline stared at him. She was now quite wide-eyed herself.

"You're guessing," she said abruptly.

"To a considerable degree, yes." He flicked a dismissive forefinger across the stack of newspapers. "Most of these are fairly wretched, and the ones that aren't come irregularly. So, yes, a lot of this is guesswork on my part." He flashed a little smile. "But on this subject I'm a very well educated guesser, you know."

"Well...yeah, I guess that's true."

"So we have some time still, you think?" That came from Baldur. It was about as far removed from an idle question as could be imagined. Ulrik could practically hear the blades being sharpened, the pistols loaded...

The outrageous lies and subterfuges, of course.

"Yes, but not all that much. The chancellor—nor the prime minister, certainly—won't take any drastic public steps or measures until they have their own people organized." He snorted disdainfully. "As much as you can organize such a sullen pack of dogs. I swear, they make even Danish noblemen look like paragons of civic virtue. But once they feel they have the wind at their back, then—yes. If we're still here in Stockholm, they'll simply have us arrested if we haven't obeyed Oxenstierna and come to Berlin already."

"You too?" asked Kristina. "Won't that make your father very angry?"

"Probably. But..." Ulrik sighed. "I am very fond of my father in most ways. But he's simply not a king you can depend on in a crisis."

"So where do we go?" asked Caroline.

"I should think it was obvious. We go straight to the heart of power. We go to Magdeburg." His voice began to rise, as the anger finally seeped through. "Let the chancellor try to dictate who rules and who does not, when the rightful heir to the land, the empire and the union had placed herself in the bosom of her people. *Let him try.*"

Kristina clapped her hands. "Oh, yes! People like me there!"

"Yes, they do. Soon, girl, they will like you even more."

Caroline Platzer finally realized the full scope of what was about to unfold.

"Prince," she said, her tone one of pleading. "She's still only a child..."

"I'm almost nine!" Kristina stamped her foot. "In a month. Month and a half. Well, almost two. Still, nine years old isn't a child anymore."

She looked up at her husband-to-be, who was almost three times her age. "Is it, Ulrik?"

He gave her a shoulder a little squeeze. "For most people, yes. Nine years old is still a child. But you're of the house of Vasa and I'm of the house of Oldenburg, We grow up much faster."

Kristina gave Caroline a triumphant look. "See?"

Caroline wasn't looking at the princess, though. She was still looking at Ulrik.

"I didn't...I hadn't..."

He cocked an eyebrow. "Yes?"

She swallowed. Then took a breath and squared her shoulders, as if she were a soldier reporting for duty. "I never understood—never realized—I didn't think..."

She took a second breath. Her shoulders relaxed a little.

"I guess I just didn't think you were this...bold."

"Oh, most certainly!" exclaimed Baldur. He clapped Ulrik on the shoulder. "In the olden days he'd have gone a-viking. Every summer! And I'd have followed him, too."

The humor went away, then. Norddahl's eyes were normally a light blue, but now they looked almost gray. Not the warm gray of ash, but the gray of arctic seas.

"Every summer, I'd have followed him," he said quietly. "Each and every one. There are not so many princes in the world—not real ones—that you can afford to let go of the one you find."

"That's very...medieval, Baldur," said Kristina. Very, very approvingly.

Kassel, capital of Hesse-Kassel

Amalie Elizabeth von Hanau-Münzenberg had access to many more newspapers than Ulrik did. Better ones, too.

But she'd let slip her lifelong habit of reading newspapers, these past weeks. She was a widow now, no longer a wife. And she'd found that the change had affected her far more powerfully than she would have believed, before her husband was killed on the banks of the Warta.

Her marriage to Wilhelm V had been one of political convenience and family advancement, originally, as were most marriages among their class of people. Neither at the beginning nor at any time since could you say they were romantically involved, in the way the up-timers used the phrase.

Still, they'd been married for years. She'd borne him a son, who would someday become William VI. She could hear him now playing in a nearby room, with all the energy and enthusiasm of a healthy six-year-old boy. He was a smart boy too, it was already obvious.

For years, the last face she'd seen most days before she slept was her husband's. And his was usually the first face she saw in the morning. Except for servants, of course, but they didn't count.

She'd almost always been glad to see the face, too. Many wives in her class dreaded opening their eyes in the morning. But she never had. Wilhelm's worst flaws had simply been irritating, nothing worse than that. If he wasn't always the cleverest and shrewdest of men, he was certainly no dullard, either. Generally good-natured, often of good cheer...

She missed him. She really missed him. There was still an ache inside.

Finally, though, just a few days ago, she'd started to resume her normal activities.

It hadn't taken her long to start feeling another ache inside. A hollowness in her stomach, this one, not a hollowness in her heart.

She got the Hamburg newspapers and journals regularly. Also all the most important ones from Magdeburg, Hannover, Mainz, Nürnberg—Grantville, of course.

The pattern was clear in all of them, if you knew what to look for.

The Swedish chancellor fixed in Berlin, like a barnacle on a piling. *Why?* Berlin was a wretched place. Miserable to live in, and a political backwater.

The badly injured king kept there, jealously guarded, the great up-time Moorish doctor dismissed. *Why?* Once the weather cleared, Gustav Adolf could have easily been moved to the capital. Or Grantville or Jena, for that matter—wherever the medical care would be the best for his condition.

General Lennart Torstensson and the bulk of the USE army, ordered to besiege Koniecpolski in Poznań.

For God's sake, why? Amelie Elizabeth was no soldier herself, but as you'd expect from a very capable landgravine of Hesse-Kassel, she understood a great deal about military affairs. Torstensson had no chance of taking Poznań, not as badly as the war had gone so far. So why keep his army in winter siege lines which would be very hard on the troops? It would be much more sensible to retreat and winter over in Gorzów and Zielona Góra.

Only one explanation made sense. The Swedish chancellor Oxenstierna—Wilhelm Wettin, formally, but Wilhelm on his own was not this ruthless—was keeping the unreliable USE soldiery as far away as possible. And he was deliberately bleeding them.

The strategy was cunning, in a reptilian way. But didn't the chancellor understand how reckless it was? Did he really think an army would just quietly starve to death?

The USE's Third Division, under Stearns, had been sent even farther away. To southern Bohemia, if the newspaper accounts were to be believed. To do what? Help Wallenstein defend himself against the Austrians?

Again, why? The last time Austria had attacked Wallenstein—just a little over two years ago, at the second battle of the White Mountain—they'd been defeated. Was it likely they would try again? Not impossible, of course, but also not at all likely. So why weaken the USE army by drawing off a third of its forces?

Then, there was the evidence she'd spent all of yesterday and half of today piecing together. This took much more time, because there was no summary to be found anywhere, in any one newspaper or journal. Just small accounts scattered across many of them—most of them, actually—of what seemed to be casual movements. This markgraf going to visit his first cousin; this freiherr off to purchase some land; this burgermeister off to do this; that reichsritter off to do that.

She didn't believe it for a minute. She *knew* many of these people. The markgraf in question only had three first cousins. One had drowned as a young man during his wanderjahr in a drunken stupor, one had married an Italian viscount and was living somewhere in Tuscany, and the third had been filing lawsuits against the markgraf for at least fifteen years.

The freiherr? Going off to buy land? With what? Just six months ago, he'd tried to borrow money from Hesse-Kassel. They'd refused the loan, of course. The man was notorious for not repaying his creditors.

The burgermeister? Oh, that explanation was particularly grotesque. He was supposedly—

"Ah!" Angrily, the landgravine swept all the newspapers off her desk.

And the final piece of the puzzle—and to her mind, the most damning. Why had *she* not received an invitation to this so-obvious conclave?

The answer was just as obvious. She called for a servant.

"Paper and ink. Then pick this up. Not now. After I'm finished with the paper and ink which you still haven't fetched for me."

The servant girl raced off. Amalie Elizabeth forced herself to calm down a bit. There was no purpose in being harsh to servants simply because they were there. Doing so just made them more impervious to discipline when it was needed.

As soon as the servant returned, she began to write.

It was almost certainly a futile exercise, but she had to make the attempt.

Wilhelm, my old and dear friend. I implore you once again—

Chapter 43

Berlin, Capital of Brandenburg

Axel Oxenstierna laid a gentle hand on Gustav Adolf's shoulder. "Be well, my old friend. You need worry about nothing. Just heal. Come back to us."

The king had seemed to be dozing. Thankfully. He'd had one of his sudden furies two hours early. They came for no reason, they left for no reason, and left everyone exhausted, including the king himself.

Gustav Adolf's eyes opened suddenly. For a moment, there seemed to be recognition there.

But if it had been there, it passed. He just seemed puzzled now. His eyes drifted away from Oxenstierna and came to rest on his bodyguard. That was Erling Ljungberg, who had replaced Anders Jönsson. For a moment, again, there seemed to be recognition in the king's eyes.

It would not be surprising. Ljungberg's facial features did not resemble those of Jönsson's very closely, but otherwise they were much alike. Both very big men, both blond, both utterly ferocious in battle. They even shared the same love of American pistols. In fact, the pistol holstered at Ljungberg's waist was the very one that had been in Jönsson's hand when he died.

If Gustav Adolf did recognize him, though, it would be hard to know for sure. His speech was still...very odd. Axel would have thought he was outright mad, except for what the Moor had explained. This might still pass away, if all went well.

"Birches? Is that folded?" the king asked. "Just move the sand under the hymns."

Axel stroked his hair. "Rest, king. Rest."

He turned away, headed for the door. It was time to attend to the king's business.

"Make sure he comes to no harm," he said to Ljungberg, then had to restrain a little laugh when he saw the man's disgusted look. Giving such instructions to such a bodyguard was quite pointless, after all. You might as well instruct the sea to be wet.

One of the palace's servants was quick to open the door. Very quick. It had not taken Sweden's chancellor long at all to make clear to the servants of Brandenburg—the servants of *former* Brandenburg—that if they wished to keep their sinecures they'd have to understand that the old sleepy ways of Berlin were coming to an end. Soon enough, this would be the new capital city of the United States of Europe.

As he walked down the corridor to the very large chamber that had served the electors of Brandenburg for a reception room, Axel mused on his long relationship with Gustav Adolf. His father had died when he was sixteen—too young to rule by Swedish law and custom. At the same time, his capabilities were obvious and no one wanted a long regency with all of its attendant problems.

Axel himself had been only twenty-eight at the time. But he was a scion of one of the great noble families and already very influential. He had been the principal engineer of the arrangement that had enabled Gustav Adolf to come to the throne on January 4, 1612. He'd been only seventeen years old at the time.

Part of the arrangement had required the young king to sign a charter of guarantees that restored most of the rights and privileges of the nobility that previous Vasa rulers had stripped away from them.

Twenty-three years had gone by since then; almost twenty-four. For most of those years, Gustav Adolf had scrupulously abided by the charter of guarantees. In letter, at least. Inevitably, a monarch as capable and forceful as he would overshadow any nobility. But no one could reasonably ask for more. A weak and incapable monarch was far worse.

Then the Americans had come through the Ring of Fire. Within a year, their alliance with Gustav Adolf had begun to take shape. It had first crystallized in the formation of the Confederated Principalities of Europe, in the fall of 1632. A year later, under the impact of the war launched by the League of Ostend, the CPE's ramshackle structure had been swept away and replaced with the much more powerful United States of Europe— a true federation, now, with real national power.

Oxenstierna had had misgivings from the start. Still, the advantages had been obvious; hard to resist, even for a nobleman, much less a king. For all his dislike of the Americans—their ways and customs and attitudes; he did not dislike all of them as people; some, he even liked—Axel was neither stupid nor blind. There was no doubt that it was the alliance with

Grantville—even with Michael Stearns, the man—that had enabled Gustav Adolf to rise so quickly to the prominence he now held in European affairs. Soon enough, Axel didn't doubt, in world affairs.

On the day of the Ring of Fire, Gustav Adolf had been the "Lion of the North." The king of Sweden, merely, but a king whose own innate abilities had made Sweden a much greater power than its population and resources would normally have warranted.

Four and a half years had gone by. Today, Gustav Adolf was still king of Sweden—and a considerably richer Sweden. He was also the emperor of the United States of Europe, a position which, despite the many republican absurdities and aggravations attendant upon it, still gave Gustav Adolf unmatched military power. Power which he'd used, among other things, to resurrect the Union of Kalmar—on a Swedish foundation this time, not a Danish one—and reunite Scandinavia for the first time since the middle ages.

All well and good. But as time went on—it was obvious, even if the king himself had been blind to it—the American elixir had become a poison. The higher the king rose, the weaker became the foundations of his rule. Before much longer, if this went on, it would all be swept away.

Axel thought the hand of God had been at work, that day on the shores of Lake Bledno. A king's life had been saved, yes, by a valiant hero. But perhaps just as important—here lay the subtlety of the Lord's work—was that the king fell into a swoon. A swoon that now looked to last for quite some time. Months, almost certainly. Possibly years. (Possibly forever, too; but the chancellor's mind shied away from that.)

Oxenstierna knew well the workings of his friend's mind. Gustav Adolf would remain loyal to a fault. He'd made his agreements with Michael Stearns, and would keep to them, even if those agreements were draining the lifeblood out of his realms.

So, Axel thought, God's hand. Let the king sleep while his faithful servitors did what had to be done.

He'd reached the door to the reception hall. Quickly, two servants opened it for him.

He stepped through. Wilhelm Wettin was waiting there.

A weak and slender reed, Wettin. A decent man, yes. Too decent, perhaps, for what had to be done. But between Oxenstierna's pressure from above and the pressure brought by his many followers from below, he'd finally acquiesced.

Again, God's hand at work. Had Gustav Adolf still been in full command of his senses, the chancellor would not have been able to bring the prime minister to this point. He was quite sure of it.

Wettin was looking pale; his face drawn; close to haggard, even.

Oxenstierna took him by the shoulder and swung him to face the crowd that was packed into the great reception hall.

"Have faith, Wilhelm," he said.

The crowd roared. Oxenstierna released his grip from the prime minister's shoulder and took two steps forward. Then, raised his hands high.

"It is time to end the anarchy! Are you with us?"

The roar was deafening.

Cast of Characters

Ableidinger, Constantin	Member of USE Parliament; leader of the Ram movement.
Abrabanel, Rebecca	Leader of the Fourth of July Party; wife of Mike Stearns.
Achterhof, Gunther	Leader of the Committees of Correspondence.
Adamczyk, Lubomir	Polish hussar.
Ancelin, Gui	French Huguenot fanatic; part of Delerue-Ducos organization.
Báner, Johan Gustafsson	Swedish general.
Bartley, David	Supply officer in Third Division; also a financier.
Beasley, Denise	Teenage girl employed as an agent by Francisco Nasi; informally betrothed to Eddie Junker.
Bose, Carl	Colonel in the Saxon army.

Brillard, Mathurin	French Huguenot fanatic; part of Delerue-Ducos organization.
Brunswick-Lüneburg, George, duke of	Major general in command of the 1st Division, USE Army.
Christian IV	King of Denmark.
Christoph, Georg, von Taupadel	Brigadier, 3rd Division, USE Army.
Delerue, Antoine	French Huguenot fanatic; part of Delerue-Ducos organization.
Derfflinger, George	Brigadier, 3rd Division, USE Army.
Donner, Agathe "Tata"	Daughter of Reichard Donner, leader of the Mainz CoC; now a CoC organizer in Dresden.
Dreeson, Henry	Former mayor of Grantville; assassinated by Huguenot fanatics.
Drugeth, Janos	Hungarian nobleman; friend and adviser of Ferdinand III.
Ducos, Michel	Assassin; leader of Huguenot fanatic organization.
Duerr, Ulbrecht	Officer, USE Army; aide to Mike Stearns.
Engler, Thorsten	Captain in USE Army; fiancé of Caroline Platzer; also the imperial count of Narnia.
Ferdinand III	Emperor of Austria.

George William	Elector of Brandenburg; Gustav Adolf's brother-in-law.
Gundelfinger, Helene	Vice-President of the State of Thuringia-Franconia; leader of the Fourth of July Party.
Hans Georg, von Arnim	Commanding general of the Saxon army.
Hesse-Kassel, Amalie Elizabeth, landgravine of	Noblewoman, wife of Wilhelm V of Hesse-Kassel.
Hesse-Kassel, Wilhelm V, landgrave of	Ruler of Hesse-Kassel.
Higgins, Jeffrey ("Jeff")	Officer, USE Army; husband of Gretchen Richter.
Hugelmair, Minnie	Teenage girl employed as an agent by Francisco Nasi; friend of Denise Beasley; adopted daughter of Benny Pierce.
John George I	Elector of Saxony.
Junker, Egidius "Eddie"	Former agent of the SoTF government, now employed as an agent and pilot by Francisco Nasi; informally betrothed to Denise Beasley.
Knyphausen, Dodo	Major general in command of the 2nd Division, USE Army.
Koniecpolski, Stanislaw	Grand hetman of the Polish-Lithuanian Commonwealth.

Krenz, Eric   Lieutenant, USE Army.

Kresse, Georg   Leader of guerrilla movement
                           in the Vogtland.

Kuefer, Wilhelm   Guerrilla fighter in the
                           Vogtland; Kresse's assistant.

Leebrick, Anthony   Officer, USE Army; aide to
                           Mike Stearns.

Levasseur, Abraham   French Huguenot fanatic; part
                           of Delerue-Ducos organization.

Linn, Jason   Soldier in flying artillery unit
                           attached to the 3rd Division.

Locquifier, Guillaume   French Huguenot fanatic; part
                           of Delerue-Ducos organization.

Long, Christopher   Officer, USE Army; aide to
                           Mike Stearns.

Mademann, Charles   French Huguenot fanatic; part
                           of Delerue-Ducos organization.

Mailey, Melissa   Adviser to Mike Stearns; leader
                           of the Fourth of July Party.

Maria Eleonora of   Queen of Sweden; wife of
Brandenburg   Gustav Adolf; mother of
                           Kristina.

Nasi, Francisco   Former head of intelligence
                           for Mike Stearns; now operates
                           a private intelligence agency.

Norddahl, Baldur   Norwegian adventurer and engi-
                           neer in Danish service; friend
                           and assistant of Prince Ulrik.

Opalinski, Lukasz	Polish hussar.
Ouvrard, Robert	French Huguenot fanatic; part of Delerue-Ducos organization.
Oxenstierna, Axel	Swedish chancellor, chief advisor of Gustav II Adolf
Piazza, Edward ("Ed")	President of the State of Thuringia-Franconia; leader of the Fourth of July Party.
Piesel, Anna	Guerrilla fighter in the Vogtland; betrothed to Georg Kresse.
Platzer, Caroline Ann	Social worker in Magdeburg; companion for Princess Kristina; betrothed to Thorsten Engler
Richelieu, Armand Jean du Plessis de	Cardinal; first minister of Louis XIII; the effective head of the French government.
Richter, Anna Elisabetha "Annalise"	Gretchen Richter's younger sister
Richter, Maria Margaretha "Gretchen"	Leader of the Committees of Correspondence; wife of Jeff Higgins.
Saxe-Weimar, Ernst, duke of	Brother of Wilhelm Wettin; regent for Gustav Adolf in the Oberpfalz (Upper Palatinate).
Saxe-Weimar, Wilhelm IV, duke of	*See:* Wilhelm Wettin.
Schuster, Ludwig	Brigadier, 3rd Division, USE Army.

Short, Andrew — Former Yeoman Warder, Tower of London; now the head of security for Rebecca Abrabanel.

Stearns, Michael "Mike" — Former prime minister of the United States of Europe; now a major general in command of the 3rd Division, USE Army; husband of Rebecca Abrabanel.

Strigel, Matthias — Governor of Magdeburg province; leader of the Fourth of July Party.

Stull, Noelle — Former agent for the SoTF government, now employed by Francisco Nasi; is being courted by Janos Drugeth.

Thierbach, Joachim von "Spartacus" — Leader of the Committees of Correspondence.

Torstensson, Lennart — Commanding general of the USE army.

Tourneau, Andre — French Huguenot fanatic; part of Delerue-Ducos organization.

Towson, Richard — Officer, USE Army.

Ulrik — Prince of Denmark; youngest son of Christian IV in the line of succession; betrothed to Princess Kristina of Sweden.

Vasa, Gustav II Adolf — King of Sweden; emperor of the United States of Europe;

also known as Gustavus
Adolphus.

Vasa, Kristina

Daughter and heir of Gustav
II Adolf.

Vasa, Wladyslaw IV

King of the Polish-Lithuanian
Commonwealth.

Welch, Patrick

Officer, USE Army.

Wettin, Wilhelm

Prime Minister of the USE;
leader of the Crown Loyalist
Party (formerly Wilhelm IV,
duke of Saxe-Weimar).

Wojtowicz, Jozef

Nephew of Grand Hetman
Koniecpolski; head of Polish
intelligence in the USE.

The following is an excerpt from:

Grantville Gazette VI

Sequels to 1632
Edited and Created by
ERIC FLINT

Available from Baen Books
December 2012
mass market

The Masque

Eric Flint

— 1 —

Anne Jefferson studied herself in the mirror, then turned sideways and spent a few more seconds with the examination.

"The colors are pretty drab," she announced. "Comfortable, though, I'll give it that—way more so than modern-day Dutch women's apparel. At least it doesn't have a ruff. I hate those things."

She giggled. "I can't believe I just heard myself say 'modern-day' to refer to the year 1635."

Her husband Adam Olearius smiled at her reflection in the mirror. "I was born in this century so I can't say that I find the expression peculiar. Although people didn't use it much until you Americans came barging into the world. Changes came a lot more slowly before you arrived, so the distinction between past and present wasn't as great."

He studied her garments for a few seconds. "With the exception of fashion, of course. That's always changed rapidly."

Still looking at the outfit in the mirror, Anne shook her head. "I'll tell you what's odd to me, though. In the world I came from, women's fashions changed all the time. But men's clothing changed slowly, and it was even more drab than this dress I'm wearing. Suits, suits, suits. The colors were black, gray, navy blue and one or another shade of white. If you were really daring, you wore a light brown suit. Whereas here! Men's clothing changes every bit as fast as women's and it's even more flamboyant."

Olearius curled his lip theatrically. "One of the great drawbacks of your democratic system! In our sane seventeenth century, male fashion is determined by princes—who are not about to bury their effulgent glory under dismal colors and sober designs. In your world, on the other hand, male fashion was dictated by businessmen. Merchants, that is to say, a class of people whose adventurousness is entirely restricted to pecuniary endeavors."

Anne chuckled but didn't argue the point. Leaving aside her husband's analysis of the causes involved, she didn't disagree with him on the substance of the matter. She thought male costuming in the here-and-now was a marked improvement over that of the world she'd come from. Thankfully, the codpieces prevalent in the last century had fallen out of fashion. That would have been . . . a bit much to take, for someone who still had a lot of West Virginia attitudes.

She turned away from the mirror altogether. "Talk about princes! I still can't believe Ben Jonson is taking a personal hand in this masque."

"Do not get your hopes too high. I've heard he's declined a great deal from his glory days twenty years ago. That's the real reason he left England, I suspect, whatever he claims himself about the enmity of Inigo Jones and the Earl of Cork."

Anne smiled. "It probably doesn't help that he's bound and determined to base the masque on that crate of stuff he got from Grantville. 'Memorabilia,' he calls it. 'Odds and ends,' is more like it."

"Or 'junk,'" added Olearius, perhaps uncharitably. He went to the door and opened it for her. "And now, my dear, we should go have an early dinner before making our appearance at the rehearsal. Even though"—his tone of voice was now definitely uncharitable—"I will be astonished if the esteemed poet has made much progress by the time we get there."

— 2 —

Ben Jonson studied the bizarre object in his right hand, his head propped up by the left. "Perhaps a token of esteem from the tritons..." he mused.

Standing behind him where the poet and dramatist couldn't see her, the young Countess Palatine Elizabeth rolled her eyes. It was obvious that Jonson was bound and determined to copy as much as he could of the masque he'd done thirty years earlier for King James, the famous *Masque of Blackness*. She thought the project was ill-conceived, herself. If for no other reason because the success of *The Masque of Blackness* had been due in no small part to the architectural genius of Jonson's partner Inigo Jones. His stage settings had been magnificent.

Jonson's *then* partner, alas. The rupture between the two men had been deep; it was now deep and bitter, since Jones had won the favor of Richard Boyle, the Earl of Cork. So now Jonson was in self-imposed exile in Amsterdam and the Dutch architects and artisans at his disposal were not really up to the challenge of designing the monumental stage settings he insisted upon.

It would help, of course, if he'd actually finish the blasted thing instead of dithering. There was another rehearsal scheduled for that evening, for which both she and her brother Rupert had donned their costumes. It would probably wind up being a disjointed semi-disaster like the two previous rehearsals.

Rupert was leaning over Jonson's shoulder. He had his chin cupped in his hand in what he presumably hoped would be seen as a gesture of thoughtfulness— but Elizabeth was quite sure her brother just wanted to stroke his beard. Still shy of his sixteenth birthday, Rupert was inordinately proud of his whiskers.

In truth, he had some right to be. He was already six feet tall and was showing that extraordinary musculature that would make him a military legend in another universe. *Prince Rupert of the Rhine,* they'd called him. Rupert had vowed he would not pursue the soldier's career he'd followed in that up-time world. But Elizabeth had noted that her brother maintained a rigorous regimen when it came to his exercises in the *salle d'armes* run by his Dutch swordmaster. Such vows were easy to make; not so easy to keep.

"I think you should rather make it a token of esteem from Oceanus," Rupert said. He pointed to the object in the poet's hand. "You could think of it as a symbol of the engirdling oceans in all their many hues."

Ben Jonson stroked his own beard. "Hm. Interesting idea, I agree."

In Elizabeth's opinion, the idea was idiotic—because *any* attempt to make the Rubik's Cube the center of a masque was idiotic. The ridiculous up-time contrivance was far too small to play that role. They'd do better to use the statue of the elf or even the club. What did Americans call the thing? A "baseball bat," if she remembered correctly.

The name was as idiotic as the Rubik's Cube. There'd been bats in two of the houses she'd lived in during her family's peripatetic existence following the expulsion of her father, the Elector of the Palatine Frederick V, from the throne he'd briefly held as King of Bohemia. The American club bore no resemblance to the creatures at all.

— 3 —

"George Monck's been executed," John Hampden announced, closing the door to the salon behind him. He came over to the big table in the center of the room around which a number of other men were seated and laid a radio message on the surface. "The news just came in. Thomas Fairfax, John Lambert and Thomas Horton were executed along with him. Horton was drawn and quartered first."

"*Bastards,*" hissed Arthur Haselrig. "What about Denzil Holles? And Fairfax's son Ferdinando?"

Hampden pulled out a chair. "Still alive, I suppose. For how long remains to be seen." He sat down. "So far, the Earl of Manchester is the only one who seems to have wormed his way into Cork's good graces."

"'Wormed' is the right word, too," said young Henry

Ireton. "Unfair to worms, I suppose, but since 'swined' or 'toaded' aren't verbs it'll have to do."

There was real anger lurking under the humor. Still only twenty-four years old, Ireton was too young to have known any of the men executed by the Earl of Cork. But like all of the men in the room, he'd studied the up-time accounts of the civil war that had begun in England—would have begun, rather, in another England in another universe—in the year 1642.

The history of that conflict weighed heavily on all of them, for all its insubstantial nature. Perhaps on none more than the man sitting at the head of the long table, Thomas Wentworth—who'd stopped calling himself the Earl of Strafford because of it.

Wentworth studied young Ireton for a moment. In this world, the man was a lawyer—as he had been in that other. But so far he was only a lawyer, not the accomplished military officer he would become—would have become, had become, could have become—the grammar was maddening—in the up-timers' universe.

The men who'd recently been executed had played prominent roles in that civil war, as had the Earl of Manchester. Would have played, it might be better to say. The reason Horton had been drawn and quartered was because, it that other universe, he'd been one of the commissioners of the High Court of Justice in 1649 and among those who'd signed the warrant for the execution of King Charles I of England.

In that universe, Horton had died of natural causes—disease, presumably; the American records were not specific—while serving in Ireland under Cromwell. In this universe, King Charles was still on the throne and his chief minister Richard Boyle, the Earl of Cork, ad seen fit to cut the matter short—along with the man himself.

In the universe the Americans came from, Horton's heirs had been deprived of their estate during the Restoration in the 1660s. Wentworth didn't doubt for a moment that they'd already been stripped of the estate in this one. Among his other charming characteristics, Richard Boyle was ravenously greedy. By all accounts, the king was mired in melancholia and paid no attention to the affairs of his realm. The Earl of Cork had become for all practical purposes the military dictator of England and he saw to it that all property seized from "traitors" wound up either in his own hands or those of his close associates and followers.

"Why execute Monck at all?" asked Henry Vane plaintively. "Or Fairfax, for that matter? Both of them helped the Restoration in the end."

Wentworth exchanged glances with the man sitting at the other end of the table. That was Robert Devereux, the Earl of Essex. He and Thomas Wentworth were more-or-less the two recognized leaders of the group. "More or less," because as yet the group itself was only more or less a group. It was still an association of like-minded individuals rather than the formally-constituted revolutionary organization that both Wentworth and Devereux were striving to establish.

Robert understood the meaning of that glance and took it upon himself to answer Vane's question—and did so a lot more diplomatically than Thomas would have himself. It was a cretin's question, after all.

"Boyle's got his own ambitions, Henry, that's why. He doesn't want anyone at the court who could make a claim to the king's confidence, besides himself. Given the king's nature—even on his best days, which these aren't—that's not unlikely. Charles is petulant. Sooner or later, the Earl of Cork is bound to annoy him. When that time comes, Boyle doesn't want anyone like Monck or Fairfax around whom the king might decide would make a suitable replacement for him."

Thomas Harrison grunted sarcastically. "Not all that likely, Robert! You're presuming that His Royal Idiocy has actually studied the up-time histories." He gave Wentworth a look that was not entirely friendly. "What actually happened is that he learned of the basic fact that concerned him—'they cut my head off!'—and then left it to Strafford here to learn the details and act accordingly."

Wentworth's jaws tightened, but he made no protest. It would be hard to do so, of course, since Harrison's account was fairly accurate. As for the harshness of the man's attitude...

Again, the weight of history. In this world, Harrison had had the good sense to flee England as soon as he heard of Pym's arrest. At the time, he hadn't read any of the up-time texts himself, but he'd sensed what was coming.

There was no guesswork involved any longer. In that other universe—and by now Harrison *had* read the texts—he'd been executed at the Restoration.

—end excerpt—

from *Grantville Gazette VI*
available in mass market,
December 2012, from Baen Books